SEDUCED BY A STEELE

BRENDA JACKSON

TOO TEXAN TO TAME

JANICE MAYNARD

MILLS & BOON

First Published in Great Britain 2020
by Mills & Boon, an imprint of HarperCollinsPublishers,
1 London Bridge Street, London, SE1 9GF

Seduced by a Steele © 2020 Brenda Streater Jackson
Too Texan to Tame © 2020 Harlequin Books S.A.

Special thanks and acknowledgement are given to Janice Maynard for her contribution to the *Texas Cattleman's Club: Inheritance* series.

ISBN: 978-0-263-27919-1

0420

MIX
Paper from
responsible sources
FSC™ C007454

This book is produced from independently certified FSC™ paper to ensure responsible forest management.

For more information visit: www.harpercollins.co.uk/green

Printed and bound in Spain
by CPI, Barcelona

SEDUCED BY A STEELE

BRENDA JACKSON

One

Mercury Steele glanced over at his mother, sitting across the breakfast table. Eden Tyson Steele, you just had to love her.

He'd just told her how awful the past few days had been for him. Not only had he lost a client but also one of his prized antique cars had been stolen. She had the audacity to say there must be a reason for the streak of bad luck he'd had lately. Of course, she couldn't resist blaming it on his womanizing ways.

"That's awful about your car getting stolen, Mercury. What did the police say about it?" his father asked with concern.

He appreciated his father's empathy, but then, Drew Steele had passed his love for antique cars on to his six sons. He'd passed something else on to them, as well. Namely his testosterone-driven genes.

In Drew's younger days he'd been quite the ladies' man. His reputation as a philanderer had been so bad that he'd been run out of Charlotte by a bunch of women out for blood—namely Drew's. He had fled from North Carolina,

where most of the Steele family lived, and made his way to
Phoenix. That was where he'd eventually met and fallen in
love with Mercury's mother.

Eden Tyson Steele, a green-eyed beauty and former international model, whose face had graced the covers of
such magazines as *Vogue*, *Cosmo* and *Elle*, had practically
snatched Drew's heart right out of his chest. Proving mir-
acles could happen.

For the longest time, it seemed their six die-hard bachelor sons had inherited Drew's philandering genes when
their womanizing reputation rivaled that of their father's.
They'd become known as the Bad News Steeles. Four of
Mercury's brothers had now married, leaving only two
brothers still single: Mercury and Gannon.

He couldn't speak for Gannon, but Mercury intended to
be a bachelor for life.

Their brother Galen was the oldest of the six and had
gotten married first. At thirty-eight he'd made millions as
a video-game creator. Tyson was thirty-seven, the most recent to marry, and was a gifted surgeon. Eli, at thirty-six,
was a prominent attorney in town and had been the second
to marry. Jonas, who was thirty-five and the third to marry,
owned a marketing business. Mercury was thirty-four and
was a well-known sports agent; and Gannon, who had recently turned thirty-three, had become CEO of the family's million-dollar trucking firm when Drew had retired.

"They will be on the lookout for it, Dad, but I was told
not to get my hopes up about getting it back. More than
likely it will be dismantled for parts. Knowing that hurts
more than anything. That particular car was my favorite."

Drew nodded sympathetically and Mercury appreciated his father's understanding of just how upset he still
was about it, even if his mother did not. He glanced at his
watch. "I need to get going if I intend to make that appointment. A possible new client."

Getting up from the table, he leaned over and placed a kiss on his mother's cheek. "Thanks for breakfast, Mom. You're still my number one girl." He then glanced over at his father. "I'll talk to you later, Dad."

Ten minutes later he was headed toward his office in the Steele Building. A few years ago, his attorney brother, Eli, had purchased a twenty-story high-rise in downtown Phoenix. Eli's wife, Stacey, owned the gift shop on the ground floor. Their brother Jonas's marketing company, Ideas of Steele, was housed on the fifth floor, and Galen leased the entire second and third floors as a downtown campus for his wife's etiquette schools. Mercury and his brother Tyson jointly leased the tenth floor. Although Tyson was the physician in the family, he'd leased the space as a gift to his wife, Hunter, for her architecture company.

Sharing office space with Hunter worked out great. Mercury liked Hunter and for now they shared an administrative assistant, Pauline Martin. The older woman was perfect and had to be the most efficient woman Mercury had ever met. She knew how to handle him, his clients and his appointments.

The moment he merged into traffic on the interstate that would take him downtown, he blinked. Three cars ahead of him was *his* car. *His stolen car.* He would recognize his red 1967 Camaro anywhere. Hell, they hadn't even bothered changing the license plates.

Moving into the other lane, he tried getting as close as he could. Finally, he was two cars behind. When the driver changed lanes, he did likewise. When the car exited off the interstate, he followed, but now he was three cars behind. He pressed the call-assist button on his car's dash. Within seconds a voice came on through the car's speaker. "Yes, Mr. Steele, how can we help you today?"

"Connect me with the Phoenix Police Department."

"Yes, Mr. Steele."

He nodded, appreciating hands-free technology. Moments later the connection was made. "Phoenix Police Department. May I help you?"

"My car, the one that was stolen three nights ago that you guys haven't been able to find, is three cars ahead of me. I'm tailing them as we speak."

"Your name, sir?"

"Mercury Steele."

"What is your location?"

"Currently, I'm in the Norcross District, at the intersection of Adams and Monroe. If the driver makes a stop, then I will, too."

"Sir, you are advised not to tail anyone or take matters into your own hands. Police in the area have been summoned."

Like hell he wouldn't tail the person who'd had the nerve to steal his car, he thought, disconnecting the call.

Mercury saw the driver making a right turn ahead and he quickly put on the brakes when the car ahead of him got caught by a traffic light.

"Damn!" He hoped he didn't lose the thief. It seemed to take forever for the traffic light to change and then he turned right at the intersection. Glancing around, he saw he was on a busy street, one that led to the Apperson Mall.

Sloan Donahue didn't have time to go back home and change her blouse, and there was no way she could wear one bearing coffee stains to her job interview. That meant she needed to dash into this clothing store and buy a new blouse and then swap it out in the dressing room with the one she was currently wearing.

She was excited. For the very first time she would be interviewing for a job without her parents' help or interference. She'd left Cincinnati, Ohio, a week ago when her parents tried forcing her into an arranged marriage, saying that in their social circles it was their duty to ensure her future and her fortune. She'd refused. Luckily, her parents' predictions that she couldn't make it on her own and would be returning home in less than forty-eight hours didn't happen. She wouldn't go back if they still expected her to marry Harold Cunningham. And she knew they would.

Sloan didn't care one iota that marrying Harold would be a financial marriage made in heaven. It was her life and future they were dealing with. She didn't love Harold any more than he loved her. For the past six months he'd wined and dined her, romanced her like a good suitor was supposed to. For a short while, she'd almost convinced herself maybe he was falling in love with her and that she could possibly fall in love with him.

Then she'd discovered he was having an affair. She'd received the text message he'd intended to send another woman. When she confronted Harold about it, he didn't deny anything. He admitted to being in love with the woman, but said he would do his "duty" and marry Sloan. However, he wanted her to know that, married or not, he intended for the woman he loved to forever be a part of his life. In other words, he would have a mistress if he and Sloan got married.

When she told her parents to call off the wedding and the reason for doing so, they felt Harold marrying her and keeping his piece on the side shouldn't matter. She should consider the boost the marriage would play in her financial future and suck it up. They'd given her an ultimatum to marry Harold or else. She told them she would take the *or else*.

She needed time away from her family, and wanting to get as far away from Cincinnati as she could, Sloan had looked up an old college roommate who invited her to come to Phoenix. But then Priscilla had unexpectedly had to leave the day after Sloan arrived. Priscilla's boyfriend had finally asked her to marry him and had sent her an airline ticket to Spain.

The good thing was that the rent was paid up and Priscilla told Sloan she was welcome to stay in the house for the remainder of the month. That meant getting a job to have funds to cover the rent for next month. For the past few days she'd studied interview videos on the internet and felt she was ready.

As she rushed into the store, she glanced back at her car. *Her car.* It wasn't the Tesla sports car she'd left behind in Cincinnati, but a car that was probably older than she was. But it ran okay, and she'd only paid three hundred for it. It was hers and that was what mattered.

Since her parents had made good on their threat and placed a hold on the funds in her bank account, she had to watch her money. No telling what else they would do in order to get her to return home. Well, she had news for them. She would rather endure the hardship of not having the finer things in life she was used to than a forced, loveless marriage.

She knew she would be making decisions she'd never had to make before, decisions her parents had always made for her, but it was time for a change. For the first time in her life she felt a sense of freedom she'd never had before, and she truly loved it.

Two

A feeling of relief swept through Mercury when he located his car. Parking in the space beside it, he quickly got out and glanced around the shops in the mall, wondering where the driver had gone.

He was pissed when he pulled his phone out of his jacket to call the police again to give them his exact location. Putting his phone back, he walked around his car and was glad not to see any dents. Other than needing a good wash job, the old girl looked good. Deciding to check the interior, he pulled his car keys out of his pocket to open the door.

"Get away from my car!"

Mercury snatched his head up and was instantly mesmerized by the beauty of the woman's dark brown eyes, shoulder-length curly hair that cascaded around an oval face, high cheekbones, the smooth and creamy texture of her cocoa-colored skin and one pair of the sexiest lips he'd ever seen on a woman.

He immediately flashed her one of his wolfish smiles and was about to go into man-whore mode until what she'd said stopped him. Then he became blinded to all that gorgeous beauty. "*Your* car?"

"Yes, *my* car. Now get away from it before I call the police."

He crossed his arms over his chest. "This is *my* car. It was stolen from me three nights ago."

"You're lying," the woman snapped.

Calling him a liar was a big mistake. The one thing he despised more than anything was for someone to question his integrity. "If you think that, then by all means call the police. However, you don't have to call them since I already have. You're the thief, not me."

"I am not a thief," she said, feeling brave enough to step closer and glare at him.

"Nor am I a liar," he said, glaring back.

Suddenly a police cruiser with flashing blue lights pulled up and two officers quickly got out. One was Sherman Aikens, one of Jonas's old high school friends. "I see you've found your car, Mercury."

Mercury frowned over at him. "No thanks to you guys who should have been looking for it. And my car was never lost, it was stolen, and she's the person who has it."

"It's my car!"

Both officers glanced over at the woman and Mercury glowered. Instead of saying anything, they just stared at her, male appreciation obvious in their gazes. "For crying out loud, aren't you going to ask to see her papers on the vehicle since she claims to be the owner?" he snapped out at the officers.

Sherman broke eye contact with the woman to frown at Mercury. "I was going to get to that." In a voice Mercury felt was way too accommodating, considering the circumstances, Sherman said, "Ma'am, I need to see papers on this vehicle, because it resembles one reported stolen three nights ago."

"It *is* the one that was stolen three nights ago," Mercury snapped while ignoring Sherman's frown. As far as Mercury was concerned, Sherman could become smitten with the woman on someone else's time.

"Stolen! That's not possible, Officer," the woman said, looking alarmed. "Why would anyone want to steal that car? Look at it. It's old."

Mercury glared at her while Sherman and the other officer unsuccessfully tried hiding their grins. "It's a classic, and if it's so old for your taste, why did you buy it like you claim you did?" Mercury asked her.

"Because I needed transportation and it was in my budget," she said, pulling papers from her purse. "I just bought it yesterday." She handed the papers to Sherman.

Mercury thought it took Sherman longer than necessary to switch his gaze from the woman to the papers. He then said in a too-apologetic voice, "Sorry, ma'am, but these papers are fake."

Shock flew to her face. "Fake? But that's not possible. A nice gentleman sold the car to me."

"That 'nice' man conned you into buying a stolen car," Mercury said, ignoring Sherman's narrowed gaze as well as the woman's thunderstruck expression.

Switching her gaze from Mercury to Sherman, she said, "Please tell me that's not true, Officer. I gave him three hundred dollars."

"Three hundred dollars?" Mercury asked, not believing what she'd said.

Lifting her chin, she added, "Yes, I knew the car wasn't worth that much, but the man looked a little down on his luck and needed the money."

Mercury shook his head. "You got that car for a steal, no pun intended. Do you not know the value of that car? It's worth over two hundred *thousand* dollars easily."

She rolled her eyes. "Don't be ridiculous."

Ridiculous? She had bought a stolen car from someone who she thought was a *nice* man, and she thought *he* was being ridiculous? He was about to give her a scathing reply, but Sherman's look warned him not to do so.

"Yes, ma'am, unfortunately that man did run a scam on you," Sherman said. "I hate you lost all that money. I need you to come down to police headquarters and give us a statement, including a description of the man who sold you the car. We will be on the lookout for him."

"Like you guys were on the lookout for my car?" Mercury said under his breath, but when Sherman shot him a disapproving glare, he knew he'd been heard regardless.

Sherman turned to him. "We're going to have to impound the car. You and Miss Donahue need to come down to police headquarters to give statements."

"But I'm on my way to a job interview," the woman said, suddenly looking distressed.

Mercury refused to feel an ounce of sympathy for her since he too would be late for an interview with a potential new client. Now he would have to reschedule. Every sports agent alive would want to sign on Norris Eastwood, but the parents of the high school senior with plans to go straight into the NBA had sought out Mercury. He hoped being a no-show this morning wouldn't be a negative against him. If it was, then he had this woman to blame.

"Are you okay with that, Mercury?"

When he heard his name, he glanced up. "Am I okay with what?" He saw the other officer had pulled the woman off to the side to take down some information.

"Giving Miss Donahue a ride to the police station," Sherman said.

"Don't you have room in the police car? That's the normal way you transport criminals, isn't it? For all we know, she could be in cahoots with the person who stole my car."

Sherman rolled his eyes. "You don't believe that any

more than I do, Mercury. It's obvious she's an innocent victim who doesn't belong in the back of a patrol car. She's no more a thief than we are. Look at her."

Mercury didn't want to look at her, but he did anyway. He immediately thought the same thing he had when he'd first seen her. She was a very beautiful woman. Her features were just that striking. And then there was that delectable-looking figure in a navy blue pencil skirt and white blouse. Sexy as hell. But still…

"Unlike you, Sherman, I refuse to get taken in by a beautiful face and a nice body. Need I remind you, the woman was caught with a stolen car, and I refuse to be that gullible." *Again.* He quickly pushed to the back of his mind the one time he had been and the lasting damage it had caused him.

"Look on the bright side, Mercury. At least you got your car back. You can't blame her for being too trusting."

He could blame her and was in just the rotten mood to do it. "Whatever."

"So, will you give her a ride to police headquarters? The sooner we can get there and plow through all the paperwork, the sooner you can get your car released to you. Then you can forget you've ever seen Sloan Donahue."

"So, where are you from?"

Sloan hadn't wanted to glance over at the man whose name was Mercury Steele, but with his question she felt compelled to do so. She had been satisfied with pretending to view all the sights outside the car's window but now that had to come to an end. It wasn't that she was ignoring him, because to ignore a man who looked like him would be nearly impossible. However, she did have a lot to think about.

Because of her naivete in trusting that man who'd sold her that car, she could have been thrown in jail. She could just imagine her parents' reactions if she'd been forced to call and ask them for bail money. Their accusations that she couldn't fend for herself would have been proved right.

Shifting in her seat, she glanced over to Mercury Steele and asked a question of her own. "How do you know I'm not from here?"

"Trust me. I know."

She raised a brow. "How? My accent?" She honestly didn't think she had one.

"No, it wasn't your accent. It's your looks. I know every beautiful woman in this town. If you were from here, we would have met already."

Was he serious? Sloan studied his profile as he maneuvered the car in traffic and figured that, yes, he was serious. "I'm from Cincinnati, Ohio."

"I represented a kid from there once."

"You're an attorney?"

"No, a sports agent."

She nodded. Although she didn't know a lot about that occupation, other than they brokered deals for athletes wanting to play certain sports for a living, she thought he fit the part. First off, he was a sharp dresser. She was convinced the suit he was wearing was the same designer brand her father and Harold often wore. And then there was this car he was driving. A Tesla, like hers. It was obvious he was a successful man. Why hadn't she noticed that before accusing him of trying to steal her car? A car it seemed was rightfully his.

Sloan released a long sigh and inwardly admitted that, considering the circumstances of how they'd met, she appreciated him giving her a lift to the police station. It was time she told him that and apologized for her earlier accusations.

"Mr. Steele?" They'd come to a traffic light and he

glanced over at her. In a way, she wished he hadn't. There was something about his green eyes that unsettled her.

"Yes?"

"I want to apologize for everything. I honestly didn't know the car was stolen."

He didn't say anything and for a minute she wondered if he would. Instead he stared at her. Finally, before turning back to the road, he said, "Apology accepted."

That made her feel better, although to her way of thinking, he'd said it almost grudgingly. "And I want to thank you for giving me a lift to the police station."

"Don't mention it." A few moments later, he asked, "How old are you, Ms. Donahue?"

"Twenty-five."

He didn't say anything, nor did he glance back over at her. Since he'd asked hers, she could ask his. "And how old are you, Mr. Steele?"

They'd come to another traffic light and he did glance over at her when he said, "Thirty-four."

He kept staring at her as if he expected her to say something, and when she didn't, he said, "When you refer to me as Mr. Steele that makes me feel even older. I prefer being called Mercury."

She lifted a brow. "Like the planet?"

He chuckled. "Yes, like the planet, and also like the chemical element. However, I was named after one of my father's favorite football players."

She nodded. "I understand about being named after someone."

He turned back to the road and asked, "Do you?"

"Yes. I was named after my grandfather. I'm Sloan Elizabeth." She missed her grandfather and often wondered how different things would have been had he lived. He'd died of cancer six years ago. She would never forget when her parents had shown up on her college campus to deliver the news to her. At least they'd had the insight to know that receiving such news over the phone would have devastated her.

She snapped out of her reverie and saw they'd arrived at their destination.

"Here we are," Mercury said.

Three

"In case you haven't noticed, Mercury, Sloan Donahue is a beautiful woman."

Mercury glared over at his oldest brother, Galen. The woman's looks were the last thing Mercury was concerned with. He had called Galen because he lived close by, and his wife, Brittany, had dropped him off. Once his car was released to him, Mercury would need someone to drive it to his place.

"If she hadn't bought a stolen car I wouldn't be here."

"True," Galen said. "Instead you could have been at the junkyard looking at what was left after thieves dismantled it, so the way I see it, her buying it was a blessing in disguise for you. Once you get off your indignant high horse, you will realize that, as well."

Galen paused briefly then added, "And another thing. Evidently you've been so into getting your car back that you failed to notice that everything about Sloan screams money. I don't know her story now, but I'd bet in her past she lived a life of wealth. That's obvious from her manicured nails all the way to those designer shoes. And if you took the time to talk to her instead of glaring at her, you would notice her refined voice. She spells high-class any way you want to look at it."

Mercury didn't want to look at it in any way. Galen was too damn observant to suit him. "Whatever," he said, glancing at his watch.

He wondered what was taking so long. He'd given his statement and now Sloan Donahue was behind closed doors giving hers. It had taken him less than ten minutes, but she'd been in there for nearly thirty.

No sooner had he wondered at that than the closed door opened, and she walked out, followed by a smiling detective. Mercury immediately noticed the man wasn't wearing a wedding ring. He would bet the detective had been in that room flirting with Sloan instead of doing his job. Or it could be the other way around. Sloan might have been deliberately flirting with the man for a lighter sentence. Regardless of the circumstances, possession of stolen property was a serious crime.

"Like I said, she's a beautiful woman," Galen leaned over to whisper.

He turned to his brother and frowned. "Need I remind you that you're a married man and the father of twins."

Galen chuckled. "I was making the observation for you, not for me. I am happy being Brittany's husband and father to Ethan and Elyse. In fact, I'm looking out for their best interests. It's about time Brittany got a new sister-in-law and the twins a new aunt, don't you think?"

Mercury's frown deepened. "Go to hell."

Galen laughed but Mercury ignored his brother when the detective and Sloan approached. "Now can I get my car?" he asked the man who was still smiling.

"Yes. I'll complete the release now." The detective then turned to Sloan. "You have my business card. If you need anything, don't hesitate to give me a call."

"I will."

The detective walked off and then Mercury heard Galen ask Sloan, "Are you okay?"

It was then that Mercury noticed the worried expression bunching her forehead. "Well, I do have a slight problem," she said.

Mercury didn't like the sound of that. "What?"

"I don't have a way home."

When she looked at him expectantly, Mercury said, "And?"

"I was wondering if you could drop me off there."

Personally, Mercury was wondering if she'd considered calling Uber, a cab or a friend. He was about to put such a thought into her head when Galen spoke up and said, "Don't consider it a problem. Mercury will be glad to drop you off."

Mercury gave his brother a look that could have turned him to stone, but Galen ignored it and said, "My five brothers and I were raised to treat all females with the utmost respect. If one is ever in need, we are there for the rescue."

Mercury fought to keep a straight face. *Respect? Rescue?* Of the six of them, Galen had been the most notorious womanizer. His reputation had extended from Phoenix all the way to Charlotte, North Carolina, where their Steele cousins lived. Hell, Galen had gotten expelled from school once after the principal found him under the bleachers making out with the man's daughter. And now he wanted to stand here and say he respected women like he'd always done so.

"Our mother wouldn't have it any other way, right, Mercury?"

Mercury rubbed a hand down his face. Galen would have to bring Eden Tyson Steele up at a time like this. "Yes, right, Galen." Mercury would give his brother hell when he saw him alone later.

At that moment the detective came back with Mercury's keys and said to him, "Here you are."

The man then turned to Sloan, smiled broadly and said, "Again, I regret what happened to you and wish you the best in the future."

"Thanks, Detective Fulton."

"And I meant what I said earlier—if you need anything else, just call the precinct and ask for me," the detective added.

Mercury fought not to begin fuming again inside. Why was everyone treating her like the victim when it had been his car that had been stolen?

"You're ready to go now?" he asked Sloan, deciding to break up the little chitchat. It wouldn't surprise him if the detective asked her for a date right then and there. The man could do whatever he liked, but not on Mercury's time.

"Yes. Mercury, I'm ready."

That was the first time she'd referred to him by name and he didn't appreciate that he liked the way she said it. He then turned to Galen and handed him the key. "Take my baby home and park her in the garage."

"Okay, and there's no reason to rush to your place. Jonas will pick me up from there. He's treating me to lunch."

There was no reason for Mercury to ask why. Those two brothers were always betting against something.

Galen then extended his hand out to Sloan. "It was nice meeting you, Sloan."

"Same here, Galen, and again, you have a beautiful wife and twins."

Mercury lifted a brow. "You know about his wife and kids?"

Sloan smiled. "Yes. He showed me photos."

Galen grinned. "I was keeping her company while you were giving your statement."

"I see." Without saying anything else to Galen, Mercury escorted Sloan out of police headquarters.

Sloan glanced over at the man walking beside her. The man who was too good-looking and she had a feeling he knew it. Otherwise, why would he assume he'd know every single woman he thought beautiful in Phoenix?

But she had a feeling every single woman in Phoenix probably knew him, as well. He was a man a woman couldn't easily forget. Tall with medium brown skin, a strong chiseled jaw and a pair of lips that looked so delicious, it would tempt you to take a lick to test their sweetness. And she couldn't forget those gorgeous green eyes.

When she had used the restroom earlier, two women were talking between stalls after having seen Mercury and Galen. They were familiar with those *green-eyed* Steele brothers. Just from eavesdropping on the women's conversation, she found out that at one time Mercury and his five brothers had been pegged the hottest bachelors in Phoenix. Some even called them the "Bad News" Steeles. Their reputations as die-hard players were legendary. Then real shockers happened when they started getting married, one at a time, leaving only Mercury and his younger brother, Gannon, to fire up women's beds.

She figured there was truth in everything the women had said, especially about the Steele brothers being hot. Although she didn't like Mercury very much and thought his attitude could handle some improvement, his looks were downright gorgeous.

Sloan wished there was a wall somewhere to knock her head against. At this point in her life, being attracted to a man, especially to this one, was ludicrous. She had enough problems on her plate without adding Mercury Steele to the menu.

Walking beside him wasn't easy. His walk was brisk,

and she could barely keep up with him, but she refused to let him leave her. He had to be wondering why she hadn't called a taxi or used Uber to get home. He would probably be shocked to know she'd never used either in her entire life. While growing up, her parents had always provided private transportation for her. Then for her sixteenth birthday, they'd purchased her first car and she'd gotten a new one every year since.

It was only after arriving in Phoenix and taking stock of her predicament that it dawned on her that over the past twenty-five years, her parents had played her right into their hands. They had taken care of her every need, given in to her every whim. She hadn't wanted for anything.

There had been more cash in her bank account than she'd known what to do with and credit cards in her name with unlimited balances. All that had made her completely dependent on them, and shamefully she would admit that for years she hadn't questioned it.

Just because she'd never used other modes of transportation didn't mean she thought she was too good to do so. Today just wasn't a good day to try something new. Especially after what had happened this morning in that dress store.

Her credit card had been declined. A credit card that had been issued through her parents' bank, so she knew who was behind that denial. Her parents were determined to put a squeeze on her so she'd be forced to run back home and be their puppet again. Luckily, after telling the nice saleslady about her job interview, the older woman had helped her get the stain out of her blouse.

With her credit cards canceled and unable to get funds from the ATM, that meant she was low on funds. She'd lost three hundred dollars buying that car and had only less than a hundred in cash on her. When she'd tried calling to reschedule her interview, she was told she would have to reapply. She tried not to feel too sad about that.

Glancing over at the man walking beside her, she noted he was staring straight ahead with a brooding expression on his face. He probably hated being bothered about taking her anywhere again, but she would ignore his mood. After all, if he'd taken better care of his car it would not have gotten stolen and she wouldn't be in this predicament. She knew for her to think that way was absurd, but she didn't care. It was just as illogical for him to think she would have intentionally stolen his car or be in cahoots with the people who had.

"I hope I'm not inconveniencing you again, Mercury."

He glanced over at her and her heart began thumping hard in her chest. The look he gave her wasn't one of annoyance but something else. Something she couldn't quite put a name to. It left her momentarily dazed. Before she could sufficiently recover, the look was gone and replaced by one of indifference.

"No problem," he muttered. "Like Galen said, we were raised to respect women and rescue damsels in distress."

"In that case, you have a very kind mother."

"She is definitely that and I wouldn't trade her for all the tea in China."

Sloan heard fondness in his tone, and she wished she could say the same about her own mother, but she couldn't. It was not that her mother was a bad person because she wasn't. She'd just never made her daughter her priority. Her father hadn't been much better. He never failed to let Sloan know she should have been born a boy, and because she hadn't been, he'd treated her like the disappointment she'd been.

"You're okay?"

She glanced back over at Mercury. They had reached his car. A serious frown marred his forehead. "Yes, I'm

fine." He nodded and then opened the car door for her.
"Thank you."

She slid onto the car's leather seat and then glanced at
him. Their gazes met, and when he stood there a moment,
she lifted a brow. "Is something wrong?"

As if her question made him realize he'd been staring,
he frowned and shook his head. "No. Nothing is wrong."

He then closed the car door and walked around to the
driver's side to get in. He had removed his jacket earlier
and she liked the way the dress shirt fit him. It was obvious he worked out. A man didn't get those kinds of tight
muscles by doing nothing.

"Your address?"

She blinked. "My address?"

"Yes. If I'm to take you home, then I need to know it,
don't you think?"

She swallowed. "Yes, of course." She then rattled it off
for him. When he started the car, she asked, "Aren't you
going to put it in your GPS?"

He glanced over at her before backing out of the parking space. "No. I'm familiar with the area. How long have
you been in Phoenix, Sloan?"

She sighed deeply. "One week tomorrow."

He didn't ask her anything else during the car ride and
she was fine with him ignoring her all the way to their
destination.

"You're having a yard sale?"

His question made her look at him. "A yard sale? No, of
course not. Why would you ask me that?"

"Because of what's going on at your address."

She glanced out the car's window and drew in a sharp
breath. Her belongings—the little she'd brought with her—
were laid out on a table for everyone to see, and it appeared
as if someone was having a sale with her stuff. As soon as
Mercury stopped the car, she was out in a flash.

Four

Mercury called out to Sloan, but she ignored him and marched with indignation toward the older woman who was still placing items on the table. Shaking his head, he quickly followed while wondering what the hell was going on.

"How dare you do this!" he heard Sloan yell at the top of her voice, while placing her hands on her hips. "These are my things."

The woman, who looked to be in her late fifties and several inches shorter than Sloan, didn't cower. Instead she placed her hands on her own hips. "I do dare. I am not selling anything, although I should since you're being evicted."

"Evicted? But why?"

"Like you didn't know the check Priscilla used to pay her rent this month wasn't good! It bounced like a rubber ball."

Mercury felt Sloan stiffen beside him and immediately realized she hadn't known what this person named Priscilla had done. "You got a bad check? I didn't know. I'm sure there's a mistake."

"Ha!" the lady said. "No mistake. Take your stuff and go."

"But you can't make me leave with no place to go,"

Sloan implored. "I'm sure if I call Priscilla, we will have this cleared up."

"Nothing is going to get cleared up. Besides, I already have someone interested in leasing this place and ready to move in. I want you gone."

"Who is this Priscilla and where is she?" Mercury asked Sloan. Personally, he didn't want to get involved, but he didn't like the rude way the woman was talking to Sloan.

She turned to him and he could see the anger in her features. "Priscilla is my roommate from college. She invited me out here but left the day after I arrived. Her boyfriend proposed and sent her a one-way ticket to join him in Spain. Luckily, it was a furnished apartment, and other than dishes and silverware, she packed up her stuff that she didn't want to take with her and put it in storage. She said I could stay here until the end of the month because the rent was paid up."

"Not with a bad check it wasn't," the woman intervened to say. "Now get your things and go."

Sloan turned to the woman. "And I told you that I don't have anywhere to go."

"Not my problem," the woman snapped.

Mercury bit down on his lip. Hadn't he thought the same when told she didn't have a car? However, hearing someone else tell her that didn't sit well with him.

"Thank you for bringing me here, Mercury. I'll be okay."

Did she honestly expect him to leave after hearing her tell the woman that she didn't have any place to go? He shoved his hands into the pockets of his pants. "You will only be okay when you stop trusting people so easily," he said, frowning. First, she'd bought a stolen car from a "nice" man, and now she'd been let down by a friend.

Refusing to let the woman listen to their conversation, he said, "Excuse us." He then took Sloan's hand and led her a few feet away from the older woman's ears. "Listen, I can't leave until I truly know you are okay."

"Thanks for your concern, but I have to figure things out on my own."

He nodded. "And how will you do that and where? Were you telling the truth when you said you didn't have any-place else to go?"

He watched her nibble on her bottom lip. She then stared into his eyes. "Yes. I was telling the truth. I've been in town just a week and don't know a soul."

He started to say she knew him and Galen. And she also knew Sherman and the overly friendly detective. The detective had even invited her to call him if she ever needed anything. It might be a good time to suggest she take the man up on his offer.

But Mercury knew he couldn't do that. He and his brothers might have notorious reputations, but who was to say Sherman and that detective were better? Besides, Galen was right. Mercury and his brothers might be known for their whorish ways, but thanks to Eden Steele, they knew how far to take them when it came to a woman in need.

"Do you have the funds to move elsewhere?" he asked. He had a feeling she didn't, no matter what Galen had pointed out about her being high-class. He refused to make any assumptions about her.

"No," she said despondently. "Getting to Phoenix took most of my money. Priscilla had offered me a place to stay until I got a job and was on my feet. I had a job interview this morning at a bank."

He had a feeling it had taken a lot for her to admit all of that. Now he wondered if she would answer his next question. "Are you running away from someone?" *A jealous boyfriend perhaps*, he thought.

She hesitated a minute and then nodded. "Yes."

Since she'd given him that much information, he decided to delve deeper. "Who?"

She paused and then said, "Controlling parents. They were pushing me to marry a man they approved of, Harold. That was fine until he told me marrying me meant he got to keep his girlfriend and that she would be a part of our marriage."

"Excuse me." Mercury was certain he'd heard wrong. He decided to make sure. "You didn't just say the man you were engaged to marry told you he intended to make his girlfriend his mistress, did you?"

"Yes, that's what I said."

Mercury was convinced that now he'd heard everything. "Why didn't you tell your parents?"

"I did."

"And they still wanted you to marry the guy?"

"Yes. I'm their only child and the marriage between me and Harold would help them with a business merger."

Mercury shook his head. It was hard to believe people actually thought that way. Although his mother had been notorious for wanting all six of her sons happily married, but all along the key words were *happily married*. She would not have forced them into anything, not that they would have let her.

"So, I decided to leave Ohio and stay with Priscilla. I found out this morning that my parents put a hold on my bank account and I can't get any cash right now. And they canceled my credit cards."

"They actually did that?" he asked, amazed at how far her parents were taking things.

"Yes. They figure sooner or later, without the financial resources I'm used to, I'll run back home to do whatever they want me to do."

"Which is to marry that prick?"

"Yes."

At that moment, Mercury knew he couldn't leave her here. He had a huge condo, but he couldn't take her there either. His home was sacred, and other than female relatives, he didn't invite women over the Mercury Steele threshold.

"I will give you a chance to go back in the house and grab anything I might have missed bringing out," the woman called, as if she was doing Sloan a favor.

"Go on," he said to Sloan. Although she was trying hard not to show it, he could still detect how upset she was. "You might as well take advantage of her so-called generosity. I will help you get your things repacked."

She slumped her shoulders. "Thanks. And then what?"

"And then we load the stuff into my car and get the hell away from here."

"And go where? I don't know you well enough to go to your place."

"I don't remember inviting you to my place." In a way, he was glad she wasn't suggesting that he do such a thing. "I'm taking you to where you'll be okay for the night."

"Where? To a homeless shelter?"

"No."

"Then where?"

He hesitated briefly before saying, "I'm taking you to my mom."

Sloan tried not to dwell on the fact that this was the third time today that she was being taken somewhere by Mercury Steele, and if he was taking her to his mother's like he said, it wouldn't be the last.

She couldn't believe that she'd broken down and told him everything. The only reason she could think of for doing so was that she needed him to understand that being needy wasn't her choice, but a situation being forced on her.

Now, of all places, he was taking her to his mother's. *His mother.* If Sloan hadn't needed a place to stay for the night, she would have refused. Priscilla's reply to the text she'd sent had said there was no way her check had bounced and that she would contact her bank about it. Priscilla wished she could send her money to tide her over, but she didn't have any extra cash.

Sloan glanced over at Mercury. "Are you sure it's okay with your mom to have an unexpected overnight houseguest?" She figured that would be all the time she needed to come up with a plan B, and she had already sent a text message to Lisa Hall, another friend from college, who was living in Miami.

The car had come to a traffic light and he glanced back at her. "Yes, I'm sure she won't mind."

Sloan raised a brow. "Have you done this sort of thing before? Taken strangers to your mom for the night?"

"No. But I know my mom. She has a heart of gold."

Sloan's mother had a heart of gold, too, but not in the same sense. Both her parents thought money was everything and the only important thing in life was more of it. "Tell me about your mom."

He chuckled. "I'll let you get to know her on your own."

"What about your dad?"

He chuckled again. "Dad loves Mom, and whatever makes her happy makes him happy."

"Your parents love each other?" she asked, surprise flitting across her features.

"Of course. Don't yours?"

"No," she replied without hesitation. "I never thought they did and they confirmed it when I told them about Harold's mistress. They felt a loveless marriage wouldn't be so bad since they'd had one for years."

"They actually told you that?"

"Yes. My parents think wealth, not love, is what makes a good marriage."

He stared at her and then asked, "What do *you* think makes a good marriage?"

She released a deep sigh. "I'm not sure there is such a thing as a good marriage. All I know is that I refuse to be forced into one."

The traffic light went to green and Mercury's attention returned to the road. Just as well, she thought. With parents like his, he wouldn't fully understand parents like hers.

"How did you and this Harold guy meet?"

She glanced over at Mercury, whose eyes were still on the road. "Our families have always known each other. Harold and I began officially dating a year ago." She paused. "He says he loves the other woman, and if he could marry her, he would. However, he's too much of a weakling to stand up to his parents."

What she'd just said was true. She was convinced Harold was so conditioned to do whatever he was told, he couldn't fathom doing anything else. But then, she had been the same way until she'd begun to see that was no longer the way she wanted to live.

"Here we are."

She looked out the windshield as Mercury pulled into the circular driveway of a house that was just as big as the one her parents owned. "Your parents' home is beautiful."

"Thanks."

She felt nervous tension line her stomach.

As if he sensed her anxiety, when Mercury brought the car to a stop, he smiled over at her and said, "Things will be fine. Trust me."

Five

Mercury walked into his parents' home, placed Sloan's luggage down and then glanced around, wondering where his parents were. Both their cars were in the driveway. Suddenly, he heard a sound upstairs in their bedroom and immediately got the picture. He turned to Sloan to find her glancing around. Evidently she hadn't a clue.

Quickly moving to the intercom system on the wall, he pressed the one for his parents' bedroom. "Mom. Dad. I'm here and I have a guest."

Turning to Sloan, he thought the last thing he wanted was for her to figure out what his parents were doing. But then he realized that maybe she should know there were some couples who loved the sanctity of marriage and all the benefits that came with it.

"Come, let me show you my mother's courtyard." He opened the French doors to the garden that held every type flower imaginable.

"It's so nice out here. Is this the house you grew up in?"

"Yes. My parents knew they wanted a large family and

decided to buy a house to accommodate their dream. Galen told you about our brothers, so if you can see the first eight years of my parents' marriage, Mom was pregnant most of the time."

"And loved every moment," his mother said, joining them outside. If she was surprised to find his guest was a woman, she didn't show it.

Not waiting for him to make introductions, Eden Tyson Steele moved toward them, giving Sloan what Mercury thought was a very gracious smile. He'd made the right decision in bringing Sloan here. Extending her hand to Sloan, she said, "Hello, I'm Eden Tyson Steele."

For a minute, Mercury thought Sloan was about to curtsy. He understood. In addition to being an awe-inspiring beauty, his mother's elegant and refined manner had an effect on people. Even now Eden looked as if she'd just stepped off the cover of *Vogue* magazine.

"Mom, I'd like you to meet Sloan Donahue. Sloan, this is my mother," Mercury said.

Eden's smile widened. "Nice to meet you, Sloan. You're a friend of Mercury's?"

"No," he answered quickly before Sloan could. "Sloan and I just met today."

His mother looked up at him. "Oh?"

"It's a long story, and unfortunately, I don't have time to explain since I have an important appointment at the office. She needs you."

Eden lifted a brow. "She does?"

"Yes. I'm leaving her here with you. She'll explain everything."

Then, not waiting for his mother's questions—or Sloan's, for that matter—he quickly headed for the door.

Sloan watched Mercury leave, feeling embarrassed that he was doing so without an explanation to his mother or even a goodbye to her. They might not be seeing each other again. She forced her attention away from the closed French doors and looked at the woman standing in front of her.

Eden Tyson Steele's eyes were the exact shade of green as her son's and she was simply gorgeous. Sloan didn't want to keep staring, but her face looked familiar. The woman still had such a warm smile on her face that Sloan felt even worse.

"I'm sorry," she finally found her voice to say. "I should not have let Mercury bring me here."

"Nonsense. I saw the luggage by the door and wondered who it belonged to. Have you had lunch yet?"

Lunch? She'd barely had breakfast. She had grabbed a doughnut and coffee at the diner on the corner. That was when she'd spilled coffee on her blouse. "No, but I couldn't possibly let you feed me, too. Mercury said I could stay the night, but it's your house and your decision. If you prefer I leave, then—"

"Of course you won't be leaving. I will show you to the guest room, where you can get settled, freshen up and join me and my husband, Drew, for lunch."

"Did I hear my name?"

Sloan turned to see a very handsome older gentleman stroll into the courtyard. Eden's son might have her eyes, but everything else belonged to the man who came over to join them and place an arm around Eden's shoulders. Galen's and Mercury's coloring was a combination of their two parents, but their chiseled, handsome looks were from this man. She couldn't help wondering about the other four brothers. Galen said all six had their mother's eyes, but did they have their father's handsome features?

"Yes, sweetheart." Sloan watched as Eden smiled up at the man with both love and adoration in her eyes. Sloan wasn't sure how she recognized such emotions, since she wasn't around them often, but in this case, she could. "Mercury brought us a houseguest. A friend of his, Sloan Donahue." Then to Sloan, she said, "This is Mercury's father, Drew."

He bestowed a smile that was nearly identical to Galen's. She couldn't say it was similar to Mercury's, since she'd yet to see him smile. "How are you, Sloan?"

She took the hand he extended. "I'm fine, but I need to correct something," she said, looking from Drew to Eden. "I'm not a friend of Mercury's."

Drew lifted his brow. "You're not?"

"No. In fact, I'm almost certain he doesn't like me very much."

"Why do you think that?" Eden asked.

Sloan released a deep breath. "His car was stolen a few nights ago and he found it today...with me driving it." At the surprised look on their faces she said, "I unknowingly bought a stolen car." She then told them about their trip to police headquarters and meeting Galen.

"And Mercury brought you here after leaving police headquarters?" Drew asked curiously.

Sloan shook her head. "No, there's more. It's a rather long story."

Eden smiled and gently patted her shoulder. "And we definitely have time to hear it. Over lunch."

Mercury got off the elevator and walked over to the woman sitting at the huge desk in the reception area. "Good afternoon, Pauline. Have the Eastwoods arrived?"

"Good afternoon, Mr. Steele, and no. They did call and say they were on their way. They got caught up in road-construction traffic."

Good, Mercury thought. The last thing he wanted was to keep them waiting again. "Thanks. I'll be in my office. Please send them in the minute they arrive."

"Yes, sir."

He entered his office and closed the door behind him. After removing his jacket and placing his briefcase aside, he placed his cell phone on his desk before easing down in the chair behind it. He then leaned back to think. Not about the Eastwoods because he felt fairly confident that was a deal in the making.

His thoughts were on Sloan Donahue.

Maybe he should have said goodbye. She would spend the night at his parents' home, which would give her a chance to convince her own parents to unblock her credit cards and bank account. And then she'd be gone.

No matter what she'd told him, he just couldn't fathom anyone's parents holding such a hard-line position when they discovered she'd been evicted. There was no way they would want her living homeless on the streets.

And even if she was right about her parents, once she explained her situation to Eden, his mother would probably make a few calls and secure Sloan a job as a live-in companion to one of the older women at his mother's church. Even if she took the position only temporarily, it would allow her to save money, get her own place and apply for higher-paying jobs.

Either way, Sloan wasn't his concern anymore.

Picking up the paperweight on his desk, he exhaled, thinking about how Sloan had dropped into his day. He would admit that he found her attractive. What man in his right mind wouldn't? However, the woman had issues, and he still couldn't get beyond the fact she'd been driving his car. His stolen car.

His cell phone rang. He clicked it on after checking caller ID. "What do you want, Galen?"

"I thought you would like to know the Camaro is parked safely in your garage. Jonas is here to give me a ride back home, and we figured we should take some of your Scotch, as a thank-you for all our help."

Mercury rolled his eyes. "Kind of early in the day for Scotch, isn't it?"

"Not if we each take a bottle."

Mercury sat straight up in the chair. "You didn't help me that much, and I honestly don't recall Jonas helping at all."

"He came here to pick me up. That's helping. And maybe I should mention that we also washed your car. It was dirty but at least there weren't any dents."

"Yes. Despite everything, I appreciate that. And I guess since the two of you washed the car, that earned you each a bottle."

"Stop being so stingy. It's not as if your booze cellar isn't stocked with enough wine and liquor to last a lifetime," Galen said.

"Whatever."

"So, did you get Sloan home okay?"

A frown touched the corner of Mercury's mouth. "Yes. Just in time to be evicted."

"What!"

"You heard me." He then spent the next ten minutes telling Galen what had happened and the information Sloan had shared with him about her parents.

"I knew it!" Galen said. "I told you she came from money. Please don't tell me you dropped her off anyway and kept going."

"Okay, I won't tell you."

"Mercury!"

"For Pete's sake, stop screaming in my ear, Galen. Of course I couldn't just drop her off, especially after that damn respect-and-rescue crap you told her."

"It's the truth and you know it. So, what did you do? Where did you take her? Please don't tell me to your place."

"You know me better than that. I don't do female sleepovers, houseguests, drop-ins or otherwise."

"So, where is she?"

"At the best place and with the finest people. They know how to deal with issues like hers."

"Ah hell, Mercury. Please don't tell me that in your haste to get rid of her you took her to a homeless shelter."

Mercury rolled his eyes. "No, Galen, I didn't take her to the homeless shelter. I took her to our folks. More specifically, I took her to Mom."

"So, there you have it," Sloan said to Mercury's parents as she finished off the last of the chicken-salad sandwich Eden had served with chips and a glass of iced tea.

"My parents refused to back down about me marrying Harold. When I left home, I had a small amount of cash and a couple of credit cards in my name. I used most of my cash when I bought Mercury's car."

Sloan drew in a deep breath. Already she could tell that Mercury's parents were different from her own. That made her wonder if perhaps they thought she'd made up the entire thing. "I know what I just told you about my circumstances might be hard to believe, but it's true."

Eden smiled and gently patted Sloan's hand. "Oh, I believe you. In fact, listening to you brought back memories of how Drew and I met."

Sloan was surprised to hear that. "Really?"

"Yes. Like yours, my parents also had money and an arranged marriage in my future. It wasn't that Mark and I didn't get along or that he wasn't a nice guy, but we didn't love each other, and I had other plans for my future. I wanted to be a model and had actually gotten an agent and was doing a few jobs behind my parents' backs right after college."

"What happened?"

"They found out and told me to quit the modeling and

instead concentrate on becoming Mark's wife…or else they would stop providing me with anything. Up until then, I'd had the best of everything. Of course, I didn't believe they would do it, try forcing me into a marriage I didn't want. But they were determined."

Eden took a sip of her tea, and the expression on her face let Sloan know she was remembering that time. "I was deeply upset when they threatened to destroy the model agency representing me, and my agent caved in under pressure and dropped me. When I still refused to do what they wanted, my parents took my car and charge cards, as well as closing my bank account, leaving me with very little to my name."

Sloan leaned forward, intrigued by what Eden was sharing and fascinated by how similar it was to her own situation. "What did you do?"

"I was determined to make it on my own, so with only a couple of hundred dollars in my pocket, I did something rather foolish. Something that these days I wouldn't advise anyone to do, especially a woman."

"And what was that?"

"I stowed away in the back of a tractor trailer at a truck stop, hiding behind boxes of auto parts the trucker was hauling from Phoenix to California. At the time I was too upset with my agent and my parents to consider the danger doing something like that involved. Luckily for me, the trucker was this guy here," Eden said, smiling over at her husband. "He said my perfume gave me away and my scent was all over his truck. He'd gone ten miles before he pulled over and found me hiding. He threatened to take me back to the truck stop, but I talked him out of it and persuaded him to take me with him to California. Less than two years later, we were married."

Sloan studied Eden and then recognition dawned. Eden

Tyson. This was the Eden Tyson who'd been a renowned supermodel right along with the likes of Christie Brinkley, Cindy Crawford and Naomi Campbell. And she was Mercury's mother? Wow!

"I recognize you now and you're still beautiful," she said in awe, complimenting the older woman.

"Thank you, Sloan."

"And I'm glad your situation had a happy ending."

Eden's smile widened. "And I have a feeling yours will, as well."

An hour later, Sloan walked out of the guest-room bath feeling totally refreshed after her shower. She appreciated Eden and Drew opening their home to her. This was such a lovely guest room. The entire house was beautiful and had the feel of a home and not just a house.

Sloan also appreciated Eden and Drew sharing their story with her. She could see by the way they looked at each other that Mercury had been right. His parents did love each other. That was how it was supposed to be. Although marriage was not in Sloan's plans, if she ever did marry it would be for love and nothing else.

She was about to blow-dry her hair when her cell phone rang. She immediately recognized the caller. Harold. Moving to the bed, she picked up her phone. "Why are you calling me?"

"Thanks to you, the folks, both yours and mine, are mad at me."

Did he honestly call to tell her that? "Not my problem."

"It *is* your problem because now they blame me for you ending our engagement. They've given me one week to have you back here in Cincinnati and planning our wedding. So, where are you?"

If Sloan hadn't known it before, she definitely knew it now. Harold Cunningham was a jackass, especially if he thought there was a chance for them to get back together.

"You don't need to know where I am because there won't be a wedding between us. Ever."

And without saying goodbye, Sloan disconnected the call.

Six

"Is it true?"

Mercury glanced up to find his brothers Eli and Tyson standing in the doorway of his office. Neither believed in knocking, and since Pauline had left early today, they'd taken advantage of not having to be announced.

He really wasn't surprised to see either Eli or Tyson today. Eli's law firm took up the entire twentieth floor and he was known to drop in and talk about his wife and one-year-old son, Elias. Like Galen, Eli had fallen into the role of family man like he'd been bred for the part.

As far as Tyson, the Steele brother who was a gifted heart surgeon, was concerned, Mercury knew, from running into Hunter earlier, that Tyson was here picking her up from work for one of their date nights.

A huge smile touched Mercury's lips. "I guess you guys heard that I signed Norris Eastwood today. It will probably make the news this evening."

"We hadn't heard that," Eli said, coming into Mercury's office with Tyson on his heels.

"Congratulations," they both then said.

"Thanks." Mercury leaned back in the chair behind his desk. "If the two of you didn't know about Eastwood, then what are you asking about being true?"

Eli eased down in one of the guest chairs. "The fact that you took a woman home to Mom. And according to Galen, she's a sizzling-hot looker *and* a prim-and-proper lady. She's just the type a guy *would* take home to his mother. What could you have been thinking? A man never takes a woman home to his mother for any reason unless it's serious."

Mercury rolled his eyes. "Galen has blown things all out of proportion. The woman was down on her luck and needed a place to stay for the night."

"And you honestly think our mother will give her refuge for just one night? If Mom likes her, and Galen is convinced that she will, chances are that woman will stay while Mom turns her into your future bride."

Mercury sat up straight in his chair. "That won't be happening."

"You'll never convince Mom of that," Tyson said. "Have you forgotten how Mom and Dad met?"

"Of course I haven't forgotten. Mom stowed away in the back of Dad's rig."

Tyson was still grinning. "And do you recall just why Mom did that?"

The line of concentration along Mercury's brow deepened. "Yes. She was on the run from her parents…"

His voice trailed off when he remembered. Clearly remembered. He gazed over at his brothers, who were staring at him. Now they were both grinning with a "you really set yourself up for that one" look on their faces.

"I need to talk to Mom," Mercury said, quickly moving to the coatrack and grabbing his jacket. The last thing he wanted was for Eden Tyson Steele to fill her head up with romantic ideas, just because she had ended up marrying her rescuer.

"It might be too late, Mercury. You might as well accept your fate."

He ignored Eli's comment as he briskly walked out of his office.

"And you're sure you'll be okay?" Eden asked Sloan again.

Sloan smiled. Drew and Eden had a prior dinner engagement that they'd offered to cancel. Sloan wouldn't hear of it and refused to disrupt their plans for the evening. "I'll be fine. Since you graciously offered me the use of your computer, I'm going to search the internet for more job opportunities."

"Well, if you're sure, then all right," Eden said, smiling. "You have my phone number if you need me and if you get hungry there's plenty of food in the refrigerator."

"Thanks. I'll be fine."

When Drew and Eden left, Sloan crossed her arms over her chest and thanked her lucky stars. She appreciated Mercury for bringing her here. His parents were super. They'd even suggested she remain with them until she was back on her feet. Of course, she couldn't do that, but she had agreed to stay an additional day. She'd sent a text to her friend Lisa, who'd quickly responded and said she could send her a thousand dollars without any problem. The only problem was on Sloan's end since she had no way of receiving the money with a closed bank account.

Another thing she appreciated was Eden letting her use the computer in her office since the battery in Sloan's laptop had died hours ago. After mentioning to Eden that she spoke several different languages, Eden had asked her if she'd ever considered working as an interpreter. It just so happened that she knew the Miss Universe pageant was looking for someone with her credentials. Eden had a friend with connections to the pageant and would arrange for the woman to talk with Sloan about it.

An hour later, Sloan pushed away from the computer feeling irritated at not being able to open a new bank account online. It seemed that her driver's license number was being blocked for some reason. She sighed, trying not to feel defeated.

She was about to try again with another bank when her phone rang. She hoped it wasn't Harold calling again. Her heart kicked up a beat when she saw the caller was her mother.

She clicked on. "Yes, Mom?"

"We expected you back by now, Sloan Elizabeth. We do have a wedding to plan, sweetheart."

Sloan swallowed deeply, knowing it was going to be one of those conversations. Why had she hoped her mother was calling to tell her that she and her father had been wrong trying to force her into a loveless marriage?

Placing the phone on the desk, she decided to put her mother on speakerphone so she could talk while maneuvering through the sites of several banks. "Sorry to disappoint you. I keep telling you that there won't be a wedding. Why won't you and Dad believe me?" she asked her mother.

"Because we know you. Why are you being difficult? You are only hurting yourself. You know your father. He is going to get his way about this or else…"

Sloan lifted a brow. "Or else what?"

"Or else he's going to make you suffer needlessly. Putting a hold on your funds and credit cards is just the beginning. Do you honestly think it was a coincidence you got evicted?"

Sloan sat up straight in her chair. "Please don't tell me Dad had something to do with Priscilla's check bouncing."

"Okay, I won't tell you."

Sloan rubbed a hand down her face, not believing this, although she knew she should.

She didn't have to wonder how he'd found out about her plans with Priscilla. Her father kept on retainer a man who owned one of the most reputable investigative companies in Ohio. She wouldn't have put it past her father to hack into her phone to retrieve all her text messages and phone conversations with Priscilla. Did he also know about the money Lisa had agreed to send her? Would he try sabotaging that, as well? She then thought about how difficult it was for her to open a bank account online. She suddenly felt uneasy. Perhaps he already had.

"What Dad did to Priscilla's bank account was illegal," she said, not caring if she raised her voice.

"You might think so, but he considers it a necessary means to an end. I don't think you realize just how important your marriage to Harold is for this family."

"And what about my survival, Mom? Better yet, what about my happiness?"

"I've discovered a person can force themselves to be happy under any given situation."

"Happiness shouldn't have to be forced."

"I blame your grandfather for putting all these foolish ideas into your head. Being born a Donahue comes with certain costs that must be paid."

"I refuse to pay them."

"Then you're only asking for trouble, Sloan Elizabeth. Not only for yourself but for any allies you drag into this mess."

A lump formed in Sloan's throat. "What do you mean?"

"What I mean is that your father can be ruthless. Please don't drive him to be that way with not only you, but also with others you might befriend in your quest to disobey us. We know Harold called to make amends. He told us you're being difficult with him, too. It's time for you to stop this foolishness. Harold is coming to Phoenix and we expect you to be nice to him when he gets there."

Like hell she would. Sloan was ready to end the call. She knew that nothing she said to her mother would get through to her, so there was no need to waste her time. "And it's time for you and Dad to stop trying to control me. I won't let you do it. Goodbye, Mom." She clicked off the phone.

"I gather your folks still are causing problems."

Sloan swiveled around in her chair to find Mercury standing in the office doorway.

"Sorry, I didn't mean to startle you," Mercury said, coming to stand in the room.

Sloan glared at him. "Are you apologizing for eavesdropping, as well?"

He leaned against a file cabinet while remembering how Galen had described her to Eli. A sizzling-hot looker who was also prim and proper. He wholeheartedly agreed with the description and found it fascinating that any woman could be both.

"I didn't have to eavesdrop. You were talking loud enough for the entire house to hear. Where are my parents, by the way?" He wasn't ready to discuss the parts of her phone conversation that he'd heard and wished he hadn't. Doing so would only make him mad about the things her mother had said.

"Your parents went out for the evening. They had a dinner date with another couple."

"Probably the Connors," Mercury said, thinking aloud. Deciding to return to his earlier comment, he said, "Sounds like your parents are trying to stir up trouble for you."

She shifted in the chair, and that was when he noticed she had changed from the skirt and blouse she'd been wearing earlier to a pretty pink sundress. Why did the color pink make her look both sexy and feminine?

"A part of me wishes you hadn't heard that, but in a way, I'm glad you did. Now you can explain to your mother why I left, when she returns." Sloan stood. "I need to go pack."

Mercury shoved his hands into the pockets of his pants. "And just where do you think you're going?"

She shrugged a nice pair of shoulders beneath the spaghetti straps of her dress. "Not sure, but I have to leave here. I don't know how much of the conversation you heard, but if my father thinks you and your family are befriending me, he will cause problems for you."

Mercury just stared at her. Did she honestly think his family needed to be protected against a man who was acting more like a bully than a father? Mercury had heard what her mother said about Sloan's father's ruthless side. He'd also heard there was a strong possibility her ex-fiancé was coming to town to talk her into going ahead with their wedding plans.

"I don't know where I'm going, Mercury, but I need to leave here."

He shook his head. "Honestly? In the middle of the night, with no place to go and no transportation to get there? And before you even think to ask me to take you anywhere, the answer is no."

He watched her nibble on her bottom lip and wished like hell he didn't feel a tightening in his gut. He didn't like the way his thoughts were going with her. He could accept being attracted to her, since it came with the territory of who and what he was. A reaction to any beautiful woman was automatic. Only problem was that he had no desire to be attracted to this one.

"Okay, I won't leave tonight, but I will be leaving in the morning. That will give me a chance to explain things to your mother."

"Good luck with that." Mercury knew his mother. There

was no way Eden would let Sloan go anywhere after she explained things.

"Regardless, I will leave first thing tomorrow for the airport."

He raised a brow. "The airport? To go where and how will you pay for a ticket?"

"I have a college friend living in Florida named Lisa. I contacted her and she said she'll be able to loan me a thousand dollars. I'll use it to hide out somewhere in another state where nobody knows me."

"Another friend you can trust?" he asked sarcastically.

She lifted her chin. "You obviously didn't hear what my mother said about my eviction today."

No, he hadn't heard that part. "What about it?"

"My father was behind that, as well."

An incredulous expression settled on Mercury's face. "You've got to be kidding me."

"Sadly, I'm not." She then told him what her mother had said.

"But how could he remove funds from someone's bank account?" Mercury asked.

"Dad is on the board of a number of national banks. Unfortunately, one of those includes Priscilla's bank. He didn't have the funds removed—instead he probably worked with the banker to have them appear as if they weren't there to accomplish what he needed to have done."

As far as Mercury was concerned, her father was worse than ruthless. He was a tyrant.

"So, as you can see, my father will stop at nothing to get what he wants. He doesn't care who he hurts or maligns in the process. I refuse to let your family become involved."

A frown settled on his face. "That's not your decision to make."

"What do you mean it's not my decision to make?"

"The Steeles can take care of ourselves."

"But you don't know my father."

"Wrong. Your father doesn't know us."

She shook her head. "Look, Mercury, no matter what you say, I *am* leaving town tomorrow."

"Aren't you afraid he will cause this Lisa retribution, as well?"

She shook her head. "No. Lisa's father is a US senator and her mother is a high-profile judge. My father isn't crazy enough to mess with their daughter." Then after she'd thought for a moment, she said, "But what Dad *is* doing is blocking my ability to open a bank account online."

Mercury rubbed his hand down his face in frustration. The main reason he had come here was to meet with his mom and quell any foolish notions she might have about any type of relationship developing between him and Sloan, because it wouldn't be happening. But now, after overhearing that phone conversation, protecting Sloan from her tyrannical father had become more of a priority to him.

"Obviously your father is tracking you with your phone. You need to get rid of it."

She nodded, agreeing. "I'll ditch it. One of the first things I will do when I get the money from Lisa is buy one of those burner phones." Then she asked him, "Do you have a way to receive funds through your phone?"

He had a feeling why she was asking. "Yes."

"Do you have a problem with Lisa sending the money to your bank account since I can't open one of my own?"

"Yes, I have a problem with it."

First of all, he didn't like the thought that she was willing to be on the run like some hunted animal. And second, he refused to believe her father had a way to block her from opening an account at every damn bank in the country.

"Why?"

He crossed his arms over his chest. Earlier today he would have pegged her as a spoiled, rich woman, used to getting whatever she wanted. He'd even felt she had gotten easy treatment at police headquarters. However, the hurt and humiliation he'd seen during her eviction had been real. He'd even felt her defeat. He was somewhat feeling it now and he didn't like it.

"I prefer not being an accomplice to your cowardice."

An angry look appeared on her face and she was out of her chair in a flash. She got right in his face. "How dare you insinuate that I'm a coward? You don't know me or my parents. You don't know how manipulative they can be to get what they want."

He wished she wasn't standing so close. His gaze suddenly became fixated on the delicious shape of her lips. He was staring at them and not her eyes. Unfortunately, she was too fired up to notice.

Not liking where his thoughts or his libido were headed, in a voice gruffer than he liked, he said, "Maybe it's time you stand up to your parents. Running away is not going to help and they will see that as a weakness to prey on."

"You think I don't know that?" she snapped. "I know my parents a lot better than you, and I'm trying to prevent all of you from getting to know them. Trust me—you wouldn't want to."

She drew in a deep breath, and when she did, the suction was like a vacuum, drawing his mouth closer…and she still didn't notice. "Whether you help me or not, I am leaving Phoenix tomorrow. I'll tell your parents when they return tonight and that's final."

Mercury wasn't sure what pushed him to make the next move. It could have been the frustration he felt at that moment or the proximity of his mouth to hers. All he knew was that he was trying to talk some sense into her, and she wanted to give in without a fight. That annoyed the hell out of him. Reaching out, he pulled her into his arms.

He hesitated only a moment—long enough for her to pull away or not—and captured her mouth with his.

He wasn't sure what he expected when his mouth connected with hers, but it definitely wasn't the way fire blasted through every part of his body. Nor had he expected the taste of her tongue to go straight to his groin. And he absolutely had not expected her mouth to soften beneath the forceful demand of his.

This was what he would call a mind-blowing kiss, definitely one for the record books. And the way she followed his lead with her tongue tugged at everything male within him.

When the sound of someone clearing their throat intruded, Sloan all but jumped out of his arms. He released her and turned to find his mother standing in the office doorway with an unreadable expression on her face. This wouldn't be the first time his mother had caught him kissing a girl and he doubted it would be the last. But he could just imagine what Eden was thinking and he knew he needed to get something straight before she got any wrong ideas.

Stepping away from Sloan, he said, "It's not what you think. I was trying to talk some sense into her."

Eden lifted a brow. "Oh? Is that how it's done now?"

Mercury released a heavy sigh. "Maybe you will succeed where I've failed. She is about to make a big mistake," he said in a curt tone. Knowing he needed to put as much distance between him and Sloan as he could, he asked, "Where's Dad?"

"In his man cave. Maybe you ought to join him there and chill a minute."

"I think I will." Without giving Sloan a backward glance, he strolled past his mother and out of her office.

Walking quickly, he took the steps down to the basement, where his father's man cave was located. His father stood in front of the huge flat-screen television holding the remote while trying to find a decent channel.

Without bothering to turn around, Drew said, "I saw your car parked in the driveway, Mercury. Do I need to wonder why you're here?"

Mercury slid down on the sofa. "It's not what you think."

Drew turned and looked at his fifth-born son. "It's not?"

"No."

His father stared at him a minute too long to suit Mercury. "Is something wrong, Dad?"

His father shrugged his shoulders. "I hope for your sake there's not."

Seven

Sloan figured she had a lot of explaining to do to Eden. But first she needed to give her head a chance to stop spinning and her body time to cease throbbing.

What man kissed like that? Definitely not Harold and certainly not Carlos Larson, that guy she'd dated in college and the only man she'd slept with.

She hadn't known someone could capture your lips in a way where you felt under siege and too filled with pleasure to do anything but be a willing participant.

"Are you okay, Sloan?"

She glanced at Eden and saw the concern in her eyes. "I guess I need to explain."

"Only if you want to."

She didn't want to, but she knew she should. "I owe you one regardless. You've been nothing but kind. And Mercury was right. He started out trying to talk some sense into me. Then something happened we didn't expect and both now strongly regret. I apologize that you were privy to our foolishness. There is no excuse for our behavior."

"No need to apologize, but why did he feel the need to

talk some sense into you?" Eden asked, coming to sit down on the love seat.

"Mainly because I've made decisions about a few things."

"Oh?"

"Yes. I got a call from my mother letting me know my father was behind my eviction today."

"He was?"

"Yes. Mom also informed me that Dad intends to make trouble for anyone who tries to help me out of the predicament they've deliberately put me in."

Sloan noticed that Eden didn't seem bothered by that revelation. Instead she said, "I think you need to start from the beginning."

Sloan told Mercury's mother everything. When she'd finished, Eden didn't say anything for a minute. "All this time I was under the assumption that when they made my father, Elijah Tyson, that they broke the mold. Obviously not, if your father is his clone."

Sloan lifted a brow. "You told me about your father at lunch. Are you saying your father was like mine?"

Eden chuckled. "Close enough. When he discovered Drew had helped me cross state lines, he tried to have him arrested. When that didn't work, he tried destroying Drew's trucking business."

"Oh, my."

"Yes. But Drew was determined not to go anywhere, even when Dad tried paying him off. Dad literally disowned me until his first grandchild was born, especially one with the Tysons' trademark green eyes. That's when he began changing." Eden smiled. "You can say Galen captured his grandfather's heart. Then I guess he figured Drew couldn't be all bad since the two of us could make a child so perfect. There was also the fact that Drew had money. He was a self-made billionaire who'd turned his trucking company into a huge success."

Eden paused and then added, "He came around, asking for our forgiveness."

"Did you forgive him?" Sloan asked, coming to sit beside Eden on the love seat.

"Yes, because we knew his apology was sincere. My mother had died and he didn't want to spend the rest of his years a mean and hateful man without any family. By the time my second child was born, I honored my father by giving my son my maiden name of Tyson. All six of my sons were very close to their grandfather until the day he died nearly eight years ago."

Sloan didn't say anything. She had lost her grandfather as well, six years ago. "Do you think I'm making a mistake by running away again?"

Eden reached out and took Sloan's hand in hers. "Only you can answer that. You are an adult and what you decide to do is your rightful decision to make. However, please don't make it on the assumption you have to protect my family, just because we are people decent enough to help a young woman in need."

Sloan took in those words and then said, "I have decisions to make."

Eden nodded. "Yes, but the good thing is that you don't have to make them tonight. Or tomorrow. Our offer still stands. You can stay here for as long as you need."

"Thank you."

Eden stood. "I suggest you get a good night's sleep. I can imagine Mercury was overwhelming. That's how he is when he cares about something—or someone."

Sloan hoped Eden wasn't thinking that way because she'd walked in on Sloan and Mercury kissing. They had just gotten caught up in the moment and the clashing of wills. "He only brought me here because he wants to wash his hands of me."

Eden waved off her words. "Don't worry about Mercury. I'm sure he'll get over it."

Sloan thought that might be true for him, but she had a feeling that kiss they'd shared had affected her in a way she wasn't sure she'd ever get over.

Mercury was trying to show interest in the basketball game on the huge flat-screen. After all, sports was his business and one of the players was someone he represented. However, at that moment, none of that mattered. His thoughts were not on the game, but on Sloan.

What if his mother failed and couldn't talk any sense into her? What if her ex-fiancé found her and tried forcing her back home? Or even worse, what if her father sent a bunch of goons to snatch her back and force her into marriage? And why was Mercury even caring when none of it was his problem?

He blamed his thoughts on that damn kiss. The one that still had his insides tingling from head to toe.

"You okay, Mercury?"

He glanced over at his father, who was looking at him curiously. "Yes. What makes you think I'm not okay?"

"You're twitching," Drew said evenly.

Yes, he was, but there wasn't a law against it, was there? Of course, he wouldn't be a smart aleck and dare ask his father that. So instead of giving a response, he tried to bring his movements under control. When that didn't work, he was about to stand and start pacing when his mother came down the stairs. He was out of his seat in a flash. "Well, did you talk some sense into her?"

Eden crossed her arms over her chest. "Yes, and I didn't have to resort to kissing her like you."

Drew glanced over at his son and frowned. "You kissed Sloan?"

Mercury drew his hand over his face. "Like I told Mom, I was trying to talk some sense into her. I got frustrated."

"And resorted to taking your frustrations out on her mouth," Drew said, nodding. "I see how that's possible."

"Don't you dare encourage him, Drew," his mother said.

Mercury fought back a chuckle. His father was keeping it honest. Of course Drew Steele would know of such things because he probably helped write the Womanizing 101 playbook.

"So, what did she say, Mom?"

Eden tilted her head to stare at Mercury. "She's staying for now, but if she gets another phone call threatening us, then she just might take flight."

"Her father threatened us?" Drew asked, frowning.

"Yes." Eden then told Drew what had happened. While she did so, Mercury began pacing. He hadn't liked what his mother said about Sloan possibly changing her mind about leaving. He didn't like that one damn bit.

"So, what's your plan, Mercury?"

He stopped pacing to look at his father. "What makes you think I plan to do anything?"

Drew gave him a level stare. "Chances are Sloan will try to hide from her parents unless you come up with a plan. What have I always taught my sons?"

Mercury didn't have to think twice on that one. When there was a problem, first up was to find a solution. However, this situation was different. Couldn't his father see that? From the way Drew was looking at him, he obviously didn't.

"Fine. I'll come up with a plan."

Eight

Sloan looked at Eden across the breakfast table. "Mercury is helping me take care of some business things?"

"Yes. I expect him in an hour, and he will explain everything." Eden looked at her watch and then smiled at her. "Today I'm spending time with my grandbabies."

Sloan heard the excitement in Eden's voice. In addition to Galen's twins, Eden had a one-year-old grandson from her son Eli and his wife, Stacey. The proud grandmother had shown Sloan a photo of the little boy, and just like her other two grands and her sons, he had green eyes.

"Good morning."

She glanced up to see Mercury walk into the dining room. He moved to where his mother sat and placed a kiss on her cheek before glancing over at Sloan.

She'd wondered how she would react upon seeing him after that kiss they'd shared last night. The thought had worried her, kept her from sleeping most of the night, until she'd accepted that Mercury Steele had undoubtedly kissed a number of women in his day—for him to do it so well—and kissing her had meant nothing.

She could have sworn she saw something flash in his eyes, but what, she wasn't sure, because just as quickly, it was gone. "Good morning, Sloan."

"Good morning, Mercury."

He then glanced at his watch. "Are you ready?"

She wondered just where he intended to take her. "Where are we going?"

"To the bank to open an account. This bank is owned by my best friend's family. So you don't have to worry about your father getting to the manager. Then I figure you can pick out a car and an apartment."

She was about to remind him she would only have the money Lisa would be loaning her when he said, "There is such a thing as building up your own credit."

Building up my own credit.

She nodded, deciding that made sense. She had to start somewhere, and it would be nice being independent the way she wanted. "Okay."

"My goodness, Mercury. Give Sloan a chance to at least finish breakfast."

"That's okay—I'm fine," she said, pushing her plate aside. The thought of building up her own credit had her excited. "I'll take my plate into the kitchen and be back in a flash."

"No rush."

Well, there was a rush, as far as Sloan was concerned. There was something in the way he was looking at her that had a heated feeling flowing through her. Grabbing her plate, she then headed toward the kitchen. When she got there, she leaned against the counter, needing to take a deep breath. Why did Mercury have to look so darn hot in yet another business suit? And the scent of his aftershave was so masculine it sent spikes of desire through her. And when she looked at him, she remembered how thoroughly he had kissed her and how eagerly she had kissed him back.

The only way she could handle spending any time with him today would be to be on her guard, because whether she wanted to be or not, she was attracted to Mercury.

Mercury watched Sloan leave the dining room and couldn't help but appreciate the gracefulness of her walk. She seemed to glide on air, perfect posture and one hell of a sexy body in a pair of slacks and a blouse.

He was getting frustrated with the way his thoughts were going. He recognized the signs whether he wanted to or not; he desired her.

"Mercury?"

He turned and discovered his mother looking at him with an odd expression on her face. "Yes?"

"I've been trying to get your attention."

He knew that was her way of letting him know she'd noticed the interest he was showing toward Sloan this morning. He didn't like the thought of that. "Was there something you wanted?" Of course there was something she wanted; otherwise, she would not have been trying to get his attention.

Eden smiled. "Thanks for taking time out of your busy schedule to care for Sloan today."

Like he had a choice after what his father had made clear last night. Sloan was his responsibility and he'd needed to come up with a plan to make sure she was taken care of. "No need to thank me. From here on out I will handle her."

The smile was suddenly wiped from his mother's face. "I don't want you to *handle* her, Mercury. I want you to take care of her. I want you to see to her needs and make sure she understands the Steeles are here for her regardless of her father's threats."

Before he could give his mother a response, he heard the sound of Sloan coming back. She had changed out of the outfit she'd had on earlier and into a pretty yellow sundress, one that showed off those appealing shoulders, those gorgeous legs. And her hair was pinned back, highlighting a face that appeared as sexy as the rest of her.

"I'm ready, Mercury."

Her words snapped him out of his intense perusal. Drawing in a deep, troubled breath, he turned to his mother. "Sloan and I will see you later."

Sloan glanced at Mercury as he backed out of his parents' driveway. This was the first time they'd been alone since the kiss they'd shared last night. Should she address it, if for no other reason than to make sure it didn't happen again?

She decided to wait and see if he would mention anything about it, and if he didn't, she wouldn't either. Like she'd told Eden, they'd both acted foolishly and sharing that kiss was something they both regretted. She was sure of it.

Last night before going to bed, she'd looked him up on the internet. He was a former NFL player turned sports agent who was doing very well for himself. And he was considered one of Phoenix's most eligible bachelors.

"Your best friend's family owns a bank?" she asked when she thought the interior was all too quiet.

He didn't answer until he came to a stop sign on the corner. "Yes. Jaye's family has been in banking for years and they own the Colfax National Bank. Most of the branches are located in Arizona, Texas and Oklahoma. Rest assured—you can open an account without fear of your father interfering."

She nodded. "Thanks, Mercury."

"You're welcome." He paused and then said, "May I ask you something?"

"Yes," she said, glancing over at him, hoping he wasn't about to ask her anything about last night. "What would you like to ask me?"

"While growing up, was there not anyone in your corner? Someone you could depend on? To protect you from your parents' craziness?"

Sloan thought about his questions before answering. "Yes—my paternal grandfather. The one I was named after. He was wonderful. My grandmother died before I was born and he would tell me often that they loved each other very much."

She paused and then added, "Pop always said that he sent my father off to college only for him to become an educated fool by getting mixed up with a woman who'd filled his head with crazy notions."

"What kind of crazy notions?"

"That their marriage was to be a business proposition to grow their wealth. My mother's family had once been wealthy, until they lost most of everything when she was fifteen. She swore she would one day regain that wealth and would never be without money again."

Sloan paused, remembering how her mother would tell her often that money was everything and that you could even buy love. "My father bought into her theory of wealth building, and together, for the past thirty years, they have been doing just that. Building wealth. They had to start somewhere and got a loan from my grandfather. That's when he made them sign a legal document that their first child would be named after him. Otherwise, whatever charity he selected would be entitled to a third of whatever wealth they accumulated."

"Sounds like he didn't take any stuff off them."

"He didn't. He also made them sign an agreement to send me to him at his ranch in Texas every summer. Although they did it, they hated doing so and said he was poisoning my mind with foolishness. As I got older, I saw that Pop was showing me just how wrong they were in trying to control my life."

When he brought the car to a stop at a traffic light, he glanced over at her. "Sounds like he tried preparing you for what your parents were capable of."

She'd thought of that same thing over the years and believed that he was. Not wanting to talk about her family anymore, she asked him something she'd been wondering about. "Yesterday, because of me, you missed an important appointment. Were you able to reschedule it?"

He smiled. "Yes. In fact, I cinched the deal. I signed on this kid who is great on the basketball court. Now I have to make sure he ends up on the best NBA team."

"Congratulations."

"Thanks. And we've arrived."

She glanced out the window and saw they'd pulled into the parking lot of a huge bank. "Thanks for bringing me here. If you'll give me your cell number, I can text it to Lisa."

He turned off the ignition and glanced over at her. "Why?"

"So she can send the money to your phone."

"That's not necessary." He unbuckled his seat belt and got out of the car to walk around the back and open the door for her. What did he mean it wasn't necessary? She still hadn't unsnapped her seat belt by the time he reached her.

When he leaned over to undo it, she said, "I can do it myself."

He straightened and looked down at her. "I figured you could, but when you hadn't, I began to wonder."

The reason she hadn't was because what he'd said had given her pause. "What do you mean it's not necessary for Lisa to send funds to your phone?"

He leaned against the open door with an annoyed look on his face. "Like I said, that's not necessary."

She frowned. "Then how am I supposed to open a bank account without any money?"

"I'm taking care of it."

She tilted her head to look up at him against the glare of the sun, wishing she'd thought to bring her sunglasses. "You're taking care of what?"

He drew in a deep breath as if he was agitated by her questions. Sloan didn't care. She wanted an answer. "I asked what you are taking care of, Mercury."

He crossed his arms over his chest and stared down at her. "I'm taking care of everything, Sloan. More specifically, I am taking care of you."

Nine

Mercury wondered if anyone had ever told Sloan how cute she looked when she became angry. How her brows slashed together over her forehead and how the pupils of her eyes became a turbulent dark gray. Then there was the way her chin lifted and her lips formed into a decadent pout. Observing her lips made him remember their taste and how the memory had kept him up most of the night.

"I don't need you to take care of me."

Her words were snapped out in a vicious tone. He drew in a deep breath. He didn't need this. Especially from her and definitely not this morning. He'd forgotten to cancel his date last night with Raquel and she had called first thing this morning letting him know she hadn't appreciated it. It had put him in a bad mood, but, unfortunately, Raquel was the least of his worries.

"You don't?" he asked, trying to maintain a calm voice when more than anything he wanted to snap back. "Was it not my stolen car you were driving?"

"Yes, but—"

"Were you not with me when you discovered you were

being evicted?" he quickly asked, determined not to let her get a word in, other than the one he wanted to hear.

"Yes, but—"

"Did I not take you to my parents' home? Did you not spend the night there?"

Her frown deepened. "Has anyone ever told you how rude you are? You're cutting me off deliberately, Mercury."

"Just answer, please."

She didn't say anything and then she lifted her chin a little higher, letting him know just how upset she was when she said, "Yes, but that doesn't give you the right to think you can control me."

Control her? Was that what she thought? Was that what her rotten attitude was about? Well, she could certainly wipe that notion from her mind. He bedded women, not controlled them.

"Let me assure you, Sloan Donahue, controlling you is the last thing I want to do to you." There was no need to tell her that what he wouldn't mind doing was kissing some sense into her again. "I'm merely here to help you."

"If you feel obligated to help, then don't."

He didn't feel obligated; he felt responsible for her. Otherwise, he wouldn't be here. Hell, when was the last time he'd been made to feel responsible for anyone? Thanks to his dad, he did now. "Look, Sloan. You need help and I'm willing to help you. What does it matter if it's my money or your friend Lisa's?"

She glared at him. "It matters because I know Lisa, but I don't know you."

He rolled his eyes. "Hell, I don't know you either, but I'm willing to help you out. I have been helping you out. Again, I will ask you—where would you have stayed last night had I not made sure you had a decent roof over your head?"

"Why do you keep throwing your help in my face?"

He stared at her, getting more frustrated by the second. "That's not what I'm doing. I'm trying to get you to see, to recognize, that I have been there for you, regardless of how well I know you or you know me."

She began nibbling on her bottom lip, and seeing her do so sent a flare of response throughout his body. It made the muscles beneath his business suit tighten with desire. And if that wasn't bad enough, remembering the taste of those lips and her tongue kicked in his body's most primal reaction with a vengeance.

Glad she was too deep in thought to notice, he moved from where he'd been standing, directly in front of her by the car door, to where his erection wasn't so obvious. "We don't have all day, Sloan."

What he wished he could say was that he could only take so much of his body's intense throbbing.

She glanced over at him. "How much?"

He lifted a brow. "How much what?"

"How much are you willing to loan me?"

He shrugged. "How much do you need?"

"Just enough to tide me over until I get a job." Then she quickly added, "And earn my first paycheck. Then I will pay you back every penny."

Because he knew she wouldn't accept things any other way, he said, "And I intend for you to do so, but I'm willing to break down the payments into installments so it won't be so hard for you."

She nodded. "Thanks. That will work better."

"Now can we go into the bank?"

He watched her unbuckle her seat belt before easing from the car, not knowing she'd flashed a portion of her thigh in the process. Heat curled inside him, threatening the control he'd thought he'd reclaimed.

Then she stood beside him, dark eyes staring up into his. "Yes, I'm ready."

* * *

"No, absolutely not! I will not let you put that much money into my checking account. I'll never be able to pay you back, Mercury," Sloan said, not caring if the man staring at her, the man who owned the bank and who was one of Mercury's closest friends, Jaye Colfax, was doing so with keen interest.

"Mr. Colfax? I'd like a private word with Mercury."

The man stood and smiled. "The two of you can certainly use my office to hash out the details of your bank account."

As far as she was concerned, there was nothing to hash out. There was no way she'd let Mercury deposit twenty thousand dollars into a bank account for her.

"So, what's the problem now, Sloan?" Mercury asked as soon as the door closed behind Jaye Colfax.

She glared at him. "There is no way I can let you open a bank account for me by putting that much money into my account. It would take forever to pay you back."

"You don't think you'll eventually get a job?"

"Of course I do."

"And were you not the one who a few minutes ago made it clear to me, Sloan, that you don't like depending on anyone?"

"Yes."

"Then what's the problem?" he asked, getting to his feet and then crossing the office floor to where she sat. She wished he hadn't done that. Every time she saw his body in motion it did things to her. Things that didn't make sense. She'd seen Harold move and it had never made her body hot in certain places. It never tempted her to glide her hands up his shoulders and abdomen to see just how tight his muscles were.

"Sloan, I asked what's the problem."

Mercury was now standing in front of her, and when

she looked into his gorgeous green eyes, her pulse actually flickered.

"Did we not discuss this out in the parking lot? Did you not agree to accept my loan and that you would pay me back in installments?"

"But that was before I knew how much you would put into my account. Lisa was only going to loan me a thousand dollars."

He tilted his head to further stare down at her. "And just how far do you think you'd get with a thousand dollars? Or do you intend to live with my parents forever?"

"Of course not!"

"Then what's the problem? I'm loaning you enough money to get started. You'd need to put money down on a car, put a deposit on an apartment, buy food and clothes. So, I'm asking for the fifth time, what's the problem?"

Sloan broke eye contact with him, knowing there was no way she could express herself logically while staring into his eyes, even if those eyes were upset with her at the moment. Licking her lips, she stared down at her lap instead, trying to gather her thoughts and not dwell on the heat curling in her midsection.

Drawing in a deep breath, she lifted her head to drag her gaze back to Mercury's face and felt her body warm again under his regard. "The problem is that I don't want to be in your debt, Mercury. I don't want to feel dependent on you."

She heard his frustrated sigh before he said in a calmer voice, "At some point, Sloan, you're going to have to accept that, to get out of this mess your parents have placed you in, you're going to have to depend on someone." He paused a moment and then asked, "Do you prefer that my parents loan you the money?"

"No! I could never accept that from them."

"Yet you were going to accept money from your friend Lisa. I'm offering you twenty times what Lisa was able to loan you. I don't understand why you're putting up such a fight. I've never before known any woman who didn't like spending my money."

His words set her off and she was out of her chair so fast it didn't give him a chance to back up, so he didn't. They were standing so close their bodies were touching, the way they had last night before they kissed. Trying to ignore how his closeness made her feel a little light-headed, she said, "I don't want to become beholden to the one man in town who claims he knows every single woman who lives here."

There, she'd said it. She'd expressed her feelings. Now all she had to do was get a grip on her heartbeat and slow it down. She wasn't sure what reaction she had expected from him, but it wasn't that he'd have no reaction at all. He was still staring down at her, those green eyes holding her captive.

"It shouldn't bother you what woman I know or don't know. I'm being generous. Are you going to let me help you or not?"

A part of Sloan knew she was being too prideful for her own good. She should accept his generous offer with the understanding that she would pay him back. Every cent. No matter how long it took. "Will you put me on a payment plan?"

"I told you that I would. Let me repeat myself. The money is a loan and not a gift."

He hadn't stepped back. Was she imagining sexual vibes that seemed to be pouring off him? And why did it seem as if the air shimmering around them was growing taut? "When?"

He lifted a brow. "When what?"

Was she mistaken or was she seeing desire in his eyes? Would she even recognize it if she saw it? "When can I have it?"

"When do you want it?"

She swallowed. They were still talking about a payment plan, weren't they? "As soon as you can give it to me."

"How about now?"

She nervously licked her lips as naked heat seemed to fill her. And did her hips just move against him? And did he have an erection?

"Now?" she asked, trying to keep up with what he was saying.

"Yes, now."

Then he lowered his head and crushed his mouth to hers.

Ten

The kiss was every bit as raw as it was seductive. That was the way Mercury had wanted it to be. He knew what they'd been discussing and in no way was this what she'd asked for, but at that moment he was unapologetically getting what he knew they both wanted.

She might not understand the heated yearning passing between them, but he most certainly did. It was there, a deep desire that pulsed and throbbed. A desire he definitely didn't want.

This was how he handled such matters, meeting them head-on. Last night he'd kissed her to drill some sense into her. At least that was what he'd told his mother. What was his excuse this time? What was the reason he'd allowed her to get under his skin enough that he'd been tempted to kiss her again? How did Sloan Donahue have the ability to arouse him even without putting forth much effort?

When she wrapped her arms around his neck, he could actually feel anticipation thicken the air. He also felt something else thickening. If he were to ease her a little to the left and then lean forward, he could easily take her on that desk.

He was then quickly reminded it was Jaye's desk. His best friend wouldn't like Mercury using his office as a make-out room. That thought reminded him of where they were and what they were doing. It also reminded him that he had to regain control of his willpower and he needed to do it now.

He broke off the kiss and took a step back. The dark heat in Sloan's eyes tempted him to come back, return to her arms and reclaim her mouth. But he didn't. He couldn't. He'd crossed another line today and that wasn't good.

"So," he said, after giving in to temptation and licking his tongue across his lips, as if to make sure her taste still lingered there. "I'm glad I've talked some sense into you, and that you've agreed to the money I'm putting into your account."

He watched her expression. His words had been a reminder of the disagreement they'd been dealing with before the kiss.

"I don't like taking your money, Mercury. I wish there was another way," she said softly, not looking at him.

"There's no other way."

"And I wish you wouldn't kiss me every time we disagree about something and claim to be talking some kind of sense into me."

Was that what she assumed was the only thing driving their kisses? Maybe he needed to enlighten her that there was more to it than that. On the other hand, it might be wiser that he just let her assume whatever she wanted. "Maybe we need to try to be of one accord, then."

"Or maybe you need to keep your mouth to yourself."

He could very well tell her it took two to tangle, and that her mouth had been involved just as much as his. "I'll try." That was the best he could do since he could no longer ignore the attraction he felt for Sloan.

Unfortunately, he was a man used to acting on attractions. Women in Phoenix knew him. They knew he was a die-hard bachelor with no intentions of ever changing. The only thing they got from him were nights of lovemaking with more orgasms than they could count.

"Maybe it's something we need to talk about, Mercury."

He didn't agree. Glancing at his watch, he said, "Let's discuss it later. Right now, we need to take care of opening that bank account and then look for a car and an apartment for you."

Mercury could tell by the mutinous look on her face that she wanted to discuss things now, but there was no way that he could. Namely because he'd done something today that he'd never done, which was to give a woman his hard-earned money. In no way was he a cheapskate when it came to women. Just the opposite. He had no problems lavishing his money on someone if it meant the outcome going the way he wanted.

Expensive dinners, weekends at exclusive and luxurious resorts, beautiful flowers, high-priced purses. You name it and he'd bought it. But never had Mercury Morris Steele dropped twenty grand into a woman's bank account knowing in the end he wouldn't be getting a single thing…except for maybe a few stolen kisses when his patience with her had run its course.

Why kissing her was becoming a habit, he wasn't sure. All he knew was that if her mouth got too close to his, he was driven to taste it. Devour it. Make a damn meal out of it. One he was enjoying way too much. Hell, he was even anticipating it happening again. He honestly liked his way of trying to talk sense into her.

The knock at the door signaled Jaye's return and a part of him was glad. Being in a secluded space with Sloan was putting ideas in his head and that wasn't good. "Come in."

Jaye had the damn nerve to walk into the office smiling. Mercury wished he could knock that silly-looking grin off his best friend's face and could only imagine what

Jaye was thinking. "Well, have the two of you reached an agreement?"

Mercury decided to speak up before Sloan did. "Yes, we have. We are opening the account."

Less than an hour later, they'd left the bank and were headed to a car dealership owned by one of his brother Eli's friends, Ronald Taylor. Mercury had called Ronald, who'd promised that one of his car salesmen would be ready to work him up a beauty of a deal.

He glanced over at Sloan. She hadn't said much since leaving the bank. He knew she was still bothered that she would be using his money, but like he'd explained to her, she had to start somewhere and this was it. He'd also had to assure her that his money hadn't come with any strings. He'd almost had to kick Jaye to remove the shocked look on his face when Mercury had made that announcement.

"Do you know what kind of car you want?" he asked now, to break into the quiet of the car's interior.

"It doesn't matter," she said, in a voice that sounded defeated. For the life of him he couldn't understand why she would feel that way. With the money he'd given her she could start the independent life she wanted.

"What kind of car did you have before?" he asked her out of curiosity. She glanced over at him and it seemed a whimsical smile touched her lips. He was so taken by it that the driver behind him had to honk his horn to let him know the traffic light had changed.

"The same kind you're driving now."

He lifted a brow. "A Tesla sports car?"

"Yes. Same year and model, but mine was blue. My favorite color."

He shouldn't be surprised. After all, her parents were loaded and had doted on her to keep her under their thumb. And he shouldn't be surprised that blue was her favorite color. It was his as well, and as far as he was concerned, nothing was prettier than blue. He'd even read once that the color blue had a positive effect on a person's mind and body. He could believe that. That was why he preferred making love to a woman on blue linen.

"No wonder you thought my Camaro wasn't worth much."

He wasn't sure what he expected her response to be, but it hadn't been her throwing her head back and laughing. It was the first time he'd heard her laugh, and the sound did something to him. Emotions within him seemed to come to life. Her laughter was so infectious that he heard himself laughing, as well. How could he laugh about her thinking that one of his antique cars, his prized possessions, was a POS? It didn't make sense. Nor did it make sense that he'd opened a bank account in her name and deposited his money or that he'd kissed her twice now or that he'd taken time away from his job to take care of her needs.

"I'm truly sorry about that, Mercury."

"About what?"

"About my reaction to finding out the car I'd purchased was stolen. That just goes to show how much I don't know about cars. About anything. I'm embarrassed to even say that opening that bank account was new for me. When I turned sixteen, I was given one for my birthday and Dad automatically deposited money into it monthly."

She paused and then added, "I never questioned how much he was putting into it or why. I never realized my parents were binding me to them in a way they figured meant I'd never want to break free. It was all about the money."

Mercury didn't say anything because he knew that was true for some people. Money meant everything. The more they had the more they wanted. Although his mother had been born to wealth, his father had not. Drew Steele was a self-made man and made sure his sons followed in his footsteps, and they all had. Nobody had given them anything, which was why Drew wouldn't agree to let their maternal grandfather set up trust funds for his boys unless he specified the age of thirty-two. By that age Drew figured they would have learned to sink or swim on their own. Luckily, all six of them had been successful, and the five-billion-dollar trust fund had been icing on the cake.

"Well, at least you had the sense to break free when you realized what they were doing. Some people wouldn't have minded being dependent on others and not thinking for themselves."

His thoughts shifted to the one-and-only woman he had thought he'd loved. Cherae Blackshear. They had met in college. He'd been in his freshman year and attending college on a football scholarship. Galen, Eli, Tyson and Jonas had warned him about those girls who hooked up with football players they thought were going places. He'd gotten injured in his sophomore year and some thought that would be the end of his football career. Cherae's family, who'd been all gung ho on their relationship, then decided she needed to switch ships since his future no longer looked bright.

Mercury would never forget the day she'd visited him during one of his physical-therapy sessions to break up with him because her parents said she had to. They wanted her to hook up with someone who would be able to take care of her and give her the things they felt she deserved. Namely money.

Cherae cutting him loose like that had messed with his mind and left him not giving a damn about his future or anything else. It had taken his brothers arriving on his college campus ready to beat some sense into him. They'd told him that his biggest mistake had been to fall in love in the first place. Bad News Steeles didn't give their hearts to women. Second, they bashed into his brain that to get even he needed to get his ass back in gear and play football again.

Taking his brothers' advice, he had worked hard, endured all kinds of physical pain during his therapy sessions. But he had gotten back in shape. By his junior year, he was in the college team's starting lineup. In his senior year, sports agents had come out of the woodwork to sign him on with the NFL.

That was when Cherae had tried making a comeback. He'd told her in a not-so-nice way that she would be the last woman he'd ever get serious about again. In fact, thanks to her, he'd happily reinstated his player card and the only thing she could get from him now was laid. He'd run into her a few years ago at one of their college homecomings, and she was still trying to find a rich husband.

"They don't look too busy today," he said, pulling into the lot of the auto dealership.

Sloan glanced around and he smiled at the sparkle he saw in her eyes. "There are so many beautiful cars."

"Yes," he said, bringing his own car to a stop. "And there's one out there with your name on it."

"I'm positive this is the car I want," Sloan said excitedly, smiling brightly at both Mercury and the car salesman. Her smile then faded somewhat when she thought of something. "But can I afford it without any credit history?"

To Sloan's way of thinking, the smile the salesman returned was even brighter than hers. "Don't worry about that, Ms. Donahue. Everything has been taken care of."

She lifted a brow, not liking the sound of that. It reminded her of what salespeople would say when they knew her parents would take care of any debts she incurred. "What do you mean by that?"

Before the man could respond, Mercury said, "What he meant is that he's in the business to make sure the customer gets any vehicle they want, even if it means adjusting the payments to accommodate the buyer. Right, Mr. Lowery?"

The man looked over at Mercury, nodded and then glanced back at her. "Yes, that's right."

"Great! Thanks, Mr. Lowery." Like Sloan had told them, she really liked this car. It was a gorgeous sky blue Chevy Camaro. Same make and model as the red car that had been stolen from Mercury, but this one was the current year and brand spanking new. The exterior was so shiny she could practically see herself, and the interior was a dark blue leather with that new-car smell.

"Now I have my very own Camaro," she said, trying to hold back her emotions. Sloan knew she would love this car forever because it was hers. It was a car she would work hard to pay for and that no one had given to her. It was hers and no one could take it away from her.

"Yes, you have your very own Camaro," Mercury said, smiling down at her.

"How much down?" she then asked the salesman.

He looked at her strangely. "How much down?"

"Yes. How much money do I need to put down on this car?" Sloan figured the more she could put down the lower her payments would be. She only had twenty thousand dollars to work with and there were other things she needed to do with that money, which included putting a deposit on an apartment. She also needed to make sure she had enough to make the first couple of car payments in case she didn't find a job right away.

The man hadn't answered yet, but another question popped in her head. "Are there papers I need to sign? What about documents showing this car is truly mine? Or do I get them in the end when I pay off the car?" Sloan wasn't sure how that worked since she'd never purchased a car before.

"You will get everything later," Mercury said. "I will make sure all the paperwork is mailed to you."

"But I don't have a permanent address yet," she said, nibbling nervously on her bottom lip. She hoped that wouldn't be a problem getting everything in order in time to make her first payment. Now more than ever it was important that she got a job.

Over breakfast Eden had mentioned her friend Margaret Fowler, the one with connections to the Miss Universe pageant, wanted to speak with Sloan on Monday. Although the pageant was held every December, the job of interpreter was year-round and required a lot of traveling the last four months of the year. The other eight months entailed working from home, communicating with pageant officials who spoke other languages.

"I'll pick it up and deliver it to you."

"Thanks, Mercury." She thought he was being nice about everything. So far, she had only two debts to worry about. The car payment and the money she had to pay back to Mercury for the bank deposit. "When do I get to take my car with me?"

"When you have a place to park it, one you can call your own, since my parents' home has enough cars in their garage already," he said.

She nodded. He was right about waiting to get her own place. "That's fine." She then looked at the salesman. "You will take care of my car until I get it, right?"

The man grinned, probably happy for a sale, Sloan thought. "Yes, Ms. Donahue. I'll take care of it until you return."

She smiled, feeling good about that. She then turned to Mercury. "How soon can we look for an apartment?" She figured the sooner she had a place of her own, the sooner she could get her car.

"Today is fine, but I suggest we go somewhere for lunch first."

She nodded, thinking that was a good idea. She hadn't eaten since breakfast and it had to be around noon now. "Do you know a place?" she asked him.

"Yes, I know the perfect spot, and it's close by."

Eleven

"This is a nice place," Sloan said, taking a sip of her iced tea and looking around.

"Glad you like it. I come here often for lunch," Mercury replied, trying hard not to stare at Sloan.

Why did she have to look so beautiful?

The waitress came to take their orders and he and Sloan discovered they liked the same kinds of foods. Since she'd never eaten there before, he introduced her to several of his favorite dishes. After they'd placed their orders and gotten refills on their iced teas, he asked her, "What are you looking for in an apartment?"

He liked the way the smile curved her lips when she said, "Definitely something I can afford. Already I'll have two bills to pay. Your loan and a car payment," she said, enthused.

He grinned. "You sound excited."

"I am." Leaning over the table, she said, "Do you know this is the first time I will have bills? Real bills? Bills that I will pay without anyone's help. And I am ready to take ownership of them. It's going to be fun learning to budget my money and knowing how much I can spend. So, to answer your question, all I need is a one-bedroom apartment. Of course, it has to have a bathroom, living room and a kitchen."

"Can you cook?"

She grinned. "No, but I can learn. In fact, I think I'll have fun learning." She took a sip of her tea, then asked him, "Can you cook?"

He took a sip of his own tea and then said, "Yes, I can."

"Who taught you?"

Watching her mouth move dredged up memories of the kiss they'd shared in Jaye's office. Mercury wished he could look at her lips and not remember taking them in a way that even now aroused him. Why did she have to taste so damn good? And why was he recalling her taste?

"I taught myself like you intend to do. I did use cookbooks and, on occasion, some of my mother's recipes. I even took a cooking class once."

"A cooking class? Was it expensive?"

There was no need to tell her that cost hadn't mattered because taking the cooking class had been his and his brother Jonas's way to meet women. Not only had they met single women, but they'd garnered invitations for free home-cooked meals with no-strings-attached sex on the menu. "I didn't think it was and thought it was worth every cent I paid. Maybe you should think about signing up for one."

Shrugging her shoulders, she said, "I will have to see if I can fit the cost into my budget."

She was serious about staying on a budget and he thought that was a smart move. Money wasn't endless. Drew had taught his sons the fundamentals of managing money. It was a lesson none of them had forgotten. Their father hadn't built his trucking business into a multimillion-dollar enterprise by accident. He'd always said, you can't spend money you don't have. Those same words still stuck with the six of them today.

"Your mom might have landed me a job where I'll be doing some traveling at least four months out of the year. I will be talking to the lady on Monday."

His eyebrows lifted in surprise. His mother hadn't mentioned that to him. "Oh, what lady is it?"

"Margaret Fowler."

Mercury nodded. He'd known Ms. Fowler for years. The older woman was a world traveler and he'd always admired her spunk. He'd heard his mother mention that after Ms. Fowler turned seventy-five, she'd liked traveling with a companion since her husband had passed away a couple of years ago. A job as a companion would suit Sloan.

"I assume you'd want a furnished apartment to avoid having a furniture bill," he then said.

"Yes, I do. What about appliances? I don't want to buy any of those either."

He nodded. "Appliances are standard items in most apartments. Even a washer and dryer." He was about to say something else when the waitress appeared at the table with their food.

"Looks good."

It was on the tip of his tongue to tell her that he thought she looked better. Instead he glanced over at her and said, "You're right—it looks good."

"Are you sure I can afford this place, Mercury?" Sloan asked, glancing around the apartment and loving everything she saw. It was just the right size for her with one bedroom, a nice-size bathroom that included both a tub and walk-in shower, a neat-and-tidy kitchen with a breakfast nook and a living room that extended from a wide foyer. The place was completely furnished.

Then there was the little work-space nook with a desk

between the kitchen nook and living room. It would be perfect when she wasn't traveling and worked from home. She wasn't sure she could handle all her good luck in one day when yesterday had been such a disaster.

"Is there anything in here you want to change?" he asked her, glancing around, as well.

"No. I love it. The view of the lake from that window is beautiful. I love being on the fourth floor and the elevator makes it convenient. Paying my first two months of rent in advance was a great idea. Thanks for suggesting it."

Now she didn't have to worry about something unexpected coming up or miscalculating her budget and getting evicted. That was an experience she never wanted to repeat. Glancing at her watch, she saw it was close to three in the afternoon. The apartment manager said she could move in as soon as she wanted.

"I got a lot accomplished today thanks to you, Mercury. Please don't forget to get me that installment schedule so I can start paying you back."

"I won't forget."

"Although I'm sure she probably doesn't need my help with anything, I told your mother I would be back in time to help her with dinner tonight."

"So, you will be there?"

Where else would she be? Was that disappointment she heard in his voice at the prospect that she would be? Eden had explained that every Thursday night was their family gathering for her sons, their wives and the grandkids. Sloan couldn't help wondering if Mercury felt her being there was infringing on the time the Steeles spent together when she wasn't one of them.

"I offered to leave for a while and go to a movie, but your mother wouldn't hear of it." Eden had told her she could use her car whenever she needed to go somewhere since she had a spare. "However, I can certainly change those plans if you prefer I not be there."

He lifted a brow. "What makes you think it matters to me if you are there or not?"

She looked him directly in the eyes. "Your tone just now gave me the impression you'd rather I not be there."

He shoved his hands into the pockets of his pants, making her fully aware of his height and masculinity. "It doesn't matter to me. It's my parents' house and they can invite whomever they want."

Sloan tried not to get frustrated with him and ruin what had been a great day. "I'm very much aware it's your parents' home and they can invite whoever they want, Mercury."

"Then why are you worrying about it?"

She honestly wasn't liking his attitude right now. "I'm not worrying about it. I just didn't want to do anything to make you feel uncomfortable. It's your family and I prefer not intruding if you don't want me there. I'm glad to know you don't care one way or the other."

She moved to walk away and he caught hold of her arm. He didn't say anything when she turned back to him. He simply stood there and held her arm while staring at her. Honestly, there was nothing simple about it. He had a way of looking at her that made something stir inside her.

Her chest had been heaving with frustration; now it was surging with something else. Something she didn't want to feel but couldn't stop herself from feeling. Passion and desire were new to her, but around Mercury she could recognize them for what they were. Only problem was that they had no place in her life now. There were more important things she needed to concentrate on. Learning how to survive without her parents' wealth topped the list. But with Mercury, temptation was hard to resist.

"Is something wrong, Mercury?"

"What makes you think something is wrong?" he asked in a voice that was so husky it seemed to make a crackle of energy flow in the room.

Duh. He was standing there holding her arm while staring her down in a way that made a deep yearning stir to life within her. However, if for whatever reason he refused to acknowledge the obvious, she wouldn't follow his lead. Not this time, even if doing so would be wise.

At that moment she was too mesmerized by the look in his green eyes. The one thing she couldn't ignore was how close he stood to her. The scent of him and the touch of his hand were making her even more aware of him.

Suddenly, he began stroking the tips of his fingers up and down her arm. She nearly closed her eyes on a groan. Fire began running through her veins. And from the heated look in his eyes she had a feeling he knew what he was doing to her and wanted to know—why?

"Why, Mercury?" She figured she didn't have to elaborate. He *had* to know what she was asking.

"I honestly don't know, Sloan. All I know is that whenever I get close to you, I have the urge to touch you. And when we're at odds, all I can think about is kissing you."

His words caused sensations to flow through her. That wasn't good. She was being aroused in a way she'd never been before. "I bet you tell that to all the women."

"Actually, I don't."

Yeah, right. There was no way she could believe him. She understood why women were drawn to him. The man was way too handsome for his own good…and for hers. "What do you want from me, Mercury?" she heard herself ask and then wondered why she'd bothered. It was obvious from the look in his eyes what he wanted.

It wasn't as if she didn't understand the attraction thing; she had just figured it would never affect her. He was proving her wrong. At any other time, she probably would welcome such a diversion as a way to claim her independence, but the timing was all wrong. The man was all wrong. She wasn't certain why she was so sure of the latter, but she was.

"I shouldn't want anything from you, Sloan."

"But you do?"

"I wouldn't be a man if I didn't."

She frankly didn't know what to say to that. He saved her from saying anything when he pulled her to him and covered her mouth with his, causing bone-melting fire to rush through her. They'd kissed three times now, and each time he did it with toe-curling expertise. When she groaned, he intensified the kiss by slanting his mouth over hers.

Had they finished their discussion? She didn't think so, but this was so much better than talking. Why did his kisses have the power to kick up her pulse, have desire flowing through her? She might not be as experienced a kisser as he was, but Sloan was determined to show Mercury she learned fast and could be just as thorough. His tongue might be swirling all around hers, but she was following his lead. If Mercury's groans were anything to go by, he was obviously enjoying this kiss as much as she was. That made her wonder who was seducing whom...

He surprised her when he let go of her arm only to plunge his hands into her hair as if to pull her mouth closer while his tongue went deeper. His mouth was firm and strong, and his lips were demanding. In the past, all the kisses she'd ever shared with a guy had been controlled, restrained and disciplined. Mercury's kisses were always uncontrolled, unrestrained and totally undisciplined.

And heaven help her, but she liked them that way.

In fact, she was liking this kiss so much that when her phone rang, she tried to ignore it, but the persistent ringing had them breaking apart. Still he managed to get in a final lick across her lips before taking a step back.

By the time she pulled the phone from her purse it had

stopped ringing. Just as well, she thought, after seeing the missed call had been from Harold.

Putting her phone back in her purse, she glanced over at Mercury. He was back to staring at her like she was a puzzle he needed to solve. Like he hadn't been the one who'd made the first move to lock lips in a kiss that still had her toes tingling.

"Ready to go? I told Mom I would have you back by four," he said, breaking the silence between them.

"Did you?"

"Yes, and I'm a man of my word."

A man of your word? Let's see about that. "Then will you give me your word that you won't kiss me again?"

"No. Like I said, I'm a man of my word, Sloan."

Twelve

"Would you like to explain what today was all about?"

Mercury took a sip of his beer. He'd known that would be the first question Jaye asked him when they met for their usual happy-hour drinks at Notorious, a popular nightclub in town. The one thing he liked about this place was that the owner opened its doors three hours ahead of the night-time crowd. On occasion, Mercury would arrive for happy hour and stay through the night, especially if there was live entertainment. The food and the drinks were great. And so was ladies' night every Tuesday.

"Don't pretend you don't know already. I'm sure one of my brothers has enlightened you."

Jaye chuckled. "Yes, it just so happens I ran into Jonas yesterday evening, and he told me what he'd heard. I'm glad you got your car back, by the way."

"Thanks."

"But still, I was surprised when you walked into the bank this morning to help the woman open an account using your own money. Twenty grand is—"

"Twenty grand. I know," Mercury said, still wanting to believe he'd done the right thing.

"I have to admit she's a looker, so I guess you consider it an investment in future benefits," Jaye said, smiling.

Mercury could understand why Jaye thought that. Other than his brothers, Jaye—whom he'd known since grade school and who had been his roommate in college—knew him better than anyone. In fact, it had been Jaye who'd sent out the SOS to his brothers after Cherae had dumped him.

"I don't plan to collect any future benefits."

Jaye nodded, grinning. "That means you're collecting them already."

"No, it doesn't mean that," Mercury said, annoyed that Jaye knew him so well that he would assume that. "In fact, I don't expect anything from her, sexual favors or otherwise."

The grin suddenly left Jaye's face and he stared at him. "Then I think you need to explain why you deposited twenty grand into a woman's account. A woman you just met yesterday, who was driving your stolen car. And while you're at it, you can explain your reasoning for taking her home to Ms. Eden."

Mercury took another sip of his beer. Had it been anyone other than Jaye, he would have told them he didn't have to explain a damn thing. But with Jaye he did.

"I guess I'll start from the beginning. My version and not Jonas's."

"All right."

It took him longer than he'd expected to cover everything with Jaye, only because Nancy Ormond showed up trying to get his attention, which he refused to give her. They'd been involved a few months ago, but he had immediately dropped her after she began hinting that her biological clock was ticking. As far as he'd been concerned, that wasn't his problem, and he'd quickly removed himself from the situation before she got any ideas about him being some baby daddy.

"So, let me get this straight," Jaye said, when Mercury had finally finished. "Drew told you to fix the problem, one you didn't make, I might add…and you figured the solution was to lay cash on her, buy her a car and put her in an apartment?"

Mercury knew that sounded kind of crazy, but Jaye was right. "The money in her account is a loan, and because she doesn't have any established credit, I had to put the car and apartment in my name."

"Does she know that?"

"Heck no. She would have had a holy cow, but putting them in my name was the only way she could have gotten them. She'll be paying me back for the car and the loan, and the apartment will transfer to her name after six months."

He took a swig of his beer, then added, "When I heard Sloan's mother talking to her that way, demanding she marry some prick she didn't even like—who has a woman he wants as his mistress, I might add—I knew I had to do something."

"Why?"

Mercury's brows arched. "Why what?"

"Why did you feel you had to do something?"

Mercury rolled his eyes. "Did you not hear anything I said? Were you not listening? The woman was in one messy situation."

Jaye shrugged. "And that was your problem how?"

Mercury stared at Jaye. His friend was not some uncaring ass, which meant he was asking him the question for a reason. He had a feeling Jaye wanted him to think through what he'd done. Jaye was late because Mercury had thought things through and was convinced, no matter how it looked to others, helping Sloan out the way he had was the right thing to do. "I told you, Dad told me to handle it."

Jaye leaned back in his chair. "Be careful, Mercury. From what I saw today, it's obvious Sloan Donahue has a problem with depending on others."

"That might be the case, but when you don't have a penny to your name, you have to start somewhere and accept help when offered." Mercury didn't say anything for a minute. Then he asked, "Is there a reason for the lecture, Jaye?"

Jaye took a swallow of his beer. "Yes. I don't want you to make the same mistake with Sloan Donahue that I made with Velvet."

Mercury noted that Jaye hadn't mentioned Velvet in months, not since she'd moved away last year without telling Jaye where she'd gone. Jaye had been warned that one day Velvet would get tired of being his bedmate instead of becoming his wife.

"Whoa, no comparison. You loved Velvet, although you never admitted you did. I don't do women to fall in love. I do women for sex."

"If you recall, that was once my attitude as well, Mercury."

"No, you never did women, at least not after meeting Velvet. I knew you loved her, Jaye, and *if you recall*," he said, repeating Jaye's earlier words, "I told you that you loved her. But you refused to believe me. For three years you dated Velvet exclusively and still you honestly thought it was only about the sex."

"Hell, Mercury, I realize my mistake and will rectify the problem. Soon."

Mercury lifted a brow. "Soon? Just how are you planning to do that when you have no idea where she is?"

"I do now. A few months ago, I hired a PI to find her. I got a call from him before leaving the office to let me know he's found her."

Mercury sat up in his chair. He'd always liked Velvet,

and although falling in love was not his thing, he'd known Jaye had cared for Velvet Spencer deeply, but refused to acknowledge that he had. Hell, everyone had known but Jaye. He'd discovered his feelings too late. "So, where is she?"

Jaye met his gaze. "She's living in a coastal town in Louisiana, an hour away from New Orleans. A place called Catalina Cove."

Mercury didn't say anything for a minute. "I take it you're going to come up with a plan to get her back."

A determined look appeared on Jaye's features. "Yes, and it has to be a good one."

"I agree, man. She gave you plenty of chances and you blew each one."

"Don't remind me." Jaye then glanced at his watch. "It's Thursday night. Aren't you going over to your folks' for dinner?"

Mercury knew this was Jaye's way of changing the subject. "Yes, I'm going."

There was no need to tell Jaye that because Mercury knew Sloan would be there, he wasn't in any hurry to get there. There was something about being around her that made him feel vulnerable for the first time since Cherae had left and he didn't like it one damn bit.

Even now he remembered Sloan's kisses. There were too many when there should not have been any. Yet the way her body felt pressed to his, the way her firm breasts and stiff nipples poked him in the chest and the way her tongue would mate with his were torments he couldn't let go of. And to see her again meant not only remembering, but also being tempted for a repeat performance.

"Mercury?"

He glanced over at Jaye. "Yes?"

"Did you hear what I just said?"

No, Mercury inwardly admitted, he hadn't heard. There

was no need to lie about it. "Sorry, my mind was elsewhere. What did you say?"

Normally Jaye would have given him a look that said he knew where Mercury's mind was...which was usually on bedding some woman or another. Instead the look he saw on his best friend's face was one of purposeful resolve.

"I asked if you think you will ever fall in love again."

"No." Mercury's attitude about love might be confusing to some, but it shouldn't be to Jaye. "If you recall, I was the first of my brothers to fall in love and you know what Cherae did. Once you've been burned you have a tendency to stay away from the fire."

"That's what you've been doing all these years? Staying away from the fire?"

"Yes, pretty much."

"Then would you like to explain your attraction to Sloan Donahue? I watched you and it's quite obvious that you're taken with her, although you're trying hard not to be."

Mercury didn't like that Jaye was so damn observant. No need to deny anything. "I'll be okay once I get a handle on things."

"If you say so, but I'm finding that hard to believe. You've only known her for two days, yet..."

"Yet what?"

"You seem smitten."

Smitten? Mercury frowned. "And I think you've lost your mind."

"Possibly, but what I saw today and how you were looking at her when you thought no one was noticing says a lot."

In all honesty, that said more than a lot, Mercury thought. That said too damn much. If Jaye could pick up on how attracted he was to Sloan, then his brothers would, too. Hell, he had a good mind not to show up at his parents' place for dinner tonight. But not doing so meant he would be allowing her to get next to him in a way he couldn't control, and he refused to let that happen.

"I'm leaving," he said, standing and glancing at his watch. There were a couple of stops he had to make, as well as going home to change clothes.

"Okay. Take care."

"And, Jaye?"

His friend looked over at him. "Yes?"

"I'm glad you found Velvet."

Jaye smiled. "Me, too, Mercury. Me, too."

Sloan stared up at the five men standing in front of her. One she knew from yesterday, but the others she did not. The one thing she did know was that they were Mercury's brothers. Four were the husbands of the very friendly women she'd met earlier—Brittany, Stacey, Nicole, who was married to Jonas, and Hunter—who'd arrived early to help Eden with dinner.

For a minute, Sloan had felt like an intruder when the women had shown up, but they, along with Eden, had made her feel right at home. And Eden and Drew's grandkids were to die for. The twins were simply adorable, just like Galen had said they were, and the youngest grand, Stacey and Eli's son, had stolen her heart immediately.

Now Sloan was eyeing the green-eyed men standing in front of her. Their eyes might have come from Eden, but their features belonged to Drew. They were the former "Bad News Steeles" minus one. Namely Mercury, who hadn't arrived yet.

"Sloan, let me introduce my brothers," Galen said, smiling. "In order of ages, this is Tyson, Eli, Jonas and Gannon. Missing is Mercury, but you know him already. He fits between Jonas and Gannon."

Sloan smiled brightly as her gaze moved from one brother to the other. Four of them might be happily married now, but she bet they'd all been pistols before marriage. "It's nice to meet all of you."

"The pleasure is ours," the one named Jonas said. "We heard about your misfortunes and we're glad the folks were here to help."

"Thanks, and Mercury helped, too," she quickly said. "If it hadn't been for him, I would not have met your parents."

Eli smiled. "Then we need to commend our brother for acting the part of a hero for once in his life."

As far as Sloan was concerned, Mercury *was* a hero.

"Speaking of Mercury, where is he?" Gannon asked, glancing down at his watch.

"He's late and Mom doesn't like us to show up late. Then she thinks you only come for the meal," Tyson tacked on, grinning.

"Someone's looking for me?" a deep voice said behind Sloan.

She not only recognized the husky tone, but a sudden jolt of sexual energy in the atmosphere had announced his presence. She turned and saw him. He'd changed from the business suit he'd been wearing earlier and was now dressed in a pair of jeans and a white shirt. He looked relaxed and handsome. In the jeans and shirt, his body was hard and muscular, and she was fully aware of the length of him. All his brothers were tall, but he was taller. Only Gannon, the youngest brother, was a wee bit taller.

"Yes, we were looking for you. We said you played the role of hero for Sloan and that was good," Tyson said.

"Only after I reminded him that Mom expected us to treat ladies with the utmost respect, and if there's ever one in need, we're there for the rescue," Galen said.

"Whatever." Mercury switched his gaze to her. "Good evening, Sloan. I hope my brothers aren't boring you to tears."

She chuckled. "No, I'm enjoying their company."

"In fact, I was just about to ask her if she'd like to take a stroll in Mom's courtyard so I can show her all the different types of flowers she has growing there," his brother Gannon said, smiling.

Mercury came to stand by Sloan's side. "No need. I gave Sloan a tour of the courtyard yesterday." He then turned to her. "I need to talk to her about something."

"What about?" Gannon asked, like he had every right to know.

"None of your business."

Sloan was enjoying this playful camaraderie between the brothers. She missed out on this sort of thing by being an only child. It was obvious the six had a fondness for each other, even when they were annoyed.

"Mercury probably has to tell me something about my new car," she said.

Eli lifted a brow. "You got a new car?"

She couldn't help but beam all over the place. "Yes. Hopefully, I'll be picking it up this Friday when I move into my apartment."

"Apartment? You have an apartment?" Tyson asked.

"Yes. I signed a lease as well today, thanks to Mercury."

"Yes, that Mercury is such a nice guy," Galen said, giving his brother a look Sloan couldn't decipher.

"Of course I am. Just like you said, Mom raised us well. Respect and rescue, right?" Mercury said, giving his brother a huge smile.

"I'll be glad to help you move into your apartment," Gannon offered, taking a sip of his before-dinner drink.

"No need—I'm taking care of Sloan."

She wasn't sure she liked the implications of that, but knew Mercury hadn't meant it the way it sounded and she figured his brothers probably knew that, as well.

"We'll see you guys in the dining room in a minute. Like

I said, I have something to discuss with Sloan," Mercury said before presenting his arm to her.

She took it and he escorted her toward his mother's office. The same one where they'd shared a kiss last night. He didn't say anything until he'd closed the door behind him.

"What's going on, Mercury?" she asked him.

After that kiss they'd shared last night and the two they'd shared today, she was somewhat nervous about being alone with him. He had a tendency to make her body feel things.

"I need to give you this," he said, reaching into his jeans pocket and pulling out a phone. "It's a burner. We didn't have time to pick one up today, so I made a stop by the store on my way here."

Getting one had been on her list of things to do. "Thanks. I appreciate you doing that for me. Please be sure to add the cost to the amount I owe you already. It seems I'm getting further and further into your debt, Mercury," she said, sliding the phone into the pocket of her skirt.

"No, you're not. And here's the number to it," he said, handing that to her, as well. "And there's something else you need to know."

She lifted a brow. "What?"

"Your ex-fiancé is in town."

Of all the things she had expected him to say, that hadn't been it. Harold had told her he was coming to Phoenix, but she hadn't believed him. "How do you know?"

"I have a friend connected to Homeland Security. As a favor, I asked her to let me know the moment his plane landed."

Sloan tried ignoring the fact this particular friend of his was a female. "How did you know he'd planned to come here?"

"I overheard that part of your phone conversation with your mother. I figured that meant he knew where you were."

"Only because my father told him." Anger tore into Sloan. Did Harold have no shame? "I've told him countless times that I won't marry him, so coming here was a waste of his time."

"That might be the case, but he may need to hear it again."

"It won't do any good—trust me. He has it in his head that he can do whatever the hell he wants to do where I'm concerned because he has my parents' blessing."

"Sounds like you have a problem, Sloan. In that case, I'm going to give you the same advice my father always gave his sons while growing up and even after we became men."

"Which is?"

"When there's a problem, first up is to find a solution."

She didn't say anything as she tried to digest his words. Good advice for anyone other than herself. She'd never had to come up with a solution to anything because her parents had always fixed her problems. Instead of helping her, she now saw they'd only been hindering her.

"But what if the solution I come up with is not well-thought-out? And ends up causing more harm than good?" she asked, seriously needing to know. She knew what he'd said was true. Her parents were her problem and she needed to take ownership of how to deal with them.

"It's fine if that happens, Sloan. We're human. We make mistakes. On the other hand, we can go back to the drawing board and start over, make new decisions, find new solutions."

She studied him for a minute. "Was there ever a very important problem you had to find a solution for?" For some reason she had a feeling there was.

He broke eye contact with her to look out a single French door that led outside to his mother's courtyard. Moments later, he glanced back at her. "Yes, there was. Finding the solution was difficult, but I did it and I'm glad I did. Taking ownership of the problem fell on me and I'm glad I made the decision that I did."

She nodded, wondering what had been the problem and the solution. It wasn't any of her business and he wasn't sharing any details. "What if my decision is impulsive?"

He chuckled smoothly. "It can happen that way. I call them temporary fixers. But even coming up with something temporary is better than not doing anything. Never let anyone know how intimidated you might be. No matter who they are. Stand your ground. Let them see you as a strong individual, even when your knees might be shaking. Have confidence in yourself even in the face of not feeling confident. Fake it. Who's to know?"

She tilted her head up and looked at him, studied his features. Handsome? Yes, but there was something else she was seeing. That realization made her smile. "You mentor a lot, don't you?"

She could tell by his expression that her question surprised him, caught him off guard. "What makes you say that?" he asked, leaning back against his mother's desk.

In a way, she wished he hadn't done that. His stance made his jeans stretch tight across a pair of muscular thighs. The same thighs that had rubbed against her today when they'd kissed. Both times. Deep feminine appreciation flowed through her. Her attraction to Mercury was becoming so intense that he could and would be placed on her problematic list. He'd become a distraction as well as a temptation. She didn't need either. As one of her problems, she would have to find a solution to deal with him, as well.

Now she wished several hot, passionate solutions weren't flowing through her mind.

Knowing he was waiting for a response to his question, she shrugged her shoulders. "Not sure. I guess it's not only what you're saying but how you're saying it. Like you've given this sort of advice before."

He gave her a look that made her think he wasn't at all happy that she'd been able to read him. But she had.

"My occupation requires it," he finally said. "I represent a lot of sports figures and sign them up for million-dollar contracts. Some have never seen that much money or dreamed of having it. It can pose problems. People they know and are better off not knowing come out of the woodwork. Most of the guys and women are young, inexperienced and not able to handle the vultures, the opportunists, the problems. I periodically give them pep talks, and when a problem arises, I am there for them. Not to solve it but to help them solve it themselves. They have to come up with their own solutions."

"And if it's the wrong one?" she asked.

"I tell them to never come up with a solution that's not reversible."

A slight frown burrowed between her brows. "So, in other words, no solution should be permanent," she said, trying to follow him.

"Remember permanent means permanent. Ask yourself if that's what you want. And if the solution you come up with seems unconventional, but it will work at the time, there is nothing wrong with doing it to give yourself time to come up with a bigger, more conventional and better plan."

She nodded. He'd certainly given her food for thought. "Thanks, Mercury. I appreciate you sharing your thoughts with me."

"No problem." He moved away from the desk and slowly walked toward her. She met his gaze and could see the same look he normally had right before he would kiss her. And she had a feeling that was his intent now.

They hadn't argued, nor were they at odds with each other like all those other times. If he kissed her, it wouldn't be driven by anything other than desire. Plain and simple.

He came to a stop directly in front of her. He glanced down at her outfit. A flowing skirt and sleeveless blouse with sandals on her feet. When he glanced back at her, he said, "Did I tell you how nice you look?"

"No."

"Then let me do that right now. You look nice, Sloan."

She couldn't help but smile at the compliment. "Thank you, Mercury."

He stared down at her for a moment. Was she imagining things or was his gaze centered on her lips? Evidently her lips thought so because she could feel them start to tingle. Nervous, she swiped her tongue across her bottom lip, then watched how his eyes seemed to lock on the movement.

"I guess we need to get back. We wouldn't want to be the ones holding up dinner, right?" she asked, barely able to get the words out.

He reached up and tucked a strand of hair behind her ear. The movement, the touch, made a shiver run down her spine. As if he'd felt it, his gaze returned to hers and locked in. "You know what I think?"

Why did he ask in that low, husky voice of his? The one that made yet another shiver pass through her.

She swallowed. "No. What do you think?"

"I think they are going to have to wait."

He moved in closer, pressed those tight muscular thighs and firm stomach close to hers and then lowered his mouth to hers. She was so ready and felt a sudden drench of desire invade her the moment his tongue mingled with hers.

Within seconds, it wasn't quite clear whether he was devouring her mouth or she was devouring his. All she knew was that they were taking each other's tongues with a hunger she'd never felt before.

She loved his taste, and from the way he was marauding her mouth, he enjoyed hers, as well. She'd never been kissed like this. Those other times had been hot; however, this was blazing. Now she felt weak in the knees and couldn't help the groan that escaped.

Mercury then ended the kiss with the same intensity he'd used to start it. She appreciated how he wrapped his arms around her, holding her as if to keep her from melting at his feet. The man had practically kissed her senseless and she had no shame in inwardly admitting that she'd liked it.

It took her a minute to catch her breath, take in the scent of him in her nostrils. She thought she could stay like this, being held by him forever, but knew in reality, she couldn't.

Slowly, she lifted her head and met his gaze. He was staring down at her with an odd look on his face. If he was deciding she was a problem just like she'd begun to think he was becoming one, then he would have to follow his own advice and find a solution. She couldn't and wouldn't help him. She had her own issues to deal with. That made her recall what had brought them into his mother's office in the first place.

"Just because Harold is in town doesn't mean he'll be able to find me, right?"

He held her gaze. "Not sure. That would depend on whether or not your father had a tracker on your phone."

His words made her frown. He did. She'd forgotten about that tracker, which at the time her father had said he'd had installed for security reasons. It hadn't mattered to her when she'd left Cincinnati because she hadn't been trying to keep her whereabouts a secret. At least at first she hadn't. Then after her mother's phone call, leaving Phoenix and hiding out somewhere had been her plan until Mercury had pretty much talked her out of it. He was right; it was time she stood her ground and came up with a solution. Even if it was a temporary solution.

"It doesn't matter if Harold eventually finds me. Nothing has changed. We aren't getting married."

Mercury nodded. "I still don't understand why your father would want you to marry him."

She shrugged. "I told you—it's all about merging the two families' wealth. Thanks to an inheritance from my grandfather, when I turn thirty I will come into a large sum of money as well as a bunch of real estate in Texas."

He nodded and took her hand in his. "Come on. Tonight, I want you to forget about your problems. Instead I want you to enjoy the Steele family."

She thought that was a nice thing to say. "Thanks, Mercury. I appreciate you sharing your family with me."

Thirteen

Mercury kept his eyes on Sloan through most of dinner. Memories of the kiss they'd shared were affecting him in ways he hadn't counted on. It didn't take much to recall how easily his tongue had slid between her lips and she'd sucked on his tongue just as greedily as he'd sucked on hers.

He'd heard her moans and was certain he'd released a groan or two himself. But that was fine with him, although he wasn't one who would usually lose control while kissing a woman. Sloan was making it obvious she was different, and he was having a hard time pinpointing just what that difference was.

There was just something about her he found fascinating and it was more than how easily she'd blended in with his family. Everyone liked her; that much was obvious. His parents, his brothers and sisters-in-law and even his niece and nephews.

Even now the look in her eyes was brimming with the kind of happiness he had a feeling she hadn't experienced much, hanging out with a family who loved each other. That didn't mean they all thought alike or got along 100 percent of the time, but it did mean they respected each other's opinions, even when they didn't agree with them. It also meant that, when the time came, they would have each other's backs and would be there for each other.

His only problem with his mom right now was that she had separated him and Sloan. The dining-room table that seated twenty-four was big and long, to accommodate their growing family. Eden had placed him at one end of the table and Sloan at the other. And she'd seated Sloan beside Gannon—the charmer, of all people.

Growing up, Gannon had been in awe of his older brothers. He'd been very impressionable, and their mother had warned them to set positive examples for their youngest brother to follow. With such a tall order, Mercury and his brothers had tried to be low-key around Gannon, but when it came to women, he'd turned out to actually be the worst of the lot. In fact, Gannon always said he was waiting for the day Mercury bit the bachelor dust so he could have all the single ladies in Phoenix to himself.

That was one of the reasons Mercury was keeping an eye on Sloan, to make sure she wasn't being taken in by Gannon's charm. It was obvious his brother was laying it on thick and the two were getting much too friendly to suit Mercury.

"You okay, Merk?"

Mercury turned to Jonas. Whereas all the other brothers had at least a year and a few months in their ages between them, that wasn't the case for him and Jonas. In fact, for three days they were the same age. Because they were so close in age, there had always been a special bond between them.

"Yes, I'm fine. Why do you ask?"

"Because you've been unusually quiet, and you've been staring at Sloan quite a bit."

"Have I?"

"Yes. By the way, I like her."

He took a sip of his lemonade, then asked in a low voice, "How can you like her when you don't even know her?"

Jonas chuckled and lowered his voice, as well. "I can ask you the same thing."

Mercury frowned. "Who said I liked her?"

"Your mouth. The one that was slightly swollen earlier. So was hers. That means the two of you did some heavy-duty kissing while locked up in Mom's office. I doubt I'm the only one who noticed. So, do you like her?"

Mercury didn't say anything because at that moment Sloan caught his attention when she laughed at something Gannon said. He glanced down the long table at her, and as if she sensed him staring, she looked at him. Their gazes locked and held. There was no way Jonas wasn't noticing, as well as Gannon. Hell, others were probably noticing as well, but he was too mesmerized to care.

Then Drew spoke and Mercury glanced over at his dad. "A game is on tonight. Anyone care to watch?"

His brothers all said yes. Mercury didn't say anything because although he'd dropped eye contact with Sloan, he was still reeling. While holding her gaze he had tuned out everything around him...except for her.

Jonas leaned over toward him. "You still didn't give me an answer to my question, Merk. But then, you truly don't have to."

"He doesn't have to do what?"

That question had come from Gannon. Mercury then noticed that his brothers were standing around him at the table and everyone else was gone. "Where's Sloan?"

"In the kitchen with Mom and our wives," Galen said, looking at him funny.

"And why are you asking about Sloan?" Gannon asked, grinning. "You need to discuss something else with her locked in Mom's office?"

Mercury frowned. Before he could say anything, Tyson's wife, Hunter, walked into the dining room to grab the plates off the table. It wasn't that he, his brothers or their dad were sexist. They could and did take their own plates to the kitchen, but those were Eden's rules. Thursday was the one night she liked pampering her husband and sons.

When Hunter left, Mercury said, "Let's speak Russian." Because Eden had been a world traveler while modeling, it had been important to her that her sons spoke different languages. That was why Mercury and his brothers had the ability to speak several foreign languages fluently. The last thing he wanted was for Sloan to walk in to discover she was being discussed.

"Fine," Eli said, dropping down in a chair.

Before they could begin their conversation, Sloan entered the room to gather the place mats. She smiled at them and they smiled back. She would probably wonder why they were speaking another language, but knowing she didn't understand them was the important thing.

"We want to know where you stand with Sloan. We don't want her to be taken advantage of," Galen said, starting off the conversation in Russian.

Mercury stared at his brothers. Why did they think he owed them an explanation about anything concerning Sloan? Besides, hadn't it been Eli and Tyson who'd dropped by his office yesterday, all but telling him he needed to do something before Eden got any ideas in her head? He took the time to remind them of that.

"We know," Tyson said. "But that was before we got the chance to meet Sloan. We like her. In fact, we like her a lot. We all do."

"I told you that you would," Galen said, smiling. "She's special."

Mercury tried listening to his brothers while watching Sloan. Damn, she looked good moving around the table gathering the place mats. And she looked like she belonged here.

Belonged here? He didn't like thinking that.

"So, what are your intentions toward her?" Gannon asked. "If you're not going to make a move, I will."

"The hell you will," Mercury said to his youngest brother. "So, back off."

Sloan glanced over at them with concern in her features. Mercury figured that although she couldn't understand what they were saying, she could probably tell he was upset. "Look, guys, we will finish this discussion later," he said, refusing to discuss Sloan with his brothers any longer. At least he'd let Gannon know she was off-limits.

At that moment the doorbell rang. Mercury glanced over at his brothers. "It's late for visitors. Are the folks expecting anyone?" he asked them, still speaking Russian.

"Not sure," Galen stated. "I'll let Mom know she has company."

"I can do that, Galen," Sloan said. "I need to carry these place mats to the kitchen anyway. You guys can continue on with your conversation." She then left the dining room.

Mercury and his brothers watched her leave, staring at her in shock and feeling the need to pick their jaws up off the floor. She had spoken in fluent Russian. That meant she had not only heard their conversation but had understood every single thing they'd been saying about her.

"Did you know she spoke Russian?" Tyson asked him when they were able to speak.

Still in shock, Mercury shook his head no. The only words he could mutter at that moment were "Ahh hell."

"Eden, someone is at the door," Sloan said, returning to the kitchen.

"Oh? Thanks. I hadn't heard the doorbell," Eden said, wiping her hands on a dish towel before leaving the kitchen.

The other women continued their talk about the latest in fashion and makeup, but Sloan was having a problem contributing. She wished she could put the conversation she'd heard between Mercury and his brothers out of her mind, but she couldn't. Because they'd assumed she didn't understand Russian, they'd felt safe talking about her. At least she knew Mercury's brothers liked her, but he never said whether he did or not.

"Sloan?"

She glanced up to see Eden had returned. "Yes?"

"There's a young man here to see you and he says he's your fiancé."

Harold was here? Mercury had warned her that he could possibly track her in Phoenix, but she honestly hadn't thought he would. He had a lot of nerve coming here. Anger consumed her. "Where is he?"

"I left him in the living room."

"Do I need to go get Mercury?" Eli's wife, Stacey, asked nervously.

Sloan shook her head. "No, I've got this." She walked out of the kitchen and headed toward the living room.

It didn't take her long to get there. Harold seemed to be standing in the middle of it and he looked annoyed. She was grateful the women hadn't followed her. This would be a conversation she and Harold needed to have alone. It was embarrassing enough that he had shown up here. "What are you doing here, Harold?"

He glanced over at her and frowned. "I'm glad your father had a tracker on your phone, or I would not have been able to find you. I called him and he texted me directions straight here."

Agitated, Sloan asked him again, "What are you doing here?"

He had the nerve to smile. "That's obvious. I came for

you. I told you that I would. We have a wedding to plan in Cincinnati."

"No, we don't. I told you that. The wedding is off. You should not have come."

He stared at her. "The wedding is on and we're getting married in August."

"Is everything okay, Sloan?"

Hearing the deep voice, Sloan turned to find Mercury, his father and brothers had entered the room. Also, the women. The living room was large enough to accommodate everyone and she didn't resent their presence, but instead felt it was reassuring. In their own way, this family she'd only known for two days was telling her they had her back.

"Yes, Mercury, I'm—"

Before she could finish her response, Harold rudely cut in and said, "Hello, everyone. Thanks for looking out for Sloan, but we have a plane to catch. Her parents have been worried about her."

Sloan wanted to laugh at that. "I'm not going anywhere with you."

Harold had the nerve to chuckle. "Sure you are, sweetheart." He then glanced around at everyone. "Sorry, I didn't introduce myself. I'm Harold Cunningham of the Cincinnati Cunninghams," he said, as if his name meant something.

"And we're the Steeles. The Phoenix Steeles," someone said behind her, and she recognized the voice as Galen's.

"And I'm Mercury Steele," Mercury said, moving forward, extending his hand to Harold. Sloan wondered why Mercury was acting like a diplomat and being so nice.

Harold shook Mercury's hand, and then Mercury proceeded to introduce Harold to every single person in the room. After doing so, Mercury then said, "Harold, we really do appreciate you coming all the way from Ohio to check on Sloan, but as you can see, she's in good hands. When you return to Cincinnati, please be sure to tell her parents that she's in my care and under my protection."

Harold frowned. "Your care and protection? What's that supposed to mean?"

Mercury didn't answer; instead he glanced over at Sloan. She immediately recalled the conversation they'd had in his mother's office. Harold was her problem and she needed to fix it.

Suddenly, an idea for a temporary fix came into her head. As long as Harold and her parents assumed there was a chance for the marriage to go on, they would keep hounding her. That was what this was about anyway. That was what had driven her away from Ohio. Her parents' insistence that she and Harold marry to expand their families' wealth.

Drawing in a deep breath, Sloan moved to stand beside Mercury. She hoped he recognized what she was about to do as a temporary fix and that he wouldn't fall flat on his face from shock. From the look on his face earlier, finding out she understood Russian had been shocking enough.

She met her ex-fiancé's gaze. "Harold, what it means," she said in a clear voice, "is that…" She paused and gave Mercury a quick please-forgive-me-for-this smile before turning back to Harold. "Mercury is my fiancé and we're getting married. In fact, we were planning our wedding when you showed up. So now will you please leave?"

Fourteen

Sloan had just told a whopper of a lie and for the longest time the entire room got quiet. She hadn't known what to expect, especially from the man standing by her side whom she refused to look at. Instead her attention was trained on Harold.

She watched the expression on his face show shock and then outrage. Outrage? Honestly? The man who'd told her his mistress would become a permanent part of their lives?

Then Harold spoke. "Don't be ridiculous, Sloan. How can you be engaged to him when you are engaged to me?"

"I *was* engaged to you, but if you recall, I broke off our engagement weeks ago."

"And now you're going to marry a man you barely know?"

"Why not? I thought I knew you and found out I truly didn't." She hated that the Steeles were privy to this conversation, but she wouldn't let that stop her.

"Your parents won't approve of you marrying anyone but me," Harold had the nerve to boast.

She lifted her chin and stiffened her spine. "Then it's a good thing I'm not seeking their approval."

Harold rubbed his hand down his face. "Do you know what will happen to the Donahues and Cunninghams without your…?"

His voice trailed off and she wasn't sure if it was because he suddenly realized they had an audience or if perhaps there was something else. "My what?"

Harold quickly shoved his hands into his pockets. "Nothing."

Yes, there was something and she was determined to find out what it was. "Let's be honest, Harold. You don't love me and I don't love you. In fact, you told me that you want the woman you do love to be a part of our marriage and I refused that."

Sloan's last statement caused a gasp from the back, she wasn't sure from whom, but she didn't care that all the Steeles knew why she'd ended her engagement. "What you do is your business," she continued. "But I won't allow myself to be manipulated by my parents any longer. I will have the freedom to choose the man I want in my life and not the one they want for me. I suggest you do like I'm doing and be your own person and marry who you want. Money isn't everything."

Harold was quiet for a minute and then he said in a somewhat subdued tone, "I need to speak with you privately. There's something you need to know."

A part of Sloan wanted to tell him that there was no room for further discussion, but a pleading look in his eyes stopped her. She would listen to whatever he said, and then she would tell him to leave and stay out of her life. "Fine. We'll talk privately." She then turned to Eden and Drew. "May I use your office?"

Eden nodded. "Certainly."

"And as your *fiancé*, I intend to be a part of this *private* discussion," Mercury said, meeting her gaze.

Sloan would rather he wasn't. However, considering that she'd given him the title of fiancé without his permission... She didn't want to think how he was feeling about that. She just hoped he remembered their discussion about solutions, and that what she'd done was a temporary fix.

"I'd rather you weren't," Harold said curtly.

"Doesn't matter. That's the way it's going to be," Mercury said.

"Mercury is right, Harold. He can be privy to whatever you have to tell me since he knows all of my business anyway," she said, suddenly realizing just how true that was.

"Okay," Harold said tersely.

"This way." Taking her hand, Mercury led her toward his mother's office and Harold followed.

"So, what do you want to talk to Sloan about, Cunningham?" Mercury asked, leaning back against the door.

He was trying to reel in emotions that were swamping him. He wasn't sure what was upsetting him the most, finding out Sloan had understood his and his brothers' conversation in Russian earlier, Stacey coming down into the dining room to announce it was Sloan's fiancé at the door, or Sloan's lie that he was her fiancé. He had wanted her to fix her problem with Cunningham but claiming Mercury was her fiancé was not what he'd had in mind.

Sloan had taken a seat on the sofa and Harold had the nerve to sit on the sofa, as well. At least the man had the decency to make sure there was space between them.

Instead of answering him directly, Harold shifted in his seat and turned to Sloan. "I don't think you understand how important a marriage between us is to your father."

"Then tell me, Harold."

Harold shot a look over at Mercury before looking back at her. "I honestly wish we could speak privately."

"That won't be happening," Mercury said, meaning every word.

Sloan glanced over at him and then back at Harold. "Mercury is right, so please answer. Why is a marriage between us so important, other than combining the families' wealth?"

Harold didn't say anything for a minute. "I think your father needs a lot of capital for some reason. I overheard a private conversation between my father and yours regarding your trust fund. The one left to you by your grandfather."

Sloan frowned. "Why would our fathers be discussing my trust fund?"

"Your father wants us to marry so they can get their hands on it."

Sloan shook her head. "That's not possible. I can't get my trust fund until I'm thirty."

"I suggest you verify that, Sloan. I gather from the conversation I overheard that might not be the case. And you, of all people, know your father. Whatever he wants, he gets. He has friends in high places. He could financially ruin these people who've helped you. Do you want that?"

"Stop trying that scare tactic, Cunningham," Mercury said, having heard enough. "Her father can't ruin my family financially. But we could ruin him. Maybe you need to let him know that."

Harold stared at Mercury and he stared back for the longest moment. Then Harold said, "And I will certainly tell him."

"Good."

Harold stood. "You've been forewarned."

Mercury moved away from the door for Harold to walk

out. There was no doubt in his mind that one, or possibly all, of his brothers would escort Cunningham to the door with a warning to never come back.

"Are you okay, Sloan?"

She glanced up at him and he could see the hurt in her eyes. "Yes, I'm okay. Sorry that I used you as my temporary fix."

He nodded. "It took me a minute to figure out that's what you were doing. I'm okay with it for now." He needed to let her know he expected her to start working on a permanent solution, but for some reason he let it go.

"I need to talk to your parents. Your family. I owe them an apology for Harold even showing up here tonight like he did and for having to listen to our issues. I feel embarrassed."

"Don't feel that way," he said, easing down beside her. "I'm sure you know by now that my family likes you, and we are here for you, no matter what."

Mercury could tell his words touched her and she was about to get emotional. He wasn't used to emotional women. For a moment he felt out of his element. Then he recalled Eli saying that he'd learned that emotional women liked to be held, when his wife, Stacey, was very emotional while pregnant. Hell, Mercury didn't hold women; he bedded them and then moved on to the next. If he showed too much empathy, they might get clingy. A clingy woman was nothing but trouble.

But for some reason, he felt compelled to give Sloan a little more consideration than he gave to most. Probably surprising her just as much as he was surprising himself, he reached over and swooped her into his arms and placed her in his lap. Then he wrapped his arms securely around her.

When she tilted her head back to look up at him, he said, "I figured everyone needs a little cuddling every once in a while, and I would be the first to admit that the last two days have been pretty damn hellish for you."

"Will they get better, Mercury?"

He released a soft chuckle that was meant to charm her. He wasn't sure why, when he wasn't a charmer like Gannon. "We're going to hope, okay?"

"Okay." And then she placed her head against his chest.

Why it was important to him that she felt safe and secure, he wasn't sure, but it was. For a long moment neither said anything. Then he asked her the one question that was still on his mind. "Sloan?"

"Yes?"

"Why didn't you tell me you speak Russian?"

She glanced up at him, her brow furrowing. "I speak seven different languages."

"Seven?"

"Yes. Besides English, I speak French, Italian, German, Spanish, Russian and Swahili. I assumed you knew, since the job I'm interviewing for is interpreter for the Miss Universe pageant."

Mercury was surprised. "An interpreter for Miss Universe?"

"Yes. What sort of job did you think it was?"

He shrugged. He certainly hadn't thought it would be that. "A traveling companion since Ms. Fowler likes to travel a lot. Mom had mentioned months ago she would be looking for one."

Sloan chuckled. "A traveling companion? I doubt a salary doing that will pay my bills, Mercury."

He'd figured that much, as well. "That job as an interpreter sounds interesting," he said.

She smiled. "I think so, too. I'm excited about the prospect of doing something like that."

She glanced at her watch. "I need to talk to your family. I hope they haven't left yet."

He doubted they had. His brothers and sisters-in-law would want to make sure she was okay before they left. "You don't have to talk to them."

"I want to. I know what you're saying about my father's scare tactics, but your brothers need to be told, as well. Harold is right—my father will try coming after anyone who befriends me."

He stood and placed her on her feet. She tilted her head back to look up at him.

"So, you and your brothers speak Russian, too?" she asked.

"Yes," Mercury said, grinning. "Besides English, we speak Russian, Spanish, German and French."

She nodded. "That's good to know."

They headed for the door, Mercury taking her hand in his. "Yes, that's good to know," he agreed.

Hours later, long after his mother and Sloan had gone to bed and his sisters-in-law and niece and nephews had left to go home, Mercury, his brothers and father were still in his father's man cave. Sloan had apologized to everyone for Harold's unexpected arrival, and like he'd known they would, his family had basically assured her that Harold's surprise appearance hadn't bothered them. She'd also told them about what a tyrant her father could be and that he had no qualms about going after anyone who would help her defy him. They'd pretty much told her to let him try.

Drew stood. "I assume you have a plan, Mercury?"

Mercury couldn't help but chuckle. "Yes, Dad, I have a plan."

"You're marrying her, right?" Galen asked, grinning.

Mercury frowned. "No. I'm not marrying anyone. Her claiming that I was her fiancé was just a temporary fix. She knows she has to come up with a permanent solution…but in the meantime, this is what I propose."

His brothers all leaned toward him. "What?" Tyson asked.

"I need to call Quade to find out every single thing I need to know about Sloan's father."

Quade Westmoreland was married to their cousin, the former Cheyenne Steele, and lived in Charlotte, North Carolina. For years Quade worked with the PSF, the Presidential Security Forces, dual branches of the Secret Service and CIA. Now he owned an elite PI firm, in addition to a network of security companies around the country and abroad. "We need to know everything about the man we're dealing with."

Everyone nodded their agreement. Quade would leave no stone unturned and his report would be thorough. Mercury then said, "I also need to find out more about Sloan's trust fund. You heard what she told us tonight. She honestly doesn't know much about it. All she knew was that she would get it whenever she turned thirty."

Mercury looked over at Eli. "Since Sloan hired you as her attorney tonight, what do you plan on doing?"

"I'm meeting with Sloan here in the morning to get more information," he said. "Specifically, I need the name of her grandfather's attorney. Then I'll be contacting him and go from there."

"That sounds like a plan," Mercury said.

"When is Sloan moving into her apartment?" Jonas asked. "Will it be safe for her to do that? I hate to say it but her parents sound like a pair of loonies."

Gannon laughed. "You can go ahead and say it because they do."

Mercury smiled and shook his head, but Gannon was right. They did. "Sloan's moving into her apartment tomorrow. The place is already furnished, so all she has to do is move in. Just to be on the safe side, I'll hang around her more often."

"More often than you do now?" Gannon asked with a smirk on his face.

Ignoring his youngest brother's comment, Mercury said, "I'll contact Quade first thing in the morning."

Fifteen

Sloan glanced across the breakfast table at Eli with an apologetic look on her face. "I'm sorry, Eli, but I don't have the answer to any of those questions. The only reason I know the name of my grandfather's attorney is because I met him a few times."

Eli nodded, pushing his folder aside. "And you don't think he's been corresponding with your parents on your behalf?"

"I would think not. Charles Rivers and my grandfather were close. I recall his father was my grandfather's friend for years, and when Mr. Rivers finished law school, he became Pop's private attorney. He knew how my grandfather felt about my parents meddling in his affairs."

"Did your grandfather know the Cunninghams?"

Sloan shrugged her shoulders. "Not that I know of. At least he never mentioned them to me. In fact, I'm almost sure he didn't. If I recall, the Cunninghams and my parents became friends after my grandfather passed away, when they moved their company to Cincinnati."

"Hopefully, I'll be able to reach out to Charles Rivers

today," Eli said, standing. "I understand you're moving into your own place today."

Sloan couldn't help the bright smile that touched her lips. "Yes, I am. And my new car is being delivered today, as well. I am so excited. Mercury is arriving around noon and I'm all packed and ready to go."

"I'll let you know if I hear anything from Rivers."

"Thanks."

A few hours later, Sloan was prepared to leave when Mercury arrived. Giving both Drew and Eden hugs, she thanked them for their generous hospitality and told them she would be inviting them to her place when she got settled. "When will my car be delivered?" she asked Mercury excitedly, as they drove away from his parents' home.

"It should be there by the time we arrive at your apartment."

"My apartment. I like the sound of that." She truly did. While living with her parents, she'd never given any thought to moving out since she basically had her own wing of the house and nobody monitored her comings and goings. At least she hadn't given leaving any thought until she'd had enough.

She glanced over at Mercury. He was wearing a nice suit. "You went to work today?"

"Yes, this morning. I had a couple of meetings. I try to wrap up things by lunchtime on Fridays to get a head start on my weekend."

"Big plans?"

"The usual."

She wondered what was the usual for him, but knew not to ask. What he did and with whom was his business. She should appreciate the time he'd given her the last two days and let it go.

But a part of her couldn't help remembering how when she'd gotten upset last night about Harold's appearance and the entire situation with her father, Mercury had placed her in his lap and held her.

She couldn't ever remember anyone doing that for her before. And the sad thing was that she'd needed it. She hadn't known just how much until he'd performed the self-less act.

"Nikki and Hunter will be dropping by later to bring over toiletries and stuff I might need. I think it's nice of them to do that."

"I have a nice family. By the way, how did your meeting with Eli go this morning?"

"I think it went okay." She spent the next twenty minutes filling him in on everything.

"Eli is a good attorney. And just so you know, I have a family member who used to work for the CIA checking out a few things on your father."

"CIA? That's a little deep, don't you think? Trying to keep me under their control is nothing like selling government secrets to other countries," she said, making light of her situation.

"You never know what motivates people to do what they do, Sloan."

"I know what motivates my parents, Mercury. Money. My grandfather would say that all the time." Not wanting to talk about her parents any longer, she told Mercury about her to-do list and how glad she was to have a car to get around town.

"So, what are your plans for the weekend?" he then asked her.

"I'm going to relax, maybe check out that mall on the corner and buy a book to read. Your mother invited me to church with her on Sunday. I figured I'd do some interview practice sessions Sunday evening for my talk with Ms. Fowler."

"Interview practice sessions?"

"Yes. Although she's not doing the official hiring for the pageant, I understand that if she recommends me for the position, then there's a good chance I'll get it. I want to make a good impression on her."

"You will. Just be yourself."

Moments later, they were pulling into her apartment complex and she drew in a huge, exhilarated breath. This would be her place. Granted, she didn't own it, but it would be hers nonetheless. The apartment would be her home.

"You okay?"

She smiled over at Mercury. "Yes, I'm okay. I couldn't be better."

Mercury stood in the living room and watched Sloan slowly walk around, moving from room to room, as if she was in awe. If truth be known, he was in total awe of her. Today she was attired in another sundress, this one a beautiful floral print. Her hair was swept up with a few loose strands framing her face. Her makeup was never heavy, always soft and subtle and barely looked as if she was wearing any.

He'd had to mentally prepare himself to see her again today, after having thought about her into the wee hours of the morning. When had he thought about another woman as much? Hell, he doubted he ever had. He'd tried convincing himself it was because of her ex-fiancé's visit last night. The man had had a lot of gall to show up at the Steeles' home.

Then there was that moment between Mercury and Sloan afterward in his mother's office when he'd placed her in his lap and held her. It was during that time that he'd felt emotions that were so unlike him. Totally uncharacteristic. Atypical. She had the ability to make him behave like a totally different guy. Like now.

Drawing in a deep breath, Mercury knew there was no

reason for him to still be here. She was in her apartment and had a car, which meant his services were no longer needed. He should be on his way to Notorious to get an early start on the weekend and check the lineup of women who were probably already there. Ready for some action, a one-night stand, a Mercury quickie or a Mercury Steele seduction.

Yet he was still here, watching her, staring as she strolled from room to room, admiring her beauty. He loved the size of her breasts and the shape of her thighs, easily displayed whenever she moved. There was a gracefulness about her stride. He figured she'd probably attended one of those finishing schools, and that was the reason she and Galen's wife, Brittany, had hit it off last night. But then, Sloan had impressed everyone without even trying to do so.

He'd meant what he'd told her in the car. When she met with Ms. Fowler on Monday she should just be herself. There was something about her that drew people in. His brothers, parents and sisters-in-law had been drawn in immediately. It had taken a little longer for him, only because of their rocky beginning. But now he was all in, and like the rest of the Steeles, he was Team Sloan.

She stopped walking, turned and gave him a smile that heightened his pulse and made a hard hum of lust flare through his veins. Her smile and his reaction to it had been so unexpected he'd immediately shifted, feeling weak in the knees. Otherwise, he might have fallen flat on his face.

What was he thinking? No woman could make him fall flat.

"Tell me about *your* apartment, Mercury."

Why did she want to know about his apartment? Usually when a woman asked about his apartment, that meant she was hinting at an invitation. However, he doubted that was the case with Sloan. "What would you like to know about it?"

"Although this place is furnished, I'm still considering decorating ideas. Nothing costly. Definitely within my budget."

He liked how she was forever mindful of her budget, trying hard not to overspend. He knew that would be something she would have to get used to since that hadn't been her way of life before now. "Unlike these white walls, mine are colorful."

"Colorful?"

"Yes. It wasn't my choice. I hired a decorator and told her to do her own thing. Unfortunately, she was into bold colors. It took me a while to get used to them, but now I can't imagine my walls any other way."

She tipped her finger to her chin and glanced around, as if thinking about it. Why did seeing her doing something so mundane look sexy as hell? He bet she would be hot in bed.

He forced back a groan, knowing he shouldn't be thinking of Sloan in a sexual way. But he had and this wasn't the first time he'd done so. And why not? She was a woman. He was a man. He'd already admitted to their attraction by kissing her. And they had been kisses he'd totally enjoyed. Kisses he'd gone to bed thinking about. Kisses that were becoming greedier and more erotic every time they shared them.

What had Jonas told him at dinner last night? It had been obvious to everyone that Mercury and Sloan had been kissing when they walked out of his mother's office because their lips were swollen. For that to happen had meant some heavy-duty kissing had gone down behind those closed doors. He would admit it had.

Normally, if he was attracted to a woman, he would have made several home runs by now. With Sloan, he hadn't even tried swinging. He'd been satisfied with going to the bat with the kisses. He'd figured she had too many issues for him. Issues he didn't want to become involved with.

Now, that was a laugh since he was involved. All the way up to his balls.

And speaking of his balls…

They were actually twitching with need for her. He could just imagine that same finger that was tapping her chin stroking them, cupping them before using that same hand to feel him all over. Just the thought of her touching him down there—hell, touching him anywhere—had him feeling the area behind his zipper expand. He needed to leave. Now.

"I've got to go," he said, moving toward the door. "There's an important appointment I need to keep. I'll see you later."

And then he was gone.

He walked quickly to his car without looking back. In fact, he nearly held his breath until he reached his car, got inside and buckled his seat belt. When had he rushed away from a woman's place instead of rushing to it? Okay, he did remember rushing from Nancy Ormond's place the night she hinted at wanting him to father her baby. That was an altogether different issue than what had him dashing from Sloan's apartment.

He checked his watch and decided that he would go home and change clothes, chill a bit and then hit Notorious. He needed a night in some woman's bed. There had been a woman he'd seen last night when he'd been there with Jaye. She had given him the eye and had even flirted with him when he'd been about to leave. Maybe he'd be lucky and hit the jackpot tonight.

In fact, he intended for that to happen.

Sixteen

Yippee! She had the job!

Sloan was tempted to do a happy dance around her apartment, but she didn't want to disturb the Hollisters, the couple living in the apartment below her. She had met them when she'd gone bike riding on Sunday. Of all things, she had purchased a bicycle on Saturday. She loved her blue bike and went riding every morning.

She thought about the phone call she'd just received. After their talk yesterday, Margaret Fowler had been so taken with Sloan that she'd immediately called the pageant committee to put in a good word for her. Yesterday evening they had called to arrange a Skype interview that she'd thought had gone well. Obviously it had, since she'd just received a call from the pageant's hiring team, who'd said the job was hers.

She had been blown away by the salary they'd offered. It was more than Sloan had thought it would be. Nearly three times as much. They'd explained it was based on the number of languages she spoke. That meant she would be able to pay Mercury back sooner than planned for the loan, and hopefully she could double up on her car payments and pay the bank off sooner, as well.

Mercury...

Sloan hadn't seen or talked to him since Friday, when he'd brought her here. She had gone to church with members of his family on Sunday. After church she'd been invited to Galen's home in the mountains for dinner. She'd figured Mercury would show up, but he hadn't. She didn't want to admit to being disappointed at not seeing him, but she was. It was Tuesday and he still hadn't called. Not even to say hello and see how she was doing.

She wished she could talk to him to tell him about her new job, her *first* job, and she was excited about it. She refused to let Mercury's absence rain on her parade. She wouldn't call him. Chances were, he felt he'd spent too much time with her already and wanted his life back, the way it was before meeting her.

Fine, she hoped he was enjoying it. She couldn't let his absence get to her. Besides, she had plenty to keep her busy. She needed to set up her office since she would begin working from home in a few weeks. The laptop she owned was old and it was time to upgrade to a more advanced model. Then she would need a printer that had both scanning and faxing capabilities. She also needed to purchase office supplies.

However, Sloan knew no matter how busy she was, she would think about Mercury. She thought about him when she woke up every morning and he took over her dreams when she went to sleep at night. Those two days they'd spent together had meant everything to her. Evidently more to her than to him. Undoubtedly those kisses had been no different than any others he'd shared with women. They'd meant nothing to him and probably didn't even compete.

No surprise, since she had limited experience when it came to men. Harold hadn't wanted to make love to her and now she knew why. And that one time with Carlos Larson had been a total waste of time. Probably not for him, but definitely for her. She'd been wholly disappointed. Sloan had a feeling a night with Mercury would not disappoint her.

A night with Mercury...

She shouldn't be thinking such things even after four kisses and a cuddling session in his lap. He'd only indulged her as his way to either chastise, comfort or talk sense into her. His methods were effective and quite enjoyable.

The ringing of the doorbell meant she had a visitor. Other than the Hollisters, who lived downstairs, the only people who knew where she lived were the Steeles. She tried ignoring the tingling sensation in her stomach at the possibility that it could be Mercury.

She checked the peephole and couldn't see the person's face for the huge green plant in front of it. Could it be Mercury? Swallowing deeply, she asked, "Who is it?"

She then held her breath. Hoping. Wishing. Wanting it to be...

"It's Gannon, Sloan. I brought you a housewarming gift."

She let out the breath she'd been holding and with it came deep disappointment. What had she expected? Had her claiming he was her fiancé made him want to put distance between them? That had to be it, although he seemed to have accepted her explanation as to why she'd done it. Had he given it further thought and decided he didn't want her to get any ideas about where their relationship was going or wasn't going? The bottom line was they didn't even have a relationship.

That had to be it. What else could it be? Was keeping his distance a way of making sure she understood that?

"Sloan?"

She blinked. Gannon had to be wondering why she hadn't opened the door yet. "Yes. Just a minute."

Pasting a huge smile on her face, she opened the door and said, "Gannon! It's good to see you. Come in. Ahh, this plant is beautiful. Thanks for my gift."

Mercury leaned back in his chair and absently tossed paper clips back and forth in the center of his desk. Then he would gather them all up and start the process all over again. It was an unproductive way to spend his time, but he would do anything to keep his mind off Sloan.

He had deliberately stayed away from her the past four days and intended to add four more. That meant he would be a no-show Thursday night at his parents' for dinner. He wasn't ready to see her and at least he had an alibi. He would be flying out Thursday morning to Dallas for a high school basketball game. His eyes were on a player by the name of Brock Dennison. Brock was only seventeen, which meant he had to complete at least two years of college before he could get signed on with the NBA at nineteen.

Any other time Mercury would be looking forward to such a trip, but he was not this time. Although he knew he should keep putting distance between himself and Sloan, part of him didn't want to. He wanted *her*. Hell, he hadn't even been able to pique his interest for any other woman. He'd gone to Notorious four nights in a row and women had thrown themselves at him; a couple of them had all but invited him out to their cars for quickies, and he'd turned them all down. Granted, he did have discriminating taste, but still, he'd never gone this long without getting laid. So why was he going through self-induced torture?

He knew the reason and had already admitted to it.

He wanted Sloan. And he wanted her bad.

He wanted to seduce the hell out of her, knowing he would enjoy every minute of doing so. However, he'd made up his mind not to cross the line with her. She wasn't one of those women a man would enjoy in bed without wanting more, more and even more. She was the kind of woman a man could get addicted to. Hell, wasn't he addicted to her taste already after just four kisses? He could close his eyes and remember how his tongue felt in her mouth, the lusciousness. Needing to savor the memories, he closed his eyes and remembered sucking her lower lip into his mouth, nipping on it a few times before their tongues dueled in one hell of a heated encounter.

He would seduce her with even more hot, deep and erotic glides of his tongue. More than once he'd been tempted to take her just where they stood and…

The buzzer on his desk had him snapping his eyes back open. He glanced at the stack of paper clips, scooped them up and placed them in the designated bowl before clicking on the buzzer. "Yes, Pauline?"

"Your brother is here to see you, Mr. Steele."

Mercury frowned. "Which one?" Not that he was in the mood to visit with any of them. No doubt they were here to get in his business, wanting to know why he'd been a no-show at Galen's on Sunday.

"Mr. Gannon Andrew Steele."

Mercury shook his head. His brothers had given up trying to figure out why Gannon wanted to gloat that he'd gotten their father's name. It didn't matter to the five of them since they were all Drew's boys. They had the looks and high testosterone levels to prove it.

"Send him in."

It didn't take long for Gannon to walk through the door, smiling broadly. Mercury wondered what the huge grin was for. "Any reason you're not working today?" he asked his youngest brother, who took a chair without being invited.

"I'm leaving in the morning to make a pickup in Santa Fe and won't be back for a week."

Mercury frowned. "It will take you a week to go to Santa Fe and back?"

Gannon's grin widened. "No."

There was no need to ask Gannon what he would be doing while he was in Santa Fe. Mercury knew it had nothing to do with taking in the sights…unless you counted some woman's bedroom as something to see.

Over forty years ago, Drew Steele had taken his small trucking company and turned it into a million-dollar industry with routes all over the United States. When Drew retired, Gannon had taken over the company as CEO. Gannon enjoyed getting behind the rig himself on occasion and Mercury and his brothers knew why.

"So, what's this I hear about you agreeing to be on the cover of Chloe's magazine?" Mercury asked Gannon. Chloe Westmoreland was someone they considered a cousin-in-law since she was married to Ramsey Westmoreland, who was a cousin to Quade.

Mercury wasn't sure how it was possible, but Gannon's smile got even wider. "I guess Quade told you about that, uh? You know what they say. If you got it, you might as well flaunt it."

And Mercury knew Gannon was convinced he had *it*. "Whatever."

Suddenly the smile disappeared from Gannon's face. "And speaking of Quade, is his firm checking out that business with Sloan?"

"I told you guys last week that I was pulling him in to check out some things for me."

"Yes, and you also said you would be hanging around Sloan more, too, but you haven't been doing it."

Mercury frowned. "I didn't need to. I have a friend who works for Homeland Security constantly checking the airline database. Cunningham left Phoenix, and if Sloan's father shows up in town, I'll know it before his plane lands."

He then lifted a brow. "And how do you know what I've been doing or not doing with regard to Sloan?"

"Because I just left her place and she said she hadn't seen you since Friday, the day she moved into her apartment."

Mercury's frown deepened. "What do you mean, you just left Sloan's place? Why were you there?"

Now the smile returned to Gannon's face. A slight one, but one just the same, and it was enough to let Mercury know the last thing he should have done was lose his cool at the thought of Gannon visiting Sloan.

"Any reason you want to know, Mercury?"

"Don't play games with me, Gannon. Why were you at Sloan's apartment?"

Gannon smiled a little more. "Hey. No need to get all jealous. I bought her a housewarming gift that I wanted to take her before I left town."

"I wasn't getting jealous."

Gannon laughed. "You could have fooled me. On the other hand, no, honestly, you can't. You like her and you know it."

Refusing to get baited by his brother, Mercury asked, "How is she?"

"Not telling. If you want to know, then go see her for yourself. But I will tell you this. Although she tried to hide it, I could see the disappointment in her face when she saw it was me and not you."

"You're imagining things."

The smile was off Gannon's face again. "No, I'm not. I suggest you make some decisions, Mercury."

"About what?"

"Not what but who. Sloan. You like her and she likes you. Get to know her or you could lose the best thing to ever happen to you."

Mercury didn't say anything for a long moment. "You know about Cherae."

Gannon rolled his eyes. "Hell, everybody knew about Cherae but you. Stop finding excuses since we all know that Sloan is nothing like her. Cherae was running toward money and Sloan seems determined to run away from it. All she wants is to live as normal a life as possible. On a budget," he said, grinning.

Gannon paused and then added, "And she thinks that car is in her name and that she got the apartment on her own. She's proud of those accomplishments. I think you need to set the record straight before someone else does. The last thing you want is for her to think you played her and cared nothing about her need for independence."

"I wasn't trying to play her, only help her."

"Let her know that. After you tell her, then all she's going to do is add it to the budget to pay you back. I've never known a woman so excited about being on a budget."

Mercury chuckled. "Yes, I know."

"Well, something else you might not know is that she got that job with the Miss Universe pageant. They notified her today and she was extremely happy about it."

"And I'm happy for her."

"Then tell her, Mercury. I believe she would appreciate hearing that from you." Gannon stood. "I'll see you when I get back."

Gannon had made it to the door when he turned back to Mercury. "And just so you know, the thought of me being the lone Bad News Steele doesn't bother me. With you out of the way here, that clears the field for me to have all the women."

"Does it?"

"Sure does. And whenever I visit North Carolina with no more single Steeles there to worry about, and with those Bachelors in Demand finally all married off, I'll be king of the road…if you know what I mean."

Unfortunately, Mercury knew. "Don't rush things with

me and Sloan. I might like her, but that doesn't mean I want things to go any further."

Gannon chuckled. "If you honestly think that, then you're only fooling yourself. You were the first of the pack to break away and fall in love with Cherae. That means you're capable of loving a woman, Mercury. All you have to do is let some of that ice thaw from around your heart and you'll be okay."

Mercury couldn't believe his baby brother was actually trying to give him advice or that he was even listening. "For Pete's sake, I've barely known her a week."

"And? If you recall, Galen was trying to convince Brittany to move in with him the same day they met."

Mercury remembered, and he also recalled how the five of them had nearly flipped their lids not only when they heard about it, but also when they'd found out Galen had talked Brittany into agreeing. In the end, Brittany and Galen had fallen in love. "I'm not Galen."

"No, but you are Drew Steele's son. Don't forget Dad almost lost Mom because he was convinced he was not ready to love her or any woman. But look at him now. If Drew hadn't come to his senses, there would not have been any of us. Hell, can you imagine being born to any other parents? Parents like Sloan's?"

Mercury cringed at the thought. "No."

Then without saying anything else, Gannon opened the door and left.

Seventeen

Sloan stood back and admired her work area. She had a new laptop, a new printer, a beautiful green plant—compliments of Gannon—on her desk, and all the office supplies she needed to start her new job, although she wouldn't officially begin working for a few weeks.

Tomorrow she had a mobile conference call with the pageant committee. They wanted to get to know her and wanted her to get to know them. The thought that they'd hired her so quickly based on Margaret Fowler's recommendations meant a lot to her.

It was just a little past eight and dark outside already. She had taken a bubble bath and changed into a pajama shorts set. Next on her list of things to do was to enjoy a glass of wine, compliments of Tyson and Hunter. Jonas and Nikki had given her a beautiful set of wineglasses, which she couldn't wait to use with the wine. Galen and Brittany had given her a starter kit of every spice that existed. Since she wouldn't begin work for another month, she figured she could take Mercury's advice and enroll in a cooking class.

Mercury...

Hadn't she told herself she would not think about him today, tomorrow or any other day? The fact that he hadn't called said a lot. She'd been tempted to ask Eden about him, but had talked herself out of doing so.

She was about to go into the kitchen for a glass of wine when her phone rang. She checked caller ID and saw it was Eli. When she'd seen him at Galen's on Sunday, he'd told her he had spoken to Charles Rivers's personal assistant, who said Rivers was out of town and wouldn't be back until Tuesday. Hopefully that meant Eli had talked to him today.

"Yes, Eli?"

"Hello, Sloan. I made a connection with Charles Rivers and I need to discuss with you what he shared. Are you free tomorrow morning? I can drop by your place on my way to the office."

She knew from Stacey that she and Eli lived in a community not far from there. "That would be great. I'm in apartment C240."

"Okay. Will nine o'clock work?"

"Yes, that will be fine."

"Okay, I'll see you in the morning."

"Thanks, Eli."

Sloan had just disconnected the call when she heard the sound of the doorbell. Immediately, there was a pounding in her chest, hoping it was Mercury. Hadn't she just convinced herself that it hadn't mattered if she saw him or not? So why was she having such an intense reaction at the possibility it was him?

Moving to the door, she inwardly told herself that even if it was him, he'd probably only dropped by to deliver the documents for her car and the payment sheet for the loan since she was yet to get them from him.

"Yes? Who is it?"

"Mercury. May I come in?"

He was asking to come in and she hadn't opened the

door yet? Erring on the side of caution, she looked out the peephole to verify it was him, although she'd recognized his sexy voice. Releasing a deep breath, she opened the door.

"Hello, Sloan."

She wished he didn't say her name in that strong, husky voice. And more than anything, she wished he wasn't standing in front of her door looking the epitome of masculine beauty in his business suit. Why did he have such chiseled good looks that looked even more so when half lit by the moonlight?

"Mercury," she said, stepping aside. No matter what, she would not ask where he'd been the last four days and what he'd been doing…or with whom. He was the one who'd put distance between them, which meant he had a problem with her.

It was his problem and he was the one who needed to find a solution.

When he walked over the threshold, the scent of his cologne was enough to make her insides shiver. He stopped in front of her and that was when she saw the package he was holding. "This is a housewarming gift for you."

She looked down at the prettily wrapped white box with a sky blue bow. "Thank you, Mercury."

"You're welcome."

He stepped back and she closed the door. "I was about to have a glass of wine. Would you like to share one with me?" she invited.

"Yes, I'd like to."

Her gaze roamed the length of him, and she thought, yes, she *would like to* as well, but the thought had nothing to do with a glass of wine. Had those gorgeous green eyes darkened just a bit?

She moved away from the door to stroll toward the kitchen and he walked beside her. Out of the corner of her eye she watched him taking note of the changes she'd made.

Flowers, new pictures on the walls and pretty curtains to replace the boring blinds. Going shopping with his mom and sisters-in-law on Saturday had been great. They had taken her to stores that kept her within her budget.

Sloan could just imagine what he was thinking. She'd been busy and she hoped he assumed she'd been much too occupied to even remember he existed. Maybe she wouldn't go that far, but she hoped he hadn't thought she'd missed him, even if she had.

When they reached the kitchen, he stopped in the doorway, probably noticing the changes in here, as well. She placed the gift he'd given her on the table before going straight to the wine bottle on the counter. Opening a cabinet, she pulled out two glasses.

"Need help with anything?" he asked.

"No, I've got this," she said, and a part of her wished she had him, too. She blamed her thoughts on his sisters-in-law. It was obvious they loved being married to their Steele husbands. It didn't take long to discover they also enjoyed bedtime with their spouses. Could sex be that exciting and enjoyable? Evidently for them it was, which made her wonder if she had made a mistake allowing Carlos to be her first and last. Was there something she'd been missing? Listening to them had given her the impression that maybe she had.

"The place looks nice," he said. "I like all the changes you've made."

"Thanks," she said, looking at him quickly before returning her attention to pouring the wine.

"You look nice, too, Sloan."

She glanced down at herself. He had to be kidding. She was in pj's and fairly decent. She wasn't wearing a bra, but she doubted he would notice.

It was only when she carried the glasses of wine over

to the table that he moved away from the doorway to join her. "Thanks."

Deciding to get her mind onto something else and off him, she asked, "Have you gotten the payment information for the car yet?"

"No."

She nodded. "What about the printout for the payment plan information for the loan? Or the papers on the apartment here?"

"No and no. There's no rush."

There was for her. "I need to be able to figure all that into my budget. I bought one of those online programs to help me keep things straight." When she sat down, he eased into the chair across from her. Before taking a sip of her wine, she decided to open his gift. "Oh, Mercury. It's beautiful." He'd given her a crystal paperweight in the shape of a globe.

"I heard the good news about your job with Miss Universe. Congratulations. I understand you'll be traveling a lot internationally. I thought that globe would be a reminder that all the world is out there for you to see."

Yes, it was, and she wished she could say she was ready for the adventure, but she wasn't. She still had to uncover things regarding her parents. Namely why it was so important to them that she marry Harold. "I have a place on my desk for it."

"Good."

Placing the gift aside, she then took a couple of sips of her wine. She tried not looking at him, but couldn't help it. When she did, she discovered he'd been looking at her. She swallowed. "Eli called right before you arrived."

"Did he hear from your grandfather's attorney?"

"Yes, and Eli's coming here in the morning to discuss it."

"I see."

Did he expect her to ask him to join her when his brother dropped by tomorrow? He had avoided her for the past few days. She assumed that was his way of letting her know that not only did she need to find a permanent solution to her problem, but that she needed to do it without him.

"Sloan?"

She glanced over at him. "Yes."

"I owe you an explanation."

She couldn't imagine what kind of explanation he thought he owed her. Hadn't he told her she needed to find a solution to her problem? Then what did she do? She used him as a temporary fix. "No, you don't."

"I honestly believe that I do."

He looked troubled by something. She hadn't picked up on it when he first arrived, but now she did. Maybe the wine had loosened him up a bit; she wasn't sure. Then it dawned on her that whatever was bothering him involved her. Why?

"Okay, if you feel that way, then what's your explanation?"

He'd been looking at her, holding her gaze in a way that made her more aware of him than ever before. When he didn't say anything but continued to stare at her, her heart raced. His look was affecting her.

Clearing her throat, she said, "So, what's this about, Mercury?"

He broke eye contact with her for a quick second. Then he met her gaze again and said, "The reason I put distance between us is because I was tempted to do something that I didn't think you were ready for."

She lifted a brow. "What?"

"To be seduced by a Steele. More specifically, to be seduced by this Steele."

There, he'd said it. He'd told her the root of his problem. However, from the look on her face he had a feeling she didn't fully understand. Did she need him to break it down further? Did he need to tell her how he went to bed dreaming of making love to her? How just sitting across from her at this table was nearly driving him insane?

From the time she'd opened her front door, his attention had been drawn to the nipples poking against the fabric of her top. His mouth had watered immediately at the thought of sliding one or both into his mouth with good, hard sucks. Then he would...

"Obviously you think seducing me is something I'd have no say about, Mercury."

A beguiling smile tugged at his lips. "The only thing you'd be saying is *Please move to the next level*, Sloan. When it comes to seduction, I'm an expert," he added.

There was no need to go into detail about how he typically didn't have to seduce women because they were often trying to seduce him. When he walked into a room, he recognized the predatory gazes, which always made things easy for him.

"So, that's where you've been? Putting your seduction skills to work," she said in a lighthearted tone.

He'd seen a flash of something in her eyes that gave him pause. Hurt. Something twisted his gut. Was that what she thought? That over the past four days he'd been holding a sex-a-thon? And why did it matter if she did think it? It wouldn't have been the first time, if he'd had one. He was single and didn't owe anyone an explanation or an apology for what he did. It was nobody's business. Definitely not hers.

Then why was unexpected guilt still twisting his gut? And why did he feel it was imperative that she know he hadn't been with a woman? That whether he liked it or not, for some reason, she was the only woman he wanted.

In his arms. In his bed. In his life...

That last thought nearly knocked him out of his chair because he didn't do the life thing. He did the sex thing with women. Why would she be any different?

Because Sloan *was* different.

He knew they were attracted to each other; that had been obvious. However, they'd managed to control things and there was no doubt they would have continued to do so… At least she would have. Temptation would have overtaken him if they'd spent more time together.

"Sorry to disappoint you, but I've been busy the last four days doing things that didn't involve women," he said. "I've been handling clients. A few hiccups came up with several players that I had to take care of."

He took a sip of his wine and watched her. Did she know his words had placed a quick smile on her lips that he probably wasn't supposed to have seen? That pretty much let him know she wasn't disappointed that his last four days had been boring.

She wasn't saying anything and then it dawned on him that she was looking at him, not with a predatory gaze but a curious one. And she'd zeroed in on his mouth. He glanced at her chest. The budded tips of her nipples were pressing even more against the fabric of her top. He couldn't help his lusty smile that shifted back to her eyes.

"I think I have a problem where you are concerned, Sloan."

She licked her lips and it was as if he could feel her doing so. "Do you?"

"Yes."

He refused to tell her anything different, not when he could clearly read desire in her eyes. Did she not know what seeing it was doing to him? That was why he'd felt it was best to stay away. Not just because she was getting to him, but because he was letting her. She was tempting him into breaking one very important rule: never let a woman get to him again.

"You know what you told me, Mercury. When you have a problem it's up to you to find a solution."

"I thought I had, which was why I stayed away," he said, not trying to mask the frustration in his voice. He then grazed his fingers across her hand and watched as her nipples got even harder. Something hot, passionate and wild moved between them. Something he wasn't sure either of them could stop.

"You might not like the solution I come up with, Sloan."

"Try me."

He lifted a brow. Had she just told him to try her? In that case...

He slowly stood from the table and came around to where she sat. He extended his hand to her, she took it, and he gently tugged her from the chair. He then eased closer to her, deliberately brushing their bodies, certain she felt the evidence of his desire for her when he did so.

She didn't know it, but being seduced by this Steele was a three-step process. TLC. Tempt. Lure. Conquer.

"Say it again, Sloan." He wanted to make sure she understood what she was saying. He had a feeling that, in the end, she wouldn't be his conquest; he would become hers. The thought of that didn't bother him.

"I said, try me, Mercury."

He still needed to make sure because there was no going back. "Do you know what trying you entails?" Maybe he needed to let her know that trying her meant doing it the Mercury Steele way.

"Yes, I know."

She thought she knew, but he definitely had a few surprises for her... He knew his expression had instantly become predatory, wolfish and seductive. He then wrapped his arms around her waist. First up was tempting her. Giving her a sampling of what to expect.

More than ready to get his plan of seduction started, he leaned in and slanted his mouth over hers, knowing this time it wouldn't stop with a kiss.

Eighteen

Sloan fought back a moan. What in the world was Mercury doing to her? Kissing her this way? Raw and possessive. They had kissed before, several times, but she'd always managed to keep up with him. Now he was leaving her far behind. But that wasn't all he was doing.

How had his body seemed to sink deeper into her when they were standing up and still fully clothed? Yet she felt the hardness of his erection pressing against her, scoping out the best spot for entry. Since there was only one possibility, she figured it was his way of trying to drive her mad. And it was working.

Never had any man taken this much time with her. No rush job like Carlos. Mercury was taking his time driving her wild with desire. It was a degree of desire she hadn't known she was capable of feeling. She was so wrapped up in their kiss that she hadn't known he'd opened the buttons to the front of her top until she felt the air hit her chest. How had he managed that when their bodies were pressed together?

And then he was finally releasing her mouth and taking a step back. She opened her eyes to find him studying her breasts like they were a piece of art. When he used the pad of his thumb to caress a nipple, she could actually feel heat flowing between her legs. Did he have any idea what he was doing to her?

Her breasts were sensitive and one of the erotic points in her body. She'd tried to get Carlos to pamper them, and he refused, saying he was a between-the-legs man. That was when she'd decided to make him one and done. But Mercury was indulging her breasts as if he'd known how much pleasure she would get from him doing so. And she *was* getting pleasure.

"You like that, Sloan?"

Unable to speak when his thumb moved to the other breast, she merely nodded her head.

"I knew you would."

How had he known? As if she'd spoken that question out loud, he said, "A man intent on pleasuring a woman makes it his business to know what turns her on. By the time I'm finished with you, I will know every erogenous zone on your body." And with that said, he leaned in and sucked a nipple into his mouth.

Sloan fought back a scream when his tongue hungrily lapped her nipple. If he only knew how he was making her feel. Maybe he did know. He'd pretty much said he was an expert when it came to seducing a woman, and it seemed he hadn't been lying.

No longer able to fight back a scream, she let it rip. Sensations tore through her, more powerful than any dreams she'd had. Never in her wildest dream could she have imagined this. Never.

Before she could recover, Mercury had left her breasts and was kneeling in front of her. Through dazed eyes she saw him jerk down her shorts. Was he shocked to discover she wasn't wearing any panties? She didn't have time to wonder because that was when he used his hands to widen her legs. The next thing she knew, his mouth and tongue had invaded her.

Heaven help her.

Was he trying to kill her? His tongue pushed inside her, then licked her like she was his favorite treat. She grabbed his head to push him away, and then when sensations began rippling through her, she tightened her hold and moved her hips back and forth against his mouth. The more she did, the greedier he became. Was she telling him in a chant not to stop?

Another orgasm tore into her and she screamed again. Her body trembled inside and out and she still held firm to him, tossing her head back and sucking in air. It was only when the last spasm had left her body that he eased back up to his feet and kissed her, letting her taste herself on his tongue. How scandalous.

He released her mouth and she opened her eyes. The look in his almost had her coming again. Never had she seen so much desire as she did in his green depths. "Sloan?"

It seemed as if he'd breathed out her name. "Yes?" she said, barely getting out the single word.

"I've just tempted you. Do you know what's next?"

He'd done more than tempted her. He had to know that. She'd never known temptation to be anything like this. "No, I don't know what's next."

"Lure. I want to lure you to your bedroom to finish what we've started. My plan of seduction is a three-part process. TLC. Tempt, lure and conquer. Now to lure you."

She watched as he crooked his finger and began walking backward. Not caring that she was naked and he wasn't, she slowly followed him, going where he lured and knowing what he had in store when she got there would be worth it.

* * *

Mercury was convinced that never had luring a woman to her own bedroom been so freaking awesome. He was walking backward, so it was a good thing he remembered the layout of her place. Sloan was holding his mind hostage.

There was just something about a naked woman following you with a look in her eyes that all but said, *I can't wait.*

Neither could he, especially while allowing his gaze to roam all over her, from head to toe. She had a beautiful body with curves in all the right places. Her breasts were perfectly formed and the area between her legs was a gift from heaven. Not for the first time he thought she had that refined walk that mothers were sending their daughters to Brittany's etiquette school to perfect.

When they finally reached her bedroom, he glanced around, noticing the changes in here as well and the dominant color. Blue, blue and more blue. He smiled. However, the decor of the room wasn't what was on his mind.

He wanted to get a naked Sloan in her bed and join her there.

"We're here," he said, slowly walking over to her. "I lured you into your own bedroom."

"Conquer is next, right?" she asked when he came to a stop in front of her. He could see the pulse rapidly beating in her neck and he felt her anticipation. He liked that.

She had no qualms about what they were about to do. Neither did he.

"Yes," he said, sliding his hand between her legs and loving the fact that she was still wet. "Do you know what that entails?"

"No. Tell me."

He had no problem doing that. "Now I want to make you come while I'm inside you."

He watched her features when his fingers eased inside

her. She was so hot and the expression on her face was just as heated.

"You have your clothes on," she said, like she was just realizing that fact.

"Not for long." He then stared at her and realized just what she'd come to mean to him over the past few days. More than he'd wanted. More than he was ready to admit.

"You're ready for my final part of seduction? Conquering?" he asked her.

"Yes."

"Good. I'm about to give you all the pleasure any one woman can handle." While saying those words he moved closer so his body could brush against her naked one. Specifically, he wanted her to feel just how hard his erection was for her. "It wants you, Sloan."

"And I want it, Mercury."

He smiled. Then, sweeping her up into his arms, he moved toward the bed.

When Mercury placed her in the middle of the mattress, he leaned in and placed a finger at her chin to lift her gaze to his. Sloan's heart beat hard at the look she saw in the depths of his green eyes.

"You have no idea how much I've thought of you these last four days, Sloan. How hard I've been fighting my need for you or how many nights I've gone to bed dreaming of being inside you. At this moment I need you with every breath flowing through my lungs."

His words, spoken so seductively, caused every part of Sloan to come alive, to want him as much as he'd just said he wanted her. No man had ever expressed a need for her the way he'd just done. Then he released her chin and moved away from the bed and she watched. She knew what they were about to share would be one of those incredible experiences that she would remember forever.

She pulled herself into a better position to watch what he was doing, not wanting to miss a thing. Her gaze followed Mercury's fingers as they went to the buttons of his shirt. As he eased each button free, she saw his chest and the curly hair covering it. She tried hard not to moan in total admiration at the sight but found it impossible.

He looked at her when he tossed his shirt aside. "You okay, Sloan?"

How could he ask her that while standing there shirtless with a body that could make a woman drool? "I think so."

"Well, I hope so. Are you changing your mind about anything?"

Changing her mind wouldn't be happening. "You don't have to worry about that, Mercury."

He smiled as his fingers went to the zipper of his pants. She couldn't help it when her breath caught. It seemed every nerve ending within her came alive as he slowly dragged down his zipper and then proceeded to ease down his pants and black briefs over a pair of powerfully built thighs.

She'd never seen a naked man before. Carlos didn't count since he'd undressed in the dark. But now she saw Mercury and knew without a doubt he was beautifully made. Seeing him in the flesh had her in a sensual daze. She lowered her gaze to his middle and shivered all over. He was big. Real big. Extra, extra big.

"It will be okay, Sloan," he said, then proceeded to sheathe himself with a condom.

She moved her gaze to his eyes. She hoped so. Had he seen the distress in her face? When he strolled back toward her she didn't have time to think any more about what he might or might not have seen. No man should have such a sexy walk.

Placing a knee on the bed, he whispered her name and then reached down and drew her naked body to his, connecting their mouths. The moment his tongue slid inside her mouth she knew what to do. She hungrily latched on to it, following his lead and returning the kiss with the same intensity he was using. The feel and scent of him were drugging her mind.

She felt him lowering her to the bed cushions without dislodging their mouths, and she experienced the moment he positioned his body over hers. Then she felt his erection right at her opening. He released her mouth to look down at her, locking their gazes together as he slowly began easing inside her. Instinctively, she wrapped her legs around him. Drawing in a sharp breath, she felt a quick moment of pain. Then he thrust into her. She drew in a deep breath, feeling him deeply.

"You okay?"

She tightened her arms around his neck. "Not sure I could ever be better."

Her response pleased him if that smile was anything to go by. Then he began moving, slow at first, as all kinds of delicious sensations overtook her. He established a rhythm for them, one she thought was destined to drive her mad with desire.

Just like with his kisses, she began following his lead. She moved her body in sync with his, arching her hips and grinding her thighs. Each one of his thrusts seemed to ignite even more passion within her, and when he increased the pace of the strokes, she broke eye contact with him to toss her head back and forth and from side to side.

He leaned in and whispered naughty words in her ear. Her entire body shuddered when he described in intimate detail what they would do all night. Then his thrusts became even more powerful, going even deeper, and she became lost in the pleasure.

Over and over again he pushed her to the edge, and before she could fall, he would whip her back again. Why was he torturing her this way? She called out his name in protest, and that was when he whispered in a husky tone, "Let's come together, baby. Always together."

His words seemed to trigger something inside her. She screamed his name at the same exact moment he hollered hers. He threw his head back. His thrusts kept coming and she kept taking them, loving the way her body exploded under his.

At that moment she knew she had fallen in love with Mercury. It didn't matter if he loved her back or if this was only a seduction by a Steele.

It only mattered that she loved him.

Nineteen

When Mercury opened his eyes, it took him a moment to remember where he was. Definitely not in his own bed with all this frilly, lacy stuff covering the bed with curtains to match. At least he approved of the color blue.

He then glanced down at the woman in his arms. He smiled, loving the feel of the warm body tucked beside him, with his legs thrown over hers. Sloan was still sleeping, which wasn't surprising, considering all they'd done through the night. His goal had been to give her all the pleasure she could handle, and it seemed she'd been able to handle a lot. He'd figured she would tire out, but she'd been determined to keep up with him. His Sloan had discovered that, when it came to sex, he had endless energy. He wholly appreciated her efforts.

His Sloan?

He closed his eyes, not wanting to think of her or any woman as his. Needing to push the thought from his mind, his gaze scanned the room. He liked her decorating ideas. She'd been busy this weekend. She probably hadn't thought of him at all, but he had thought about her. He hadn't known a woman he'd met less than a week ago could have such an impact on him. But she had.

His gaze returned to her. She looked beautiful while she slept, but then, she looked beautiful while being made love to, as well. More than once he had watched her come, and the way her features contorted in pleasure filled him with so much enjoyment.

Glancing at the clock on her nightstand, he saw it was close to eight in the morning. It had not been his intention to spend the night, but things had turned out that way. He had no complaints.

"Good morning, Mercury."

Her sleepy-eyed smile was beautiful. *She* was beautiful. He thought about how they'd met and everything that had transpired since. The woman had entered his world on a series of misadventures. But he would gladly experience them all again if he could be assured that he would have another night like the one he'd shared last night with her.

"Good morning. Are you okay?" He knew he'd asked her that a lot, but her well-being meant everything to him. She pulled herself up, fully stretching, seemingly not at all bothered by her nakedness. If it didn't bother her, it certainly didn't bother him. In fact, he liked looking at her sexy body.

"Yes, I'm wonderful. You were wonderful, Mercury."

He'd heard that before from other women, but hearing it from her meant a hell of a lot. "Thanks, and you were wonderful, too."

"You're just being kind because I didn't know what I was doing most of the time. I was basically following your lead."

And she'd done a good job of it. "Trust me—you were wonderful."

His words brought an even brighter smile to her lips.

"And just to think last night was the first time I've ever had an orgasm."

He blinked. "Excuse me?"

"I said I never experienced an orgasm before last night. Couldn't you tell?"

No, he couldn't, considering she'd had her first one with him while his mouth had been on her breasts while in her kitchen. "Are you saying Cunningham dropped the ball? No pun intended."

She laughed. "None taken since Harold and I never shared a bed. I would suggest it, thinking it would be the thing to do since we were engaged, but he wasn't interested. Of course, I eventually discovered why. He was into a relationship with someone else. At least he wasn't trying to sleep with the both of us. Some men would have, you know."

His mind was reeling at what she'd just said. "You weren't a virgin last night, right?"

Hell, he hoped not. He'd never wanted to be any woman's first, thanks to his mother's lectures and her psychological analysis of what that meant for a woman. According to the Principles of Eden, a woman never forgot her first guy. She would remember him forever. He hadn't wanted to be remembered by any woman that long.

"Virgin? Heck no. I had sex with Carlos in college once. It was awful."

He nodded. "Carlos was your boyfriend?"

"Yes, at the time. For me it was one and done." She broke eye contact with him to glance over at the clock. "And speaking of time, I need to get up and get dressed. Eli is dropping by at nine. I have extra toiletries under the vanity in that bathroom."

Did she want him to leave? There was only one way to find out. "Will this be a private meeting between you and Eli?"

She glanced back at him. "No. You're welcome to stay if you want. Like I told Harold that night, you already know most of my business anyway. I'm surprised Eli didn't mention anything to you."

Was she kidding? Sloan evidently didn't know how Eli functioned as an attorney. His brother operated on a strict code of ethics. When she'd hired Eli, his by-the-book brother wouldn't share any details of his findings without her permission. "He didn't, but that's fine as long as you don't have a problem with me being here."

She leaned up and wrapped her arms around him. "I don't have a problem with you being here, Mercury."

"Glad to hear it." He then leaned in and captured her mouth with his.

Eli stared hard at his brother when Mercury opened the door to let him into Sloan's apartment. "Why aren't I surprised to find you here?"

Mercury smiled. "I don't know. Why aren't you?"

Before Eli could give a smart-ass answer to Mercury's smart-ass question, Sloan came out of the kitchen, smiling. "Good morning, Eli. I just made a pot of coffee. Would you like a cup?"

He smiled over at Sloan. "No, thanks. I had a cup earlier. I'd like to go into my report since I have another appointment in a couple of hours."

"Okay," Sloan said, easing down on the sofa with Mercury sitting beside her. "What did Mr. Rivers have to say?"

Eli slid down in the wingback chair opposite of them. "To protect you, the terms of your grandfather's will stated that you will get the proceeds from your trust fund at thirty...unless you marry before then. Then you get it the day after you marry, to do with as you wish."

Sloan's eyes widened in surprise. She hadn't known. "So, Harold was right. My parents are banking on our marriage not only to combine the family's wealth, but for me to bring a dowry."

"Yes, it looks that way," Eli said, standing. "If you need me to do anything else, let me know. I like Charles Rivers. It's obvious he intends to handle business the way your grandfather wanted him to do."

"Thanks, Eli," she said, walking him to the door.

When she returned to the living room, Mercury was standing in the middle of the floor. "Come here," he said, opening his arms to her.

She walked into them, needing a hug and grateful he was there to give her one. He tightened his hold on her and she snuggled closer to him. They'd made love again this morning and then they'd showered together. What she'd told him was true. He was a fantastic lover and had made her feel things she'd never felt before. Things she hadn't thought she'd been capable of feeling.

"Go out of town with me tomorrow."

She leaned back to look up at him. "You want me to go out of town with you?"

"Yes. I'm flying to Dallas for a few days to meet with a potential client. I think getting away will do you good."

She didn't want to think about just how good it would be with him. Another thing she didn't want to think about was how she felt for Mercury.

She loved him.

Drawing in a deep breath, she accepted that, love or no love, a serious relationship was the last thing she needed. She was starting a new life and a new job. She needed time for herself without being crowded by emotions for someone else. But she knew loving Mercury wasn't anything she could put on a shelf to take down when it was convenient.

And she knew that, although she loved Mercury, he didn't love her. Hadn't he told her more than once that he could never love a woman? She had no reason not to take him at his word.

Even so, the thought of spending a couple of days with him sounded nice.

"Sloan?"

She smiled. "I'd love to go to Dallas with you."

Twenty

Mercury sat at his desk steepling his fingers while studying the beautiful view of the mountains outside his office window. Had it been two weeks since he'd persuaded Sloan to go out of town with him? Two whole weeks? He still thought about just how wonderful their trip to Dallas had been and how his life with her had changed since then.

He had never invited a woman anywhere with him and had surprised himself by asking her. But once the shock had worn off, he'd looked forward to spending time with her. When it came to meeting people and putting them at ease, she'd been a natural. He was convinced Brock Dennison's parents would not have entertained signing their son with Mercury if it hadn't been for Sloan. The Dennisons were farmers, and not used to urban ways of life. Because she'd spent so much time with her grandfather on his farm in Texas, Sloan had been able to relate and put the Dennisons at ease. They had loved her.

And he loved her.

That admission had Mercury's heart pounding hard in his chest. He closed his eyes, knowing he'd never expected to admit to feeling those emotions toward any woman ever again, yet here he was, admitting to loving a woman he'd known less than a month.

At that moment she was a woman he couldn't imagine living without.

That was the reason why, since returning to Phoenix, he'd done everything to make her an intricate part of his life. He'd decided to do something he'd never done before, which was to court a woman. He'd taken her to dinner, to the movies, and he'd even shown up at church last Sunday, much to his mother's shock and delight. And he never assumed he had a right to spend the night. He asked or she would ask. Well, she never really asked, since now she was the one using his TLC approach and seducing him with such finesse that he got a hard-on thinking about how she'd go about it.

Unlike the other women in his past, with Sloan it had never been about just a physical attraction. It had been more. Spending time together was what they needed to do to get to know each other better. She'd talked about her grandfather and he could feel the love in her words. He'd also discovered that trust was important to her and it hurt her to find out about her parents' deception. More than once, he'd been tempted to tell her about the car and the apartment and how his name was on both. But he hadn't wanted anything to ruin their time together.

He looked at the packet Pauline had given him this morning, the one that had arrived while he was out on Friday. Namely the payment plan for the loan from his accountant, the paperwork for the car and the lease agreement for her apartment. The time had finally come. He would deliver the packet to her this evening and tell her everything then.

When the buzzer on his intercom went off, he pressed the button. "Yes, Pauline?"

"A Ms. Beverly McClain is on the line for you."

Beverly was the one-night stand that never was. They'd met on a flight to Florida eight years ago, and when they discovered they would be staying at the same hotel, they had agreed to hook up. He hadn't known her divorce from her husband had become final that day, and instead of burning the sheets, he had taken her to dinner, where she'd cried while telling him what an asshole she'd been married to for three years. The next morning they'd met up again for coffee and decided they could be friends, and for the last eight years, they had.

Since then, she'd remarried a great guy who'd made her happy and they had two kids. Beverly worked for the government as one of the heads of Homeland Security. If she was calling him, that meant…

"Please put her through."

When he heard the click, he said, "Beverly?"

"Hello, Mercury. How have you been?"

He smiled. "Great, and you?"

"Pregnant again. You know what that means. Morning sickness is kicking my butt, but I'll survive."

"Of course you will. You always do."

"The reason I was calling was to let you know of activity with the names you gave me. A plane carrying Carter Haywood Donahue landed in Phoenix less than an hour ago. He didn't have any checked luggage."

Mercury nodded. That meant the man didn't intend to stay in Phoenix long. "Thanks. I appreciate the information."

Moments later Mercury stood and reached for his cell phone to let Sloan know her father was in town. Chances were, he'd found out where she lived and would go straight to her place. He quickly changed his mind about phoning Sloan. There was no way he would let her face her tyrant of a father alone.

He had stood and was reaching for his jacket when the buzzer on his desk sounded. "Yes, Pauline?"

"Quade Westmoreland is on line two."

"Thanks."

Sitting back down in his chair, Mercury said, "Quade? You have something for me?"

"Yes, man, I do."

Sloan ended her conference call with the pageant committee feeling excited about what they'd told her. She had two more weeks to enjoy life as she now knew it before her work with them officially began. She had been assigned five countries. All five were now holding their individual pageants that would determine the woman to represent their country in the Miss Universe pageant in December.

She leaned back in her chair and thought about her five days in Dallas with Mercury and the time they'd constantly been together since. More often than not, he would spend the night after taking her to dinner or to the movies or just hanging out at her place watching television. And she'd been invited to his place more than once to spend the night. He'd told her that he'd never invited a woman overnight before.

More than once she wondered if there had been a reason for him telling her that. Had he been insinuating that she was special in some way? That he could possibly love her as much as she loved him? He'd even invited her to attend his parents' Thursday dinners and she felt right at home. No one had questioned their relationship. It was as if his family was giving them the time they needed to build the relationship they wanted. At least the one she wanted.

Did he?

Mercury saw to her every need, both in and out of the bedroom. She was feeling like a woman who was living the independent life she'd always wanted. She had to answer to no one. And she was involved with a man who understood how much her feelings of self-worth and her happiness mattered. She was free of dependency and she felt like a new person. A person in love.

She wanted to believe the last two weeks were the beginning of something special between her and Mercury. She wanted to believe the more they got to know each other the stronger their relationship would grow.

She wanted to believe she could have both her independence and Mercury, too, because he understood how much not depending on anyone meant to her. He respected her desire for liberation.

A smile touched her lips when she remembered how he'd even helped by allowing her to test her dominance in bed. She'd loved it. He'd loved it. She had a lot to learn and he'd happily volunteered to teach her.

She heard the sound of the doorbell. It wasn't even noon yet. Who would be visiting her? Mercury had said he would be going into the office this morning to get caught up on work. She then remembered that she had ordered a few things from an online office-supply store and figured the delivery was being made.

Going to the door, she looked out the peephole and her breath caught. She felt like someone had kicked her in the gut. It was her father. What was he doing here? It didn't matter because he was here.

For the first time in her life she would not let him intimidate her. Thanks to Mercury, she was more self-assured than ever and wouldn't let her father treat her like less than the adult she was.

Opening the door, she faced the man she loved but who for years never knew how to show or return that love. "Dad, come in."

He didn't say hello. He just walked past her like the thought of even being here agitated him. When she closed the door and turned, she saw him glancing around her apartment with disdain.

"Dad, what are you doing here?" There was no reason to ask how he'd found her. He kept one of the best detective agencies in Ohio on retainer.

His scornful gaze switched to her. "I am here to take you home, Sloan Elizabeth. I expected Harold to be man enough to handle you, but it seems you're being difficult."

At any other time, his harsh reprimand would have brought her back in check, would definitely have made her lower her head in shame, but not this time. Carter H. Donahue was going to discover that his child who had been a disappointment was more like him in some ways than a son could ever be. The one thing she had inherited from him was his stubbornness.

"News flash, Dad. I am not going anywhere with you. Did you not listen to what I told you when I left Cincinnati? What I'm sure Harold told you I said when he returned to report back to you? Harold and I aren't getting married."

He rolled his eyes. "Of course the two of you can't get married in June now. That's not enough time to plan for the huge wedding the two of you deserve," he said irritably. "You'll be happy to know that the Cunninghams, your mother and I have decided that an August wedding for you and Harold will work."

She would be happy to know…? Sloan just stood there and stared at her father. His assumption that he had her unwavering obedience was her fault. In the past he'd given her a mandate and she'd marched to whatever beat he played.

She'd changed.

"Dad, read my lips. I am not marrying Harold. I love my life here and I am not leaving."

There was no way she would tell him about her job with the Miss Universe pageant or else he would ruin that, too.

That was why she'd made sure all her employment information was listed under S. E. Donahue.

"So you'd rather be a kept woman than the wife of an honorable man?"

She frowned at her father. "What are you talking about?"

He eased down on her sofa without her having issued an invitation for him to do so. "You think I haven't checked out Mercury Steele and his family?"

Sloan's heart began pounding again and she tried hard to remember what Mercury had always said. Her father couldn't touch his family. "So, you've checked them out. Then you know they don't scare easily."

"Yes, and under any other circumstances I wouldn't mind doing business with them, but for your future I'm betting my money on the Cunninghams."

Doing business? She wasn't surprised that he saw any marriage for her as a business deal. "You're not the only one who can have people checked out. I know all about my trust fund and the reason you want me and Harold to marry. You think you can get your hands on it."

"Of course I can. I'm your father and will look out for your best interest."

"No, Dad, you are looking out for your own interest. There's no way I'll let you or the Cunninghams touch what Granddad left for me."

His facial features contorted in anger. "So is this how you claim the independence you want so much, by being Mercury Steele's kept woman? Do you think he will make you anything other than his whore? You'd rather be a man's whore than his wife?"

He paused as if he needed a moment to catch his breath before continuing. "Regardless of what you told Harold about Mercury Steele being your fiancé, his reputation proves he's not going to be any woman's husband. If you think he will marry you, then you are a fool. Your mother and I raised you for more than being some man's kept woman."

That was the third time he'd referred to her as being a kept woman. "I have no idea what you are talking about."

Her father's features suddenly changed, and his mouth actually seemed to twitch in amusement. As if it suddenly occurred to him that he knew something she didn't. "You don't know, do you?"

"I don't know what?"

"That you aren't the independent woman you think you are. You left home because you thought your mother and I were being manipulative and you wanted your freedom and didn't want to be dependent on anyone. Yet you are dependent on Mercury Steele."

She frowned. Evidently that detective agency he retained had found out about the twenty-thousand-dollar loan Mercury had made to her. "So, he loaned me money to help get me on my feet. Big deal. I am paying him back."

"What about that car you're driving and this apartment. Both are in his name."

"They aren't."

"Yes, they are."

Sloan's frown deepened. That wasn't true, but she didn't have the paperwork to prove otherwise because Mercury hadn't given any documents to her.

What if her father's claim *was* true?

She refused to believe it because, of all people, Mercury knew how much she wanted her independence. Why would he keep something like that from her?

"So, what do you have to say to that, Sloan Elizabeth?"

When she didn't reply because she was still reeling, in his authoritative voice he said, "Now do what you're told and go pack. I've reserved a ticket in your name. Our flight leaves for Cincinnati in three hours."

"I hate to disappoint you, Mr. Donahue, but Sloan isn't going anywhere with you."

Sloan jerked around to find Mercury standing by the door. Legs braced apart with his arms folded over his chest, he had a fierce look on his face. How did he get in when she'd locked the door? Then she saw the key in his hand. A key to her apartment that she hadn't given him. At that moment she knew her father had been telling the truth.

Twenty-One

Mercury refused to look at Sloan's father. The man was of no significance, but his daughter was, and Mercury's gaze was trained on her. She meant everything to him and he refused to let anyone, including her father, devalue her or put ideas in her head about her meaning nothing to him.

When he saw the pain in her eyes, he knew his mistake had been in not telling her the truth weeks ago. "It's time you left, Mr. Donahue."

"Oh, I guess you do have the right to put me out since this apartment is leased to you and not to my daughter."

Mercury ignored the man's words. "We need to talk privately," he said to Sloan.

"My daughter has nothing to say to you."

Mercury glanced at the other man. Mercury knew his gaze reflected the anger he felt. "Sloan can speak for herself." He had a mind to kick the man out, literally, but figured even if he was an ass, he was Sloan's father.

"You're right—she can, and I'm sure she will make the right decision." The older man then moved to Sloan. "I'm going back to the airport and will wait for you. Here's your ticket," he said, placing the ticket on the coffee table. "I expect you to make that plane with me, Sloan Elizabeth."

Carter H. Donahue then walked to the door and slammed it shut behind him.

Mercury couldn't help but stare at the door the man had just walked out of, not believing what he'd witnessed. No wonder Sloan had needed to escape her father's control. The man was worse than a tyrant. He was a damn dictator.

"Is what my father claimed true, Mercury? Do you own my car and is this apartment in your name?"

"Yes," he said, without hesitation, turning back to look at Sloan. "Remember our discussion on temporary fixes? I made decisions to use a couple."

He then came to stand in front of her, but not before tossing the package he carried onto the same coffee table where her father had tossed the plane ticket. "I had planned to explain things to you tonight when I dropped by. If you care to check that packet, you'll see the car and the apartment are both in your name now."

"B-but why?"

He shoved his hands into his pockets. "Because I knew how much both meant to you, and without me handling things the way I did, you would not have gotten either. I wanted to see you happy."

Sloan broke eye contact with him to look at the package. She then looked back at him. "Why didn't you tell me?"

Mercury knew he needed to make her understand. "Because the one thing I had gotten to know about you was that being independent meant everything to you. It boosted your confidence in yourself, and I wanted to help make it happen. Had I told you then, you would have fought me on it. Look how you didn't want the money I gave you to open that bank account. I'm used to women wanting my money more than not wanting it."

She placed her hands on her hips and glared at him. "Then maybe you need to know better women."

"True, and I found that out the hard way—trust me." He moved past her to look out the window at the lake. He then turned to her. "While in college I fell in love with a woman who I thought loved me back. I later found out that all she wanted was to hook up with a football player who she thought had a future in the NFL. Like you, she had parents with goals established for her. They wanted their daughter to marry for money."

She eyed him speculatively. "What happened?"

He drew in a deep breath. "I was injured and was told I would never play football again. That's when I discovered my purpose in her life. She moved on to another player."

Sloan raised a brow. "But you did play again?"

"Yes. I was determined to show her that she'd written me off too soon. It took me an entire year of rehab and therapy, but I came back better and stronger than ever. And I told myself I would never love another woman. All they see are dollar signs. Not one proved me wrong...until I met you. You're the only woman I know who prefers being poor to being rich."

She rolled her eyes. "I wouldn't take it that far, Mercury. I like nice things like anyone else. I just never want money to define me."

"Most women wouldn't care about such a definition."

Spine straight and her chin tilted high, she said, "When are you going to realize I'm not like most women?"

Leaving his spot by the window, he slowly walked over to stand in front of her. "I realized it the moment I accepted that I had fallen in love with you."

She released a shocked gasp. "You love me?"

He nodded. "Yes, I love you," he said, thinking the shocked look on her face was so painfully beautiful. At that moment nothing mattered more than for her to believe what he was saying. "I absolutely, positively, undeniably, unequivocally love you, Sloan."

She didn't say anything, but he saw the lone tear that fell from her eye. "You love me even knowing what kind of parents I have?" she asked in a voice filled with emotion.

He drew her into his arms. "Your parents have nothing to do with you other than that they created you. I just hope you're not going to rush off to the airport and leave town with your father. I couldn't handle it if you left me."

"Oh, Mercury," she said, leaning up on tiptoe to brush a kiss across his lips. He was about to slant his mouth over hers when she said, "And just so you know, I already love you. I love you so much, Mercury."

Surprise lit his eyes and he smiled before taking her lips in an open-mouth kiss that seemed to last forever. When he finally released her mouth, she buried her face against his neck.

Mercury closed his eyes and inhaled her scent. He was thankful for the misadventures that had brought her into his life. However, there was something he had to tell her. Something she needed to know that Quade had found out.

Lifting her off her feet, he held her securely in his arms, carried her over to the sofa and sat down with her in his lap. "There is something I need to tell you. It's about your father."

She lifted a brow. "What?"

"I told you that my cousin Quade, who used to work for the CIA, was investigating your father for me."

"Yes, you told me that."

"Well, Quade called me right before I came over here." She nodded. "And?"

"Your father is being blackmailed. That's why he needs money. He's borrowed as much as he could get and now you're the only source he has left. Namely your trust fund. That's why he needs you to marry Cunningham."

"Why is he being blackmailed? What has he done?"

Mercury paused and then said, "A couple of years ago, he and a couple more bankers took what was supposedly a business trip to this island off the Caribbean. The entire weekend they were sexually involved with underage girls who'd been kidnapped to pleasure them. Some as young as eleven."

Sloan's hand flew to her mouth. "No!"

"Yes. What these businessmen didn't know was that cameras had been installed in the bedrooms to deliberately blackmail them later. All the businessmen who participated in the orgy have received calls demanding money in exchange for the blackmailers' silence."

Anger flared in Sloan's eyes. "How could any of those men have participated in such a thing?" She then said, "If your cousin found out about it, that means…"

"Yes, the FBI is on it, and it's just a matter of time before arrests are made. That will include your father and I just wanted you to be prepared." He paused again. "And I wanted you to know I will be here for you. In fact, all the Steeles will be. My family loves you as much as I do."

"Oh, Mercury." He saw tears shimmering in her eyes. In the future he would put more smiles than tears in her eyes.

He then leaned in and captured her mouth again before standing with her in his arms and heading for the bedroom.

At twenty-five Sloan finally knew how it felt to be loved by a man. To be totally cherished. And when Mercury placed her on the bed and stood back and stared at her, she knew how it felt to be desired.

She didn't have to sense his need for her. She saw blatant evidence of it. Then there was the look in his eyes that held so many sexual promises. She knew she was in for a wild ride. And a very satisfying one at that.

"What are you thinking about, sweetheart?" he asked her.

She couldn't help but smile. "I'm thinking about how much I love you. How grateful I am for having you in my life and how I'd give anything if you stayed."

A serious expression appeared in his features. "I'm not going anywhere. Neither are you. We're stuck in this crazy thing called love together."

Yes, they were stuck in it together.

She reclined into a comfortable position and watched as he began removing his clothes. She always enjoyed this part, which left her wondering how any man could be so well toned, so powerfully built and so masterfully sexy. She wished she could concentrate on other things, but when he removed his clothes, his body always had her full attention. And when he finally stood in front of her, splendidly naked, she couldn't help but be in awe of his masculine beauty.

"Now for your clothes," he said, drawing her attention to his mouth. It was a mouth she totally enjoyed kissing. Over the past weeks, he had shown her how to kiss him in so many enjoyable ways. He was right; she wasn't going anywhere. She honestly pitied her father if he truly believed she would be showing up at the airport to return to Cincinnati with him. That wouldn't be happening.

She watched Mercury move to the bed and she leaned toward him. He always took his time undressing her, removing every piece of her clothing, then meticulously touching the areas he uncovered. He enjoyed fulfilling all her sexual needs. Making up for lost time and making sure she got everything she wanted and then some.

She drew in a deep breath when his hand slid beneath her T-shirt, felt the braless breasts and unerringly went to her nipples. The moment his fingers touched them, she felt a tingling sensation between her legs. "Mercury..."

"Tell me what you want, baby."

He'd first asked her that on their trip to Dallas and she'd had a bucket list. But not tonight. More than anything, she needed the feel of him buried deep inside her. The feel of him claiming her as his and her making him hers. That was what she both wanted and needed.

"I need you inside me. Now," she said in a desperate tone before leaning in to nip at his jaw.

He must have heard the urgency in her voice because he suddenly ripped her T-shirt over her head and then grabbed the waistband of her shorts. In one lightning-quick motion, he removed both the shorts and her panties. Reaching out, he swiftly positioned her body against the mass of pillows, bedcovers and cushions and immediately joined her there, straddling her.

He captured her wrists in his hands, held them over her head and looked down into her eyes. "If my lady doesn't want seduction this time, I have no problem bypassing that part."

Sloan smiled. She had been seduced by this Steele more times than she could count. This time she wanted to go straight to being conquered. "Take me, Mercury. Make me yours."

The gaze staring down at her was fiercely possessive when he said, "You're already mine, Sloan."

And then she felt the full length of the huge, solid erection slide into her. In response, her inner muscles tightened around him, holding him and squeezing him. She knew he'd felt it when a satisfying grin covered his features. "I love it when your body tries holding me hostage like that."

She smiled up at him. "Just getting all I can." He had stopped using a condom the last time he'd made love to her, after establishing the fact that they were both healthy and she'd been on the pill for some time.

"And I plan to give you all you want."

Then he began moving, just the way she liked and, more

important, the way she needed. The feel of his shaft stroking inside her had her moaning his name over and over again. He released her hands to grab hold of her hips, lifting her up to assure she received every one of his hard thrusts. Their bodies were so in tune. She closed her eyes as he began pushing even deeper inside her, setting a rhythm and giving her everything she craved.

His male scent filled her nostrils, stimulating her senses. When his thrusts grew harder and harder, she moaned more than just his name. She said words she'd heard him say while climaxing with her. Naughty words. Erotic words. Words she hadn't known existed until he'd said them. Words she now found so wickedly sexy.

"Do I need to start washing your mouth out with soap?" he asked her, leaning close to her ear and not missing a beat with his steady stream of thrusts.

"Not with soap, but I can think of something else," she told him, remembering how just last week he'd taught her to please him with her mouth. He said she was too good a student and would be the death of him yet.

When he threw his head back and hollered her name, his actions triggered an orgasm of gigantic proportions. In that instant she wasn't sure what was the loudest. His holler or her scream. It didn't matter. Nothing mattered but this and each other.

She knew at that moment that Mercury Morris Steele was all she wanted and needed in her life.

"Will you marry me, Sloan?"

She opened her eyes to stare up into his. She felt his shaft stretching her again. "Marry you?"

"Yes."

What man could ask a woman that in the middle of making love? She smiled. Mercury could. Mercury would. Mercury just did. Her answer would be just as spontaneous as his question had been. "Yes! I will marry you."

He smiled down at her before capturing her mouth with a long, deep, thorough kiss. And then he began moving again, putting her inner muscles to work once more. Both of them were determined to drive each other off the edge. They had tonight and the rest of their lives to make it happen. And they would.

Epilogue

One month later

Mercury smiled when he entered his condo to the aroma of food. Since finishing her cooking class, Sloan enjoyed coming over to his place and surprising him with different dishes. So far, he hadn't convinced her to move in with him.

He'd known she still needed the little bit of freedom and independence that came with having her own space, and he loved her enough to understand the need and give it to her. Just as long as he had this: her occasional surprise visits that often lasted for days.

They would be getting married; they just hadn't set a date yet. Understandably, she didn't relish a large wedding and promised to let him know when she was ready. Hell, he was ready but refused to rush her.

He walked into his kitchen and the woman he loved with all his heart was bending over to check something in the oven. His gaze roamed over her backside. She had the most delectable and sexiest behind of any woman he knew. It was perfect. As far as he was concerned, everything about Sloan Elizabeth Donahue was perfect.

"Something smells good."

She jerked her head up. She smiled, closed the oven and raced across the room to jump into his arms. His hands immediately went to that backside he'd just been admiring to support her in place.

She wrapped her arms around his neck and smiled brightly at him. "You're early."

He returned her smile. "No, for you I'm right on time. Always."

Her smile seemed to brighten even more. "Yes, always."

And then he kissed her with all the love in his heart. She was his and he was hers. Both he and his family had been there for her two weeks ago when her father had been one of ten businessmen arrested. She had called to talk to her parents but they tried shifting the blame. Saying that if she'd married Harold when they'd wanted her to, then they would have had the money to pay off their extortionist.

Mercury knew some people were better off not becoming parents, and the Donahues were a prime example of those who shouldn't. But then they would not have created this beautiful woman in his arms. Then where would he be? Still a Bad News Steele with the only direction in his life being to some woman's bedroom.

Now he had a purpose, which was to make Sloan happy. Hell, he'd even made his mother happy by becoming an engaged man. Eden was just waiting for them to give her word so she could start planning what was supposed to be a small wedding. She claimed all she needed were two weeks, and knowing his mother, he had no reason not to believe her. He'd warned Sloan about how big the Steele family was and not to be surprised if a small wedding became a rather large one.

No matter how hellish his days might have been, it was

nice knowing he had this. He had her. He broke off the kiss and smiled when he saw how desire filled her eyes.

"I love you, Mercury."

He leaned in and pressed another kiss on her lips. "I love you, too."

"And I'm ready for Eden to start planning our wedding."

He went momentarily still. "You sure?"

She threw her head back and laughed. "Yes! I've never been so sure of anything in my life. I'm ready to be your wife, move in here with you, proudly wear your ring, one day have your babies, take your name, be your life partner in everything. I want it all."

"And I'm going to make sure you get everything you want."

And then he was kissing her again, knowing their lives together would be filled with plenty of love and happiness.

* * * * *

TOO TEXAN TO TAME

JANICE MAYNARD

For Caroline and Anna.

You two are the best mothers I know. :)

Love always,

Mom

One

Vaughn Blackwood would do just about anything for his baby sister, Sophie, even if it meant returning to Royal, Texas. Again. He'd been back far too often lately. A New Year's Eve ball—because Sophie had begged. Before that, for his father's funeral. And, of course, the reading of the will. Hell, that had been a disaster.

His father's legal adviser, Kace LeBlanc, was Vaughn's age, give or take. But if LeBlanc had any sympathy toward the heirs who had come up empty-handed, he hadn't shown it. After all, the guy was a lawyer. He probably wouldn't bleed if you cut him.

LeBlanc wasn't a bad guy, but he sure as hell was a pro at handing out bad news. Buckley Blackwood hadn't left his dear children so much as two pennies to rub together. His entire estate had gone to Miranda Blackwood, the second of Buckley's ex-wives.

The whole situation was a travesty of justice. Just because Vaughn didn't want anything from his father didn't mean it was okay for his siblings Kellan and Sophie to get the shaft.

He gripped the steering wheel, absently noting the familiar landmarks as he got closer to town. In between his bouts of indignation, other feelings simmered uncomfortably. Vaughn hadn't adored his father. No warm, fuzzy childhood memories lingered. But he'd never wanted the man dead. In fact, when he first heard the news that Buckley "Buck" Blackwood had passed, Vaughn actually felt something twist in his chest. A sharp pang of regret. The bittersweet knowledge that some fences would never be mended now.

Then he'd attended the will reading and had been sharply reminded of why he and the old man were never close. His father had been a hard-nosed son of a bitch. So it wasn't entirely surprising that even from the grave, Buck was manipulating and shortchanging his own flesh and blood.

Vaughn had done his damnedest to avoid all the inheritance drama back home. As far as he was concerned, Miranda, the stepwitch, as they called her, could spend the old man's riches however she wanted. It was a sweet pot of gold, for sure. First, there was Blackwood Bank—the family business. Then a series of homes all over the globe. The seven-figure fortune. And last but not least, Blackwood Hollow, the sprawling ranch outside Royal.

If Vaughn had any regrets at all about being shut out of his father's will, it was only the thought of never visiting the ranch again. He'd met Brielle there. Some days those memories were sweet. Other days they made him angry. And occasionally, like today, they made him ache.

Stubbornly, he pushed all thoughts of Brie aside. She was a mistake. Relegated to his past. For his peace of mind, she needed to stay there. Vaughn had left Royal, Texas—and Brielle—a long time ago, and he had set out to make his own mark in the world, away from his father's long shadow. He'd earned his first million buying up land in the Fort Worth area and selling drilling rights. His company, Blackwood Energy Corp., was worth $500 million by most recent estimates. Royal, Texas, might be where his life began, but Vaughn had moved on.

He parked his late-model Mercedes—the one he kept in a fancy garage at the airport for his visits—in front of the elegant country guesthouse that would be his base for the next week or so. His hostess, Dixie Musgraves, owned this building and all of Magnolia Acres. As a longtime friend of the Blackwood family, she had supported Kellan, Sophie and Vaughn since they were kids. She had also stepped in as a second mother when their own mother died of a stroke a few years ago.

Now, the attractive fiftysomething redhead came out to meet him. She hugged him tightly. "I've missed you, sweet boy."

"Hey, Dixie." Vaughn grinned, returning the warm embrace. This "boy" towered over her by almost a foot. Dixie had been a dear friend to Donna-Leigh Blackwood since before Vaughn and his siblings were born and had loved and cared for Donna-Leigh all the way to the day she died. Actually, the name had been Donna-Leigh Westbrook by then. Vaughn's mother had taken back her maiden name as a postdivorce jab at her controlling ex-husband. The public action had made Buck seethe, but Donna-Leigh had been beyond his touch by then.

Buck Blackwood was a distant parent on his best days, a harsh, punishing father on his worst. Since Donna-Leigh's passing, Dixie had been the closest thing the Blackwood kids had to a nurturing figure in their lives.

She grabbed his smallest bag. "Come on in, honey. I've got iced tea and beer and anything else you want."

Vaughn reached for his high-end leather backpack and

large suitcase, following her into the house. It had been months since he felt so relaxed. Despite the many family situations brewing, it was good to be home…to be back in Royal.

He set the luggage at the foot of the stairs. "I'm still thankful the wildfires spared Magnolia Acres," he said. "Is everything here going well?" He sprawled in an easy chair and accepted the glass she handed him. "Thanks, Dixie."

"Yep," she said. "We're right as rain, pardon the pun. Word has rippled through town about the two fire crews you funded and sent. And that you came yourself. People are grateful."

Guilt curled in his stomach. "Well, it seemed the least I could do," he muttered, grimacing.

Dixie cocked her head and gave him the stink eye. "And now here you are. You didn't want to come again so soon, did you?"

He shrugged. "Not particularly. But when a man's sister gets married, he doesn't have much choice."

Her gaze softened. "Sophie will be so glad you're here. Your brother will, too. And Darius is coming with Audra."

"We keep missing each other."

Her sympathetic gaze told him she saw his inward turmoil. "He's a great guy. You'll like him when the two of you have the chance to bond."

"I'm sure I will." His words were deliberately bland. These last few months had been filled with too much drama. Too many surprises. Like discovering he had a half brother. He hadn't fully adjusted to the status quo. So he decided to change the subject.

But Dixie wasn't going to let him act like his normal taciturn self. "Is that all you have to say?" she asked.

"I feel bad about Dad's will," he muttered, shrugging. "I never wanted anything of his for myself, but why give it all to Miranda? She must have done something to manipulate Dad."

"Give me your glass," she said. "You need some more tea. And maybe a scone. Low blood sugar is the only excuse I can think of for such crazy talk."

"She's Kellan's age, for God's sake. How can you stand up for her? She's nothing more than a gold digger."

Dixie handed him another drink and cuffed the side of his head. "Listen to me, you hardheaded Blackwood. Lord knows I loved your mother. She was like the sister I never had. But when Miranda hooked up with your father, the first marriage was legally over. Barely. You know it was."

"Doesn't mean Miranda is a saint."

"She signed a prenup. Walked away after the divorce without a penny of Blackwood money. And she's made a name for herself in the big city."

"What's your point?"

"Even though she had a heads-up before the will reading, I think Miranda was as shocked as any of you that Buck made her his sole heir."

He swirled the tea in his glass. "Maybe. It still seems fishy."

"So you're going to join Kellan and Sophie in contesting it?"

He looked up, shocked. "Me? No. I've got everything I need."

Dixie gave him a mysterious smile. "Maybe you do, and maybe you don't." She glanced at her watch. "Oh, shoot. I've gotta run. Make yourself at home, Vaughn. There's no one in the other bedroom. I know how you love your privacy."

He frowned. "What does that mean?"

"Not a thing, sweetie. Don't be so touchy."

He followed her to the porch. "Thanks for the hospitality, Dixie. I really appreciate it. With my brother a newly-wed and my sister in the midst of wedding fever, it's nice to have a place to myself."

His hostess nodded. "Glad I can help." She paused on the bottom step, shielding her eyes from the sun and staring up at him. "Did you know Brie is back in town?"

The news kicked him in the chest like a horse. Vaughn kept his expression neutral, but it wasn't easy. "Oh?"

Dixie grinned smugly. "About six weeks ago now. She's opened up a private practice veterinarian clinic on Main Street. Mostly for pets. Calls it Happy Trails. Seems to be doing well."

"I thought she liked large animals and ranching."

"I wouldn't know about that. Your daddy sure was fond of her when she worked at Blackwood Hollow."

So was I, Vaughn thought bleakly. But Brie had wanted and needed things he couldn't give her.

Again, he kept his face and his tone carefully noncommittal. "She definitely had a way with horses. You won't find many ranch hands as gifted or as overqualified."

"True. I suppose she was wasting her talent working for Buckley. He never did recognize her education or her value…at least not when it came to giving her a fair paycheck."

"Tightfisted until the end." Vaughn rubbed the back of his neck. Talking about his father and Brielle wasn't helping the knot in his stomach. "I think I'll grab a shower and go see Sophie."

"You're welcome to join me for dinner. I always have plenty."

"Not tonight, but I appreciate it. I'll take you up on that invitation another evening. Thanks for rolling out the welcome mat."

Her grin was a tad wistful. "Maybe I'm hoping I can convince you to come home for good."

Vaughn shook his head slowly. "Not in the cards, Dixie."

She waved as she walked toward the main house, tossing a last shot over her shoulder. "Never say never."

Vaughn stood in a corner of his sister's enormous living room and eyed the crowd that ebbed and flowed around him. He'd been hoping for a private word with his sister. Apparently, private moments were in short supply during the days and weeks leading up to a wedding.

He was glad, at least, to see that Sophie looked amazing…and happy. The buttoned-up English fellow on her arm was her fiancé, Nigel Townshend.

Fortunately, the man seemed completely smitten with Vaughn's baby sister. It was a good thing, because if Vaughn had sensed any duplicity in the guy, he'd have been forced to beat the Brit to a pulp.

Sophie was innocent and sweet. Far too trusting. Not only that, but Buckley Blackwood had done a number on his only daughter's self-esteem, because he didn't know how to parent a girl.

Fortunately, Sophie had matured into a caring, lovely woman in spite of their father, and she deserved every bit of happiness she seemed to have found. Even so, the thought of this wedding to come made Vaughn jumpy. So much damn money and time and effort for a ceremony and a noose that experts predicted had a fifty-fifty shot at success.

Vaughn wasn't a pessimist. He was a realist.

Monogamy was not a natural state for the human species. His own father had sucked at marriage. Vaughn was briefly tempted once, but the woman had wised up and ditched him after he repeatedly insisted that wedded bliss wasn't his thing.

Remembering the expression on Brielle's face when she said her goodbyes eviscerated Vaughn to this day. But he couldn't regret his honesty with her. He'd only told her the unvarnished truth.

Moments later when Kellan appeared with his gorgeous Russian bride, Irina, at his side, Vaughn slammed the door on his negative thoughts and hugged his older brother. He kissed Irina on both cheeks. "Congrats on the baby-to-be."

Irina beamed. "We are so happy," she exclaimed. "Your brother is a wonderful man."

Kellan puffed out his chest. "Keep talking, sweet wife. I want Vaughn to hear all about how wonderful I am."

Vaughn snorted. "Somebody's been brainwashing her."

In the laughter that followed, Kellan kissed his wife's cheek, making her blush. Then he turned his attention back to Vaughn. "Did you know that Brielle is back in Royal?"

Seriously? This again? Why was everyone so obsessed with keeping Vaughn up-to-date about his ex-lover? He shrugged. "Dixie mentioned it."

Kellan lifted an eyebrow. "And?"

"And nothing. Brie and I were never serious." The lie caught in his throat.

Kellan shook his head. "I'm not buying that. You were mad about her."

Irina pinched her husband's arm. "Why are you being so mean to your brother? Leave him alone."

Vaughn was both touched and amused. "Thanks for the backup, Irina, but I can handle Kellan. We've been sparring partners since I was five—Kellan might have been three years older, but even then, I could hold my own. I've been able to bust his ass since I turned twelve."

"Not true," Kellan insisted, bristling theatrically.

Irina shook her head, rolling her eyes at both of them. "We will leave you on that note, dear Vaughn. It's good that you are home where you belong."

"I'm not *home*," Vaughn insisted. But it was too late. They didn't hear him. While the other couple walked away to do more socializing, Vaughn sighed and maintained his position.

As good as it was to see his family, this kind of crap was what he didn't need. Come back to Royal for good? Not a chance.

Sophie breezed across the room in Vaughn's direction. Earlier in the evening, Vaughn had met the British fiancé briefly. But now Sophie was on her own.

"Great party, sis," he said. "Any chance you and I could have some time alone later?"

She waved a hand. "Maybe tomorrow. Noonish. We *do* need to catch up." Despite her glowing mood, there were dark shadows beneath her eyes.

He curled an arm around her waist. "You look exhausted, Soph. Everything okay?"

She leaned her head on his shoulder and yawned. "Everything is perfect now that you're home. Did you know Brie is back in town?"

His jaw clenched. "Yeah. I heard."

"She's opened a vet clinic. I took Mr. Boots there for his shots last week. The whole waiting room was full."

The niggling headache Vaughn had earlier was turning into a full-blown drum line chorus. Before he could think of yet another innocuous response, a young, uniformed maid appeared. "Ms. Blackwood? There's someone at the front door asking to see Mr. Blackwood." The employee glanced at Vaughn. "Mr. *Vaughn* Blackwood."

Sophie yawned again. "Tell them to come in."

The maid fidgeted. "They don't want to intrude."

Vaughn interrupted. "I'll deal with it, sis." There was no way the mystery caller at the front door was Brielle. Why would she show up uninvited at Sophie's house? And looking for him, no less?

Despite the uneasiness in the pit of his stomach, he strode through the crowded rooms, not making eye contact with anyone. Maybe this was his chance to escape and go back to the blessedly quiet guesthouse.

When he put his hand on the doorknob and pulled, his spine tingled. As if lightning was about to strike the cold metal in his fingers. Nonsense. Absolute nonsense. "Can I help you?" he asked gruffly as he swung open the door.

Two

Brielle sucked in a shocked breath. She had asked to speak to Vaughn, but she hadn't held out much hope that he would come. "It's me," she said. And then realized that her words were foolish and bumbling. *Of course* Vaughn knew who she was.

He still held the edge of the door with one hand, the fingers white-knuckled. "Brielle."

Just the one word. Hoarse. Disbelieving.

Her lips twisted. "You seem shocked. I thought surely someone would have told you I've moved back to Royal."

"Oh, they have," he muttered. "A whole parade of 'em."

There was an odd note in his voice. And though it was hard to tell in the harsh glow of the porch light, he seemed pale.

He was as beautiful as she remembered. Thick brown hair, intense green eyes. And a clean-shaven jaw that would make a sculptor weep with envy. Her insides turned all shivery.

She shifted from one foot to the other. "I stopped by Magnolia Acres and asked Dixie where you were. One of my friends said she heard you blew into town last night."

"No secrets in Royal." Now he sounded almost bitter.

"I was sorry to hear about your dad. And his crazy will."

"No great loss. Clearly, we kids didn't mean that much to him."

"Surely he had his reasons."

"Did you come tonight to discuss my father?" The question was curt.

"You don't have to be rude."

He lifted his chin, closed his eyes briefly, then pinned her with a stare that practically froze her on the spot. "Why are you here, Brielle?"

She gnawed her lip. "I need to talk to you."

He waved a hand in a "go on" gesture. "Knock yourself out."

"Not now," she said. "Not in public."

His gaze narrowed. "I think you said everything I needed to hear the last time we were together. I'm a selfish Peter Pan with no compassion, no heart and no real purpose on the planet."

Brie winced. Hearing her own words quoted back to her made her feel slightly ill. "I was angry," she said.

"No kidding." Vaughn's steely-eyed gaze flayed her.

"I really do need to talk to you. It's important," she whispered, suddenly close to tears. She had never seen a man less open to mending fences. Animosity rolled off him in waves.

Vaughn glanced at his watch impatiently. "I need to get back to the party. The bride-to-be will be wondering where I am. Surely whatever this is can wait."

"I have a half day at the clinic tomorrow. Could we do lunch?"

He shook his head. "I already have a date with Sophie.

And honestly, I'm not going to have much free time while I'm in Royal."

Wow. She hadn't expected this. It almost appeared as if her defection had actually hurt him. But why? He'd been the one dead set on making sure she knew the rules when it came to their relationship. Strictly temporary. Recreational sex. No promises. No future.

It wasn't as if he had been in love with her. "Never mind," she said dully.

As she turned to leave, he grabbed her arm. Not hard. But firmly. As if he really didn't want her to go. "Wait," he said. "I'm sorry. You caught me off guard." He closed the door behind him and led her down a couple of steps to the driveway below. "Is it really so important? I thought you hated my guts."

"I never hated you, Vaughn. We were simply too different to make things work."

Almost against his will—or so it seemed—he cupped her cheek in one large, warm palm. "You look beautiful, Brie." Something hovered between them for five seconds. Ten. Her legs trembled. Her breath lodged in her throat.

"I'm a mess," she protested. It was true. She had come straight from the clinic. It was her late night. She had put on a clean top, because her lab coat had been spattered with blood. Her hair was caught up in a loose knot. She hadn't had time to fix it.

His body was warm and male close to hers.

Just when she thought for sure he was going to kiss her, he stepped back. "I'll be free by two o'clock tomorrow. We could go for a drive."

The sudden concession dissipated some of the heavy, leaden feeling in her stomach. "What if I drop by the guesthouse?" she said. A drive wouldn't work for what she had in mind.

He raised an eyebrow. "Are you propositioning me,

Brie?" His sardonic jab was meant to make her uncomfortable.

Her cheeks flamed—not that he could tell in the dark. "Don't be silly. You're not so irresistible that I have to jump your bones hours after you come back to town."

"I'm devastated," he said, clearly not serious. "The Brie I remember was not so cruel."

"I have to go," she said. "Will you be there when I show up?"

The sharp note in her voice didn't affect him at all. He had the gall to lift an eyebrow and give her a tight smile. "I'll be waiting, Brie. Can't wait to see what happens."

Vaughn stood on the porch and watched Brie's little car disappear down the driveway. He believed he'd put on a good show of being totally relaxed, but inside, he was less so.

What did she want from him? And why all the secrecy?

It occurred to him that she might need an investor for her veterinary practice. It wasn't easy these days to get a new business off the ground. But if that was the case, why ask *him*?

The questions swirled unanswered in his head as he went back inside and mingled. He had about reached his limits for socializing.

Nigel, Sophie's fiancé, and Irina, Kellan's pregnant bride, were holding court on the far side of the living room in a circle of admirers. The aristocratic television executive and the Russian former model were both magnetic personalities.

Meanwhile, Kellan and Sophie stood huddled in a nearby alcove, whispering. Vaughn joined them. "I think I'll head out," he said.

Sophie's face fell. "So soon?"

"I was up early," Vaughn said. "For a work meeting. I barely made it to the airport on time."

Kellan leaned against the wall, clearly keeping tabs on his wife across the expanse of expensive carpet. "I wish you had returned sooner and been able to meet Darius. He had an important meeting he couldn't miss in LA, so he and his girlfriend, Audra, headed to California a few days ago. They'll be back for the wedding, of course, but it would have been great if you could have spent time with him before then."

Vaughn experienced a jolt of relief. Things were complicated enough at the moment. He wasn't sorry to delay that odd family reunion with a stranger who shared his blood.

"What do we think of our half brother?" Vaughn asked.

Sophie and Kellan exchanged glances.

Kellan shrugged. "I like him. He's a straight-up guy. The DNA test results were conclusive."

Sophie nodded. "Darius is honestly as rattled as the rest of us. Can you imagine what it was like to hear that his biological father was Buck Blackwood?"

Kellan snorted. "And that despite the dramatic reveal, the old man left him nothing?"

"Where does Miranda fit into all this?" Vaughn asked. "I have a hard time imagining that she wants to deal with the ranch or the bank when her whole life is back in New York. She's got the TV show, for one thing. Plus, New York is the home base for her exercise empire. And since everyone knows she got the inheritance while we were left out in the cold, Royal can't possibly be a fun gig for her right now. Surely she doesn't need the money."

"Well, you do know that *Secret Lives* has been doing some filming here. Audiences love the whole Western angle," Sophie said.

Vaughn shook his head, filled with admiration and love

for his sister. "I still can't believe you infiltrated the show and posed as a consultant."

Kellan grinned. "And got a husband out of it besides when you fell in love with the production company's CEO."

Sophie's smug smile told Vaughn that she didn't regret a thing. "I went there trying to dig up dirt on Miranda, but honestly, I think she's not as bad as we've painted her all this time."

Vaughn scowled. "And yet somehow she managed to inherit *everything* from a man who wasn't even her husband anymore. I'm not buying the innocent surprised act."

"I get where you're coming from," Kellan said. "But Miranda has dropped a few hints that the inheritance drama might not be over yet."

Sophie nodded. "When I was over at the house making last-minute wedding arrangements, she mentioned the word *caretaker*. As if something in the future will be different."

"Well, thank God it has nothing to do with me. As soon as you and Nigel are legally wed, I'm getting back to Fort Worth. I'm not waiting around to see if my dearly departed dad has some Machiavellian plan for my future."

Kellan sighed. "He died virtually alone. Didn't even let anyone know he was near the end. And because he had alienated his friends and family, he was left with nothing that mattered. Makes you feel kind of bad for him, doesn't it?"

Vaughn shook his head slowly. "You two are more forgiving than I am. He brought his troubles on himself."

"Maybe so," Sophie said. "But Kellan and I are so happy now, it's hard to hold a grudge."

Vaughn put an arm around each of them, closing the circle. "He may have been a wretched excuse for a father, but he and Mom gave us each other. I love you both. Now get back to the party and let me be an old curmudgeon in peace."

* * *

A half hour later, Vaughn pulled up in front of the guest-house, got out of the car and stretched. The sky cradled a million stars tonight. Quite a change from the view he was used to. The Dallas/Fort Worth metroplex was his home these days. He loved the energy and vitality of the cities.

Even so, Royal's slower pace and laid-back charm drew him in, restored his sense of balance.

He couldn't help thinking of Brielle at this moment. How many times had the two of them indulged their love of amateur astronomy? How many times had they spread a quilt in some private field and made love under the stars?

The memories swamped him, coming as thick and fast as a flash flood in a dry gulch. She had been everything to him at one time. But he had been too driven, too ambitious. He'd let the relationship wither on the vine, leaving Brie to point out his shortcomings and ultimately to leave him.

Ah, hell. It was all for the best.

Gloomily, he fished out the key Dixie had given him and unlocked the door to the guesthouse. But he nearly stumbled when his toe connected with something unexpected.

A manila envelope, thick and menacing, lay on the ground. Vaughn picked it up, saw his name scrawled in black marker. Inside the house, he tossed the envelope on the table and poured himself a drink. His luggage still sat at the foot of the stairs.

The master suite was on the top floor. A second, smaller bedroom was tucked away at the back of the main level. Because Dixie had saved the entire place for him, he wouldn't have to bother making small talk with any additional guests.

He was damned glad. Exhaustion went bone deep. Sometimes he wondered why he worked so hard. He'd already made more money than he could spend in a lifetime.

Yet still, he had to accumulate more. It was the Black-wood way.

After finishing his scotch, he carried his bags upstairs. Then, unable to help himself, he went back down the stairs and picked up the envelope. Inside was a copy of his father's will. He'd never actually read the damn thing—or even heard it read, come to think of it. At the reading of the will, Kace LeBlanc, Buck's lawyer, had cut straight to the heart of it and told them all, flat out, that Miranda had gotten everything. But the document in Vaughn's hands now was conveniently folded back to a page that addressed him personally.

He sat down hard, felt his stomach pitch and began to read.

Dear Vaughn,

If you're reading this, you're probably pissed that I didn't leave you anything. The truth is, of all my progeny, you're probably the most like me. You love the open road—not being constrained by anyone's expectations. You have a keen business sense, and you're a bit of a renegade. You don't want to settle down.

Unfortunately, all those characteristics make you a bad risk when it comes to relationships. I suffered the same weaknesses, and I ended up alone and lonely. Does that admission surprise you? I learned my lessons the hard way. I'm dying now with no one at my side to hold my hand.

So, I'm not leaving you any money. I'm hoping this letter from beyond the grave will convince you that the one thing you lack is the love of a good woman. I had two, and I lost them both.

Be angry with me if you must, but try to learn from my mistakes. Miranda will be the arbiter of what comes next. I've asked her to watch over my children

and decide when and if each of you has matured
enough to make good lives for yourselves.
   I do love you, son. Don't be afraid to change.
Dad

Vaughn cursed and tossed the sheaf of papers aside. What a load of crap. This was why he had stayed far away from all the lawyer shenanigans.

Who had dropped off such a bombshell? Dixie? Surely not. She was more inclined to face problems head-on.

Vaughn was too jumpy and irritated to sleep, even though the hour was late. Instead, he changed into shorts and athletic shoes and left the house to outrun his demons.

The ranch was dark and quiet and mostly peaceful. Periodically, a lowing moo broke the silence. It was probably foolhardy to run in the dark, risking a broken ankle. But he was angry and upset and, though he was loath to admit it, hurt.

Maybe most men would be pleased to hear they were like their fathers. Not Vaughn. His dad had alienated his mother. Then married a woman young enough to be his child. Divorced her, too. At the end, he'd succumbed to cancer with no close family member at his side.

Vaughn ran faster, harder. He wasn't like his father. He wasn't. Maybe he was a loner, and maybe he liked keeping his emotions under control. Nothing wrong with that. It didn't matter what his father or *anyone* thought of him.

He lived by a set of rules that made sense. He was charitably generous, and he had a brother and a sister he cared about. His life was perfect.

Three

After a restless night, Vaughn sent Dixie a text to see if she would join him for coffee. Half an hour later, she showed up carrying a freshly baked coffee cake that smelled of cinnamon and culinary delight. He inhaled deeply. "Did you make this?"

She reached into a cabinet for plates and forks. "I could have, but I didn't. I have a new cook who enjoys reproducing our family recipes. I'm paying her a ridiculous salary so she won't leave me."

"Stick with that plan," he said, swallowing his first bite. "This is amazing."

Dixie joined him, and they ate their impromptu breakfast in harmony. When the last crumbs were gone, she eyed him wryly. "You haven't even been home twenty-four hours. What's wrong, Vaughn? You're so tense, you're giving *me* a headache."

He shrugged and pulled the sheaf of papers from underneath a stack of magazines. "I found this on the doorstep when I got home last night."

Dixie glanced at it. "Ah."

"That's all you have to say?"

"I didn't leave it there," she said. "Though I have seen it. Both Kellan and Sophie have copies."

"If it wasn't you, then who?"

"Probably Miranda. She knows you don't like her, so she wouldn't have wanted to make waves."

"Yet she's sticking her nose in my business." Vaughn's mood teetered between resigned and angry.

"If it was her, then she was just trying to carry out the terms of your father's will. Cut her a break."

"Forgive me if I'm not feeling particularly sympathetic toward Miranda right now." He stabbed his finger at the paragraphs that had given him a sleepless night. "Do *you* think I'm like my father?"

Dixie hesitated. Long enough to give him heartburn. His surrogate mother was honest to a fault.

She shook her head slowly. "You're *not* your father, Vaughn. But you do share some of his traits."

"Like what?"

"You've never learned how to open yourself up to other people. Even your brother and sister have a hard time knowing you."

"They said that?" He was startled and chagrined.

"Not in so many words. But we all worry about you, Vaughn. You're like a superhero with deep psychological wounds. You wear the cape or the mask, or you simply hide from the world. It's not healthy. I want more for you."

"I think you have a wonderfully caring heart, Dixie, and I'm glad you love me enough to worry about me. But if you're thinking that I need some big love story in order to be happy, think again. Just because Kellan and Sophie have wallowed in romance lately doesn't mean I will. I'm here for the wedding. That's it."

"Fair enough." She stood and gathered the dishes. "How was Sophie last night?"

The obvious change in subjects relieved him. "I thought I was just dropping by for a casual visit. But you know Sophie. There was a party underway. I had a few minutes with her and Kellan. Met Nigel. It was...nice."

He couldn't quite bring himself to mention Brie or that he was seeing her again this afternoon. Dixie would jump to conclusions, but there was nowhere to jump. Nowhere at all.

Brie closed the office for the lunch break and handed off the keys to her brand-new partner. Dr. Brody had been a veterinarian in Royal for over four decades. Since his retirement, he'd been at loose ends. When Brie had asked if he'd be willing to cover for her occasionally, Dr. Brody jumped at the chance.

He was thin and stooped, but his mind was as sharp as ever. Plus, he had a wealth of experience that could only enhance Brie's fledgling practice. It was the perfect solution for both of them.

Brie scooted home as quickly as she could and relieved the babysitter. Danika was already down for her nap. Brie missed her daughter fiercely when she was at work, but Brie was their sole financial support. No matter how much she would have loved to be a stay-at-home mom for a few years, it wasn't in the cards.

She eased open the bedroom door and slipped inside to watch her baby sleep. Not really a baby anymore. Danika would be two very soon. Where had the time gone?

Her daughter's hair was pale blond like Brie's. But the little girl had her father's vivid green eyes. Anyone looking closely could deduce the truth easily.

Brie had realized when she returned to Royal that she

would have to face Vaughn sooner or later. He didn't live here anymore, but with his sister getting married, of course he was going to come home for a visit.

It might have been possible to avoid a confrontation for a week or ten days—long enough for him to leave town again. But Brie had known for some time now that she needed to make a concerted effort to connect father and daughter.

Vaughn didn't want family ties or obligations. That was fine. His choice. Still, Brie had to tell him the truth.

This move back to Royal was fraught with possibilities for happiness or for heartache, but Brie was convinced it was what was best for her little family. Brie wanted Danika to grow up in the wonderful town where she had spent her own childhood. Though Brie's parents had relocated to south Florida for their retirement, Royal would always be home. She wanted that sense of belonging for her daughter.

While Danika was still napping, Brie carried the baby monitor to the bathroom so she could shower and change. When her hair was dry and her light makeup redone, she chose black dress pants and a crimson silk blouse that lifted her spirits while suiting the weather. Royal was on the cusp of a mild winter and an early spring. Dressy black sandals gave her a couple of extra inches and completed her outfit.

Danika stirred just as her mother was ready. After a snack of applesauce and goldfish crackers, Brie dressed her daughter in a knee-length dress with short sleeves. The fabric was pale blue gingham. The white band of smocking across the upper chest incorporated a cute pattern of yellow ducks chasing brown bunnies.

Danika squirmed. The child's boundless energy didn't take well to hair brushing.

"Easy, baby," Brie said, expertly catching up the fine silky-blond strands into two small pigtails and adding blue bows. "Mommy's almost done."

Danika giggled when Brie lifted her little skirt and tick-
led her bare tummy. The baby had been wearing tights all
winter, but today was balmy, so Brie put the child in a diaper and sandals and nothing else but her dress.

At last, both she and her daughter were ready to go.
Brie had skipped lunch. Her stomach was in knots. Anxiety. Tension.

She was doing the right thing. No question.

But how would Vaughn react?

By the time Brie strapped Danika into her car seat, and
they were headed toward Magnolia Acres, her forehead
was damp and her hands were almost too shaky to drive.

She hadn't been this nervous since the day she sat in a
doctor's office and heard the news that she was going to
be a mother. She'd been all alone in a little suburb outside
Houston.

After quitting her job at Blackwood Hollow she had
fled Royal. Though Vaughn lived in Fort Worth, he came
back and forth to Royal frequently. Their breakup had been
ugly—too ugly for her to be comfortable with the idea of
seeing him again. She'd been convinced that she had no
choice but to leave Royal and start over.

Just as she was reliving her past, a car ran a stop sign
and nearly clipped her bumper. Brie took a deep breath, sat
up straight and concentrated on her driving. This looming
confrontation was like ripping off a Band-Aid. The anticipation was always worse than the real event. Hopefully…

Besides, Vaughn wouldn't want anything more than a
cursory relationship with little Danika. He might offer to
write a check for child support. Brie would decline, and
her responsibility to inform him would be over.

By the time she reached Magnolia Acres, her pulse was
racing. Fortunately, Danika played happily with books in
the back seat. She already spoke multiple words and short

sentences and was picking up additional language skills every day.

Would Vaughn be impressed with his daughter? Or was fatherhood going to be nothing more than an inconvenience to him? Brie braced herself for the fact that he might simply be uninterested.

That would be the worst blow of all…

She bypassed the turn to the main house and headed for the guest quarters. The clock on the dash read three minutes before two. A rental car in the driveway told her that Vaughn had returned from his earlier plans with his sister.

After checking her reflection in the visor mirror and smoothing her hair, she got out and freed Danika from her car seat. "Showtime, sweet baby. Please be on your best behavior." The child might not understand the seriousness of the situation, but hopefully she would be in her usual good mood.

Brie balanced her daughter on her hip, hefting the bag against her other side. The diaper bag went everywhere with them. It held toys and snacks and extra clothing, and it was easy to tuck her small purse inside. She didn't relish arriving on Vaughn's doorstep burdened down with the huge navy-and-white tote, but it wouldn't be smart to leave it.

Was Vaughn watching them out the window? A trickle of sweat rolled down Brie's spine. Her mouth was so dry she wondered if she would be able to speak.

She had rehearsed this speech a hundred times over the past two years. Now that the moment had come, her mind was blank.

At the door, she set down the diaper bag and cuddled Danika for moral support. Then she rang the bell.

Vaughn answered almost immediately. He was wearing dark khakis with a cream dress shirt and a fashionable tie, navy with tiny gold medallions. His navy sport coat looked wildly expensive.

"Hello, Vaughn." She spoke first, because his gaze had skidded over Brie and locked on the baby.

When Vaughn didn't say anything, her heartbeat lurched and thudded wildly. "This is Danika. Your daughter. I call her Nika for short."

Still, he was silent. As she watched anxiously, every ounce of color drained from his face, only to be replaced with two dark slashes of red on his cheekbones. She saw his Adam's apple flex visibly as he swallowed.

For a second, his incredulous gaze snapped back to meet Brie's, but then immediately he focused on Danika again. He didn't reach for the little girl. He didn't move. He simply stared.

At last, when the silent standoff seemed as if it would never end, he shot a piercing glance at Brie. An angry, in fact furious, stare. "You didn't think I had the right to know?"

"Whoa, whoa, back up the truck," Brie hissed, trying not to upset her daughter. "I *tried* to tell you. Several times. But apparently, you changed cell service providers, and I wasn't one of the chosen few you notified."

A flicker in his expression told her he remembered. "We had a data breach at work. The tech guys started all my team over from scratch with new phones. But you could have called the office. The main line. That number was no secret, Brie."

"I did," she insisted. "At least half a dozen times. Twice, I even got through to your administrative assistant. Do you have any idea how humiliating that was? Begging her to connect me to your line. I told her it was a personal matter. But apparently you've trained her to be very efficient when it comes to protecting your privacy."

"Well, hell…"

"Yeah. Tell me about it."

He seemed at a loss for words now. The situation was

so novel—Vaughn Blackwood not knowing what to say—
it was as if time stood still. Finally, he stepped back. "You
should come in," he muttered. "She has such fair skin. Don't
want her to get sunburned."

As Brie leaned down to grab the bag, Vaughn intervened. "I've got it. You hang on to her."

"Okay. Thanks."

Brie had been inside Dixie's guesthouse a time or two.
She found herself fiercely glad that she and Vaughn were
going to have this conversation on neutral ground. A lot
was at stake.

"This place isn't childproofed," he said, looking around
the room, his expression still half-dazed.

"I'll watch her. She'll be fine. Maybe you and I could
sit on the sofa. That way she can play at the coffee table.
I'll need the diaper bag, though."

When she said the word *diaper*, she was pretty sure
Vaughn's eyes glazed over again. Brie took out a small set
of colorful stacking cups, Danika's favorite soft baby doll
and a sippy cup of water.

With interesting distractions, the little girl was happy
to stand at the table while her mother sat down opposite
the strange man. Now they mimicked a real family—the
two grown-ups on either end of the sofa and the child in
the middle.

Vaughn raked a hand through his hair, laughing softly,
though without any real humor. "I thought you wanted to
borrow money."

Brie's eyes widened. "Why would I want money?"

"For the new veterinary practice?"

The way one of his eyebrows went up reminded her
of a dozen arguments they'd had over the year and a half
they had dated. With Brie working at his father's ranch
and Vaughn based mainly in the Dallas/Forth Worth area,
their affair had been full of obstacles from the beginning.

Brie had been willing to fight her way past all of them—
at least at first. Back when she'd thought there might be a
future for them together.

The first time they made love, Vaughn had spread a
quilt in the hayloft and coaxed her into spending most of
the night with him. It had been intimate and wildly romantic. Too bad it had all been for show.

"I don't need your money," she said, perhaps a little too
sharply. "My parents invested a modest sum in my practice, and I qualified for a small business loan. The clinic
is doing fine."

His body language was guarded, arms folded over his
broad, masculine chest. "Then why are you here?"

She gaped at him. "Seriously? I'm here so you can meet
your daughter. Is that so odd? I know this whole parenthood
gig probably means less than nothing to you, but a healthy
child benefits from having two parents. I don't want her
waking up one day and hating me because I never told her
who you were."

"So this is really about *you* and not Danika. Certainly
not me."

"God, you're a sanctimonious jerk. Some things never
change." She inhaled sharply, reining in her temper and
reminding herself she didn't want to upset Nika. "I don't
need or expect anything from you, Vaughn Blackwood. But
my baby girl carries no blame here. If she wants a daddy,
I'm going to make sure she knows who he is…even if he's
an absent parent."

"I see."

"You can deny paternity. If you wish. But a court of
law would find in favor of your daughter. Look at her
eyes, Vaughn. She's yours. Through and through. If we're
lucky, maybe she won't have inherited your stubborn, bull-
headed need to push everyone away so you can always be
in control."

Four

Vaughn's hands were cold. His insides were a mishmash of anger and incredulity.

In control? He would have laughed wildly if the situation had been less fraught. He'd never felt less in control during his entire adult life.

One minute he'd been a dutiful brother showing up for his sister's wedding. The next he'd been blindsided by the woman and the past he had put behind him.

He stared at the child, searching for something, anything to tell him she was his. Brie was right. The eyes were a dead giveaway. Besides, he knew Brie. She wouldn't lie about something like this.

"How old is she?" he demanded.

"Almost two. Her birthday is coming up. You can do the math. I didn't know I was pregnant when I left Royal. By the time I found out, I was working in Houston. At first I wasn't going to tell you at all, because you'd been so adamant about not wanting ties. But after a few weeks, my conscience kicked in, and I felt I had to share the truth. By then, it was too late. I couldn't reach you by phone."

"You could have come in person," he said stubbornly, still wanting to play the injured party.

"No. We were done. I wasn't going to crawl to you and beg for support, either financial or emotional."

In Brie's eyes, he saw the pain and trauma she had experienced since they parted. But he also saw her love for her daughter. *Their* daughter. He pressed two fingers to his forehead. "What have you told her about me?"

Brie shrugged. "Nothing yet."

He reached out a hand and touched the child's hair. It was silky and soft, though not as thick as her mother's. "Hello," he said quietly.

Danika sidled closer to Brie and put her thumb in her mouth, her eyes wide.

"It's okay, sweetie." Brie petted her. "Mr. V is our friend."

Vaughn raised an eyebrow? "Mr. V?"

"*Vaughn* is not easy for a toddler to say, though my daughter *is* super verbal. She can already name most of her alphabet letters—even if they're out of order."

"Why not *Daddy*?" He saw the flash of alarm that flitted across Brie's expressive sky-blue eyes.

"I don't think that's wise," she said quietly. "Not yet. No sense in confusing her with something that may be temporary."

He clenched his jaw, battling a host of conflicting emotions. "I want to see her."

"See her?" Brie's puzzlement was evident. "She's right in front of you."

"I want to see her while I'm here," he said, clarifying the notion that even now seemed foreign to him. "I want to spend time with her."

Brie's protective body language wasn't hard to read. She

curled an arm around her daughter's small waist, pulling the girl against her legs. "You told me you weren't going to have much free time while you're in Royal," she snapped, her expression stormy now.

Vaughn shook his head, smiling ruefully. "You have the damnedest way of throwing my words back in my face, don't you?"

His humor seemed to ease something in Brie. She didn't turn warm, but she seemed less defensive. Now she was just sad and wary. "I'll be honest, Vaughn," she said quietly. "My hope is that I'll eventually fall in love with a man who will want to adopt Nika. That would be best for all of us. I don't really want her to get attached to you."

Vaughn took the hit stoically, at least on the outside. How could he complain about Brie's assumptions when he himself had shown absolutely zero interest in settling down?

He'd had a crappy example for a father. If genetics were any indication, Vaughn was probably more like the old man than he cared to admit. But when he looked at this tiny little girl, something cracked inside his heart. Something ached. Something hurt like hell.

He and Brie had created this quiet, precious child. Whether he wanted it or not, fatherhood had come knocking. Quite literally.

"Will she let me hold her?"

Brie gnawed her lip. "Maybe not today. But soon. She'll warm up to you if you play with her."

"Play?" The word was not in his repertoire, not in this innocent context.

"You know. Help her build a tower. Talk to her doll. Anything."

He sure as hell wasn't going to play ventriloquist with the doll. Not with Brie watching. Instead, he picked up a blue cup and an orange cup and fit them together. "Will you give me the red one?" he asked, smiling at the little girl whose eyes matched the ones Vaughn saw in the mirror every morning.

Danika wriggled free from her mother's embrace and took a step in his direction. She studied the cups solemnly, then picked up the one he had requested. "Red," she said proudly, handing it to him.

Vaughn added it to the top of the tower, his throat tight. "Good job," he croaked. He'd never given much thought to replicating his DNA...to passing on a living legacy for another generation.

Perhaps he was overreacting. He wasn't a sentimental man. Just because a tiny sprite of a girl carried his genes didn't make him a father. Not really. He knew better than anyone that parenting was more than a onetime sperm donation. Buck Blackwood had taught him that.

Vaughn shifted his attention to Brie. She'd been watching the brief exchange between father and daughter with pained, cautious interest. If he was reading her correctly, she was torn. Brie wanted him to care about his daughter, but at the same time, she didn't want to make room for him in the child's life.

"Thank you for bringing her," he said. He wanted to do more, to say more, but he was still in shock. This news wouldn't be absorbed in a day or even a week. He had a baby—a toddler now. Somehow he had to figure this out. Could he bear to spend the rest of his life knowing that somewhere in Texas another man was sleeping with Brie and parenting Vaughn's baby?

He stood up abruptly, startling Danika. The child looked up at him towering over her, and her bottom lip trembled. "Mama," she said tearfully.

Brie scooped her daughter and stood, as well. "We should go," she said.

He stared at the two females. Now that the initial shock had worn off, he was able to focus on the woman, not the baby. "I do appreciate you coming. Thank you for being honest with me. And…" Would it be weird to say that motherhood suited her? Because it did. She looked good. Really good. Stunning, in fact. Her crimson top flattered her pale, creamy skin. Despite the many hours she had spent outside as a ranch hand at Blackwood Hollow, her complexion was flawless. "I'm glad to see you doing so well," he finished, feeling awkward.

Brie gave him a small smile, almost reluctantly, as pink tinged her cheeks. "You, too, Vaughn. I've read several articles about your company. You've accomplished a lot for your age. Your father must have been really proud of you."

He shook his head slowly. "Nope. Not even close. You remember him, surely. I don't think he cared about anyone but himself."

"That's pretty harsh."

"But accurate."

Brie stroked her daughter's hair. Something about that slow, tender motion mesmerized Vaughn. For a split second, he flashed back to being in bed with Brie, sated and happy, while she stroked his chest with that same, gentle touch.

The memory took his breath. His body hardened in an instant. Lust and passion roared in his veins, as if some ancient lock had been broken, some wild, destructive spirit set free.

He trembled with wanting her. But he couldn't seduce Brie for the hell of it, even if she was willing. There was another person in the mix now. Small but significant.

"I'd like to visit her at your house," he said. "Do you object?"

After a long, fraught moment, Brie shook her head. "No. That's fine. If you're free tomorrow night, you could have dinner with us and help with bedtime."

His libido revved again. Everyone knew what mommies and daddies did when the kids were finally in bed. "What time?"

"Five thirtyish?"

His eyes widened. He hadn't dined that early in years. But then again, an early dinner and the baby's early bedtime meant plenty of extra opportunity for Vaughn to hash things out with Brie.

He pulled a business card from his wallet. "Text me your address. I'll be there," he said.

After Brie gathered Danika's toys and snacks and said a stilted goodbye, Vaughn watched the small car disappear down the driveway. He exhaled. Had he been holding his breath? Trying to keep himself in check? The past half hour had winded him emotionally.

Suddenly, he needed to talk to someone. Though he preferred keeping his own counsel as a rule, his world had been knocked awry. Sophie would be the perfect confidante as long as she didn't have another social event right now.

Vaughn drove to his sister's house in Pine Valley on autopilot. It was a relief to see the driveway empty, indicating that there was no shower or bridal tea or any other nonsense going on.

Nigel Townshend opened the door. The Englishman stepped back and ushered Vaughn into the foyer. "Hello, Vaughn." He glanced at his watch. "Sophie is resting, but it's time for her to be up. Let me go get her."

"Is she ill?" Vaughn felt mildly alarmed. His sister was always bubbly and energetic.

"No, just tired." Nigel grimaced. "The wedding preparations have been nonstop. And to be honest, damned stressful at times. She hasn't been sleeping."

"Ah. Makes sense." Vaughn shoved his hands in his pockets and leaned against the door. "I realize we don't know each other well. Or at all, really. But I want you to know how glad I am that she found you. My sister deserves the best life has to offer. If you ever hurt her, I'll neuter you."

Nigel grinned. "Duly noted." He waved a hand. "Make yourself at home. She'll be down in a minute."

Vaughn wandered into the elegant living room and paced. Sophie had redecorated since last year. Though the decor was sophisticated, the furniture looked comfortable. Unfortunately, Vaughn was too wired to sit.

When Sophie appeared, Nigel wasn't with her. The other man was sharp. He must have recognized Vaughn's unspoken urgency.

Sophie yawned and shoveled her hair from her face. "Sorry," she said. "I'm not usually this lazy. The party lasted pretty late. I'm paying for the indulgence."

He kissed her cheek and led her to the sofa, but when Sophie sat, Vaughn couldn't. He resumed pacing the length of the room twice and then stopped to stare at her. "I have news," he said. "Brace yourself."

Sophie's eyes widened. "Okay. What is it?"

Somehow, his throat closed up. It was almost impossible to force the words from his lips. "I have a daughter. Brie told me today. I'm a father."

His sister's smile was sweet. Compassionate. "Then my guess was right. When I first saw Brie in town with her little girl, I wondered if the baby was yours. Why did she wait so long to tell you?"

"It's complicated." He jingled the keys in his pocket, his body rigid with nervous energy. "I don't know what to do. I don't have room in my schedule for a kid. I'm a workaholic. You know that. The whole reason Brie and I broke up was because she wanted a normal family. A simple, uncomplicated life. That's not something I can give." He pretended to study a picture on the wall. Would his sister judge him for his shortcomings? Was he a disappointment to her?

Sophie stood and hugged him from behind, resting her cheek on his back. "Don't be afraid to change."

He stiffened. Sophie had read the letter from his father, too. "I'm not afraid," he said automatically. "Maybe I just don't *want* to change."

"You have this persona you show the world, Vaughn, but I know better. My brother is sweet and honorable and has a huge heart."

He turned around and grinned. "You take that back. Where would I be if word got out that the head of Blackwood Energy Corporation had a heart? My reputation would be shot."

"Very funny." She paused and cocked her head. "So where does Brielle fit into all this?"

"She's my child's mother—nothing more. At this point she has to agree to my spending time with Danika, but that's it."

"And you really believe that?"

"Brie and I were over a long time ago. I know exactly what she thinks of me, and it isn't good."

"I'm more concerned about what you think of her."

Sophie's probing irritated him, but he had opened himself up to this personal intrusion by coming to his sister for advice. "Brie is a lovely, capable, independent woman. She doesn't want or expect anything from me. The fact that she's the mother of my child complicates things, but I can handle it."

"Have you thought about the fact that your daughter, your flesh and blood, has been disinherited?"

"Of course I have…from the moment I found out about the baby. I know I said I wasn't interested in being part of the suit with you and Kellan to challenge the will, but things have changed now. I'm going to confront Miranda and demand that Danika receive her fair share—my share."

"I'm afraid you've missed your opportunity," Sophie

said. "Miranda flew back to New York this morning. The Twitter feed for *Secret Lives of NYC Ex-Wives* was all over it."

Vaughn snorted. "Please tell me you're not an actual fan of that stupid show."

"It's not stupid. Don't be so narrow-minded."

"If it's actually any good, then I can't believe Miranda is involved."

"Maybe she thinks it's good press for her company and her charity. Besides, it's harmless fun."

"Nothing about Miranda Dupree is harmless."

Sophie shook her head slowly. "That's your biggest weakness, Vaughn Blackwood. You get locked on an idea and you don't want to let go, even when you're wrong."

Five

As soon as Vaughn left, Sophie grabbed her keys and purse and headed out the door.

Nigel called after her. "Where are you going?"

She waved at her gorgeous English hunk of a fiancé. "Running an errand. Won't be long."

Guilt gnawed at her, but she kept driving. If she had asked Nigel's opinion, or even Vaughn's, they both would have said the same thing. *Don't rock the boat. It's not your business. Stay out of it, Sophie.*

Pooh. Men never understood the really important things in life until you beat them over the head with them. Sophie was an *aunt*! She wasn't going to sit on this news for a single minute longer.

It wasn't like she and Brielle were strangers. They weren't what you would call bosom buddies, but Royal was a small place—especially when someone was working on your father's ranch. When Vaughn and Brie had been dating, Sophie had interacted with her brother's girlfriend on a fairly regular basis.

The breakup and Brie's subsequent move had put an end to that budding female friendship. But today was a new day.

Sophie parked in front of the neat blue-and-white cottage Brie had been renting since her return to Royal. It was small but charming. When Sophie rang the doorbell, Brie answered almost immediately, the baby on her hip.

"Sophie." Brie's eyes widened. "What a surprise."

Sophie couldn't help herself. She reached out and touched the child's pale blond hair. "Vaughn told me," she muttered.

"He did? I wasn't even sure he had decided to claim her."

"How could he not? Look at those eyes. I've seen you and the baby around town and guessed she might be a Blackwood, but I was never close enough to see the eyes. That moss-green color is not common, you know."

"I do know. Would you like to come in?"

"Yes, please. She's gorgeous, Brie."

"Thank you. Sorry for the mess. I just fed her a grilled cheese, and I haven't had time to clean up the kitchen."

"Don't be silly. I'm family. Will she let me hold her?"

"You can try."

Sophie summoned her most winsome smile. "Hi, baby girl. I'm your aunt Sophie. Would you like to play with my necklace?" The chunky silver and cobalt beads were just the right size to fascinate a tiny child.

Danika held out her arms, and Sophie scooped her close, her heart melting. "You're so lucky, Brie. She's an angel."

Brie laughed and began loading the dishwasher. "Most of the time." She paused. "Does Vaughn know you're here?"

"Oh no. I'm sure he wouldn't approve. My dear brother likes to keep all the parts of his life in neat little boxes."

"Ouch." Brie looked chagrined.

"Sorry. I don't mean to be rude. But you must know how he is."

"I threw him a curve today. A huge one. I'm sure he's struggling with the information."

"You could say that."

Brie paled. "Is he super upset?"

"No. I'd call him flummoxed. I don't think he knows *how* to react."

"To be clear, I didn't ask him for anything. I just thought he should know. One day Nika may want to find out who he is."

"You're assuming Vaughn won't be around as an active part of her life."

"I am, yes. He's made no secret of the fact that he doesn't want to be a father."

"But now he is one. Things change. People change."

Brie folded her arms across her waist and leaned against the counter. "I'm not sure they do. Vaughn is a stubborn Texas male and set in his ways."

"Give him a chance, Brielle. He may surprise you."

"Maybe."

"You don't want him to change?"

"It's not that. I don't want my daughter to become a pawn in the Blackwood family dynamics. No offense, but you rich people have some serious issues."

Sophie laughed. "Fair enough." She snuggled Nika, giving her a theatrically loud kiss on the cheek, making the child giggle. "I have a favor to ask, Brie. It's very important."

Brie's eyes rounded. "Oh?"

"I've wanted all along to have a flower girl in my wedding. But everybody told me kids are too unpredictable. That they would be an extra layer of complication I didn't need."

"I won't argue with that. I've seen several weddings

where tiny ring bearers and flower girls dissolved into tantrums."

"I don't care. I want my niece to walk down the aisle in front of me."

Brie winced. "Oh gosh, Sophie. I don't think that's a good idea at all. The wedding is almost here, and Vaughn would have a coronary. No matter what he decides about being part of Danika's life, I'm darned sure he doesn't want to parade her in front of everyone he knows at the wedding."

"We don't have to announce that she's my niece. You and I are friends. Maybe I just asked you because you have a sweet little girl exactly the right age."

"I'm beginning to see that Vaughn's stubborn streak is genetic."

"Please say yes. I'll take care of her dress and everything. Size two?"

"Are you sure, Sophie? I would feel terrible if my baby ruined your wedding."

"Can't happen. The only thing that could ruin my day is if Nigel changed his mind. And that's not in the cards." She smiled smugly. "He adores me."

Brie grinned, though it looked a little forced. "Lucky you."

By the time Sophie departed and Brie got Danika in bed and to sleep, Brie was exhausted. The highly emotional day had left her with a host of conflicted feelings. While she was glad Vaughn wasn't averse to knowing his daughter, this new relationship would put Brie in dangerous territory.

It was one thing for a single woman to have a crazy fling with a gorgeous millionaire. But Brie was a mother now. She had responsibilities. Even if her libido went crazy when Vaughn was nearby, she had to keep her priorities straight.

Still, all the lectures in the world couldn't erase her excitement and anticipation about the following evening. She slept restlessly and barely made it to work on time the next morning. Fortunately, her schedule was tight. Her furry patients and their owners were demanding.

Though she loved what she did, the day felt like it was about a million hours long. By the time she made it home, she had only forty-five minutes to get ready. She had put a roast in the slow cooker that morning along with carrots and potatoes. It was a simple meal for a man accustomed only to the best, but Danika liked it, and that was all that mattered.

Since the babysitter was still on the clock, Brie was able to grab a quick shower and change into jeans and a soft, navy V-neck cotton sweater. She added small pearl stud earrings that had been a twenty-first-birthday present from her parents along with a dainty silver chain that supported a third pearl only slightly larger than the others.

It was a far more casual outfit than the one she had worn to take Danika to meet her father. Adding the jewelry dressed it up enough to be presentable for an evening at home…with the man who had gotten her pregnant.

Unbidden, her mind went back to all those long, lonely months before Nika was born. Brie had yearned for Vaughn so badly she thought her heart would break. The only way she had disciplined herself was to repeat over and over that the Vaughn she *wanted* him to be was not the real one. And the man he was would never be willing to change—certainly not just to please her.

She needed a lover in her life who was devoted to her and willing to do anything to make the relationship work. Vaughn was virile and incredibly masculine and phenomenally talented in bed, but he didn't *need* anyone.

That was ultimately why Brie had walked away. Long before she knew she was going to have a child, she recognized that sooner or later, Vaughn Blackwood would break her heart.

Though *Brie* had been the one to leave, the breakup was no less painful. After she left Royal, she had planned to start dating immediately…to quickly wipe the memories of Vaughn from her head and her heart.

The plan was flawed from the beginning. She found out she was pregnant, and suddenly, Vaughn was a part of her in a way she could never erase. When the baby was born, the invisible intimacy grew more intense.

All those nights Brie nursed Nika at her breast, her mind was free to wander. In her fantasies, Vaughn was there in the bed beside her, his gaze warm and loving as he stroked his daughter's downy head…as he gently kissed Brie's cheek and told her how much he loved her.

Those daydreams, those fictional vignettes, kept Brie going. It probably wasn't healthy. But it was all she had.

With one last glance at her reflection in the bathroom mirror, she cataloged every bit of stress and excitement duking it out in her stomach. Why did Vaughn want to spend time with Danika? He'd made it very clear over the months he and Brie had dated that he was a free agent.

Maybe tonight was nothing more than simple curiosity.

When Brie made her way to the living room, the babysitter was standing beside the front door holding Nika and chatting with Vaughn. When the older woman said her goodbyes, Brie tensed. She wasn't sure how to play this.

Vaughn took the decision out of her hands. Casually, as though they hadn't been separated by two years and countless miles, he leaned forward, cupped her face in his big, warm hands and kissed her on the forehead. "Hello, Brie. I like what you've done with the house."

The affectionate greeting flustered her. She didn't trust his good humor.

"Thank you. I was lucky to find a suitable rental so close to my office."

Boring. Something about this reunion made her gauche and awkward. She felt as if this moment was some kind of test, and she was failing miserably.

She wanted to roll back the clock, fling her arms around Vaughn and kiss him until he was dizzy with wanting. What followed next would be good for both of them. For the moment, at least.

But that wasn't going to happen.

Swallowing her disappointment that Vaughn seemed far more calm about this shared meal than she was, she managed a smile. "Dinner's almost ready. Would you like to open the wine?"

"Of course. If you'll point me to the corkscrew and crystal, I'll do the honors."

Brie set Danika in a quiet corner of the kitchen and gave her a wooden spoon and a plastic mixing bowl. It was a combination guaranteed to keep the child happy for at least fifteen minutes.

Vaughn poured the merlot as promised and handed Brie a glass. "To surprises," he said, his expression enigmatic.

Her throat was tight, but she managed to swallow. "To surprises." She paused. "I don't mean to disrupt your life. I hope you know that. And hopefully, this won't create too many complications for you. It might be awkward if you lived here, but you don't."

She studied him while he sipped his wine, his gaze downcast as if he were studying the shine on his expensive Italian leather dress shoes. His dark slacks and pristine white shirt were topped with a tweedy sport coat that matched his thick brown hair.

And that square jaw. *Oh, lordy.* She remembered pressing kisses across Vaughn's face and along that gorgeous chin.

At the moment, he leaned casually against the cabinet,

his long legs crossed at the ankle. He swirled his wine and studied the resultant pattern as if it held answers she couldn't give him.

Finally, he looked up. "I don't live here, that's true. But Royal is my home. And Danika is my child. I have some opinions on the matter, as it happens."

Brie stiffened. She heard the veiled threat clearly. Now that she had involved Vaughn, he wasn't going to quietly disappear. Questions hovered on her lips, but she restrained herself. It was almost impossible to win a battle of wits with Vaughn. With the full day she'd put in, she was physically tired—and all the fretting she'd done over this dinner had her emotionally exhausted. Needless to say, she was not at her best, not to mention the fact that she had a meal to get on the table.

"I'm sure you do," she muttered. "But Nika will start fussing if I don't feed her soon. When she's ready to eat, she's ready."

He nodded slowly. "Very well. My opinions will keep for the moment. What can I do to help?"

She shot him a startled glance. The Vaughn Blackwood she remembered rarely frequented the kitchen. He was the least domesticated man she knew.

Her skepticism must have been visible. His wry smile took him from handsome to heartbreaking. "Do I seem so incompetent to you, Brie?"

She weighed her words. "Not incompetent. More like uninterested. And that's fine," she said quickly. "I don't need any help with the meal. Just keep an eye on the baby, please."

She worked quickly. The small house didn't have a formal dining room. But the kitchen was fairly large and accommodated the slightly scarred oak table the landlord provided per the "mostly furnished" portion of her lease.

Brie set out neutral place mats and the brightly colored Fiestaware that had been her grandmother's.

Soon, everything was on the table, including a spinach salad with warm bacon dressing and the yeast rolls she had purchased at a local bakery on her lunch break. She scooped up the baby, washed Nika's hands and popped her in her high chair.

Vaughn watched the entire exercise in silence, waiting to seat Brie. His innate courtesy brought him far too close. His warm breath brushed her cheek. "Are you comfortable?" he asked, scooting the chair an additional inch.

Brie squirmed inwardly. Was he joking? The last thing she wanted to do was eat dinner right now. He was too handsome, too tempting. Too everything…

Six

Vaughn wasn't comfortable, not in the least. He'd been half-hard since he walked in the front door and saw his ex-lover. He had vivid memories of making love to Brie, her beautiful body naked, wearing nothing but that single-pearl necklace.

Was the jewelry choice intentional? Was Brie trying to spark a reunion? It seemed unlikely. Despite that, she looked so damned sexy and seductive tonight, he could barely remember why they had argued and split up. Until his gaze landed on the toddler happily shoving mashed carrots and potatoes into her mouth.

Brie hadn't been kidding about the kid's appetite.

He hadn't thought he was hungry, but the aroma of roast beef and all the trimmings made his stomach growl. "I didn't know you were such a good cook," he said. Now that he thought about it, the two of them had never done anything so ordinary as enjoying dinner and a movie at home. When their affair was at its peak, he had wined and dined her at the finest restaurants around when he wasn't making love to her under the inky Texas night sky.

Then it was over.

Brie's smile seemed genuine. "Thanks. This is an easy meal. I try to feed her healthy stuff, but I'll admit I sometimes resort to chicken nuggets on days when I have to work late."

"You shouldn't have to work at all," he said. "She's my child. I can pay for her support entirely."

Now his dinner companion bristled visibly. "I *like* my job. Not more than my child, obviously. And I'll admit, it would be a luxury to stay at home with her. But being a vet is what I've trained for, what I've dreamed of since I was a kid. Moms can be moms and do other things, too. This is the twenty-first century, Vaughn. Try to keep up."

Her snappish response amused rather than insulted him. "I'm as evolved as the next man. But even you have to admit that money makes life easier."

Both of her eyebrows went up at the same moment. "*Even me?* What does that mean?"

He shrugged. "When we were dating, you didn't like me showering you with gifts. You said it made you feel weird. Like I was paying for your affections."

"I had a chip on my shoulder about your money. It's true." Her cheeks took on a rosy hue, making her look younger and more vulnerable. "I was a ranch hand on your father's property. Literally no one thought we were a good match. And they were right."

"Maybe they were, maybe they weren't. But we were talking about money. Regardless of what relationship I have with my daughter, my moral obligation is to support her financially. I certainly have the means. There's no reason the two of you should ever want for anything."

Brie's gaze narrowed. "You're forgetting how well I know you, Vaughn Blackwood. In that scenario, you'd be expecting me to do things *your* way as soon as I cashed the first check. You can set up a college fund for her. And we can talk about things like insurance. But Danika and I are fine."

"The offer stands," he said calmly. "Child support aside, there's a bigger angle to consider."

"Oh?"

"I want Nika to have every opportunity to receive what's due her when it comes to my father's holdings. I've said loudly that I don't care about my father's money, and that's true. Danika changes everything, though. Kellan and Sophie have already started a legal process to challenge the will. I wasn't planning to join them, but I won't disqualify myself if it means possibly securing Danika's future. Her university studies, a wedding one day. She's a Blackwood. She deserves to inherit a portion of her grandfather's estate."

Brie set her fork on her plate and stared at him. "I've never really thought of her as Buck's grandchild. That's odd, isn't it? I think of her as *my* baby and your daughter. It's been just the two of us, me and my little one. Until Sophie showed up yesterday, I honestly hadn't realized that your siblings might care about her, too."

"Sophie came here?"

"Yes. She wants Danika to be a flower girl in the wedding. I told her it was your call. Sophie said even if you don't want to claim Nika just yet—or ever—she could simply say to anyone who asks that she and I are friends, and that I agreed to let Danika play a part in the festivities."

Vaughn frowned. Did his own sister think he would be such a moral coward as to hide the fact that he was Danika's father? "The child is mine. I'll do my duty by her, regardless. I won't let anyone say I've shirked my duty."

Brie wrinkled her nose. "Lovely."

"I'm sensing sarcasm."

"What do you expect?" Stormy blue eyes judged him and found him wanting. "The only reason I decided to tell you about Nika is that she may seek you out one day. Emotionally, if for no other reason. Little girls need their daddies. If nothing else, they should know who their daddies are."

"I thought you had plans to get married." It was a cheap shot under the circumstances, but he was in the midst of a battle.

Brie blinked and speared a carrot. She looked at it blankly as if she had forgotten they were all having dinner. "I do. I want to. But I can't guarantee I'll find someone."

Vaughn disagreed. Even if Brie and Danika were a package deal, it was a foregone conclusion that any number of men would want to wrangle a spot in Brie Gunderson's bed. Vaughn certainly had at one time. He'd been obsessed with her.

Echoes of that maddening physical insanity swirled in his gut. It had been sexual attraction back then, nothing more. And though the pheromones might still be the same, he and Brie were different people now.

The adults finished their dinner mostly in silence. Nika babbled constantly. Even Vaughn was beginning to pick out words and phrases. And while he was hardly an expert on toddlers, he thought her vocabulary was wider than he would have expected. She really was smart…he could already tell. Pride swelled in his chest. Totally ridiculous, of course. Even so, he was damn proud that he had fathered such a delightful child.

Without warning, the baby chortled and flung her arms wide, hitting Vaughn square in the chest with a blob of mushy carrots. For a split second, nothing happened. Danika's eyes opened wide, as if she realized she had broken some unspoken rule.

Brielle, on the other hand, burst out laughing. She laughed so hard her face turned red, and her cheeks were wet.

"I'm sorry," she gasped, trying to compose herself and failing miserably. "If you could see the look on your face…"

Vaughn stood and grabbed a paper towel, wetting it and dabbing the front of his shirt. "I'm glad you find me so entertaining," he muttered.

When he began unbuttoning his shirt, every trace of amusement fled from Brie's face. "What are you doing?" she asked. The last word came out as more of a gasp.

He unfastened his cuffs one at a time. "I thought it was obvious. I'm taking off my shirt so you can help me get the stain out. This one is brand-new, damn it. And it's one of my favorites."

Brie stood suddenly, almost knocking over her chair. "No, no, no," she sputtered. "Stop that." She shoved his hands away and tried to pull the sides of the shirt together. "It can't be your favorite, surely. It's nothing but a white shirt. I'll buy you another."

He'd been about to tug the tail of the shirt from his pants, but now he stopped. When Brie's fingers touched his skin, he froze as his erection came to life again. He swallowed. "Does my bare chest bother you that much, Brie?"

She was so close to him he could smell the tantalizing scent of her light perfume. Something with roses and magic and other things designed to make a man go mad with lust.

Her bottom lip trembled visibly. "Of course not," she said unconvincingly. "But I can't have a half-naked man wandering around my house."

"Why not?" He moved slowly, waiting to see if she would protest. But her gaze locked on his, and she leaned forward the slightest bit. He tugged her a few feet away, out of Nika's line of vision, and kissed Brie's chin, moved below her ear for another kiss. Then one cheek and the other.

Brie stood like a deer in the forest hoping a hunter won't notice its presence. Her chest was rising and falling so rapidly she might be in danger of hyperventilating. One of her hands gave up the battle to realign the sides of his shirt and instead flattened against the center of his rib cage.

"There's a baby here," she said. "I don't want her to see you like this." She stroked his collarbone slowly, clearly unaware that she was driving him crazy.

"Are you worried about *Nika* or you, Brie?"

Her mouth opened and shut. "You know the answer to that," she said wryly. "Kiss me, Vaughn."

He settled his lips over hers, groaning inwardly. God, she was sweet. His tongue stroked hers coaxingly, feeling and hearing the little catch in her breath.

Suddenly, the calendar rolled backward, dragging them toward a time when nothing had mattered but the physical pleasure they could find together. Brie was warm and soft in his arms. He shuddered hard, as if hit by an electric shock. The kiss went from sweet to carnal in a white-hot flash of heat.

Brie kissed him back. Unmistakably. Her arms linked around his neck. Her teeth nipped his bottom lip, then suckled it.

His knees threatened to buckle. He reached for the button on her jeans, intent on only one thing. He had to have her.

When his fingers brushed the downy skin of her belly, Brie screeched and jumped back, nearly falling. She covered her cheeks with her hands, her expression aghast. "Are you mad?" she whispered. "The baby."

Danika, in her total innocence, had no idea that the adults were contemplating doing naughty things on the kitchen table. Or at least *one* of the adults was. Vaughn's heart galloped like a Derby winner. "I forgot," he said. Then he winced when he heard the words aloud. What kind of parent *forgot his own kid*?

Brie backed away another few inches, her gaze not meeting his. "I have to bathe her and get her ready for bed. Make yourself comfortable in the living room. We can… talk when she's asleep. And please button your damn shirt."

The tiny pause before the word *talk* gave him hope. Was Brie thinking the same things he was thinking? "I can help bathe her," he said, wanting to hurry things along.

Brie shook her head. "No. She's slippery and small. You're not used to it…"

"How can I ever learn if I don't practice? I was pretty good at holding on to a football when I quarterbacked in college."

A wry smile twisted Brie's lips. "If you're comparing our little toddler to a piece of sporting equipment, I have a feeling you're not ready for the nighttime routine."

He winced. "Bad choice of words." Perhaps he needed to back off and give Brie some breathing room. That little *moment* between them had clearly rattled her. It sure as hell had rattled him.

He held up his hands. "Fine. But do I at least have permission to load the dishwasher?"

She looked uneasy. "I suppose so. But it's not necessary."

"I think I can handle it."

Brie scooped up her daughter, brushed what looked like a pound of crumbs into the high chair and stripped the baby down to her diaper. Danika laughed and pulled her mother's hair.

Again, Brie gazed at Vaughn with hesitation. "Go," he said. "I've got this."

Moments later, he heard water running in the hall bathroom. The house was small. Sounds carried. The conversation between mother and daughter was strangely sweet. Completely ordinary, but tender and heartwarming.

As he went about his task on autopilot, he couldn't help thinking about all the nights like this he had missed. Anger stirred again, mixed with searing regret. No one was to blame for what had happened. That didn't make it any less painful.

Would anything have changed if he had known Brie was pregnant? It was a difficult question to answer. Two years ago he had spent a great deal of time pushing her away, making it clear that he wasn't interested in a serious or lasting relationship. He had told himself he was being honest. A straight shooter.

The truth wasn't so clear-cut. When Brie broke up with him and disappeared, he had been forced to face up to his own duplicity. Why had he let her go? And worse, why had he really gotten involved with her? Had he gone out with her initially to get in his father's face? To make the old man angry? One of the Blackwood heirs consorting with a ranch hand?

The fact that Vaughn couldn't say a definitive no made him ashamed. With most of the kitchen tidy, he made his way down the hall and leaned against the door frame of the bathroom. Brie was on her knees beside the tub trying to shampoo the baby's hair.

Danika was having none of it. She wriggled and squirmed and then howled when she got soap in her eyes. Brie shot him a glance over her shoulder. "Hand me that towel, will you?"

He reached for the white terry cloth with the yellow duck-face hood. "Is it always like this?"

After wiping the baby's eyes and rinsing the lather from her hair, Brie leaned down and picked up the wet, constantly-in-motion child and wrapped her in the towel. The dead lift made *Vaughn's* back hurt. And he wasn't even helping.

She nodded. "Usually. Nika loves playing in the bath

with all her foam toys, but when I have to get serious with the soap, she's never happy about it."

Vaughn followed the two females into the nursery. The walls were pale green with thin yellow stripes. He wondered if the paint job had come with the house or if Brielle was one of those moms who was not a fan of all pink for girls all the time.

When the toddler was diapered and clad in soft one-piece pajamas, Brie sat her in the crib and handed her a teething ring.

"Whew," she said, fanning herself. "That exercise burns a lot of calories."

Vaughn stared at her, his heart pounding. "Your shirt is all wet," he said hoarsely. "I can see…"

Brie looked down at her chest. The red in her cheeks deepened. Though the navy fabric was not at all transparent, her puckered nipples were outlined beneath the soft cotton.

"I'm cold," she said. "I should change."

"You just told me in so many words that you were hot."

Her chin jutted, her eyes flashing. "And now I'm cold. What's your point?"

He took her wrist and reeled her in. "No point, beautiful mama. Except that you still want me, don't you?"

Seven

Brie could have pulled away. Vaughn's grip on her wrist was loose. But she went to him so easily, he must have thought she was sex starved. She would never tell him she hadn't had sex with anyone since he'd made her pregnant. That was too much ammunition for a man who was already shockingly arrogant.

He gripped a handful of her hair and tipped back her head so he could sink his teeth into her throat. "I want to strip you bare," he said roughly. "Your breasts are bigger. I can feel them. God, Brie, it's been an eternity since I've been inside you."

The gruff, carnally explicit words turned her into a shuddering mess. She was so desperate for him, her whole body trembled. Suddenly, they were racing toward a precipice she had sworn never to face again. This was madness, pure and simple.

Drawing on every ounce of strength she possessed, she pulled away and wiped her mouth. "Excuse me," she said, her tone ridiculously formal. "I need to rock the baby to sleep."

Vaughn was visibly shaken. He took several deep breaths and raked his hands through his hair. "I can do it," he said gruffly. "I won't drop her, I swear."

She couldn't read him. Not at all. Other than the lust. That was clear. And yet every time she redirected his focus to Nika, he jumped to help with the baby. Was he curious about this whole fatherhood thing? Was he testing the waters?

"Fine," she said abruptly. "I'll be in my bedroom if you need me for anything."

One dark eyebrow went up. Green eyes sizzled with heated amusement. "What a lovely offer."

"Not that, cocky man. You know what I mean." She escaped before she could say something else stupid.

Grabbing a shirt from her dresser drawer, she hid in the bathroom to do the quick change. Even her bra was wet. When she removed it and didn't bother to replace it with a dry one, she knew she was making a choice.

Who could blame her? She hadn't felt a man's touch on her body in almost three years. It had been so long she wasn't sure she remembered what it was like to be a woman consumed with arousal.

When she was decently covered in a fresh shirt, she returned to her daughter's room and lingered quietly in the doorway. Vaughn was reading the toddler a book. Nika must have asked for it. Her eyes were heavy. She nestled trustingly against her father's chest.

A baby couldn't possibly know the truth, could she? Was there some instinctive connection Brie didn't understand? Was the power of blood strong enough to bind child to man?

Brie kept silent, loath to intrude on the scene. Vaughn wasn't entirely comfortable. She could see that. But he plodded on. As crazy as it sounded, his clumsy rendering of the story made Brie's heart turn over. At least he was trying.

When the story wound to an end and Vaughn closed the book, Brie stepped into the room. "I'll take her now. Why don't you go grab yourself a drink and relax?"

He nodded, his expression inscrutable. Moments later, Brie was alone with her daughter. Danika's body was limp, her breathing heavy. There was really nothing left to do but lay her in bed and tiptoe out of the room.

In the hallway, Brie leaned against the wall and put a hand to her heart, trying to still the wild thumping. Nothing was going to happen right now. Not until she made up her mind.

Vaughn was a gentleman to the core, despite his libido. He wouldn't force himself on her.

But what if the tables were turned?

She found him in the living room sprawled on one end of the sofa, his expression moody as he channel surfed. For safety's sake, she chose an armchair several feet away. "It's still early," she said. "I'm sure you have things to do. Thanks for dropping by. You're welcome any time."

He shot her a fulminating glare. "You don't have to lay it on so thick, Brie. If you don't want me here, I can take a hint."

For a moment she thought she might have bruised his feelings, but that was absurd. "I don't think it's wise for us to be alone together." There. That was plain enough.

He sat up straight and tossed the remote aside. "So because I noticed your nipples, you're kicking me out?"

She crossed her arms over her chest. "Don't be absurd. You wanted to spend time with your daughter. And you did. Now she's asleep. End of story."

His expression softened. "You're not wearing a bra, Brielle, even though you were before you changed clothes.

What is a man like me supposed to take from a thing like that?"

Chewing her lip, she stared anywhere but at him, feeling her face flame. "It was wet."

"Ah. And you only own the one?"

He had her there. Why was she being such a coward? She wanted to have sex with him. When she'd omitted the bra, she thought she knew where the night would go. But she was allowed to change her mind. She didn't want to get sucked into his masculine force field again. She couldn't let herself be vulnerable to his charming, rakish ways.

"Fine," she snapped. "I'm not wearing a bra. Big deal. Lots of women take their bras off when they get home from work."

He rolled to his feet, all six feet plus of him. "Do you want me as much as I want you, Brie? You don't have to be afraid to say it." The taunting tone in his voice lit her temper.

"I'm *not* scared of you, Vaughn Blackwood. Feel free to go."

The fact that she took two steps in his direction dampened her dismissal.

Vaughn's shirt still hung open. In fact, it barely clung to his shoulders. She could see almost every inch of his tanned, muscular, yummy-enough-to-lick chest.

The arrogance faded. His smile was kind now, alarmingly so. "I'm not going anywhere, sweet Brie. Not unless you walk over to that front door, unlock it and tell me—unequivocally—to leave. Are you going to do that?"

If he had been a jerk about it, she might have followed through on kicking him out. But he was letting her see how much he wanted to stay. That sincerity, in the end, tipped the scales.

She sighed. "It's only seven forty-five. Isn't that too early for hanky-panky?"

He chuckled. "I'd say it's about two and a half years too late. I've missed you in my bed, woman."

"We'll be in mine this time," she warned. "It's only a queen, and the mattress sucks."

"I think I can handle it."

"And we both agree this means nothing." Somehow, it was important to lay that out there.

"Whatever you say." He shrugged out of his shirt and tossed it aside.

Dear. Sweet. Lord. Gooseflesh broke out all over her body. Erogenous zones she had forgotten about beat out a chorus of pulsing, erotic intent.

"I, uh…"

He grinned widely. "The Brie I remember didn't used to be so shy."

"I'm not shy," she protested. "I'm just not sure of the protocol for scratch-an-itch sex."

Without warning, he scooped her up in his arms and strode toward the hall. "Well, for one thing," he said, breathing a tiny bit harder than her weight should have warranted, "it doesn't usually get off to such a slow start."

She laid her head against his chest, feeling weepy for no particular reason, so she cracked a joke to lighten the mood. "As long as you get *me* off, big guy, I won't complain." This was what she had missed…what she wanted and needed. Laughter and verbal sparring with the man who had been such a pivotal part of her life.

But that relationship was over now. Whatever was left was so much less than what she had once hoped to have in a partner.

He kicked open her bedroom door and tossed her onto the center of the mattress. "Don't go anywhere." With impressive speed, he stripped out of his clothes. When he was bare-ass naked, she inhaled sharply. Vaughn Blackwood was one big, bad, gorgeous male.

His wicked smile made her squirm. As he sprawled onto the bed beside her, he began unfastening buttons and such.

Brie lay perfectly still, her fingers clenched in the covers. Every muscle in her body was rigid.

At one point, Vaughn stopped and looked at her with a little frown creasing the spot between his brows. "Brie? Are you sure this is what you want?"

She forced herself to relax. "Yes," she whispered. "Sorry. I'm just nervous."

He leaned over her on one elbow. "Why, sweet thing? It's like riding a bike." His droll comparison was meant to make her smile, but she was too tense.

"Bicycle crashes hurt. I don't want to get hurt again. I need you to know that I don't expect empty words or romantic gestures. All I want from you is an orgasm or two. So don't get the wrong impression. We're not picking up where we left off."

His frown deepened. "Are you finished?" he asked, his green-eyed gaze glacial.

"With what?"

"Reading me the fine print."

She had made him angry. Too bad. There had to be ground rules. Otherwise, having her baby's father back in her life would destroy Brie. They weren't playing house.

"I'm finished," she said.

He moved half on top of her with an audible groan. The man was fully aroused and ready to go.

So was Brie. Her body wept for him. The fact that she now had stretch marks and a stomach that was no longer taut and firm made her self-conscious for about thirty seconds. After that, Vaughn's voracious appetite told her more loudly than words that he wanted her exactly as she was.

He spread her thighs, poised to enter her.

"Wait," she cried. "Condoms?"

Vaughn seemed shocked. "You're not on birth control?"

"No. Single moms with full-time jobs don't have much time for extracurricular activities. Sorry. I wasn't expecting this."

His hunger for her blazed in his eyes, making her shiver. "Neither was I," he grumbled, "but I do have one condom in my wallet." He retrieved the protection and rolled it on.

The fleeting disappointment Brie felt at knowing this was a one-shot event amazed her. Was she really so lost to reason? Apparently, the answer was yes.

When he entered her, reality narrowed to Vaughn's face—his fierce, brilliant green eyes—the flash of white teeth when he smiled. The labored sound of his breathing.

In that moment when their bodies joined completely, flesh to flesh, heart to heart, there was a hush in the room. Almost as if everything that had been out of kilter in Brie's world finally settled into place. Such thinking was self-defeating, but she couldn't shake the notion that this man was her soul mate.

How pathetic was that?

Thinking and reasoning were a lost cause, anyway. All she wanted to do right now was *feel*. And heaven help her, there were *so* many feelings. His skin was hot against hers, his breath warm on her cheek. When he buried his face in the curve of her neck and groaned, the sound reverberated throughout her body.

She loved making him lose control, always had. In the past, they had made love often two and three times a day. She'd had no way of knowing precisely when he actually made her pregnant. She used to imagine which time it had been. Where they were. How it had felt.

The result of their passion lay sleeping just down the hall. Brie and Vaughn had created that—how perfect, how wonderful, how unbearably poignant.

She dragged her attention back to the present, more than content to live in the moment, at least for now. A lock of Vaughn's hair had fallen across his damp forehead. She pushed it back, so close to him she could see the tiny flecks of amber in his deep-emerald irises.

"I've missed being with you," she whispered. Maybe later she would regret her honesty, but it was true.

He kissed her again, bruising her lips, thrusting his tongue against hers in desperation, the same desperation she felt. "God, yes."

He felt huge and hard inside her. Intimidating. In charge. But she wanted this. More than anything. She wasn't afraid of Vaughn Blackwood. Not at all.

Nothing he had ever said or done to her had made her fear his physical domination. Despite his size and the fact that he outweighed her significantly, his care with her during their lovemaking—past and present—made her feel safe and cherished even in the midst of their wildest passion.

Then, in a flash, it was over. They were both too close to the edge, both too needy to make it last.

Vaughn cursed ruefully. "Sorry," he muttered. "Were you…did I…" His uncustomary awkwardness surprised her.

"I'm good." And physically, she was. Emotionally? The weirdness was back. Two years apart. A baby. A man who wanted to be free.

Tears stung her eyes.

Vaughn nuzzled his face between her breasts. "It's not enough," he said hoarsely. "I want more."

"We don't have any more condoms."

She saw on his face that he had forgotten. "There are other ways," he whispered, licking her nipple until it budded hard and tight. "Why don't I go clean up and then we'll improvise?"

When he separated their bodies, Brie felt the disconnect as a physical pain. "Okay." She should have said an emphatic no. Any smart woman would have. But Brie was caught up in an erotic web of longing and need. "I'll wait for you."

Eight

Vaughn staggered into Brie's tiny hallway bathroom, hoping she hadn't noticed that his legs were rubbery. He felt drunk. Out of control. Completely off his game.

Was he insane to stay the night and keep fooling around? They had no more protection. None. He couldn't slide inside her warm, tight body and empty himself in spasms of intense pleasure.

He was no teenage kid willing to come any way he could manage. A grown man had needs.

But if the alternative to full sexual contact with his lover was to walk out of this house right now, he couldn't do it. Not when Brie had finally burst back into his life.

Vaughn dealt with the condom and washed up, finishing by splashing water in his face. When he looked in the mirror, his eyes glittered with strong emotion.

Was it exhilaration he saw? Simple lust? How could a man not understand his own responses?

He needed Brie. He wanted her. Nothing beyond tonight mattered. He would deal with the future later.

When he returned to the bedroom, he found Brie huddled up against the headboard with the sheet pulled to her chin. Her eyes widened as her gaze dropped to his erection. Was it excitement or fear he saw in her baby blue irises?

He joined her on the bed. "I won't do anything you don't like, Brie."

"That's what I'm afraid of." Her wry smile touched him.

The note of humor defused some of the tension in the room but did nothing to reduce his hunger for her. Slowly, he dragged the sheet away. Even though he'd already memorized the feel of her body against his, there was nothing he could do to muffle his sharp inhalation at the view. The sight of her was a punch to the gut. He wrapped two hands around her ankle and slowly pulled her down in the bed.

"Turn over," he said softly.

After a moment's hesitation, she did as he asked, her arms stretched over her head.

Now he didn't have to disguise his reactions and his intent. Lord, she was beautiful. Her body was lithe and strong, her waist narrow above flared hips that had cradled their baby.

He put two hands on her ass and massaged her heart-shaped backside. Brie made a tiny noise, but she didn't try to stop him. Her skin was soft and smooth.

Though he wanted to pounce and gobble her up, he focused on giving her pleasure. Moving his hands slowly, he kneaded her tense muscles from waist to shoulders, coaxing her body into limp surrender. She worked hard. For tonight, he wanted to make her forget everything but how good it felt to be naked in bed with a lover. With him.

The more Brie responded to his massage, the harder he got. *She* might be relaxed, but this exercise was having the opposite effect on Vaughn. He changed positions and started on her thighs and calves.

His breathing roughened. His hands shook. When he couldn't bear it a second more, he rolled her onto her back and kissed her with long, slow, drugging kisses.

He came perilously close to sliding inside her without protection. His arousal was a living, breathing ache. Doggedly, he clamped down on his carnal impulses. He'd promised they could improvise. He was a man of his word.

When he parted her legs and kissed the inside of her thigh, Brie squeaked in shock. "Relax, sweetheart. You'll ruin the effects of the massage."

Her fingers clenched in the sheet. "How can I relax with you doing that?"

They had often enjoyed this game in the past. While the act embarrassed her initially, experience said that she'd warm up to it quickly. He knew exactly how to give her what she wanted. In minutes, she was crying out his name and arching into his caress.

With her shoulders pressed to the mattress and her hips lifting to his touch, she came beautifully. He could have watched her forever…held her forever.

He cuddled her against his body, warming her chilled limbs. "Good?" he asked, though the question was perhaps self-serving.

She nodded sleepily, nuzzling his hair-roughened chest. "Oh yeah. As soon as I can breathe again, I'll return the favor."

He could have said no. She was a single mom with a small child and a full-time job. Brie needed her sleep.

But apparently Vaughn was a selfish bastard, even now. When Brie knelt over him with her silky hair brushing his shoulders, he groaned aloud. In some ways, what they were about to do was more intimate and arousing than before.

When she slid down his body and began circling the

head of his shaft with her teeth and nibbling gently, his scalp tightened. Everything else in his body from the cell level on up tensed in helpless anticipation.

Brie was inventive and determined to torture him. Every time he was on the verge of exploding, she drew back... slowed the pace.

He cursed and begged.

Her low laugh made the hair on his body stand up, his skin tingling. This was why they had practically screwed themselves to death during their wild and wanton association when she worked at the ranch. Their relationship may have failed, but when it came to *this*, they were incendiary together. Perfectly matched.

At last, when he was incoherent with lust, she leaned back on her heels, took him in a firm grip and finished him off. His climax was painfully intense.

He groaned her name.

When he came to his senses, Brie was at his side, curled into him, one leg sprawled across his thighs. She stroked his chest. "You have to go home," she said. There was no inflection in the words.

"I know." He wanted to argue. Wanted to stay right where he was. But he was a pragmatist. No matter how much the truth sucked, it was still the truth.

When he thought his legs would support him, he rolled out of bed, gathered his shirt and pants and the rest, and made a second trip to the bathroom. This time when he returned, Brie was *not* in the bed. She had donned a silky nightgown and a fleecy robe and was standing by the dresser brushing her hair.

Nothing about her stance was deliberately provocative. Didn't matter. He wanted her still. With as much desperation as he had an hour before. Being with her tonight hadn't appeased his hunger. It had only reminded him of everything he was missing.

She stared at him from across the room, her expression sober. "I can't have an affair with you, Vaughn. Even if I wanted to, it would be impossible. You see that, right?"

"I suppose." He felt sulky and out of sorts. Which was a damned shame considering his recent euphoria. "But there's more at stake here than our physical relationship."

"What do you mean?"

"In my father's will, there was a letter to me. And something he said… I don't quite understand it, but I got the sense there may be twists and turns when it comes to Dad's inheritance. Like maybe we were all on probation. Kellan is happily married now. Sophie will tie the knot soon. If I'm the only one left, I think you and I should get engaged. Not really," he said quickly. "Only for show. So Miranda can see that I'm as stable and settled as the rest of them."

"Why? You said you don't care about the money."

"I don't, for myself. But when Dad died, he had no idea Danika existed. My daughter—*our* daughter," he said, "is entitled to my share of the money. I want her to have it."

"You and I both have good jobs. We don't need Buckley's money."

"I agree. We don't. But that inheritance will secure Danika's future. It doesn't make sense to let it slip through our fingers."

"If you trot out a fake engagement, everyone in town will be talking about us. It's not the kind of thing Royal will keep quiet."

"True. But you and I can stand a bit of gossip. For our daughter's sake." His throat tightened with unexpected emotion. "I've missed almost two years of her life, Brie. I want to do this for my child, my own flesh and blood. You can understand that."

Brie didn't seem convinced, but he wouldn't back down on this point. She nodded slowly. "If you're sure."

"As soon as the inheritance is settled, I'll set up a trust

fund for Nika. Then we can break off the engagement, and
I'll head back to Fort Worth. End of story."

Brie stared at him, her head cocked to one side. "Aren't
you afraid people in Royal will expect you to marry me?
That's why we broke up before. You wanted absolutely no
ties or responsibility."

His heart skipped a couple of beats and settled into a
sluggish rhythm. Sweat dampened his forehead. "That
wouldn't happen. You wouldn't use the court of public
opinion."

"Never underestimate an enemy. You taught me that,
Vaughn. It's high on your list of business maxims." Perhaps
sensing his unease, she chuckled softly. "Don't worry, big
guy. I'd never force anyone to marry me. When I get engaged for real, I want a man who is one hundred percent
invested in our relationship. That's not too much to ask."

He studied her for a long time as the silence between
them grew. It wasn't too much to ask. Not at all. But Vaughn
wasn't that guy. Still, when he tried to imagine Brie, blonde
and beautiful in a wedding dress, walking down the aisle to
meet the man of her dreams, his stomach curled in dread.

Maybe this engagement wasn't a good idea after all. It
would put the two of them in the midst of a fake intimacy
that might coax him into doing something dangerous.

But no, he couldn't back down out of base fear. He had
to do this—for his daughter's sake. He cleared his throat.
"So you agree? To the engagement, I mean."

She nodded slowly. "I agree. But what about Sophie's
wedding? And the flower girl thing?"

"I think we go ahead with it. It will cement our..." He
trailed off, unwilling to say the word.

Brie had no such scruples. "Cement our lie. That's what
you wanted to say, right?"

Why did she keep pushing him? "My sister wants Nika

in the wedding, so that's what we'll do. I'll tell Sophie we're engaged."

"And what about Kellan? If Sophie knows, you wouldn't keep him in the dark, would you?"

"No. I'll swing by there in the morning and fill him in."

"And Dixie?"

Damn. This was getting complicated already. "Her, too."

The fact that he didn't have a longer list of family and friends in which to confide underscored Dixie's description of his personality. He couldn't decide if that was a bad thing or a good thing.

Brie yawned. The smudges beneath her eyes did nothing to detract from her wholesome beauty, but they told him she was exhausted. Time for a graceful exit.

He wanted to kiss her again. Badly. He was on the way out the door, so surely indulging his impulse wouldn't lead him astray.

Crossing the room in two strides, he removed the hairbrush from her hand and set it aside. When she seemed startled, he grimaced. "A good-night kiss. That's all."

As he pulled her against his chest, Brie sighed and groaned. That sound encompassed every bit of frustration and resignation he felt at the thought of stepping away from her and walking out that door. Even clothed, her body was an almost irresistible temptation.

Her arms wound around his neck. Her hair, silky and thick, tumbled down her back. He tangled his hands in the strands, gripping convulsively as if he could make the moment last.

She tilted back her head, and their lips met, almost tentatively at first. This chaste farewell was something beyond his experience. He was filled with awe and tenderness. Passion was there, simmering beneath the surface. But for long seconds, he offered her his...*affection*, not his male hunger.

This woman had given him a daughter. A child who might well be the only legacy he had to leave behind one day.

"Brie…" he muttered her name, not at all sure he had anything to say that would please her, but infinitely certain he didn't want to hurt her with his silence.

She stroked the back of his neck, sending chills throughout his body. "It's okay, Vaughn. You can't be something you're not. Neither can I. You'll be leaving soon. I'm happy we're not at odds anymore."

Her speech unsettled him in ways he didn't understand. But more importantly, the way her body clung to his gave him a rush of exultation. In spite of everything that had gone wrong between them, her body still wanted his.

He pulled her more tightly against him. In her bare feet, she was small. Vulnerable. But when he looked into her eyes, he realized he was at risk, as well.

"Kiss me again," he begged. "One for the road."

"You're not going off to war," she teased.

He moved his mouth over hers softly. "If I go head-to-head with the stepwitch, it might as well be mortal combat."

She cupped his face in her hands and petted him, her fingertips exploring the late-night stubble she found on his chin. "Hating Miranda has become a habit for you, Vaughn. She's not evil. I doubt if she's even avaricious."

"Maybe. Can we quit mentioning my former step-mother?"

"You brought her up, not me."

Vaughn nipped Brie's bottom lip, then stroked the tiny sting with his tongue. "I don't want to go," he said roughly, undone by the hour and the woman and the many months they had spent apart.

Brie broke free of the embrace and stepped back, putting physical distance between them to mirror the emotional distance he had always insisted upon. Light. Casual. Nothing to tie a man down.

Suddenly, Vaughn flashed to a vision of his father, wasting away in his bed. The old man's once-sturdy frame frail and helpless. Alone at the end. Vaughn shuddered, more shaken than he cared to admit by the grim image.

You're probably the most like me. Buckley's words echoed in Vaughn's head, haunting him from beyond the grave. Vaughn hadn't actually *witnessed* his father on his deathbed. A housekeeper had discovered the body and called the coroner.

Buckley Blackwood had been ensconced in a pricey casket at the funeral home when his children saw him next. The patriarch, dressed in a tailored suit, had looked imposing even in that situation.

Vaughn swallowed hard and shook off the feeling that a ghost had crossed his path. Buckley wouldn't be here tonight trying to influence the outcome. Two years ago, Buck had hated the idea of his son having *any* kind of a relationship with Brielle. He'd believed the Blackwood clan was Texas royalty. Better than most folks. Certainly far above Brielle's station in life.

The woman in question frowned slightly, looking concerned. "Are you okay, Vaughn? You zoned out on me there for a minute."

He cleared his throat. "I'm fine," he said gruffly.

"I don't suppose we'll see each other much between now and the wedding rehearsal," she said.

"I'll be around."

Her lips twitched in a reluctant smile. "Threat? Or promise?"

He walked toward the door. "You'll just have to find out."

Nine

Sophie poured milk into her Cheerios and stirred them glumly. "Tell me again why we didn't just elope?"

Nigel dropped a kiss on top of his fiancée's head and joined her at the small table in the breakfast nook. His plate of perfectly browned toast with butter and marmalade was arranged neatly. "Because you, my love, wanted a big wedding with all the frills."

"Why didn't you stop me?" she wailed. "What was I thinking?"

Unfortunately, Nigel had heard this lament before. "It's going to be brilliant, darling girl. You're just getting cold feet. I'm told it's a common problem for brides."

"I *want* to marry you," she insisted. "But why do we need the big ceremony? You've never been to Vegas. We could be there before nightfall."

Nigel gave her a British version of the stink eye. "Eat your breakfast." He turned up his nose at her choice. "If you can call it that."

"Cheerios are healthy," she said indignantly.

"Not when you dump six teaspoons of sugar into the bowl." His shudder was theatrical.

The Englishman had her there. She'd always had a sweet tooth. Not that he seemed to mind her fuller curves—especially when they were in bed together. Her cheeks heated as memories of last night flashed through her brain.

Nigel's smirking grin told her he knew exactly what she was thinking. The man had an annoying habit of reading her mind.

"I need a break," she said. "From all the wedding nonsense. Vaughn wants to take Brie to Dallas overnight. I sort of promised to keep the baby while they're gone."

Nigel blinked, his smile fading. "As in babysit?"

"Yes. We're both intelligent adults. Surely we can muddle through. It will be fun."

"She's not even two, is she? I wouldn't have the slightest notion of what to do with her. Besides, my family will be here soon. We've lots to do in the meantime."

"Don't you see? That's why I'm freaking out. We'll be showing everyone around, wining and dining them. And after that, it will be time for the wedding rehearsal. I need to take my mind off the madness. I want to play house with you. Who knows, maybe we'll decide we want a little one of our own."

He paled. "Good lord, Sophie. Are you trying to tell me you're…?" He swallowed hard and dropped his toast.

"Pregnant?" She laughed softly. "No, silly man. But I don't want to wait long, do you?"

He stood abruptly, scooped her out of her chair and carried her toward the bedroom.

Sophie pretended to be outraged. "Put me down. My cereal will get soggy."

Nigel tossed her onto the bed and started ripping off his

clothes. "You said you didn't want to wait too long. I'm here to fulfill your every whim."

Sophie's heart overflowed with happiness. How had she gotten so damn lucky? She blinked back tears. "I love you, Nigel Townshend. Till death do us part."

His smile was tight and feral. "And I you, my crazy, gorgeous American bride. Now quit talking so I can ravish you."

Brie felt as if she was balanced on the edge of a precipice. The view was incredible, but she was terrified of falling.

Vaughn was true to his word. He'd made getting to know his daughter a priority. But he also had insisted on bringing dinner in most evenings, so Brie wouldn't have to worry about cooking after a long day at the veterinarian office.

Not only that, but the meals hadn't been pizza and burgers, which were her usual go-tos when she needed a break. He'd tracked down a private chef who catered to families with organic farm-to-table foods that kids would eat.

His thoughtfulness touched Brie.

Even so, she was cautious around him. Their breakup before Nika was born had traumatized her. She'd felt adrift. Completely lost. No matter how much she tried to convince herself otherwise, those strong feelings for Vaughn still simmered below the surface.

She was older now, though. Stronger. She had a responsibility to Danika that had to come before anything and everyone else.

Oddly enough, Vaughn didn't press the physical issue. He was affectionate and amusing and an all-around entertaining guest time and again. It wasn't his fault that Brie spent hours each night tossing and turning because she missed him in her bed.

What was he waiting for?

Maybe, like Brie, he was feeling cautious, because their behavior affected more than just themselves.

Brie and Vaughn *had* argued over the issue of childcare. Vaughn insisted that as his daughter, Danika should attend the state-of-the-art day care center at the Texas Cattleman's Club. Brie thought such an arrangement was too public a declaration of something she wasn't entirely ready for the world to know.

The thing that convinced her in the end was not Vaughn's persistence, but rather the fact that Brie knew it was time for Nika to begin playing with other children. The almost two-year-old was smart and happy and well-adjusted, but she needed more opportunities for socialization. The Club's childcare was second to none.

In the end, Brie agreed that Vaughn could pick up Nika two mornings a week and drop her off at the club. Since he had bought an expensive car seat for his vehicle, there wasn't much else Brie could find to protest.

The babysitter had actually been relieved to cut back on her hours. She was an older woman, and Nika's nonstop energy could be tiring to deal with.

So now, Brie's days were running even more smoothly.

The big change today was that Vaughn had unexpectedly asked to meet her for lunch. Thursdays were her half days at the clinic. Brie closed up shop at twelve thirty sharp, knowing that Dr. Brody would reopen the office at two. She slipped out of her lab coat and into a black blazer that matched her pants.

Tomorrow and every other Friday, Doc Brody covered for her. That usually gave Brie a chance to spend more time with Danika and to catch up on life in general.

Vaughn was in the reception area leafing through a magazine when she found him. "Hey," she said, wincing inwardly at the breathless tone in her voice.

He stood slowly and looked at her with that masculine smile that melted her knees. "Hey, yourself. Are you hungry?"

"Actually, starving." She flipped her hair from underneath her collar. "We had more appointments than usual, probably because it's right before the weekend. People don't want to wait any longer if they're worried something is wrong."

He took her arm as they exited the building. "You love what you do, don't you? Even though you used to work with big animals at Blackwood Hollow?"

She nodded. "I do. Horses were always my favorite, but a general veterinarian practice is more practical for a mom with young children. Normal hours make a huge difference. And besides, this work is rewarding, too. Pet owners are wonderful people. It gives me a lot of personal satisfaction to make someone's cat or dog well again. Or even the occasional ferret."

Vaughn fell back a step and stared at her. "Seriously?"

Brie laughed. "Of course. I've dealt with boa constrictors, parrots...you name it."

He took her arm again and steered her toward the restaurant where they had reservations. It was a quiet, out-of-the way French bistro. Definitely a special-occasion kind of restaurant. Not the kind of spot where construction workers dropped by on their lunch breaks.

Brie had never actually eaten here. When she walked inside and saw the upscale decor and elegant furnishings, her internal radar went off. Why was Vaughn taking her to lunch at such an unabashedly romantic venue?

He held her chair for her, his hand brushing her shoulder as she was seated. The fleeting touch sent shivers down her spine.

She picked up her menu and studied it intently, unable to meet his gaze. He watched her with a small smile that made her toes curl. Finally, she'd had enough. "What?" she demanded quietly, conscious of other diners nearby.

Vaughn lifted one shoulder in an elegant shrug. He was wearing a dark suit with a yellow tie and a pristine white shirt—hopefully not the one Danika had ruined.

"I like looking at you," he said. "When we're with our daughter, we tend to make her the focus of our attention, as it should be. And we're always careful not to wake her. But I thought it would be nice to have a few minutes alone together away from the house."

She chewed her lip, not trusting his casual amiability. The old Vaughn would never have wanted time alone in the midst of other people. He would have found a much more private spot for the two of them to get naked and slake their mutual need.

"I appreciate the invitation," she said, her tone carefully noncommittal. "I only had a banana for breakfast."

Immediately, Vaughn summoned their waiter. "The lady would like to order, please."

Over the salad course, Brielle could contain her curiosity no longer. She lowered her voice and leaned toward him. "You might as well tell me what's going on. I know you, Vaughn Blackwood. You've got something up your sleeve."

He buttered a piece of crusty bread and handed it to her. "I have a request, I'll admit. I thought you'd be more open to my proposal if you weren't hungry."

"Am I so predictable?" Though she was loath to admit it, Vaughn knew *her*, too. Which made it hard to hide her feelings and reactions from him.

"Don't be grumpy, Brie. I have a surprise for you. If you're willing."

Her knees pressed together under the table, and her palms got sweaty. "I don't like surprises."

"I remember," he said ruefully. "Canceling those tickets to the Fiji Islands at the last minute cost me a bundle."

"You should have known better. There was no way I was going to simply run off to Vanua Levu with you for two weeks."

"Too many rules, woman. Living a spontaneous life is more fun."

"Sorry. The idea never held much appeal for me. Which is just as well, since it's not an option anymore. Any shot I had at living a spontaneous life ended when Danika was born…at least for several years in the future. Small children thrive on familiar routines and boring schedules. You're free, Vaughn. I'm not."

He drained his wineglass and raised his hand for more. The quick frown that shadowed his face when she talked about not being free vanished quickly, but Brie had witnessed his discomfort with the topic.

Before the discussion could resume, a waiter returned with their perfectly cooked filet mignon and twice-baked potatoes. The food was stunningly good.

Brie dug in, happy to have a respite from the awkward conversation. "Danika is loving the childcare center at the club," she said. "Thanks for suggesting it."

Vaughn chewed and swallowed, then took a sip of wine. Brie knew she was in trouble when she fixated on the ripple of muscles in his tanned throat. She had a terrible urge to nibble his neck all the way to his beautiful mouth. And stay there.

Forcing herself to look away, she concentrated instead on finishing her meal. It was easier to eat than talk. No land mines in culinary excess. Silence was golden.

Her dining partner responded at last. "You're welcome. I thought she would like the center. Kellan and Sophie and I have several friends who have already started families. For the couples where both parents work outside the home, it's very comforting to know your child is in good hands. Or so I'm told."

Brielle couldn't wait any longer. Who knew how soon dessert would arrive? "Tell me," she said, sitting back in her chair and dabbing her lips with a snowy-white linen napkin. "What's the surprise?"

Vaughn reached across the table and took her hand. Brie was so startled she didn't even take it back. His grasp was warm and firm. Perhaps she should pull free, but it was so much nicer to let the man take charge just this once.

"I want you to go to Dallas with me. Overnight." His green eyes gleamed.

That last word was fraught with meaning. "Why?"

He grinned. "For fun. Or more accurately, for work and play. I have two meetings I need to be there for. One will include you. You'll need to bring fancy clothes. Or I can take you shopping."

That sounded delightful, but Vaughn's pricey gifts always came with strings. "I have plenty of clothes," she said wryly. "But it's a moot point. I can't leave town on a whim. I have a daughter and a medical practice."

"I've got it all under control," he said. "Tomorrow is Dr. Brody's day to cover for you, remember? Even better, Sophie and Nigel have volunteered to keep Nika overnight. Sophie is thrilled."

"But what about all the wedding festivities? Nigel's whole family is arriving from England Sunday evening. We can't ask them to babysit when they have so much going on. It's too much."

"It was my idea, but Sophie's jumped on it. She's sick to death of all the wedding details. She swears that focusing on keeping Danika for thirty-six hours will give her a much-needed break. We'll be back to put our daughter to bed Saturday night. Sophie and Nigel will have time to catch their breath before all the revelry continues."

"I can't imagine Nigel Townshend changing Nika's *nappies*, as they say."

"You misjudge my future brother-in-law. I've watched them together. That poor bloke will do absolutely anything for my sister. He's head-over-ass *smitten* with her."

"I can't decide if that makes you happy or if you think less of him for his devotion."

"Of course I'm happy. She's my sister."

"But you would never be all gaga over a woman, would you, Vaughn?"

His gaze narrowed. "Are you trying to pick a fight with me, Brielle?"

She stared at him, torn in half a dozen directions. Trusting Sophie with Danika wasn't a huge obstacle. Vaughn's sister had a natural affinity for children. She used to babysit all the time as a teenager.

Even being away from Royal and the vet clinic wasn't a problem. Vaughn was right. Brie had already planned to be off tomorrow. So why was she hesitating?

It all boiled down to one simple fact.

"You mean for this trip to include sex, right?"

He blinked, and his neck turned red. "I hadn't planned on announcing it to the whole restaurant, but yes. Is that a deal breaker?"

He was ruffled. Brie liked that. A lot. "Yes, I'll go," she said. "And yes, we'll have sex. Spontaneous trysts are romantic. Count me in."

Ten

Miranda Dupree was desperately glad to be back in the Big Apple. She loved Royal. Always had. But now that half the town thought she was a scheming hussy, it wasn't much fun anymore.

The three official Blackwood offspring were angry in varying degrees. As for Darius, the illegitimate son—he and Miranda had a good working relationship, necessary for the planned partnership between their businesses. But as he'd told her, he sided with his half siblings in his frustration over the whole tangle with Buck's will. From an adult child's perspective, she supposed it made sense. Their father had created an impossible situation and dragged Miranda into the middle of a mess, whether she liked it or not.

Worst of all, Buck's convoluted plan meant that everyone viewed her as a villain without knowing the truth of what Buck wanted her to do with her inheritance. Sometimes, she wondered why she was putting up with it all. The fact that Buckley had made a huge bequest to her charity, Girl to the Nth Power, was the only thing that made the past few months at all palatable.

It was noon, and Miranda had already stopped in at the Girl Power offices. Things always got a little sloppy when she was out of town. Probably because she was a micromanager. She had tried to do better in that regard, thanks to urging from her therapist.

Girl to the Nth Power and Goddess Inc., her burgeoning health and lifestyle brand, were her babies. When she walked away from her marriage to Buckley Blackwood, she'd wanted to make her own way in the world. An airtight prenup gave her little choice.

Fortunately, wise investments on her part when she was still *Mrs.* Blackwood meant she had a safety net. She was proud of the life she had built in New York. But her therapist was right. The pace she kept these days was in danger of ruining her health and her happiness.

Both organizations needed capable, trustworthy CEOs at the helm full-time. Miranda needed and wanted to step back. It had been so long since she'd had a day off, she'd forgotten what it was like to go to the Hamptons for the weekend. Or simply to hole up in her three-thousand-square-foot apartment near Seventy-Sixth and Madison and do nothing but enjoy a bubble bath and a good book.

Unfortunately, that day off wasn't coming any time soon. Until she discharged her responsibilities as Buckley's heir, she had *more* work to do, not less.

Things were chugging right along at Goddess Inc., though the staff seemed startled to see her. Not a bad thing. Miranda believed in running a tight ship. She was strict but fair.

Unfortunately, the daily business of health and lifestyle centers seemed to be doing fine without her. Which meant she had to face the truth. The only reason she was still puttering around in her office with the view of Central Park was that she was afraid to face Kai Maddox.

"Kai." She whispered the syllable out loud, trying to reduce its power.

Once upon a time, before she was married to Buck, Kai had been her whole world. With his scarred jaw from an old motorcycle accident and neatly inked tattoos covering his muscular biceps, he was the epitome of the bad boy who drew women like bees to honey.

Dark brown hair. Brown eyes. His olive complexion, courtesy of his Mexican roots, added to his moody charm. Though a scowl was his habitual expression, when he smiled… *Oh, lordy.* The man was gorgeous.

He was also a skilled hacker. Though he had come perilously close at one time to ending up on the wrong side of the law, he was now a widely respected cybersecurity expert.

Miranda was worried about Blackwood Bank. Since inheriting the business from Buck, she'd looked into the paperwork and noticed a few irregularities recently. Enough to make her realize that she needed Kai's help. Her covert snooping had established that Kai was actually in New York this week, speaking to a high-profile meeting of police officers and detectives from all over the country about the kind of tech stuff that made Miranda's head hurt.

Her plan was to show up unannounced at Kai's hotel later tonight and ask for his help. She was hoping that enough time had passed for him to forget the fact that she had gone from his bed to Buckley's.

In her defense, Kai had checked out on the relationship months before Miranda let herself be enticed by Buckley's determined courtship. But the end result was still the same—she'd married Buck and left behind the life she'd known before. If Kai was holding on to any resentment over that, working with him would be…challenging.

To say Kai had issues was an understatement. The chip
on his shoulder was large enough to start a hundred fires.
Build a dozen ships. Maybe if Miranda had met him at a
different time in his life...

The next hours passed with agonizing slowness. Even
Madison Avenue shopping, one of her go-to stress reliev-
ers, didn't do the trick. She bought a new outfit just for the
heck of it, ignoring the huge wardrobe that filled a closet
and a half in her apartment.

This meeting with Kai was important. The fire-engine
red strapless dress fit her almost too well. Her ample breasts
were in danger of spilling out. When she added black pat-
ent leather stilettos with tiny rhinestones on the heels, she
couldn't decide if the image she presented was bodacious
bombshell or tacky tramp.

Either way, Kai was in for a shock.

In the cab heading across town, she found herself wishing she had downed a good stiff drink to give her courage.

It had been years since she and Kai had been face-to-
face with each other. Would she be able to convince him
to help her?

Thankfully, she had the advantage of surprise. Kai
wasn't the only one with street smarts. Miranda still knew
guys from the old days. One of them, ironically named
Digger, was a huge Yankees fan. Miranda had bought a
couple of behind–home plate tickets yesterday for the season opener and offered them to Digger. All he had to do
was hack into the hotel's database and find a room number.

Digger loved it. He thought he was facilitating a lovers'
tryst. Or at least a booty call. Miranda didn't care what
Digger thought.

In the mirrored elevator, she checked her hair and
makeup. With her fiery tresses, the dress probably clashed,
but she had never let that bother her. The more wince-

worthy realization was the way her cleavage looked, well...deep.

Kai had always been a boob man, by his own admission. Perhaps subconsciously Miranda had picked this dress for just that reason.

Her legs were wobbly when she stood in front of room 8902. It was a suite. Of course. The man had come up in the world. Way up.

She took a deep, decidedly unsteady breath and knocked. Kai answered immediately. His hair was ruffled as if he had been sprawled on the sofa watching TV to relax. That sounded like him.

But any relaxation faded when he saw her. His eyes flashed, and the permanent furrow in his brow deepened. "Oh, hell no," he said.

When he tried to close the door in her face, she stuck a leg through the opening, risking amputation. "I need to speak with you," she said. "About business."

Perhaps the fact that her voice went all low and husky made her claim slightly unbelievable.

He shook his head in disbelief. "Only you, Miranda. I can't believe you had the balls to come here after everything that has happened. Am I finally gonna get an apology from you?"

Her blood pressure shot to the stratosphere. "Me? Apologize? For what? For walking away from a relationship you'd already killed? You were the distant, angry one." She stopped short and took a deep breath. "I'm here with legitimate business. Will you talk to me? Civilly?"

A spark flamed hot in those rich chocolate pupils. "I don't do business with cheaters," he said roughly. "There's only one thing women like you are good for."

"So you do remember that part?" she taunted. She ran a fingertip along his bottom lip, helpless to resist the feelings his nearness evoked.

"You'd better leave right now," he said, his gaze wild with strong emotion.

"Or what?"

He dragged her close against his body, tilted back her head and slammed his lips down on hers. As kisses went, it was world-class. Volcanoes erupted. Flash fires ignited. The earth's orbit accelerated.

Miranda never would have believed such heat could remain between them after so many years. She went soft and limp in his embrace. Kai was anything *but* soft. She might have whimpered embarrassingly when he cupped a breast in one big palm and squeezed.

Ten seconds passed. Maybe thirty. Time became fluid. He tasted exactly the same. And for a brief, insane moment in time, she became the young, naive girl she had been when they first met.

He could have dragged her into the room and onto the bed and she might not have stopped him.

But he didn't.

Kai broke the kiss abruptly and wiped his mouth. His face lost all expression, though muscles rippled in his throat, and his chest heaved. "The answer is no, Miranda. Not me. Not you. Business be damned. I wouldn't cross the street for you. Not anymore."

Then he set her gently into the hall, closed the door and turned the dead bolt. The loud *snick* snapped her out of a trance.

Humiliation and regret washed through her like the flu, churning her stomach and giving her a headache. There was nothing to do but retreat. She would have to find another way to protect Blackwood Bank. But how?

Kai had been her only real hope for someone she could trust to investigate without causing gossip about the bank.

Her spine stiffened, and she wiped her eyes, careful not to smear her mascara. He hadn't heard the last of her. She hadn't gotten where she was in the world by letting herself get pushed around. He *would* help her. Eventually.

Because she wasn't going to give up on him. Not this time.

Brie strapped herself into the seat beside Vaughn and wondered if all mothers felt the same when going on a trip with their partner and leaving their child behind. Torn between love for their babies and the men they cared about. Husbands. Lovers. Fathers.

She had never left Nika overnight before. When she and Vaughn dropped Danika off at Sophie's house and swapped the car seat, Brie nearly cried. She felt guilty, because she was excited to be going to Dallas with Vaughn.

Nika, on the other hand, had barely said goodbye to her mother. She was already playing with the pile of toys Sophie had somehow procured in an incredibly short time.

Now, Brie was sitting in the front of a terrifyingly small plane while her daughter's father went calmly through a preflight checklist. "I had no idea we weren't flying commercial," she said.

His cocky sideways grin amused her. "I might have omitted that info, because I wasn't sure you would come if you knew. But I promise, you can trust me. I've logged hundreds of hours of flight time. And besides, once we're airborne, you'll see how wonderful it is to chase the clouds."

He sounded almost poetic. If she hadn't been anxious and uncertain about her decision to join him, she might have appreciated his promises more. As it was, her hands were clenched on the armrests and her teeth had chewed a raw place on her bottom lip.

Though takeoff left her stomach on the ground, Vaughn was right. In this small plane, it felt as if the two of them were dancing across the sky. They didn't talk to each other, but the silence felt comfortable and natural. It was enough to watch Vaughn's big, masculine hands on the controls and to take in the view outside.

The flight was uneventful until they were thirty minutes outside Dallas. Suddenly, Vaughn cursed, his jaw tight.

"What's wrong?" Brie cried.

"I'm not sure," he said, flipping dials and switches. "The fuel indicator has gone all wonky, and my oil pressure is dropping. We may have to make an emergency landing."

The way he said those words was exactly the tone of voice a man would use to say *I may have to pull off the road and get some gas.*

Brie's brain spun wildly, trying to process the words. Even she could tell that their airspeed was dropping. "Can we make it to the airport?"

"Doubtful." He picked up the radio and called the tower. A flash of incomprehensible conversation left her more worried, not less. When the radio went silent, Vaughn reached out and squeezed her hand. "I've done this in a simulator."

Her eyes rounded. "Done what?"

"Put a plane down in a field. If my calculations are right, we'll be just short of the runway. But the surrounding acreage is flat. We should be fine."

Every disaster movie she had ever seen flashed through her brain. The fire engines and rescue squad vehicles tearing down the runways, sirens blaring. The escape slide being deployed. But this tin can they were in barely even had a door, much less an escape plan—or at least, one she could visualize.

Brie's prayer life took a real turn. "Tell me Nika is not going to be an orphan," she begged.

"Not if I can help it." The words were terse. This time he didn't look at her. He was too busy for that.

The next ten minutes unfolded with both agonizing slowness and terrifying speed. He reached in a cabinet beside him and pulled out a folded blanket. "Put your face in this. All the way down to your knees. Hands over your head."

When she hesitated, he shouted at her, "Now."

The ground rushed up at them. There was nothing in sight but a stubbly cornfield.

Vaughn cursed and shouted a Mayday call into the radio.

Then they crashed. Hard.

Intellectually, she understood that Vaughn had deployed the landing gear. But without a smooth runway, it felt as if they were catapulting nose over tail.

The world spun dizzily, filled with the noise of screeching metal. The impact went on and on. Like a nightmare from which she couldn't wake up.

At last, it stopped. Everything stopped. Her heart was beating so hard, she thought she might throw up.

Gingerly, she lifted her head and straightened. The sirens she had anticipated wailed in the distance.

"Vaughn?" She reached for his hand, looking over toward him, and cried out. He had a gash on his forehead, and his face was dead white, his eyes glassy with shock.

"We're okay," he said automatically.

She squeezed his fingers. "Yes, we are. Hold on. Help is coming."

After that, time blurred, and the world went crazy.

Rescue personnel swarmed the plane, separating Vaughn and Brie in their haste to get them away from the smoldering wreckage. One set of EMTs worked on each of them in separate vehicles.

Brie waved away their concern with mounting frustration. "I'm fine. Seriously. Go see about Mr. Blackwood."

At last, they released her. She clambered out of the vehicle and ran across the rough ground to where Vaughn was still being evaluated. He smiled when he saw her, but the flash of white teeth lacked its usual wattage.

"Are you hurt?" he asked, his gaze sliding over her from head to toe.

"I'm fine. What are they saying about you?"

He shrugged. "A mild concussion. Couple of stitches. They don't want me to drive until tomorrow."

"So no meeting this afternoon?"

"It's important," he said. "I have to go. We'll grab a room near the club instead of staying at my place like I planned."

"I want to take care of you," she said.

He held out his hand. "Maybe we'll take care of each other."

Eleven

Vaughn lived in Fort Worth, but he was serving a term as vice president of the Dallas branch of the Texas Cattleman's Club. The clubhouse was where the big meeting and gala were to be held tonight. The two cities were half an hour apart, give or take. Under the circumstances, staying in the area made more sense than adding extra driving by going to Forth Worth just to come right back.

Brie nodded. "Sounds good." As the medics finished up their assessments, she watched Vaughn. His posture was *careful*, as if he was trying not to jostle anything that might give him pain. His head was surely the worst of his injuries.

"Does he need to go to the hospital?" Brie ignored Vaughn's quick frown. Sometimes men could be stupid in these situations.

The male EMT gave her a reassuring grin. "It wouldn't hurt, but we couldn't get him to agree. Just be on the lookout for excessive drowsiness or any noticeable change. Garbled speech, sudden clumsiness. You know what I mean."

"Can he have painkillers?"

"As long as he's not driving, he could get his primary care physician to call something in."

Vaughn hopped down from the truck and took Brie by the arm. "Come on, Clara Barton. I told you. I'm fine." He thanked the team who had been working on him and then pulled out his phone. "I'm calling the car service I use. They'll pick us up at the terminal."

Brie was wearing heels. The ground was uneven. She wasn't dressed for hiking. "How do we get to the terminal?" she asked.

The same EMT waved a hand. "If you don't mind perching in the back, you can ride with us."

Fortunately, the firemen had determined the plane fuselage was stable, so they were able to retrieve Vaughn's and Brie's bags from the plane. Two carry-ons, two small suitcases.

The trip to the airport was quick. Brie and Vaughn sat side by side on the gurney, holding on to the metal edges as the vehicle bounced and lurched through the field. Behind them, the little plane lay crumpled and forlorn.

"What happens now?" she asked. "I'm assuming we don't simply walk away."

Vaughn shook his head and then cursed quietly when the motion clearly caused him pain. "We'll have to deal with the FAA, but I don't think it will take long. I have good insurance. They'll file reports." He paused and grimaced. "And we'll have to book return tickets for tomorrow on a commercial flight."

"I can deal with booking the return tickets while you're tied up," she said. Her heart still raced in her chest. They had come far too close to dying. A miscalculation on Vaughn's part, no matter how small, could have spelled disaster.

She leaned her cheek against his shoulder. Now that the adrenaline was fading, she felt weak and shaky.

He curled an arm around her waist, his expression sober. "I'm sorry, Brie. I never meant to put you in harm's way. I've flown thousands of miles in my own plane. But this was a rental. Never again. I should have known better than to trust someone else to maintain things properly."

His words unsettled her. Not the part about the plane—nothing could be done about that. But the other part.

Vaughn had always kept his own counsel, gone his own way. He kept people at arm's length, preferring to handle everything himself rather than count on anyone else. Even when he and Brielle had been sleeping together, he had given her his body, but not his heart and soul.

Despite her relative youth and inexperience at the time, she had recognized the difference.

Was he any better now at opening up? Did discovering he was a father do anything to loosen the tight control he kept over his emotions? She hadn't seen much evidence of a changed man.

Just minutes ago in the midst of a crisis, a near-fatal accident, Vaughn had kept his cool under pressure. If he had been scared, he hadn't shown it. While *Brie* had been sick with terror, Vaughn had simply done what had to be done.

That kind of mental focus in a critical situation was a great quality for a man to have while trying to save your life. He was the guy you counted on in an emergency. But she wanted more from him than superhero behavior. Maybe it was unfair, but she needed to know he could be vulnerable. Otherwise, he had no need for her at all other than sex. And a man could get that almost anywhere.

In the end, the FAA report was more than Vaughn had counted on. It was an hour before he and Brie were able to leave the airport. Despite his protestations to the contrary, Vaughn was *not* okay. After purchasing tickets—on Vaughn's credit card—to get them home tomorrow afternoon, she used the phone number he gave her to contact the transportation service he had summoned. The hired car had been waiting outside all this time.

After touching base with the driver, she scoped out the Cattleman's Club's location and booked rooms at a nearby hotel, an upscale chain that would be comfortable and quiet, two things she and Vaughn both needed after their traumatic morning.

When they exited the airport at last, Vaughn was gray faced and exhausted. Brie took over quietly, ushering him into the car and speaking to the driver. She did the same thing at the hotel during check-in, dealing with the desk clerk and shielding Vaughn from annoying questions.

The bellman loaded their few bags onto a cart and escorted them upstairs. Vaughn extracted a $100 bill and thanked the young man. Then—when the door closed behind the jubilant kid—Vaughn shrugged out of his jacket and face-planted onto the mattress.

Brie shook her head in wry amusement. "At least take off your shoes," she said. "And tell me when we need to leave later. I'm not going to let you sleep more than thirty minutes at a time because of the possible concussion."

Vaughn lifted his head and glared. "I don't need a nurse."

"You need something," she said, putting a bite in her retort. "You look like hell, and you're getting mean. Either you cooperate with me, or I'll pull the plug on this meeting tonight."

Vaughn gaped. "You wouldn't. You couldn't."

She put her hands on her hips. "Try me."

To her utter astonishment, the man actually cooperated. Perhaps because he saw the sense in her words. Or more likely because he felt dreadful and arguing was too much of an effort.

He stood and stripped down to his shirt and knit boxers. Brie hadn't been prepared for how the sight of him half-naked would affect her. His legs were long and muscular and lightly dusted with hair. Vaughn was a gorgeous man in any situation. But right now, with his reserve temporarily at bay, she saw him as more approachable than usual.

Though she wanted to join him in the bed, she also wanted to feel clean again. She probably smelled of cornfield dust and antiseptic. "I'm going to take a quick shower," she said. "And wash my hair. Will you be okay?"

He had resumed his prone position. "Humph…" The guttural syllable was supposed to be an affirmative.

It bothered her to leave him, but surely the EMTs would have insisted on hospitalization if the head injury were dangerous enough that he couldn't be left unsupervised, even for a minute. With one last worried glance at the man sprawled on top of the covers, she grabbed her luggage and made her way to the bathroom.

Looking in the mirror was a mistake. Her face was milky pale, highlighting every bruise and scrape. She resembled somebody who had wrestled with an alligator and lost. Even the scratches on the side of her neck were unfamiliar.

Twenty minutes later, she was drying her hair and feeling hunger pangs. Because of the accident, they had forgotten to eat lunch. She thought about donning a hotel robe, but she needed more armor than that. It was far too early to dress for the evening, and her original outfit was crumpled and dusty.

Fortunately, she had thrown a pair of black yoga pants and an oversize turquoise T-shirt in her bag. When she was dressed and decent, with her hair twisted up in a neat knot on the back of her head, she checked on Vaughn again.

He had rolled onto his back at some point and now lay staring at the ceiling. His head turned when she walked into the bedroom. "Will you get me some acetaminophen?" he asked gruffly.

"Of course." Her heart clenched in sympathy. She knew that he hated asking for help. Instead of riffling through *his* things, she grabbed some tablets from her own toiletry case and brought him one of the complimentary water bottles from the mini fridge. "Do you feel like sitting up?"

Vaughn scowled. "Of course. It's a tiny cut with two stitches. That's all."

"Don't snap at me," she said calmly, handing him the meds and then the water. "You're the one determined to go out this evening. Couldn't we just go back to Royal?"

He swallowed the medicine and wiped his mouth, then ran his hands through his hair. "No. Because Cal McCready won't wait forever. I have a chance to get in on the ground floor of a land deal that could double or triple my business."

"But you're rich already. Why does it matter? There will be other deals, surely."

"These drilling rights are up for grabs, and I want them. McCready has convinced some old guy to sell a huge tract of land for an incredible price."

"McCready. I've heard that name. From you, I think. Didn't you tell me a long time ago that McCready was a snake?"

"I probably did. And he is. But don't worry. He won't pull anything over on *me*. He wouldn't dare. Sometimes business makes strange bedfellows."

"I'm more concerned about the old guy than you. Are you sure McCready is on the up-and-up?"

"My head is killing me, Brie. I'm not really in the mood for a lesson in ethics from you."

"Fine," she said, her throat tight. "I'm going down to the lobby to buy a magazine."

"Wait," he muttered, reaching out to snag her wrist and bring it to his lips. He kissed the spot where her pulse thrummed visibly. "I'm sorry I snapped at you. Forgive me. This has been a hell of a day."

She allowed him to pull her down onto the bed, but she perched on the edge of the mattress instead of pressing against him. Both of them were upright. His fingers still encircled her wrist. It would be so easy to fall back into the covers and let nature take its course. Nothing mattered outside this room. It would be just the two of them, naked and needy.

Instead, she kept her spine straight and her impulses under control. "How about something to eat? Room service, not a restaurant." She spoke calmly, but being near him made her breath catch in her throat and her pulse accelerate.

They were so close, she could see the tiny dark lines of forest green that outlined the brighter irises so much like his daughter's sparkling emerald eyes.

"I could eat," he said.

He made no move to release her. Instead, he put a hand behind her neck and pulled her in for a kiss. It started out as light and playful, maybe meant to punctuate his apology. But in seconds, he had her panting and weak with wanting him.

Common sense said this relationship was going nowhere. Why else had the two of them not slept together every night they'd had a chance? They still weren't trusting each other enough to open up about what they really wanted.

Was he rethinking the faux engagement? He had never mentioned it after that first time. Brie told herself it was dumb to feel hurt, either for herself *or* for her daughter's sake.

Vaughn was who he was. Maybe this quick trip was a chance for Brie to get him out of her system once and for all. When they returned to Royal, she would break off even this tentative connection. Tell him that she and Danika didn't need him.

After all, no one believed Vaughn wanted to be a father. Least of all Brie.

All that aside, in this moment there was nowhere else she would rather be. He was big and broad and utterly male. Everything inside her yearned to get even closer.

Vaughn was the first one to pull back. He rested his forehead against hers, breathing heavily. "You're all clean, and I'm a mess," he said ruefully.

She gently touched the small bandage at the side of his forehead. "How does it feel?"

He rubbed a thumb over her bottom lip. "Sore. Manageable. I'll be fine." He hesitated. "I want you, Brie. More than anything. It makes me ill to think I might have hurt you, or worse."

"But you didn't," she said quietly. Because she couldn't help herself, she ran her fingers through his thick, springy brown hair. "Go grab a shower if you want to. I'll have the food waiting when you get back. Steak? Chicken?"

His crooked grin was more like the old Vaughn. "A little bit of everything. I'm starving."

He took his bag and disappeared down the hall. Soon, Brie heard water running. It dawned on her then that he had never actually said when they needed to leave. Maybe he wasn't thinking clearly. She didn't want him to miss his oh-so-important meeting.

Though it was embarrassing, she knocked on the bathroom door, leaning a shoulder against the frame. "Vaughn? How much time do we have? I'm going to set an alarm so we won't be late."

The door opened so suddenly, she stumbled.

Vaughn hadn't gotten in the shower yet. His hair and his skin were still dry, but he was completely naked except for one of the hotel's plush towels he had wrapped around his hips.

His eyes sparkled with humor. "Did you decide to share?"

Her throat went dry. They were standing so close together she could have leaned forward and licked his collarbone. Heat radiated from his body. It was no wonder she had fallen in love with him all those years ago.

Whoa. No, no, no. She wasn't in love with Vaughn Blackwood. Maybe once upon a time when he was pursuing her hard and fast. But that was before their breakup. Before Danika. Before Brielle became a responsible mother to her child.

Not now...

Even as she voiced the mental denial, her hands reached for him. Placing both palms flat on his hard, sculpted chest, she ran her fingers up to his throat and then down to his navel...tracing ribs, tracking his heartbeat.

"Don't take too long," she muttered, not quite able to meet his mocking gaze. He knew exactly what he did to her.

Vaughn sucked in a sharp breath when she touched the edge of his towel. "Either stay or go, Brie, darlin'. Your choice. But make up your mind."

Twelve

Vaughn cursed his own stupidity in giving Brie a choice. What he should have done was pull her into the shower with him for a long, leisurely round of hot, wet lovemaking. If he'd made the decision for them, he was sure she would have gone along with it. A man knew when a woman was interested.

What held him back was the knowledge that Brie was conflicted. He could see it in her eyes and in her body language. She wanted him. But she didn't *want* to want him. It was a fine distinction and one that unsettled Vaughn.

Unfortunately, her doubts mirrored his own. Why had he brought Brie with him to Dallas? The ostensible reason was to show her off as his new fiancée and let the gossip begin filtering back to Royal, so Miranda would find out.

However, that could have easily been accomplished without leaving town. The truth was, he needed to deal with this very important business meeting, and he wanted Brie by his side.

And then there was Danika. Those mornings when he drove her to day care had shown him that the beautiful child with the bright temperament was a delight. Any father would be lucky to have such a smart, curious kid. Did Vaughn even deserve to call her his own? He wasn't dad material. Again and again, he had asked himself if it wouldn't be better to let another—better suited—guy adopt the precocious little girl.

That was the part that stuck in his craw. He could almost convince himself that Nika was better off without Vaughn as a dad. But when he imagined Brie with another man, his blood pressure skyrocketed. Despite all evidence to the contrary, Brie was *his*.

His whole life he had always known how to get what he wanted. Years ago, when he was getting his business off the ground, he might even have stepped on people and things to meet his goals. He liked to think he had matured along the way, become more compassionate.

The careless arrogance he had evidenced as a twenty-five-year-old had altered and tempered. But he hadn't gone soft. Not at all. Which was why he was determined to make this enormous land deal with McCready happen.

He couldn't let himself be distracted by his need for Brielle.

Under the hot sting of the shower spray, he debated his options. She was the one question he couldn't answer, the one thorn in his flesh he was never able to excise.

Being intimate with her so soon after they reconnected in Royal had been a mistake. He knew that now. Sex complicated things, especially with a baby in the mix. But God, he couldn't bring himself to regret it.

His body hardened as he remembered that first incredible night. Never in a million years had he imagined that coming home for Sophie's wedding would end up with him in Brie's bed. The exhilaration of being inside her again had momentarily silenced all his discontent with his father's will and the drama with Miranda.

Making love to Brielle had seemed natural…inevitable.

But then morning had come, and with it, the harsh light of day. The inevitable voice of reason. Brielle was not the kind of woman a man picked up and put down when the mood struck him. She was decent and capable and kind. She had gone through nine months of pregnancy alone. Then she had spent two long years juggling the demands of a tiny baby, now a toddler…with no backup. No father to share the incredible load of parenting.

Vaughn could argue that it wasn't his fault. He hadn't known Danika existed. But the truth was more layered than that. If he hadn't been so adamant in the beginning that he didn't want anyone or anything to tie him down, Brie would never have broken up with him. She wouldn't have faced almost three years of unimaginable challenge without receiving any help or support from him.

Vaughn was culpable in that scenario, no matter how you sliced it. There were amends to be made.

Could he change? Was he willing to make the necessary sacrifices? He honestly didn't know. Even more daunting was the fact that he might not be who Brielle needed.

That last one was a gut punch.

As the water began to run cold, he washed his hair gingerly and then rinsed off, careful not to make contact with the bandage covering his stitches. He probably wasn't supposed to get the area wet, now that he thought about it.

Too late. His head had been killing him when the EMTs gave him instructions. He hadn't been thinking clearly.

With a glance at his watch, he realized that he was running out of time. Though he wanted to sprawl on the sofa and close his eyes, he went instead to his suitcase and pulled out his tux and neatly folded dress shirt.

When he appeared in the living room, Brie's eyes widened. "Wow," she said. "For a man who crashed a plane today, you look pretty darn great."

He sat beside her on the love seat and surveyed the plates of food. "It was a hard landing, not a crash," he said wryly. "Give me some credit."

For a moment, hunger took precedence over other considerations. He and Brie split the steak and ribs and baked chicken. Vaughn took the mashed potatoes. Brie chose the spinach salad, washed down with coffee.

When they were almost done, he curled a strand of her hair around his finger. "As much as I would love to stay here and goof off, we do have to leave in about twenty minutes. Does that give you enough time to get ready?"

Her eyes rounded, and her cheeks turned pink. "Next time, a little more warning would be nice."

He leaned over and kissed her softly, tasting the coffee on her lips. "You always look gorgeous. Throw on your fancy dress and some shoes, and you'll be good to go."

Slipping out of his arms, she stood and rolled her eyes. "Men. Glamour doesn't just happen. We have to work at it."

He chuckled as she disappeared down the hall, but humor was the last thing on his mind when she returned exactly eighteen minutes later, looking like a million dollars.

"Holy hell." He sucked in a breath.

Her face fell. "Too much? I asked Sophie what was appropriate. Was she wrong?"

How could Vaughn answer that question? "No," he said, his throat tight. "She wasn't wrong." On the other hand, Vaughn was not looking forward to other men seeing Brielle like this. She was stunning and sweet and drop-dead sexy.

The filmy white dress she wore was ethereal and sensual at the same time. Off the shoulder and fitted from breasts to knees, it almost made her appear to be naked. Because it was lined in a fabric that matched her skin tone, the whole effect was innocently suggestive. And sexy as hell.

Brie probably didn't even realize.

She wore the simple pearl necklace and earrings he had seen before. Her long, wavy blond hair was caught up in some kind of complicated knot, but with a few wispy pieces left loose to frame her face.

Turquoise eyes accented with mascara and smoky eye shadow turned his no-nonsense veterinarian into a femme fatale. Add spiky silver sandals and toes painted blush pink, and a man would be hard-pressed to decide where to start feasting on her.

He put his hands on her shoulders and massaged her soft skin, because he couldn't help himself. "You look beautiful, Brie. I'll be the envy of every man there. Let me message the driver, and we'll be on our way."

She smiled up at him, her excitement contagious. "It's been a very long time since I've had the opportunity to dress up and go out for an evening. An *adult* evening. Thanks for inviting me. I wasn't sure about leaving Danika, but I suppose there has to be a first time."

"My sister will spoil her rotten."

Brie chuckled. "I'm sure she will."

Vaughn found himself distracted during the brief drive to the TCC. Tonight was mostly about business, but that didn't keep him from anticipating the later parts of the evening when he and Brie would be alone together at the hotel.

She was the one who had made the hotel reservation while he was dealing with airport red tape. Since Brie had only booked the one room, she clearly hadn't changed her mind about them sleeping together. The realization made him hot and itchy.

His head still ached, but it would take far more discomfort than that for him to miss a chance to make love to this fascinating woman.

At the club, he was hailed as a conquering hero. Word about the forced landing had spread. People wanted to ask him about the experience.

Brie hung back as he fielded one conversation after another. She wasn't particularly shy, but everyone waiting to talk to him was male, not female. The club had accepted women as full members for some time now, but in many ways, it was still a man's world.

When there was a brief moment of privacy, Brie tugged on his arm. "What's the schedule?" she whispered.

"McCready has reserved a conference room from five until six. He's brought several of his board members."

"And what about you?"

"My lawyer is coming. But it's my company. I can negotiate on my own. Besides," he said, grinning, "I have you. My secret weapon. You'll dazzle and distract them, which will give me the edge."

Brie's lips twitched in amusement. "I'm sure I should be offended by that statement, but I'm feeling mellow, so I'll let it pass."

"Good." He curled an arm around her waist, inhaling her light perfume. "The gala officially starts at six thirty. They'll have heavy hors d'oeuvres and dancing. We can stay as long as we want…or we can head back to the hotel early."

As he watched, Brielle's face flushed dark pink. He loved that he could embarrass her so easily. She wasn't blasé about life, or anything else, for that matter. Being with her was fun. He'd never thought about it in those terms, but it was true.

They made their way down the central hallway to the back of the club and into the formal conference room. The decor relied on lots of polished wood and a traditional chandelier overhead. Cal was already in residence. His eyes widened when Vaughn walked in with Brie on his arm.

"Well, this is a surprise, Blackwood."

Vaughn lifted an eyebrow. "I'd like you to meet my good friend Brielle Gunderson. I thought she would enjoy the gala."

McCready was only a year younger than Vaughn, but he seemed older, because of the sleaze factor. The man wore Prada suits with lizard-skin loafers, an expensive cowboy hat and a killer smile that was supposed to disguise his cutthroat personality.

Brie was polite, but she didn't seem overly impressed. Vaughn relaxed inwardly. McCready wouldn't be above using a weapon against Vaughn, even if it meant dragging Brie into the middle of their business negotiation.

McCready had brought a team of six with him. Four men. Two women. One of the female VPs offered Brie a seat at the long oval table. Vaughn and his lawyer, Trent Matthews—who arrived at the last moment—sat at the head with McCready.

After that, it was game on.

McCready leaned back in his chair. "I've got a big fish on the hook. He trusts me. I'm ready to move on this, but we need plenty of capital to seal the deal."

"Money is not a problem," Vaughn said calmly. "But I want to see everything in black-and-white before I make a decision."

McCready smirked. "You don't trust me, Blackwood?"

"I don't trust anyone," Vaughn said lightly, smiling deliberately to let everyone know he was kidding. Sort of… "When it comes to this many zeroes, it doesn't pay to take unsubstantiated chances."

Cal waved a hand at his VP of acquisitions. "Show Blackwood all your fancy charts and graphs."

For the next half hour, conversation ebbed and flowed across the table. Vaughn didn't entirely trust McCready, but in this instance, it did seem as if the time was ripe to snap up an unprecedented amount of land. The drilling rights alone were incredibly valuable.

No matter how impressed he was with the bottom line, Brie's concerns rang in his ears. Was this a dirty deal? Or at the very least immoral?

Brie seemed content to watch and listen. At one point, though, he saw her ask a question of the woman sitting beside her. What was she thinking about all this?

Finally, Vaughn was satisfied he'd gotten all the information the others were willing to share. "You've given me plenty to consider, Cal. I won't stall. I'll have an answer for you in a week or so."

The workday was over, and the room emptied quickly except for the two men with the most to gain or lose. And Brie. She read the situation quickly. "If you'll excuse me, Vaughn," she said, "I need to make a phone call."

He knew she wanted to check on Danika. "Of course. Just come back here when you're done."

When the door closed behind Brie, Cal turned off the charm. "Fraternizing with the help again, I see. Isn't Gunderson the same little cookie who used to be your father's ranch hand? I always was envious of that revolving door to your bedroom."

Vaughn's temper boiled, but he kept his cool. "Shut up, McCready. We're here to talk business."

McCready shrugged. "Romantic entanglements can be *bad* for business. I'm not sure I like you bringing your lady friend to a private meeting."

The urge to punch the guy in the face was strong, but Vaughn reined in his fury. He would bide his time. There were other ways to get even with a snake. "Brie is my fiancée."

"I don't see a ring on her finger."

Cal's sneer was meant to enrage Vaughn, perhaps throw him off his game in the negotiations. And it almost worked.

But with an effort, Vaughn tamped down his ire and kept his voice calm and even. "My personal life is not your concern, McCready. To be honest, you're one of the last people I'm interested in doing business with. But you seem to have something to offer, so I'm willing to play this out. For the moment."

"And that sweet piece of as—?"

Vaughn chopped the air with his hand. "Watch yourself, Cal."

Thirteen

Brie put a hand to her mouth, her stomach churning. As soon as she walked out of the room, she had remembered that her phone was in the pocket of her shrug sweater. But when she turned to go back in, she heard Cal McCready mention her name, so she froze and stayed just outside the partially open door.

They say eavesdroppers never hear good of themselves. That was certainly true today. She could understand McCready's crass statements. He was the kind of scumbag lowlife who somehow managed to stay just inside the fringes of polite society.

What was less understandable or pleasant was the fact that Vaughn hadn't exactly defended her honor.

He'd called her his fiancée, that was true, but he hadn't denied Cal's assessment of their past.

Should he have? Or did he believe that Cal McCready was not worth the effort?

The longer she stood there, the harder it was to contemplate going back into the room. She felt small and hurt inside. As if everything was different now. She had been so sure Vaughn was changing. Seeing him interact with Danika had made Brie believe money and success were no longer the driving forces in his life.

Maybe she was kidding herself.

Before she could summon the courage to walk into the conference room, the two men exited. Vaughn's smile warmed some of the cold edges of her soul. He handed over her shrug and phone. "There you are," he said. "I was about ready to send out a search party."

Cal's lecherous assessment of her face and figure made her feel unclean. Vaughn appeared not to notice.

"I think the gala has started," she said. "I hear music."

Vaughn turned his back on the other man. "I'll be in touch soon."

Brie sensed that Vaughn's careless dismissal made McCready furious, but rather than retorting, the other man spun on his heel and walked in the opposite direction. She was glad to see him go, though no less unsettled by the words that had been spoken. Vaughn's inner thoughts remained a mystery, unfortunately.

Vaughn took her arm and steered her toward the wing that housed the TCC ballroom. The party was already in full swing. Men in formal wear and women in gorgeous dresses crowded the food tables and filled the dance floor. A seven-piece orchestra played classics from the '40s and '50s.

The gala's theme was Blast From the Past. The planning committee had decorated the walls with vintage photographs, and some men had even come wearing old military uniforms.

It was fun and interesting, but best of all, there were plenty of romantic slow dances. Brie's toes tapped out a rhythm as Vaughn introduced her to one group of people after another…as his fiancée. Though she knew the ruse was for Miranda's benefit, Brie's heart jumped every time Vaughn said the words.

All of the people she met were cordial and respectful. After all, Vaughn was the current vice president of the club. Of course, there were more questions about the plane crash. Vaughn answered them all calmly, with good humor. But as she watched, she spotted the way Vaughn held himself just slightly aloof. A layer of reserve between him and everyone else.

Not arrogance in this situation. No desire to snub anyone. Just the slight postural discomfort that perhaps only Brie noticed.

At one point, Brie left him momentarily to make a call home. Sophie sounded happy and upbeat. Nika, about to go to bed, was cheerful, too, when Sophie held the phone so Nika could hear her mother. "I'll be home tomorrow, sweetie," Brie said. It was a useless reassurance. Kids that age had no sense of time. But it made Brie feel better as she returned to the party and found her date.

After talking to what seemed like hundreds of people, Vaughn led her to the buffet. They filled their plates with delicious appetizers and found a tiny table tucked away in a corner where they were able to eat without being disturbed.

For the first time that evening, Vaughn seemed to wilt visibly. She touched his hand. "Is your head bothering you?"

He scowled. "I'm fine."

Men were such cranky patients. "You're clearly *not* fine," she said. "It's been long enough since you took that last dose of medicine. Did you bring any with you?"

"No. I did not." He cut into a bacon-wrapped scallop fiercely, as though the poor shellfish was to blame for what was likely a crushing headache.

"Oh, for heaven's sake. Here," she said, reaching into

her small evening purse for the vial of ibuprofen she carried with her. "Your wound will only feel worse if you don't stay ahead of the pain. To be honest, I'm sore, too, and I don't have stitches in my skull."

Vaughn's head shot up. His expression turned to concern. "You don't feel well?"

She grimaced. "A few twinges here and there. I think the seat belt is to blame for most of it. We hit the ground, Vaughn. There were bound to be consequences."

Suddenly, that laser-like emerald gaze focused intently on *her*. "I see it," he said, frowning. He touched her bare shoulder with a gentle fingertip. "I see the beginnings of a purple shadow. Why didn't you tell me, Brie?"

"There's nothing to tell. They checked me out after the accident. I'll have a few bruises—nothing more. All I was trying to say is that you're not any less of an alpha male if your head is bothering you. I know you're probably tougher than most, but even you have limits. Here," she said. "We'll *both* take something. Is that less threatening to your masculinity?"

He downed the tablets with a swig of champagne. "Done," he said. "Are you satisfied? Let's hit the floor."

What he probably needed was rest, but she knew she wouldn't win that battle. "Sure," she said. "I'd love to."

For some reason, she didn't expect Vaughn to be a good dancer. Maybe because he wasn't a social animal. He proved her wrong in a big way. When he took her in his arms and slid into the music seamlessly, she was charmed and enchanted.

Vaughn held her like she was a princess. As he steered her around the room, he kept her tucked close to his chest. She could feel the thud of his heartbeat where her fingertips rested against the side of his neck. His warm breath brushed her ear.

Wearing her three-inch heels, she was only a few inches

shorter than he was. They matched perfectly, every step in sync. It was magical and dangerous at the same time.

How could a woman not yearn to hang on to a man like this? Vaughn was her Prince Charming. Or she wanted him to be. She wasn't sure *what* Vaughn wanted.

One song led into another. Occasionally, someone would try to speak to them. Vaughn kept right on dancing, pretending not to hear or notice. Brie rested her cheek on his shoulder and smiled. She knew tonight was a fairy tale. Knew it wouldn't last.

Reality consisted of her job at the vet clinic and her small daughter, who had years of growing up to do with only her mother to raise her and care for her. Brie wouldn't be free to pursue her own selfish interests for a very long time.

Now that Danika was to be a flower girl, Brie and Vaughn would be enmeshed in wedding festivities for the upcoming week. But when Sophie's big day was over, there would be no more reason for Brielle to let herself be tempted by Vaughn Blackwood.

If Miranda was truly going to hand over money to Buckley's offspring, surely that would happen soon. If there was anything for Danika, great. Brie would invest it for her daughter. If not, that was fine, too. They'd get by without it. That was the easy part.

Sadly, for Brie, the bigger picture was becoming more clear every day. Vaughn's life and work were in the Dallas/Fort Worth area.

Though Vaughn had made an effort to come to Royal for his sister and was showing up for special events and supporting Sophie, he wouldn't be *staying* in Royal. He was committed to his other life, the one that didn't include Brie and Nika. That much was clear. Brie would only be courting more hurt and heartache if she let herself be persuaded otherwise.

Sometime later—time had ceased to matter—Vaughn

nuzzled her cheek and whispered in her ear. "Are you ready to go back to the hotel, Brielle?"

She pulled back and looked up at him. Though he was not a hundred percent the old Vaughn, a naughty gleam in his eyes belied his bandaged head.

"I think that's a fabulous idea."

She had no idea how much Vaughn was paying his car service, but the driver seemed to appear instantly anytime they were ready to go somewhere. Almost like a pumpkin carriage with tiny animated footmen. Brie could get used to this level of pampering.

Back at the hotel, shyness momentarily overtook her. She knew why *she* was indulging in this romantic overnight adventure. Her daughter was elsewhere, safely cared for. Brie was seizing the opportunity to feel like a woman again.

In her heart, she realized that this interlude with Vaughn had to be the end of any physical relationship. It was painful to contemplate, but she had no doubts. She was at peace with her decision.

If she had been weaving any dreams about him going down on one knee and declaring his undying love for her, the words she'd overheard at this afternoon's business meeting had put an end to that. Vaughn was a pragmatist. He was even willing to do business with a creep like Cal McCready if it meant a huge windfall for Blackwood Energy.

No doubt, Vaughn's fake engagement ploy was more of the same dispassionate, expeditious behavior of a calculated businessman.

He ushered her into their room and locked the door. Then he loosened his bow tie and pulled it free of his collar. As he struggled with the button at his throat, Brie moved closer. "Let me," she said huskily. He smelled amazing. She'd been enjoying the crisp scent of starched cotton and citrusy aftershave all evening.

He froze when she went toe-to-toe with him, invading

his space. She saw his tanned throat flex as he swallowed. "I could have done it myself," he muttered.

She freed the stubborn button and moved on to two more and then two more after that. Soon, she was ready to lift his shirttail from his pants. His taut abdomen was warm and hard beneath her curious fingertips. "I'm happy to help," she said, kissing the center of his chest and drawing his shirt upward from his belt. "After all, you saved my life today."

He chuckled hoarsely. "I was technically the one who put you *in* jeopardy, so I'm not going to brag about the whole savior thing. For the record, though, the FAA thinks it was likely an engine malfunction."

"Maybe I should be in charge tonight…you know…since you've been injured."

His green eyes flashed with heat. "I'm listening."

"Think about it," she said. "In the old days, you always called the shots. I was naive about men when I met you. I suppose I could say you taught me everything I know."

"You weren't a virgin."

"No. Did that bother you?"

"Of course not. I don't believe in double standards."

"Still, you were light-years ahead of me in experience."

"Did that bother *you*?" He threw the question back at her, his expression hard to read.

"Sometimes," she admitted. "I knew I was the flavor of the week. You had a reputation. Still have one, I guess. There were a lot of women giving me the death stare tonight. I couldn't tell them you weren't really off the market."

"As long as we're engaged, even if it's a faux engagement, I won't do anything to dishonor you, Brie. You have my word."

"Thank you. Hopefully, this arrangement will be resolved before long. If Miranda is about to spring a few surprises about the estate, I think it will be soon. Her life is in New York now. She's already spent far longer settling your father's affairs than most people thought she would. I heard that Buckley made a huge donation to her charity."

"Probably the only decent thing he ever did."

The shadows in his eyes bothered her. "It's okay to love people, Vaughn, even when they disappoint us. Your father had his faults, plenty of them, in fact. But you loved him. I know you must have been grieving in your own way."

He rested his forehead against hers. "Mostly, I've been angry. At him. At Miranda. At myself."

She cupped his cheek, feeling the late-day stubble, the warm skin. "Why yourself?"

Vaughn pulled free and crossed the room, pausing to stare out the window at the twinkling lights of Dallas. Their suite was on the top floor. Brie had requested a simple king room. The hotel had upgraded them after she'd given Vaughn's name.

He leaned his forearm against the glass and sighed. "I was a punk-ass adolescent. Even if he had wanted to be a good father, I made sure he knew I didn't need him or anybody. And once that distance between us was in place, it stuck."

"You're feeling guilty because he died alone." She made it a statement. Vaughn didn't deny her claim.

Instead, he searched out a bottle of wine and released the cork, pouring two glasses and handing Brie one. "Enough serious talk," he said. "We came here to have fun."

She wrinkled her nose. "I thought you came to make a deal with Cal McCready."

"You don't approve?"

"It's not my place to approve or disapprove. But if you're asking my opinion, the man gives me the creeps."

"Fair enough. I probably shouldn't have taken you to that meeting. I'm sorry, Brie."

"It wasn't bad. I was intrigued. It was my first opportunity to see you in your natural habitat."

The corners of his mouth ticked up in a rueful grin. "My natural habitat? I think I've been insulted."

She drained her wineglass and kicked off her shoes, groaning when her bare toes dug into the plush carpet. "Not at all. I thought you were very sexy. Everyone in the room hung on your every word. It must be a kick to have so much power."

He set his glass aside, still half-full. "You should know, Brie. You've always had that kind of power over me. In the bedroom."

She gaped at him. "That's absurd."

"Is it?" He stood there, cocky as hell with his bare chest and his ruffled hair, and gave her an emerald-eyed look that sent heat coursing through her lower abdomen.

"Why are you teasing me?" she stuttered.

He reached for her hand and dragged her close. "It's called foreplay, my sweet Brie. I'm surprised you haven't heard of it."

Fourteen

Vaughn had always enjoyed sparring with Brielle Gunderson. But not as much as making love to her. If he hadn't been hard as an iron pike, he might have been amused by her slack-jawed astonishment. Under the circumstances, he didn't enjoy winning this round as much as he should have.

"Kiss me, Brie," he said. "Like you mean it."

Her lashes lowered, hiding her expression. But her lips met his without hesitation. There it was again. The jolt. The blow. The all-out shock to his system.

He lifted her off her feet and shoved his mouth on hers roughly. His plan had been to woo her, to coax her into giving him her trust, her hunger, her soft woman's body.

Instead, he lost his mind. "How does this damn dress come off?" he groaned.

Brie leaned into him, arms encircling his neck. "Over my head. It's stretchy. You know…"

He did *not* know. But he was about to find out.

Releasing her was an effort. He made himself set her

on her feet. "Lift your arms," he said as he grabbed the hem of her skirt.

She obeyed, but as he dragged the fabric to her hips and higher, he floundered. Her tiny panties revealed everything. And his lover wasn't wearing a bra. Because the dress was two thin layers instead of one, he hadn't noticed. He must be slipping.

Now Brie was naked from her toes to her neck, except for a tiny scrap of nylon at her hips. Her voice was muffled. "I'm suffocating," she complained.

He had unwittingly stopped short of pulling the dress off completely, gobsmacked by the sight of Brie's naked body. Most of the dress was swathed around her head. "Sorry," he muttered. He kept at it, and moments later, tossed the dress aside.

"My hair's a mess now," she said.

Vaughn took her hands and lifted them one at a time to his lips. As he kissed each palm, he inhaled sharply, feeling his chest wobble in a weird way. "You're perfect."

Slowly, he removed all the hundred and one pins holding her artful hairstyle together. Then he winnowed his fingers through her silky blond tresses until they fell across her bare shoulders.

Brie put her hands over his. "Make love to me, Vaughn."

"Yes." The single syllable was guttural. It was hard to talk with a boulder in his throat.

He scooped her up and carried her to the bed. Brie looked at him so intently it made him nervous. "What?" he said, sprawling beside her. "Why are you looking at me like that?"

She shrugged with a small smile on her lips. "I like looking at you. But I notice you're still wearing pants."

He glanced down, surprised to see that she was right. "Maybe I do have a concussion," he said ruefully. Or maybe he was distracted because he was suddenly coming to realize just how much Brie meant to him. He couldn't tell her. Not yet. Not when he didn't understand it himself.

"Five seconds," he promised, stumbling to his feet and removing the rest of his clothing.

"And not to be picky," she said, "but I'm really hoping for more than one condom."

"Duly noted." He'd taken care of that item back in Royal before he did anything else for this trip.

When he joined her a second time, he pulled her close, burying her face in his shoulder and inhaling the scent of her shampoo. He ran his hands down her back, stopping when he reached the tantalizing curves of her cute butt.

Brie stirred restlessly. "You're smothering me again."

He pulled back and chuckled. How could he be so aroused and yet feel such an enormous wave of emotion for this woman? "I think I've lost my mojo," he said, not entirely kidding. Knowing that she could have died today affected him deeply.

"Because of the bump on your head?"

"That could be it." Or more likely, he was navigating unknown territory. This *thing* with Brie was about more than sex. His gut tightened. He'd never admitted that, even if it was true three years ago. When she walked out on him— because he pushed her away—he'd been devastated.

But his attitude at the time had been *to hell with women, this one in particular*. He'd buried himself in his work and convinced his heart (if he had one) that he was better off without her.

For almost three years, he had believed the lie. Right up until the moment Brie showed up on Sophie's doorstep.

And now he had a daughter.

The whole situation was a huge, tangled train wreck.

But now was not the moment to look for solutions. Now was the chance to play.

He took his time with her. There was no one knocking at

the door, no urgent phone calls. Danika was safe and happy with Sophie. Vaughn was free to make Brie as insane with hunger and desire as she made him.

She was on her back now. He leaned over her, resting his weight on one elbow. Big aquamarine eyes scanned his face. The uncertainty he sensed in them shamed him. No wonder she was not entirely comfortable with this relationship. He had never given her any reason to think he was a guy who could be counted on to stand beside her and make a real commitment.

But a man could change. His sister believed it. Dixie, too. Slowly, Vaughn was coming to understand that perhaps he wasn't as much of an independent loner as he had once thought.

He kissed her forehead, her nose, her delicate throat, each pert raspberry nipple. "Tonight was fun," he said. "We should do it more often."

"The club gala was great." She paused. "I can't do this kind of thing on a regular basis, though. I like spending time with you, Vaughn, but it's complicated and messy. I'm at a point in my life where I need structure and stability. Let's concentrate on the here and now."

Her speech winded him, nicked his pride. Did she not even want to try anymore?

"Carpe diem," he whispered, bending his head to find the vulnerable indentation below her ear. When Brie whimpered and arched her back, he exulted. *This* he was good at. This he could do.

He spent the next half hour worshipping every inch of her creamy, smooth skin. No tiny spot went unnoticed.

Brie begged. She moaned. She pleaded.

He had wanted her for so long now, his unappeased erection might do him in. Crippled with lust and blinded by the need to make her admit how much she wanted and needed him, he drove her higher and higher, using every trick in his arsenal.

When he kissed her again, she bit his lip. Hard. Enough that he tasted the tang of blood on his tongue. He jerked back. "Hell, woman. What was that for?"

"Quit torturing me. I want you inside me. Now."

Her urgency sent his arousal an impossible notch higher. He rolled off the bed so fast he nearly landed on his head. While Brie had the audacity to giggle, Vaughn located the protection and waved a strip over the bed. "Think this will do it?"

Brie pretended to consider the question seriously, trying not to grin. "Maybe for the first hour."

After that, things blurred. Vaughn rolled on protection, not waiting for Brie to help. He didn't even let her touch him. He was so wired that any little bit of stimulation from her was going to flip his switch.

Instead, he moved between her thighs, spread them farther and tried to catch his breath. He entered her slowly, bracing himself on his elbows to spare her his full weight. She seemed precious to him. Fragile. When he reached the head of her womb, they both sighed in unison, as if they had made it through dangerous waters to a final destination.

But Vaughn was just beginning. Brie's body was tight and warm, wrapping him in incredible heat, caressing his sex with inner muscles. He withdrew once, intending to stroke slowly, again and again, until he made her come.

Instead, Brie locked her ankles behind his back and canted her hips. "Harder," she pleaded. "More."

That did it. He snapped. If she wanted harder, he could oblige. The bed shook as he thrust wildly. Brie cried out his name.

Dimly, he realized she was climaxing. He wanted to pause and appreciate her excitement, but his own orgasm slammed into him and yanked him into a dark place where pleasure was so overpowering that it bordered on pain. He groaned aloud, shuddering at the intense release.

Then exhaustion claimed him, and he let oblivion roll over him.

At 3:00 a.m., Brie shifted and looked at her phone. Her legs ached, her sex was tender and she had a goofy smile plastered all over her face. Thankfully, it was dark and there was no one around to see.

No one but Vaughn, and he was still dead asleep. Her inventive, flatteringly desperate lover had rocked her world and then collapsed. She was vaguely worried about his head, but surely no one that virile and *accommodating* could be seriously hurt.

Gingerly, she slid out of bed. After using the bathroom, she washed up—everywhere—and examined her reflection in the mirror. Some of her aches and pains were from the plane crash. The bruise on her shoulder was turning a darker shade of purple.

The idea of boarding a jet later today made her slightly queasy, but she knew waiting would only make the fear worse. Instead of thinking about what was to come, she returned to the bedroom and scooted back under the covers.

The air-conditioning had chilled her skin. Spooning Vaughn's big, warm body was like huddling up to a campfire. Instant bliss.

He mumbled something. She stroked his hair. "Go back to sleep."

Vaughn had set an alarm. It was a good thing, because he and Brie were sound asleep when the damned phone went off. He silenced the annoying chirp and groaned.

Sometime before dawn he had awakened and found a soft, sleeping woman beside him. It wasn't long before he was making love to Brie. Again.

Then more blissful sleep. When was the last time he'd had such a restful night? Maybe never.

He was starting to get the idea that he might want to sleep like this forever.

He turned on his side and faced her. There was just enough ambient light to see her features outlined in shadow. Her lashes were dark crescents on her cheeks.

"Brie. Wake up, sweet thing."

She mumbled and buried her head in the pillow. He grinned. Though Brie was accustomed to getting up early every morning with a busy toddler, she *wasn't* in the habit of being disturbed during the night by a hungry male in her bed.

"I've got a meeting with my lawyer at nine thirty," he said quietly. "It won't take long. Just a few loose ends so he and I are on the same page. This deal with McCready may need to be tied up while I'm still in Royal."

"Mm-hmm." Still her eyes were closed.

"Checkout isn't until noon. I'll be back in plenty of time."

One arm raised. She waved a hand. "Go. I'll order room service. Don't worry about me."

He rolled out of bed. "If you order in a hurry, I'll eat with you. But I have to be out of here in forty-five minutes."

Vaughn had a hard time concentrating on business. The vision of a sleepy Brie wrapped in a hotel robe eating strawberries was a hard one to shake. He'd had twelve minutes to wolf down an omelet and a flaky croissant before he'd had to run. He'd taken his coffee in a to-go cup in the car.

His lawyer, Trent Matthews, was droning on now about something. The man was two decades older than Vaughn. They had different outlooks on life. Vaughn should probably have found other representation long ago, but his father had fired Trent way back when, and Vaughn had felt sorry for the man.

The guy wasn't a bad lawyer. The women certainly seemed to like him. The charming, aging Brad Pitt type, still had influence in the Dallas/Fort Worth area, so he had more going for him than looks.

Vaughn focused on the task at hand. "Are we clear how to proceed with McCready?"

"Sure," Trent said heartily. "Where do things stand on your father's will? Have you thought about challenging Miranda Dupree in court?"

Matthews was definitely overstepping. Vaughn kept his cool. "There *is* a slight possibility that things aren't final yet. And you should know that my fiancée and I have a daughter together. I plan to pursue any possible share of my father's inheritance for my daughter's sake. She's currently Buckley's only grandchild."

Trent blanched. "I see. Well, then, I can amend these documents."

Vaughn scowled, feeling his skin crawl in warning. "What documents, Matthews?"

The lawyer didn't meet his gaze. Instead, he shuffled piles on his desk. "When I heard yesterday that you were engaged, I drew up some papers to protect you in this deal we're working on. Not a prenup, per se. Simply an acknowledgment that Ms. Gunderson is not entitled to any of the proceeds from the McCready deal, because it was already in process before she became your fiancée. Pretty standard stuff. In case you were to marry and divorce. Look for yourself."

Vaughn took the papers automatically, his brain spinning. He perused the sheaf of legalese with growing distaste. According to this, Brie would be cut out even *when and if* she and Vaughn were married.

He handed them back. "Why in the hell would you do this without asking me? My wife will be entitled to everything I own. No. A thousand times no."

Trent's gaze widened. "Because I didn't put the kid in yet?"

Vaughn's glare was furious. "The *kid's* name is Danika. Whatever I have is hers. You can shred all of that, Matthews. I don't need it."

As Vaughn stormed out of the building, sick to his stomach and incredibly frustrated, he recognized this watershed moment for what it was. He'd spent his entire career making decisions based on the financial bottom line…putting money before relationships.

Those days were gone. No matter what happened between Brielle and him, he was no longer capable of being an island. A man with a daughter had to change.

Whether he liked it or not…

Fifteen

Brie put Sophie's call on speakerphone and continued loading the dishwasher. Danika played at her feet. "I don't know why you're so upset, Sophie. You went to England. Shrewsbury Hall, right? These people aren't strangers."

Sophie voice quavered. "You don't understand. This is different. Nigel's family has never been to Royal. He and I are going to walk into the Bellamy and watch British aristocracy go smack up against Texas cowboy culture. Tea cozies and mechanical bulls. Centuries of history and culture versus twenty-four-ounce steaks and silver-dollar bars."

Brie laughed in spite of Sophie's distress. "And to make matters worse, under the roof of that same five-star resort are four reality TV actresses." Who, as everyone in Royal knew, were Miranda's larger-than-life costars from *Secret Lives of NYC Ex-Wives*, all back for the wedding.

Brie dried her hands and picked up the phone. "Relax, Soph. Talk to Nigel if you're freaking out. I'm sure there won't be *actual* bloodshed." When she hung up a few moments later, she was still chuckling.

Brie was really excited about Sophie's wedding. What woman didn't enjoy the spectacle of a huge ceremony with an enormous crowd of well-wishers? She had taken Danika to Natalie Valentine's bridal shop and had her fitted in the adorable flower girl outfit Sophie had selected. Plenty of eyelet lace and grosgrain ribbon and ruffles.

Nika loved her new costume, even if she didn't fully understand what was to come.

Vaughn had been curiously quiet and withdrawn on their return to Royal. Perhaps he was being careful to protect Brie's reputation by not staying at her house overnight. Some folks in Royal were pretty conservative. While she appreciated his courtesy and circumspection, she missed him desperately.

His reticence was aligning with Brie's plan to end their sexual relationship. She should be happy. But she hadn't expected it to hurt quite so much.

Still, life was too busy to dwell on what might have been. Because Nika was in the wedding, Brie was now on the guest list for the rehearsal dinner. Which meant finding a dress for that occasion *and* the wedding. She had planned to wear something already in her closet, but while she'd been at the bridal shop, Natalie had pulled out all the stops and talked Brie into two entirely new outfits that were too beautiful to pass up.

Brie's credit card took a hit, but with her childcare costs reduced, she could afford to splurge. Though it was humbling to admit, she wanted Vaughn to see her in her new dresses. She wanted him to know what he was missing.

Sophie and Nigel must have been living right. The weather forecast for the wedding weekend called for blue skies, warm temps and low humidity. The excitement in

Royal was off the charts. It wasn't often that an actual English dame showed up.

Not that Nigel's grandmother was stuffy at all. Brie had met her briefly. The elderly lady was quite a character. And she certainly didn't stand on ceremony.

Closer to home, Brie and Vaughn had argued over the schedule for Friday afternoon and evening. Brie thought Vaughn ought to be out at Blackwood Hollow ranch to help his sister and the rest of the family with any last-minute emergencies that might arise.

Vaughn stood in her living room and scowled. "You and Nika should come with me. No sense in having two vehicles. Parking is going to be a zoo."

Brie held on to her patience by a thread. She was exhausted already, and Vaughn was still not acting like himself. "Believe me," she said. "The important thing is to make sure that Danika is in good shape for the wedding. Two-year-olds have a narrow window of cooperative behavior in situations like a wedding rehearsal. My plan is to give her a late nap and then drive her out there just in time for the wedding director to start lining everyone up."

Vaughn shook his head slowly. "It's only throwing a few rose petals from a basket. How hard can it be?"

She went to him and touched his arm. "This will be a stressful day for everyone. Trust me on this, Vaughn. Please."

He exhaled. "Okay. But I don't like it. I wanted everyone to see us together."

"And they will," she said. "But we're not going to be the focus. This weekend is all about your sister, the bride."

His handsome mouth quirked in a smile. "As if she would let either Kellan or me forget it." He paused. "Nigel is a good guy—right? I want Soph to be happy."

"I think he's wonderful. You're gaining a brother-in-law

who will be very good to her. I can already tell. He dotes
on Sophie. Surely you've noticed."

"I have," he admitted. "It's sickeningly cute."

"Don't be such a cynic. Love makes the world go round,
haven't you heard?"

"I'm not sure I know what love is. Do you?" He shocked
her with a serious answer.

The room fell silent. Nika was only a few feet away happily playing with her building blocks.

Brie swallowed. Maybe now was the time to let Vaughn
know that it was okay to live his life on his own terms. "I
think love means letting the other person be who they are.
Love isn't love if you're always trying to change someone.
When two people are in love, they should care more about
their partner's happiness than their own." She paused self-
consciously. "I guess that's more than you wanted to know."

His gaze was guarded. Intense. "Not at all. I think it
makes perfect sense. And I'll bow to your wisdom about
Danika. You're her mother. You know her best."

"Thank you for understanding."

He glanced at his watch. "In that case, I suppose I should
head on out to the ranch. I'll take other clothes with me and
shower at the bunkhouse. Kellan and I have volunteered
for manual labor. I don't know if Darius has arrived yet."

Brie followed him to the door. "And it wouldn't hurt
to keep an eye on Nigel's family. They're great, but a bit
overwhelming with the lot of them all together. Sophie's
intimidated, I think. Let her know you're in her corner."

Vaughn curled an arm around her and tugged her in for
a quick but thorough kiss. "You're a good person, Brie."

His unexpected affection caught her off guard. She
would have been happy to linger over the kiss, but Vaughn
was already on the way out the door.

"I'll see you soon," she said.

He turned, with the sunlight grazing his masculine profile. "Call me if you need me. I mean it, Brie. I want you to enjoy tonight. You deserve a pleasant evening, even if you are the mother of the flower girl. You work hard. It's time for some play."

Kace LeBlanc was suffering from wedding fever. He was as surprised as anyone to find out he was susceptible. It didn't help that his office was near Natalie Valentine's bridal shop. Every time he glanced out the window, he was treated to a view of women and girls parading in and out, excitedly choosing finery for the wedding of the season.

Considering the fact that only months ago the entire Blackwood family was in a deep funk, it was nothing short of miraculous that at least two of them had found happiness. First Kellan, now Sophie.

The weddings made Kace feel a little less guilty.

To be honest, he was tired of being considered the town scrooge just because he was one who'd delivered the bad news about a certain controversial will. He had a job to do, and he did it well. It wasn't his fault that the dead sometimes left chaos in the wake of their passing.

Buckley Blackwood had certainly put his kids though the wringer. And left a mess for his personal lawyer and his ex-wife to negotiate. Kace sometimes wanted to get his forehead tattooed—*Don't shoot the messenger.*

At the moment, though, his professional life wasn't the problem. Kace was horny. And confused. And about to do something utterly un-Kace-like.

Even worse, he had no idea at all how Lulu was going to respond. They had never talked about getting serious. Or even about being a couple, for that matter. The TV star had dazzled him from the moment he met her, early on when *Secret Lives* first began filming in Royal. But their relationship had not exactly gone smoothly.

He patted his pocket and pulled up the daily calendar on

his phone. Timing was everything. Kace had been forced to bribe one of the *Secret Lives* cameramen in order to pull off this coup. The fact that the outcome was uncertain left his stomach in a knot.

When he checked his watch, he saw that it was eleven forty-five. In exactly fifteen minutes, Lulu Shepard and three of her costars were supposed to meet at the Royal Diner, have lunch and then head over to Natalie's to pick up their gowns for the wedding tomorrow.

Kace was planning a rendezvous.

He stared down the street, remembering the day he and Lulu first met. It was last December. The entire town had been decked out in Christmas finery. Kace hadn't been feeling any particular holiday spirit, but his office was being painted, so he had camped out in the diner with legal papers spread all over his table.

In swooped one of the most beautiful and appealing women he had ever seen. He'd noticed her warm brown skin and wild, glorious hair immediately. Her deliberately provocative personality had taken time to warm up to.

The infuriating woman had sassed him and made fun of him and generally driven him up the wall at their first meeting.

But she had made an impression. Lord help him, Lulu Shephard had burst into his life like a whirlwind, and he hadn't been the same since. Half the time he wanted to smack her. The other half he was mad with lust for her curvaceous, sexy body.

What was a highly trained legal mind supposed to do with that conundrum?

At exactly eight minutes before twelve, he shut off his laptop and stood to fasten the top button of his shirt and straighten his tie.

His palms were sweaty. His heart raced. There was no going back from this. When his nerve nearly failed him, he summoned an image of Lulu in his bed…screaming, as she had once promised him in jest. Hearing her groan his name when she came was one of the highlights of his life.

Hell. His body tightened. It was too late to remember that he needed a haircut. In an ill-fated attempt to tame his rumpled look, he scraped two hands through his hair.

By the time he made it to the diner, his forehead was damp. Couldn't blame the weather. It was Kace who was a mess.

He was a very private man as a rule. Lulu lived her life, at least for the moment, under the ever-watchful eye of the cameras. Being a reality TV star meant little privacy during the day.

Thankfully, there had been zero witnesses when Kace had taken her to bed. Not that he was ashamed of what they were doing. Oh no. But certain things were sacred between a man and a woman. To his relief, Lulu had been equally discreet, working with him to hide their rendezvous from the ever-present cameras that followed her everywhere.

As he opened the door of the diner, he met the gaze of the cameraman, Sam, who was already set up to film the women as they entered the eatery. His cohort, Henry, would be bringing up the rear of the group, so there would be plenty of different shots to build an episode.

Sam grinned and gave Kace a thumbs-up.

Kace managed to nod and tried not to puke. He hated the limelight. This entire endeavor was supposed to show his luscious Lulu that he was meeting her on her terms.

The regular folks in the diner had obviously perked up when they saw Sam. You would think after all this time that Royal's citizens would be sick of having snippets of their lives show up on TV, but they all seemed to be enjoying the notoriety, even now.

The door swung open, and the cameras started to roll. Rafaela was first, of course. She was invariably intent on capturing the most screen time. Her raison d'être was fame, and her biggest concern was how the *Secret Lives* show was going to propel her to the big-time.

Next was party girl Zooey, and then Seraphina, who was Lulu's best friend and the fiancée of local rancher and former war hero Clint Rockwell. Kace had briefly entertained bringing Fee in on the secret, but she and Lulu were tight. He wasn't sure the other woman could keep quiet.

Miranda was the only ex-wife missing. She had been kind of busy lately with real-life drama.

Finally, the woman he wanted to see breezed in. She was wearing tight black leather pants, five-inch stilettos and a tangerine sweater that emphasized her bountiful breasts.

Kace was hard instantly.

When she saw him, her ever-ready confidence faltered. "Kace. What are you doing here?" She stepped in front of him, obviously trying to shield him from the cameras.

He slid his hands beneath her hair, tilted her head to one side and put his lips on hers, tasting the seam of her mouth, probing for entry. When he'd kissed her quite thoroughly, he finally pulled back. "Hi," he said huskily.

Lulu was completely thrown off stride. She pulled back and glanced over her shoulder, making a slashing motion with one hand, telling the cameras to stop rolling. Sam and Henry ignored her.

Her gorgeous almond-shaped eyes widened as Kace grabbed her a second time.

"I haven't seen you in two days," he complained. "I've missed you."

Lulu melted into him for a full thirty seconds, moaning quietly as he let her know how *much* he had missed her. But this time she broke free, agitated now.

"They're filming us," she hissed urgently. "Let's slip out the back, and we can talk."

"I don't want to slip out the back," Kace said stubbornly.

"It doesn't matter who's watching." One glance told him that Sam and Henry were ready.

Kace went down on one knee and pulled a sapphire velvet box from his pocket. He flipped open the lid, exposing the large, flawless solitaire he had picked out. "Lulu Shephard, will you marry me?"

A unison gasp swept around the diner. Lulu's costars uncharacteristically held back from displaying any drama, their expressions wobbling between awe and envy and delight.

Lulu put her hands to her cheeks, tears glistening, threatening to spill over. "Are you crazy?" she whispered. "You're a by-the-book lawyer. I'm a reality TV star."

He got to his feet, still holding the box. "Don't cry, Lu, my sweet girl. You'll ruin your makeup." Using his fingertip, he gathered her tears carefully and wiped them on his pants leg. "This is our big moment. Editing can only do so much," he chuckled.

Lulu sucked in a breath. "I can't believe you're doing this, especially right now."

"Romance is in the air this weekend," he said. "I wanted in on the excitement. Lulu, my love, you're the piece of my life I never knew was missing. You make me laugh. You make me want your insanely hot body. You make me proud to know you. Say you'll marry me, Lulu. Say you'll be my wife till death do us part. Say you want me, too. Please."

From a few feet away, Fee's excited voice called out encouragement. "Say yes, Lulu. Do it."

Everything in the room blurred and went still. All Kace could see was his lover's face. "Do you love me, Lulu? Will you wear this ring and make me a happy man?"

His larger-than-life, vulnerable-beneath-the-surface sweetheart wiggled her hand in front of his face. "Yes, yes, yes!" she cried. "Oh my gosh, I'm engaged." Her beaming smile could have powered a small city.

Kace slipped the beautiful ring on the third finger of her left hand. He leaned close to her ear, dropping his voice so that even the powerful mics couldn't eavesdrop on his words. "No take-backs, Lulu. This is for now and for always. I'm never letting you go."

When she kissed him, he forgot the cameras were recording. He forgot he liked an orderly, dignified life. Everything he had ever wanted was right here in his arms.

According to the networks, there was no such thing as too much good TV, but eventually, the diner manager cleared his throat loudly. "Um, break it up, you two. We've got customers waiting on their orders."

Kace and Lulu stepped back from each other sheepishly and grinned. Her smile faltered. "I love you, too, Kace. I'm sorry I said lawyers lacked a sense of humor and had no talent for joy in their lives. I was wrong."

"Actually," he muttered, "you didn't say that about *all* lawyers…just me."

"Oh, lordy." Her expression was mortified. "Are you always going to remember every mean thing I say?"

"Probably. But don't worry, sweetheart. You can make it up to me later. In bed," he clarified, just in case she wasn't paying attention.

One of the townspeople shouted encouragement. "Kiss her again, LeBlanc."

"Don't mind if I do…"

Sixteen

Brie looked in the rearview mirror to make sure Danika was doing okay. Of all days, Nika had chosen today to nap longer than usual. Brie was forced to wake her up at four, which was guaranteed to put her daughter in a grumpy mood.

Now, the little girl had a sippy cup of water and a bag of animal crackers in her lap and seemed to be content, at least for the moment. The rehearsal was at six. Which meant Nika's dinner would be late. Brie was trying to ward off a meltdown.

When they got to Blackwood Hollow, Brie followed directions Vaughn had sent in a text. Two huge white tents stood against the indigo of an early-evening sky. One was set up for the rehearsal dinner, the second for the ceremony itself—hundreds of chairs and a very long center aisle.

Brie had her doubts about being able to coax her daughter all the way to the front, much less throw petals the way she was supposed to, but Sophie was dead set on having her niece play a part, so whatever happened would happen.

One glance at her watch told Brie she had timed her arrival as closely as possible. She lifted the hatch of her little car, stripped Danika down in the back and quickly dressed her in a cute, comfortable sundress. Sophie's wedding director would have the basket of rose petals. Fake ones for tonight, and the real deal for tomorrow.

Vaughn met her at the back of the tent. His shoulders visibly relaxed at the sight of them. "I was getting worried."

"We're here," she said, squeezing his hand.

He bent to pick up Danika. "How's my little girl?"

As Brie watched, openmouthed, Nika cuddled up to Vaughn's shoulder and giggled when he pretended to tickle her tummy. Father and daughter had been spending time together, but Vaughn hadn't been by the house in several days. Brie was surprised by her daughter's openness. Pleasantly so.

Sophie joined them, vibrating with excitement. "We're about to start. Do I look okay?"

Vaughn kissed his sister's cheek. "You look gorgeous. Is everyone here?"

"One of the groomsmen is on a delayed flight, but we have a stand-in."

The director scurried over. "Ms. Blackwood? I'm ready if you are."

After that, it was controlled chaos. The bridesmaids and groomsmen practiced processing in and walking out. An eight-piece orchestra played "Pachelbel's Canon" over and over.

The adults decided not to wear out the flower girl, so only when the rest of the bridal party was sure of their parts did the director turn to Danika. "Okay, little lady. It's time for you to walk in front of the bride."

The plan was for Kellan and Vaughn to flank their sister on either side going down the aisle. But already Danika was showing signs of being overwhelmed by the setting and all the strangers.

Brie and Sophie both talked to her, but it was Vaughn who saved the day. He squatted in front of his daughter and spoke to her at eye level with a gentle smile. "Here's what I'll do, Nika." He pointed toward the length of the ivory satin runner. "I'll sit on the end of that aisle way up there and you can walk to me. How about that? And you can drop the flowers while you're coming to meet me."

Something in the tone of his voice or in his words reassured the not-quite two-year-old. Brie's heart melted at the interaction between father and child. She didn't know Vaughn had it in him.

Sophie and Kellan quickly moved into position. Vaughn loped to the front of the tent. The director gave a wave to the orchestra, who started playing once again.

Brie handed Danika her basket and gave her a little nudge. "Go to Mr. V. He's waiting for you."

As Brie watched, fingers crossed, Nika started walking and tossing flower petals as if she had been doing it her entire life. Sophie began to cry sentimental tears. Kellan gave her a handkerchief.

It took a while. But the bride was in no hurry.

Eventually, the woman of the hour and her hesitant petal tosser made it into position in front of the minister. Everyone breathed a collective sigh of relief.

After a quick conference with the bride, the director deemed the rehearsal satisfactory.

Vaughn hoisted Nika on his shoulders and came back to where Brie was standing. "How did it look from back here?"

"Perfect. Charming. Now, if she'll only do it tomorrow."

Vaughn grinned. "I have faith in her."

Brie lifted Danika down from her perch and took her

daughter's hand. "I've got her dinner in the car. As soon as I feed her, I have a friend who is going to swap cars with me and take her home so I can stay for the rest of the evening."

Vaughn frowned. "A friend?"

"A college student home on spring break, actually. I've known her and her parents for a long time. Tabitha will put Nika to bed and stay with her until I get home."

"How do we know she's trustworthy?"

It was Brie's turn to smile. "Good grief, Vaughn. I'm not sending my only child home with a stranger. Tabitha knows Nika and me. And I know her. She's as good as it gets when it comes to babysitters. Nika will be fine."

Seventeen

Vaughn didn't like it, but he could see the sense in Brie's plan. There was no way a two-year-old could make it through a long, fancy dinner. Instead, Danika was soon settled, eating a cheese sandwich, enjoying the novelty of being perched in the back of the car and, at the same time, ignoring the adults.

"Okay. If you've got this covered, I'm going to go back in and talk to Sophie. Apparently my big-hearted sister has invited the stepwitch to the rehearsal dinner, God knows why."

Brie stared at him oddly. "Well, Blackwood Hollow *is* Miranda's home now. And she's been kind enough to let Sophie have her wedding here. I really don't see what you have against Miranda, Vaughn. It's not her fault that your father made that crazy will."

"Doesn't mean I have to like her." His chest tightened, thinking about the injustice of it all.

Brie leaned against the car, hands propped behind her.

She studied his face. "Is it so terribly hard to be back here at Blackwood Hollow?"

He thought about it. So far today, he'd been running on adrenaline. Now he gave the question serious consideration. "Yes and no," he said slowly. "This is the first time since the will reading for me. I don't know about the others. There are plenty of bad memories here—but there are good ones, too. I like remembering Mom when she wasn't sick. When she was happy and productive and all of us kids were running around. Those were good days."

"Isn't that why Sophie wanted the wedding here? To remember your past and honor your mom?"

"Yes."

"So maybe Sophie is grateful to Miranda for making that possible."

"I suppose." He glanced over his shoulder at the tents and made a snap decision. "If Miranda is here, I don't want to miss our chance to establish Danika's claim to the inheritance." He reached in his pocket. "Here. Put this on."

Brie's expression was not what he had anticipated. She seemed both shocked and horrified, if that were possible.

"This was one of my mother's rings," he said. "We want this engagement to look like the real deal." Since Brie was making no move to take the heavy piece of jewelry, he slid it onto her finger. "I want you to keep it when this is all over. The stone will look good with your eyes." Donna-Leigh Blackwood had been a stunner in her day. The engagement ring was a huge, perfectly rectangular aquamarine surrounded by a rim of sparkling diamonds.

Brie seemed *stricken*, or something. He couldn't read her. "I can't keep this," she said. "It's far too valuable, not to mention impractical for a vet to wear to work."

"It will be Danika's someday. Wear it. Don't wear it. But tonight, it's important." He glanced at his watch. "I've got to get back over there and see what's going on."

Brie nodded, her expression unreadable. "I'll text you when I'm heading back inside."

Vaughn strode away from the two females, feeling out of sorts. In his heart, he had thought Brie would be happy to wear his mother's ring, even if for only a short while. Instead, he had the distinct impression he had insulted her.

Women. No wonder he had stayed away from entanglements all these years. They were too much trouble.

When he rejoined the bridal group, everyone had moved from the tent where the ceremony was to take place into the second tent that had been set up for a lavish dinner of prime rib and all the accoutrements. The spread looked amazing. But no one seemed to be in charge of crowd control.

The Brits were obviously flagging. They hadn't been here long enough yet to be over their jet lag, and it was late back in England. By contrast, all the bridesmaids and groomsmen were laughing and talking and enjoying the open bar.

Vaughn found Sophie, Nigel and Kellan. "I think everyone is hungry. Why don't we get them seated so the servers can begin?"

Nigel nodded. "Indeed." He put his fingers to his lips and gave a loud, perfect whistle.

The crowd stilled instantly. Nigel waved a hand. "Find your place cards, ladies and gentlemen. The meal is about to begin. Thank you for joining us this evening."

With that taken care of, Vaughn took Sophie's hand. "Is Miranda really here?"

Sophie's gaze narrowed. "You will *not* cause a scene, Vaughn Blackwood. This is my wedding weekend."

"Not to worry. I'll be good as gold. I just need to tell her something."

Sophie pursed her lips. "And you might as well know, Kace is with her."

"Kace?" Vaughn scowled. "Why? Isn't he newly engaged to that Lulu person?"

Nigel intervened. "Come on, old chap. Lighten up. This is a party. No one is going to upset my angel."

"Sorry," Vaughn muttered.

In that instant, Brie appeared. As she approached from a distance, Vaughn's heart kicked in his chest. He'd been so focused on his master plan and Miranda, he hadn't stopped to appreciate how damned beautiful Brie looked.

She had worn her hair down tonight, masses of golden waves that framed her face and made her look both appealing and vulnerable. The gown she wore was dressy but perfect for an outdoor event—a frothy confection of royal blue and silver tulle over satin. The bodice was fitted at the waist, where the dress fanned out in a full skirt that stopped just above her knees. When he glanced at her hand, he saw that she hadn't removed the ring.

The jolt of pleasure he got from seeing the ring on her finger was concerning. Why should he care that his mark of possession was on her hand? It wasn't as if any of this was real.

A tiny voice inside his head told him it *could* be. Real, that was. Real and permanent and life changing.

It was that last bit that worried him the most. He liked his life. Didn't he? Why tinker with something that had been working extremely well? This deal with McCready was a perfect example of why Vaughn was so successful. He knew how to negotiate and when to step back.

He was a damned good businessman.

Three steps in her direction, and he could take her hand. "I didn't say it before, but you look amazing tonight."

Her smile was shy. "Thanks. We were both busy earlier. I can relax now that Danika's part is over."

"Indeed. Shall we go find our seats?" He tucked her hand in the crook of his arm.

Before they could follow Sophie and Nigel and Kellan, Vaughn saw Miranda Blackwood and Kace LeBlanc appear. Along with Darius Taylor-Pratt and Audra. Vaughn recognized Darius and Audra from pictures Sophie had sent him.

Vaughn's stomach tightened, but he gave his new sibling a curt nod in response to Miranda's introductions. "Hello." Darius reciprocated with a subdued greeting.

The expression on Kace's face stopped them all in their tracks. "I know this is a special occasion, but Miranda has some very important news. Kellan, you'll need to get Irina. Sophie. Nigel. Vaughn. Let's step into the other tent, since it's empty now. Darius, you and Audra, too."

Vaughn bristled. "Slow down a minute. If this is family business, then Brie should be there. You should all know—Brie and I are engaged." He held up her hand to show off the ring. "And Danika is our daughter."

After a moment of pregnant silence, Miranda spoke, smiling wryly. "I'm happy for you. And of course, Brie should join us, as well."

Moments later, the ten adults stood inside the tent where Sophie and Nigel would become husband and wife tomorrow.

Kace LeBlanc, Miranda's lawyer, was less brusque than normal. If anything, his quiet words were conciliatory.

"Miranda has asked me to share some news with you. When your father died, he left a convoluted will, as you know. The truth is, Buckley made Miranda the temporary caretaker of his estate—not his true heir. He died old and alone because of a series of bad choices he made, particularly in the realm of relationships. He was most insistent that the same fate not befall each of you. Miranda was charged with protecting and running the estate until such time as Buckley's three children—Kellan, Sophie and Vaughn—showed evidence of personal growth, maturity and the ability to connect meaningfully with another human being. I'm quoting, by the way."

Miranda nodded. "My instructions came in the form of three letters. The initial set of demands was in the first letter, just as Kace has explained."

"And the second?" Vaughn asked sharply.

Miranda gave him a level stare. "The second letter involved finding Darius and legitimizing his claim to the estate."

"Which Darius knew nothing about," Kace reminded them.

Sophie was pale. "And the third letter?"

"It will be revealed in good time," Miranda said. "But you should know that it's the least significant of the three. The contents of the last letter won't impact anyone in a significant way. It's my instructions from the first one that I'm ready to put into action now." She grimaced. "I know what you all thought of me when it looked like I'd gotten all of your father's estate, but I didn't *want* anything of Buckley's. I still don't. Kace and I have determined that by every benchmark, you each have met Buckley's requirements. Vaughn, I didn't know you were engaged, but you have certainly made a point of being supportive of Kellan and Sophie during these difficult months."

Kace picked up the story again. "Kellan, the ranch is yours, free and clear."

Kellan blinked and muttered a shocked curse. "What about the others?"

Kace continued. "Blackwood Bank and all its assets go to Vaughn. Sophie, you inherit several houses and a large sum of cash. You can let me know how you want the payout, since it will affect your tax status."

"And Darius?" Sophie asked.

Miranda smiled. "He's to receive a lump sum of cash as well, which I'm guessing he'll invest in his business."

Darius nodded, looking stunned.

Kace sighed. "That's the gist of it. Any questions?"

No one moved at first. Then Sophie stepped forward and shook Miranda's hand briefly. "Thank you for doing this impossible job. And thank you for allowing Nigel and me to get married at Blackwood Hollow in spite of the way I treated you after the will reading. That was very generous of you, under the circumstances. I hope we can all eventually be friends."

Kellan chuckled. "Or at least not enemies."

Irina punched him in the arm.

Vaughn didn't know what to think. His head was spinning. "We should get back to the party," he said, keeping his tone cool, hoping to let Miranda know that he didn't forgive as easily as *some* people in his family.

Nigel nodded. "Vaughn is right. Kace and Miranda, you are invited guests, as Sophie has told you. I hope you'll stay and help us celebrate. This weekend is a time for looking to the future."

Moments later, Vaughn and Brie were the only two lingering in the tent. "Are you okay?" she asked quietly. "I thought you would be happy and excited. And as it turns out, our little fictional engagement was not even necessary."

He shook his head slowly. "I'm not sure I know *what* I feel. I never liked being manipulated by my father in real life. Having him do it from the grave is almost as demeaning."

Brie shook her head disbelievingly. "You're the only person I know who can inherit a fortune and still be miffed about it."

"I'm not miffed," he said, "but I don't appreciate having to prove my worth."

"In all fairness, Miranda and Kace were handing over the bank to you even before you told them you and I are engaged. So I'd say they definitely gave you the benefit of the doubt."

"I suppose so."

"Let's go eat," Brie said. "I'm starving."

"Okay. But afterward, I'd like to drive around the ranch and visit old haunts."

Brie's eyes widened. "You mean like haylofts?"

He lifted one shoulder and let it fall, feigning innocence. "Whatever takes our fancy."

For the next hour, Vaughn talked and ate and gave a winning performance of the man without a care in the world. He and Kellan both toasted the bride and groom.

But old words came back to haunt him. *You're probably the most like me.*

Was it true? The question made his stomach queasy. On bad days, he had hated his father at times. Even on good days, he'd disdained him. How would Danika look at Vaughn one day?

The uncomfortable question tormented him.

And what about Brie? She was seated beside him, of course. But somehow he sensed a distance between them that hadn't been there before.

Kellan and Irina were on the opposite side of the table. At one point, late in the evening, Kellan yawned and leaned back in his chair. "It's been great having you in Royal for so long, Vaughn. When do you have to go home?"

"I'm flying out tomorrow evening...after the wedding. Business calls," he said lightly.

Eighteen

Brie sat stunned, trying to control her facial expressions. Vaughn was leaving town tomorrow? This was the first she had heard of it. The fact that he hadn't thought to mention it told her more loudly than words that Vaughn Blackwood hadn't changed a bit.

He had a cash register—a calculator—where his heart should be. Sure, he might have warmed up to Danika, but he had no plans to alter his life in any meaningful way, no intent to include Brie and her daughter in his sterile, business-centered sphere.

The hurt ran deep. Anger, too. She was angry at herself for weaving dreams that had no basis in reality. What a fool she was. Not only had she blinded herself to Vaughn's true nature, but she had fallen in love with him again.

Perhaps that last part wasn't quite true. Maybe she had never *quit* loving him. Maybe she had been in denial for almost three years. Pregnant and alone. Giving birth. Rearing a baby with little emotional or financial support.

And all along, deep down inside, she had held out hope for the future. Wasn't that ultimately why she had moved back to Royal? To be near his family and thus be sure she and Vaughn would eventually cross paths again?

The depths of her own self-deception were stunning.

Even recently, she'd pretended that she knew Vaughn was the proverbial rolling stone…that she had to end their physical relationship because he would be leaving.

But somewhere deep in her vulnerable woman's heart, she had thought she could change him.

Her skin felt cold and clammy. The meal she had consumed rolled in her stomach. She wanted to go home to her baby, to the one person who loved her unconditionally.

Abruptly, she stood and made her way to Sophie and Nigel's table. "I need to head out," she said, feigning cheerfulness. "Danika will be up very early, and I want to make sure our day gets off to a good start in the morning, so she'll be fresh for the wedding."

Sophie and Nigel stood to hug her and extend their thanks. Then Brie turned and fled, only to run into the solid bulk of her faux fiancé. "What are you doing?" he asked, frowning. Did the man ever do anything *but* frown?

She couldn't meet his eyes. She kept walking quickly toward the tent exit, forcing him to follow. "I have to relieve Tabitha so she can go home."

Outside, he took her arm. "You told me she was prepared to stay until midnight. It's only ten o'clock. What's your rush, Brie?"

Tears burned her eyelids. She blinked them back, determined not to reveal her weakness, her incredibly hopeless yearning.

She sucked in a deep breath of the air that was far cooler here than that in the tent and exhaled slowly. "I'm tired," she said simply. "Today was a long day, and tomorrow will be the same. Good night, Vaughn."

He shackled her wrist with one big hand and drew her close. "You're upset. I know you that well. Tell me what's wrong. Did I do something?"

It was impossible to answer without incriminating herself. "No," she lied. "It's not you."

He stroked her hair, gentling her as he would a spooked filly. Brie knew the drill. She had done the same thing a hundred times on this very ranch.

His voice was low and rough when he spoke. "You wanted to know how I felt about being back here. I should ask you the same question. Is that what's bothering you, Brie? Does being here bring back too many memories?"

Gradually, she let the cool night air and Vaughn's steady touch settle her. "Yes," she said simply. "Being here reminds me of all my mistakes. I was young and not ambitious enough. I knew I wanted my own vet practice, but I let Buckley take advantage of me."

"Why?"

She shrugged. "Because I loved the ranch and the horses…" *And you.*

He was silent for a moment. "Will you get in the car with me? I won't keep you long. We both need some closure. Perhaps exorcising a few ghosts will help you sleep tonight."

Brie knew he wasn't talking about their relationship. But on a deeper level, she could hear his question in those terms. Vaughn was flying home tomorrow. Tonight would be her last chance to make love to him.

Was that what she wanted?

"Okay," she said, feeling the noose of inevitability tighten around her throat. "Sure. Let's drive."

Vaughn's car was parked nearby. He helped her in and shut the door, careful not to catch her skirt.

The night was perfect for a convertible. He put the top down so they could enjoy the stars. Gravel crunched beneath the tires. In the distance, the ranch house loomed.

Not a single light shone. With Buckley dead and Miranda at the party, there was no one left to walk the halls.

Vaughn passed the house and drove on to the collection of barns and outbuildings where Brie had worked so many long, hard hours. Despite the drawbacks, it had been good experience for her. She knew that now. But letting the old man's son seduce her had been a mistake.

Still, Brie had gotten her beloved Danika out of the bargain, so even that long-ago mistake wasn't so bad in retrospect.

The convertible rolled to a halt in the shadow of the largest and fanciest of the barns, the one with an entire double row of stalls. The one where Brie had honed her talents and enthusiasm for horses into the skills that made her such a good vet. She loved their beauty and spirit, loved keeping them healthy and productive.

Both adults got out of the car. Far in the distance, Brie could hear that the music had started for dancing. Not the orchestra anymore, but a rowdy country band. Who knew how Nigel's family would take to that? Perhaps his grandmother would learn how to line dance.

Vaughn strode toward the barn, not waiting to see if Brie was following. When he hauled back the heavy wooden door and turned on a track of diffused light, a host of smells and sounds wafted out. Simple. Familiar. Evocative.

Hay and feed. Old wood and new leather. The soft whicker of a mare. The deeper snorting of an alpha stallion.

It was like stepping back in time.

Until this very moment, Brie honestly hadn't realized how much she missed this place. Buckley might have been a difficult man, but he had built an impressive empire. He'd also helped raise three adult children who were each outstanding in their own right.

Vaughn had walked on ahead, stopping under the center pitch of the roof. As he looked up, Brie saw him in profile.

His shoulders stretched the tailored seams of his charcoal-gray suit. His features were classic, masculine.

No broken nose or shaggy haircut to mar his physical perfection and make him seem more human. Everything about him was crisp and professional and…unreachable.

Maybe Vaughn didn't need a woman in his life at all.

She closed the gap between them, assailed by memories that wrapped around her heart and squeezed. There were no more poignant words in the English language than *if only…*

Leaning her head against his shoulder, she gave herself permission to let him go. Vaughn represented a time in her life when she was footloose and free. Nothing to tie her down but the need for a paycheck.

Brie was a different woman now. Motherhood had changed her priorities. Unfortunately, the only part of her that remained the same was the hunger for Vaughn's touch.

He slid an arm around her waist, his gaze still fixed on the high point of the vaulted ceiling with the open rafters. "I walked the roofline of this barn once," he said. "Did I ever tell you that?" He pointed over his head. "Had to shimmy out that small window right there and drag myself on up to the top."

"No. You never told me. Sounds dangerous."

"Oh yeah," he chuckled. "It was. I was fifteen and dumb as a bag of rocks. My father had made me angry about something, and in my convoluted adolescent brain, I decided that literally looking down on him and his stupid ranch would give me the advantage."

"Did it?"

He rubbed the back of his neck with his free hand and gave her a rueful grin. "Not that I can remember. What I *do* remember is sitting up there for more than three hours, because I couldn't figure out how to get down without killing myself."

"What did your father do?"

"Not a damn thing. He never knew. Actually, he took the truck into town that afternoon. While he was gone, Sophie and Kellan got an extension ladder to help rescue me. Soph cried the entire time. I felt like a jackass."

"Are you jealous that Kellan inherited Blackwood Hollow and not you?"

He hesitated. "It gave me a twinge to hear it wouldn't be mine," he admitted. "But Kellan deserves it. Besides, my life is in Fort Worth. What would I do with the ranch other than get someone else to run it for me? It's all for the best."

"I suppose."

He turned her to face him and kissed her softly. "What do you say, Brie? Are you up for climbing the ladder?"

The hayloft didn't run the length of the barn. It barely covered one corner. The majority of the ranch's hay was stored in a separate facility, but a couple dozen bales were kept nearby for convenience's sake.

Vaughn and Brie had found them very convenient indeed.

She kicked off her shoes. "I am."

His gaze flared with heat. She saw the muscles in his throat ripple.

While he shrugged out of his jacket and loosened his tie, she told herself she needed one last walk on the wild side before she settled down to be a typical middle-class mom with bills and a kid in school and dreams of what might have been.

The truth was even simpler. She loved Vaughn and didn't want to say goodbye.

He pulled her toward the ladder. "You first," he said. "I'll catch you if you fall."

She put one bare foot on the bottom rung and quickly scooted up the ladder, feeling self-conscious about her bare legs and other parts. Vaughn was right behind her.

He had more upper-body strength and was taller, so he wasn't breathing hard at all when they stepped out onto the solid platform.

Nothing much had changed. Even the old, faded quilt was still there, shoved over in a corner.

Brie wrinkled her nose. "I'm not sitting down on that."

Vaughn laughed, looking remarkably carefree for once. "I'll be the one sitting. Wouldn't want to damage that beautiful dress." He caught her wrist and reeled her in. "Kiss me, Brie."

The mood shifted in a heartbeat. Up to this point, they both had been dealing with nostalgia and perhaps regret. Now, deeper emotions surfaced.

His lips were firm and warm and coaxing, as if he knew she was conflicted. Strong arms encircled her waist. Big hands cupped her bottom and lifted her against his chest.

She felt dizzy and breathless. His skin smelled warm and male. It seemed like they were the only people in the world. No one knew they were here. Everyone else was occupied.

Her heart thumped in her chest. She wound her legs around his hips, nipping his chin with a sharp, quick nibble. "I could never say no to you," she complained. "You dazzled me."

"Wrong." His quick frown was dark. "*You* were the one who bewitched me, Brie. I came home one weekend to conduct some necessary business with my father. The next thing I knew, I was commuting back and forth twice a week, trying not to let anyone know why I was suddenly so enamored with being back in Royal. I panted after you like a puppy dog, but you were maddeningly hard to read. I used to wish you came with a manual so I could figure out what the hell you wanted."

His sudden burst of frustration shocked her. "I wasn't playing games, Vaughn. I was just happy to be with you."

"But it wasn't enough, was it?"

She couldn't answer that. They both knew the truth. Brie had wanted and needed promises. Security.

Vaughn had been unable to deliver any of that and unwilling to pretend he could be that kind of man. So their relationship had unraveled, and Brie had moved away.

With a sigh, she rested her forehead against his. "Life is always about timing. You and I had something wonderful back then. Let's not ruin the memories by arguing. I want to be with you tonight. But I have to go home soon."

His muffled grunt wasn't an answer. He carried her to the nearest, newest-looking bale of hay and sat down with her in his lap. His hands settled on her waist. "You outshone the bride tonight, Brie. Even if she is my sister."

"Thank you." What would happen if she told him she loved him? If she begged him to give up his life in Dallas/Fort Worth and stay in Royal with her?

To be fair, she would have to think long and hard if he turned the tables. Could she abandon her brand-new, thriving practice and move to Forth Worth? For a man with no track record in regard to long-term commitment?

The urge to blurt out three words was strong. *I love you.* If Brie had been on her own, the only risk would be heartbreak. But Danika was a factor in this equation. Even now, Brie couldn't tell if Vaughn wanted to be a father or not.

She sifted her fingers through his thick, healthy hair. "I hope you came prepared."

His chuckle sounded hoarse and breathless. "You can bet on it, Brie."

She sucked in a sharp breath when his thumbs caressed the insides of her thighs, making her legs quiver. The subtle torture sent her higher. Wiggling so he would get the idea, she mentally urged him closer. Needy and urgent, she wanted it all.

Her breasts ached for his touch, for his possession. "Please," she croaked, shaking.

At last, he moved. He fumbled in his pants for the condom and applied it quickly. Then he gave her a smile that was both sweet and searing hot. Her undies ended up on the floor with Houdini-like speed.

"I've been waiting for this all day," he said, the words barely audible. With one hard push, he was inside her, huge and hard and crazy wonderful.

Her body tightened instinctively around him. "Yes," she whispered, her eyes squeezed shut. "Yes."

Something told her this would be the last time. Grief and joy mingled, odd bedfellows indeed. Vaughn's big, warm hands kneaded her ass, his labored breath warm on her neck as he buried his face in her shoulder.

"Brie," he muttered. "Brie."

She could almost tell herself he loved her. But he had never said the words, and she had come too far to believe in fantasy now.

Instead of wishing for the moon, she closed her eyes and gave in to the moment. It was enough. It had to be.

Nineteen

In the midst of sheer, physical bliss, Brie found herself sad…resigned. Vaughn held her close against his heaving chest—not saying much at first. "We have to talk about a few things before I leave town tomorrow," he said eventually.

Brie stiffened. "It's going to be a busy day."

"I know. But this is important."

Brie stood and reached for her missing item of clothing. "I have to get back to Danika," she said quietly. "I'm sorry to rush away."

"I understand. Why don't I drive you? I can get someone else to follow us with the babysitter's car."

His expression was impossible to read in the dim light. "Thank you, but no," she said. "Sophie is your only sister. You've already skipped out on the party for too long. Go back. Play your part. Nika and I will see you at the wedding in the morning."

After that, the silence grew. Their lovemaking had been

off-the-charts good by any standard. Brie cried out his name when she came. But they might as well have been miles apart.

As she descended the ladder with him right below her, she swallowed her dismay. At the bottom, she found her shoes and rummaged for a small towel to wipe her feet.

Vaughn wanted to do it for her. She stepped away and handled it herself.

Then she walked out of the barn to the car. She was waiting for him in the passenger seat after he turned off the lights and closed the big door.

Not a word was spoken during the brief drive back to the sitter's parked car. Danika and Tabitha had taken Brie's vehicle with the car seat.

Brie fished keys out of her evening purse. "Good night, Vaughn."

He took her wrist. Gently. No coercion. "We'll figure this out. Danika deserves the best of both of us."

"I know."

This time, he kissed her forehead. The international symbol for *I think we should just be friends.* "Be careful going home."

"I will."

When she couldn't bear the awkward tension between them any longer, she stepped back and seated herself in the unfamiliar car. Vaughn was little more than a shadow in the darkness.

Brie reversed, pulled out and drove away.

Danika woke up all smiles the following morning. The evening with the sitter had been a novelty, and Tabitha had reported it went very well.

Brie was far less perky than her daughter.

Three cups of coffee and she was still not herself. It hadn't been smart to lie awake for hours thinking about

Vaughn. Not smart at all. Now, not only was she facing a stressful day, but she was going into it with an exhaustion hangover.

They made it out to Blackwood Hollow right on time. Some of the pictures were being taken beforehand, including the ones with Sophie, all her bridesmaids and Danika.

Brie was relieved that her daughter cooperated. The ceremony itself would come and go, but pictures lasted forever.

A light breeze kept the temperature in the tent comfortable. Sophie seemed in good spirits, laughing and beaming. The men were sequestered in the other tent where the rehearsal dinner had taken place the night before.

Vaughn being absent was a good thing. Brie didn't know what to say to him. She was all out of words.

Brie still thought Vaughn should be at his sister's side going down the aisle, but the siblings had discussed it and decided it was more important for Vaughn to coax his daughter to the front.

Suddenly, without warning, it was time.

Brie had witnessed the influx of guests, hundreds of them, laughing and chatting excitedly as the crowd swelled. Most fit into the space for the ceremony, but perhaps three dozen latecomers were tucked away in the rear tent watching on a video feed.

The groomsmen and bridesmaids lined up two by two. Then Danika, then the bride.

The prelude music began.

Tears filled Brie's eyes. She was happy for Sophie.

As the attendants played their parts, moving with measured steps along the satin runner, Kellan and Sophie exchanged a hug. Two siblings out of three happily married. Those were good odds.

The wedding director gave Brie a harried smile. "Time for the flower girl."

Brie crouched and tucked a curl behind Nika's ear.

"Walk to Mr. V," she said, her throat tight. "Just like you did last night."

Danika beamed and stepped out, suddenly ready to perform. Her dress was perfect, her sweet smile adorable. The crowd loved it and responded audibly.

Brie met Vaughn's gaze over the long distance that separated them. He gave Brie a thumbs-up, or perhaps the gesture was for the two-year-old.

Then Sophie and Kellan took their places. The music swelled. The crowd stood. The bride walked down the aisle.

During the brief but meaningful ceremony, Brie stood at the back of the tent, feeling a bit lost. Danika was safe and happy with her father. Brie was superfluous at the moment.

Was this how it would be if she and Vaughn shared custody? Would Brie spend half her days feeling oddly at loose ends whenever it was Vaughn's turn to have Nika?

For one selfish moment, she hoped he would bow out completely. It would be so much easier to rear Danika on her own. And Brie wouldn't have to see Vaughn over and over again.

But even as the thought flitted through her mind, she knew it was wrong. Nika needed her daddy, and though he might not realize it, Vaughn needed his daughter.

It was Kellan's wife, Irina, who took Danika's hand after the ceremony and walked the little girl back to Brie. Vaughn had disappeared with Kellan.

Brie thanked Vaughn's sister-in-law. "What's up with the guys? Where did they run off to? Don't they know this is a special occasion?"

Irina rolled her eyes. "Something about an important business deal in Dallas. Now that Kellan for sure has the ranch, he wants to invest in Vaughn's company."

"Ah."

The two women exchanged wry glances. Irina shook

her head. "I've learned you can't tame a Texan. We're the ones who have to change and adapt."

"But you look radiant and happy."

Irina grinned. "Oh, I am. Kellan is the love of my life. He may be stubborn, but he dotes on me."

After the woman walked away, Brie stayed put for a minute, pondering Irina's words. Was Brie willing to make compromises for a shot at happiness? She honestly didn't know. How much was too much to bend?

Unlike last night, the reception was not nearby. All the guests had to load up and head across town to the posh Bellamy resort, where the wedding brunch was to be held.

The bride and groom had arranged for fully staffed babysitting—by reservation—at the TCC childcare center. The new Mr. and Mrs. Townshend had even catered munchkin-friendly food for the little ones' meals. Having the option was a relief. A formal wedding brunch at the elegant Bellamy was definitely not the place for kids.

Brie dropped Danika off at the center on the way. Nika was comfortable there by now and went without protest.

At the Bellamy, the scene was organized chaos. A larger-than-normal staff of valets was parking cars. Brie handed over her keys and tucked the claim ticket in her small beaded purse.

On one side of the entrance, Nigel's unmistakably upper-crust family gathered as they were dropped off. Coincidentally, the opposite portion of the driveway had been overtaken with the cast and crew of the *Secret Lives* show.

Nigel and Sophie had invited all the wives and even granted camera access to the reception, within reason. Brie spotted Miranda entering the hotel alone. Something about Miranda's dignified posture made Brie feel sorry for her. Miranda had done her best in a difficult situation.

As Brie made her way to the salon where the brunch was

being served, a warm male hand descended on her shoulder. "There you are," said a familiar voice.

She felt her cheeks go hot. "Hello, Vaughn."

He cocked his head, his lips twitching. "That's all you've got to say after last night?"

"I have no idea to what you are referring," she said primly.

She was wearing an ankle-length gown spangled with tiny, tiny bugle beads. The halter neck left her shoulders bare.

Vaughn traced her collarbone with a fingertip, his gaze hooded. "This tangerine color suits you. I have a few ideas for getting you undressed later."

Her spine stiffened. "You're flying out later. Remember?" Perhaps he heard the tart bite in her voice.

"Details, details." He took her elbow. "Come on. I found our seats already. And for the record, I'm starving."

The long, gorgeous room had been decked out as a conservatory. Lush plants, everything from hibiscus to orchids, lined the corridors and graced the tables. Nigel and Sophie's table was slightly raised, so the bride and groom could see all their guests.

Champagne flowed like water. Waiters with trays of mimosas in Baccarat crystal flutes circulated among the crowd.

At last everyone was seated, and the meal began. After the main course of raspberry crepes, eggs Benedict and honeyed dates, Nigel's grandmother stood and regaled the group with rather saucy tales of his childhood. Brie smiled inwardly at seeing the proper Englishman be mortified by his own granny.

Vaughn and Kellan had their own set of stories about Sophie. The bride pretended to be insulted, but Brie could see that she loved the attention from the brothers she adored.

Then it was time for dessert. Someone from the kitchen

wheeled out an enormous cart laden with the most beautiful wedding cake Brie had even seen. It was covered in pastel-pink-and-white fondant and adorned with tiny, handmade sugar ribbons and roses.

After Sophie and Nigel cut the cake, feeding each other in the process, the kitchen crew quickly sliced and served the masterpiece to every guest…with more alcohol for those who wanted it.

Vaughn whispered in her ear, "You have icing on the side of your mouth," he said softly, leaning forward and removing it with his thumb. Then he sucked his thumb and smiled. "Delicious."

Beneath the pristine linen tablecloth, Brie pressed her knees together. The man was a devil. "Stop that," she hissed. "People are watching us."

It was true. Nigel's large family and Sophie's smaller one, including Dixie Musgraves, were seated on either end of the dais, facing the rest of the guests. It was impossible to adjust a bra strap or remove food from your teeth without someone noticing.

After the cake cutting, there was a brief lull. Sophie and Nigel had exited for a brief moment alone, promising to return shortly for the obligatory bouquet toss.

Brie needed a breath of air. Though she had only consumed a single mimosa, her head was spinning. "I'm going to visit the ladies' room," she said. "Be right back."

The lobby of the hotel was oddly silent. Most of the resort's rooms had been overtaken by out-of-town wedding guests, so the most likely explanation was that everyone involved was occupied with brunch.

Just as Brie was crossing the wide expanse of lush carpet, a man intersected her path. He was a couple of decades her senior. His longish, dark blond hair wasn't her preference, but he still possessed an attractive boyish charm.

It took Brie a moment to recognize him as Vaughn's lawyer. Her stomach clenched. "Mr. Matthews. I didn't expect to see you today." He was dressed in a worn tux.

"Ms. Sophie is kind to an old guy like me. I appreciated the invitation."

Brie manufactured a smile. "If you'll excuse me…"

She turned to pursue her original errand, but the lawyer halted her with a hand on her arm. She shook off his touch. "I'm in a hurry," she said curtly, no longer willing to feign social niceties now that she remembered who he was.

"Wait," he insisted, touching her a second time. "I have something for you." He pulled a standard-size manila envelope from his inside breast pocket. It was folded in half lengthwise. "Vaughn wanted me to give you these."

Brie felt a chill on her skin. A premonition. Automatically, she took the envelope and flattened it where it had been folded. Almost without thinking, she withdrew the stack of pages. Not that many. Ten, maybe. Twelve at the most.

"What is this?" she asked, nausea rippling through her stomach as she took in words and phrases.

"Just a standard business thing," Trent said breezily. "Mr. McCready and your fiancé have to protect the integrity of their very important deal. All we're doing is asking you to sign this and verify that you and the kid aren't going to make any kind of claims on the profits. Which is only fair," he said quickly, "since this acquisition was underway before the two of you came on the scene."

"My daughter's name is Danika," Brie said carefully.

Her heart lay in ashes at her feet. She had anticipated getting hurt because she was more invested in this relationship than Vaughn. What she had never seen coming was such careless cruelty. She'd hoped Vaughn had changed…that his relationship with her and with Nika had become more important to him than profit or a bottom line.

Even in the midst of her distress, she paused, unwilling

to convict her faux fiancé unfairly. She stared Trent Matthews straight in the eyes. "Has Vaughn Blackwood seen these papers?"

Matthews never hesitated. His head cocked to one side, a mildly puzzled smile on his face. "Of course."

Twenty

Vaughn checked his watch for the third time. Brie had been gone twenty-five minutes. He assumed she would call the TCC to check on Danika, but even so, she should have been back by now.

Absently, he noticed that Trent Matthews was standing on the opposite side of the room near a doorway. The man's expression was equal parts affable and satisfied. Why had Sophie invited him?

And then it dawned on Vaughn—she probably hadn't. Trent Matthews was exactly the kind of man who would crash a wedding. Something wasn't right.

Just when Vaughn was ready to go in search of Brie, she appeared, sliding into her seat with an apologetic smile.

"Everything okay?" he whispered. She was pale, and her forehead was damp.

"Yes," she said, reaching for her water glass. "Shh. Nigel is about to say something."

The bride and groom were inviting everyone into the

adjoining ballroom for dancing and more festivities. The crowd rose as one, eager to continue the party.

In the commotion, Brie slipped something into his pocket. "When I called the TCC center, they said Danika has been asking for me. I'm going to take her home for a nap."

Vaughn frowned. "I'll go with you."

"No, no," Brie said. Her gaze didn't quite meet his. "You have to be here for your family. It's a big day for the Blackwoods."

She went up on tiptoe and kissed him on the cheek. "Tell Sophie that Danika loved her gig. Goodbye, Vaughn."

People jostled on both sides. He reached for Brie's arm, but she eluded him, getting lost in the crowd.

Vaughn cursed. But he was trapped. He and Kellan were both supposed to dance with the bride in a moment, during what was usually the father/daughter dance. Brie was right. He couldn't go.

In the ballroom, the crowd thinned out, lining both sides of the dance floor. Sophie and Nigel had the first dance, of course. Then it was Kellan's turn. Vaughn wanted to see what Brie had tucked in his pocket, but he was in a visible position and had to play his part.

When Vaughn took Sophie in his arms, his immediate frustration eased. "Have I told you how gorgeous you look, Soph? It was a great day."

She rested her head on his shoulder, smothering a yawn. "And it's not over yet. Nigel and I have to finish packing a few last-minute items. Our flight to Europe leaves tonight at six."

"And the Townshend entourage?"

"They'll all be heading out in the morning." Sophie leaned back and studied his face. "Are you okay, Vaughn?"

"Of course," he said automatically.

"Are you and Brie…" She trailed off, clearly unwilling to press him.

"I don't know what Brie and I are," he admitted.

"You're my brother. I want you to be happy."

He kissed her forehead. "I'm as happy as I deserve. Don't worry about me, sis. I always land on my feet."

The song ended, and a chunk of the guests surged onto the floor, eager to join the fun.

For Vaughn, this was his cue to cut out. Unobtrusively, he made his way toward the exit, pausing now and then for quick conversations when he couldn't completely elude someone.

At last, he made it out into a quiet corridor.

When he pulled an envelope from his pocket, his heart stopped. It was a piece of hotel stationery. The seal had barely held because of something bulky inside.

He ripped it open, catching the aquamarine and diamond ring that tumbled out. He wasn't entirely surprised. Brie had never wanted to keep it from the beginning.

With shaking hands, he unfolded the single piece of paper inside.

Dear Vaughn,

I hope you have a safe and pleasant return flight to Dallas/Fort Worth. Once your life is back to normal, please give some thought to the Danika situation. I won't judge you, whatever you decide. Your choice has to come from the heart. If you feel unwilling or unable to play a role as her father, I understand.

I'm returning the ring. Please tuck it away in a safe somewhere. Perhaps you'll want to give it to Nika one day.

I have signed the McCready papers and left them at the front desk. But I didn't want to take a chance with something as valuable as the ring.

Wishing you all the best,

Brie

Vaughn was in shock. This was a goodbye note, plain and simple. Brie had no intention of ever seeing him again.

And what the hell were the *McCready papers*?

He dashed to the lobby and had to cool his heels for fifteen minutes, waiting. One couple checking in, two checking out. At last, it was his turn.

He practically snatched the manila envelope from the desk clerk and found a semiprivate corner behind a potted plant. When he got his first look at the contents, despair washed over him. These were the documents Trent Matthews had tried to get him to sign at the lawyer's office after the meeting with Cal McCready. The papers Vaughn had flat-out refused.

But Brie didn't know that.

Vaughn shot to his feet, fury replacing his despair. He was going to fix this. Now. Fortunately for him, Trent Matthews happened to pick that very moment to slip out the front door. Vaughn followed on his heels.

"Going somewhere?" he asked menacingly.

Matthews turned and gasped. Every ounce of color left his face. "Blackwood. I thought you were at the party."

"I'll bet you did. You gate-crashed, right?"

The idiot lawyer had the balls to bristle with indignation. "It's not a crime. I'll pay Sophie for the meal if that's a problem."

"And Brie?" Vaughn asked silkily. "What will you do about Brie?"

Matthews goggled. "I didn't do anything to your woman. You can ask her. I was super polite."

Vaughn kept approaching. Trent kept backing up. Now the circular fountain blocked his escape. The large expanse of driveway with concrete and brick pavers was oddly empty save for two bored valets a couple hundred yards away who were smoking and trying to stay out of the sun.

"What did you say to her?" He took Matthews by the shirt collar and lifted him two inches.

Even then, the clueless lawyer tried to brazen his way through. "I told her you wanted her to sign the papers. She asked if you had seen them. I said yes. I did you a favor, man. You need to keep your eye on the prize. Broads and babies? They're nothing beside the money you can make on this deal."

"Damn you to hell, Matthews. You're fired. But I don't suppose that matters to you, because I'm pretty damn sure you're on McCready's payroll. Am I right?" The guilty flicker in Matthews's furtive gaze gave Vaughn his answer and blinded him with rage. He gave the slick lawyer a quick blow to the chin, toppling him over the low wall into the bubbling water.

Matthews cursed and floundered.

Vaughn's chest heaved. "And because you're on McCready's payroll, I'm texting him right now to let him know that his lackey is no longer employed by me."

Trent clambered to his feet, dripping and pathetic. "No, no. Don't do that. We'll work something out."

Vaughn hit Send. "Too late. There's nothing to work out. You and I are through, Matthews. The deal is off. Some things in life are more important than money."

While Vaughn strode toward the valets and produced his claim ticket, his brain whirled. When the car was brought around, he seated himself behind the wheel and squealed out of the exit. He had to fix this. But how?

He knew where to find Brie. Or he was fairly certain he did. She would be home by now, and Danika would be napping.

The reading on his speedometer slowed him down. Literally. He pulled off in a public parking area and tried to formulate a plan. First he needed to take care of some urgent business. Twenty minutes wouldn't make the situation better or worse. Brie wasn't going anywhere.

After two brief phone calls and three longer conversations, he felt the constriction in his chest ease. Now, at least his close friends and associates knew not to trust McCready and Matthews. The slimy duo had messed up badly this time. They might still be able to operate, but word was out. No reputable businessman or woman would give them the time of day.

Vaughn shifted into gear and pulled back out onto the highway. Ten minutes later, Brie's little house was a welcome sight. Her car, thankfully, was in the driveway. He parked behind it, hemming her in. No reason to give her an escape route.

He couldn't remember the last time he had been this nervous. As a rule, *he* was the one who made *other* people nervous.

Did he know what he was going to say? If he had to guess, he was pretty damn sure this was his last chance with Brielle Gunderson. A flub-up at this juncture would ruin everything.

He wiped his damp palms on his pants legs, got out and locked the car. Then he strode up the sidewalk and rang the bell. The baby slept with a small fan in her room for white noise. She wouldn't hear.

When the door opened without ceremony, his heart cracked wide-open. Brie had been crying. Dear God. And all because of him. Because he had given her no reason to doubt that he would draw up those papers or ask her to sign them.

"May I come in?" he asked quietly.

Brie had nothing left. Emotionally. Physically. This day had taken whatever energy and joy she had and flushed it down the drain.

As soon as Nika had fallen asleep, Brie lost the battle to keep her emotions under control. She had sobbed uncontrollably, grieving the loss of a dream that was never real in the first place.

She had hoped her note to Vaughn would be an end to things. Apparently, he still had something else to say.

"You'll miss your flight," she pointed out, not opening the door any wider.

He was gray faced and haggard, his posture slumped. She had never seen him like this. "Please, Brie. Let me in."

She lifted her shoulders and let them fall in a shrug of resignation. "Fine. Suit yourself." She had peeled out of her beautiful dress as soon as she got home. Now she was wearing faded gray sweatpants and an old concert T-shirt. If she had deliberately tried, she couldn't look any worse.

Not that Vaughn noticed. Once she let him in and moved toward the living room, he prowled, pacing back and forth.

Brie waited him out. She had said everything she had to say. If he was looking for an apology, he was out of luck.

Finally, after wearing a rut in her carpet, he sat in the chair opposite her spot on the sofa, leaving the coffee table between them. It reminded her of the coffee table where Nika had played soon after Vaughn discovered he had a daughter.

Today there was no child to defuse the tension.

Vaughn rubbed his face with his hands. "First off, those papers weren't from me."

She blinked. "Your name was on them."

"Not on the signature lines," he said curtly. "Matthews showed the papers to me the morning after the gala in Dallas. I told him to destroy the contract, plain and simple. He and McCready were worried that I was being distracted by personal matters, so when I said no, they went behind my back. As it turns out, McCready had Matthews on his payroll, too, and was pulling the strings. Do you believe me?"

The fire in his eyes was more like the Vaughn she knew. "Yes," she said. "I believe you. As it turns out, I wasn't willing to accept Matthews at face value, but when I asked him outright if you had seen the papers and he said yes, he really didn't seem to be lying. I didn't know what else to think."

"I did see them—so the only lie he told you was that I *wanted* you to sign them. His blend of truth and fiction must have been convincing."

She swallowed. "Yes. It was."

"I am sorry that happened to you," Vaughn said. "Sorrier than you know."

"I was humiliated," she admitted, wincing at the memory.

"Well, if it's any consolation, Trent Matthews ended up in the fountain at the Bellamy. I hope his humiliation outlasts yours. The skunk deserved it."

"How did he end up in the fountain?"

Vaughn shifted his gaze away, looking as guilty as a kid caught stealing a candy bar. "I might have punched him. Just once," he said hastily. "It wasn't a brawl."

Even in the midst of Brie's bleak grief, the image made her smile. "Fair enough. I should thank you, I guess."

"We need to talk," he said soberly.

"You mentioned that before, but I'm not sure why. You and I both know where things stand."

"No," he said carefully. "Not anymore."

"I'm confused."

Vaughn stood and paced again. "In my father's will, he said that I was the child who turned out most like him. When I read those words, I was furious. Shocked. Hurt. I've been processing that information for weeks now, and as much as it pains me to admit it, the old man was right. I didn't see it—but now that I do, I know I don't want to be this way anymore. It's not easy to turn things around.

Even now, I'm struggling to change. But I want to, Brie. I don't want to be my father. I won't."

His eyes glittered with emotion when he turned back to face her.

Seeing him so hurt and vulnerable destroyed her. Despite everything he had done to break her heart, she couldn't bear to witness him like this. She went to him and hugged him the way she would comfort a hurting friend.

"You're *not* your father," she said. "I could have told him that. And for the record, Miranda and Kace never thought you were, or they wouldn't have released your portion of the inheritance."

"Maybe. Or maybe Miranda was tired of dealing with it."

"You're a good person, Vaughn. Single-minded, perhaps, but that quality has served you well in the business world."

He stepped back, breaking the embrace. But he took both her hands in his. "I'd like another chance with you."

Her heart sank. "To what end? Everything will wind up exactly the same. We're too different."

"I've made some changes," he said slowly.

"I know. And it's been wonderful watching you with Nika. She brings out your softer side. I've enjoyed seeing your gentler, nurturing qualities."

"But?"

She pulled away, putting the distance of the room between them. "We've been over this a dozen times. I can't have a long-term affair with you. I have a daughter who has to be my first priority."

"And what if you and I were married?"

A sob lodged in her throat, making it hard to speak. "It wouldn't matter. A piece of paper won't solve our problems." The prospect he had raised was so unbelievably sweet that she wanted to throw caution to the wind. But it was dangerous.

His voice was low and determined when he spoke again, as if to underline the importance of what he was saying. "I resigned as vice president of the Dallas TCC this afternoon. I've called several of my key business associates and told them I'll be leaving the Fort Worth area, possibly selling off a big portion of my company."

"I don't understand."

He gave her a sweet, uncomplicated smile. "I'm moving back to Royal, Brie. To be near my daughter and the woman I love."

Her jaw dropped. "You love me?"

"Dear lord, sweetheart, you shouldn't even have to ask. I can't believe I messed up so badly that you don't believe me when I finally say it. I'm the slowest man on the planet, but I can be taught, I swear. *Yes.* I love you. I'm fairly certain I always have. That's why it hurt so much when you ended our relationship and moved away. I told myself I didn't care. I kept on doing the things I knew how to do. But underneath it all, I was turning more into my father every day. Cold. Distant. Alone. I'm so sorry I let you down three years ago."

"Oh, Vaughn." She put her hands to her cheeks, caught up in a maelstrom of emotions. "You can't move to Royal. Your life is in Dallas and Fort Worth."

"It was," he conceded. "Now it's not. For one thing, apparently I own a bank."

"Small potatoes for a man like you."

He grinned. "Maybe I'll turn it into a financial empire. Once I sell off a chunk of Blackwood Energy, I'll have plenty of capital to invest. It will be a challenge."

"I see."

"Don't you want to ask me why I'm really moving back?" he said gently, closing the distance between them.

"I'm afraid to," she admitted.

He pulled her into his arms and rested his chin on top

of her head with a long, weary sigh. "Don't be afraid, my sweet love. Not now. When the time is right, I'd like to marry you. And claim Danika legally. I want us to be a family. We'll build a big-ass house or maybe buy *another* ranch and give Kellan a run for his money. Whatever you want. In the meantime, I plan to make life a little easier for a full-time vet and a single mom."

She searched his face. "If this is a dream, don't wake me up."

He pinched her butt. Hard.

"Ow," Brie said.

"Are you convinced this is real?" His lopsided smile was the most beautiful thing she had ever seen.

"Kiss me, Vaughn. Make me believe it."

His lips were warm and firm, his body hard and perfect against hers. They were incredibly different as human beings, but where it counted, their hearts were perfectly in sync.

The kiss lingered, deepened.

Vaughn shuddered. "How much longer until Nika wakes up?"

Brie chuckled ruefully. "Not long enough."

"Damn." His long-faced expression amused her.

"But we have tonight," she reminded him. "If you can wait that long."

"Tonight and every night," he said, the words sounding like a vow. "Whatever life throws at us, Brielle Gunderson, we're a team now. I plan to love you until we're both old and wrinkled and cranky."

"Cranky?" She lifted an eyebrow.

"That will probably be me. But you'll always know how to tame your grumpy spouse, my love."

She looked him straight in the eyes, trying to communicate what was in her heart. "I don't want to tame you, Vaughn. I fell in love with the hard-edged guy who destroys me in the bedroom. You are who you are, and I adore you."

He kissed her again, hard and sweet and passionate all at the same time. "We'll compromise, then," he promised. "I'll be fully domesticated as a husband and father and upstanding member of the community."

"But when the lights go out?" she teased.

"All bets are off, Brie. All bets are off…"

* * * * *

COMING SOON!

We really hope you enjoyed reading this book. If you're looking for more romance, be sure to head to the shops when new books are available on

Thursday 2nd April

To see which titles are coming soon, please visit

millsandboon.co.uk/nextmonth

LET'S TALK
Romance

For exclusive extracts, competitions
and special offers, find us online:

f facebook.com/millsandboon

🐦 @MillsandBoon

📷 @MillsandBoonUK

Get in touch on 01413 063232

MILLS & BOON

THE HEART OF ROMANCE

A ROMANCE FOR EVERY KIND OF READER

MODERN

Prepare to be swept off your feet by sophisticated, sexy and seductive heroes, in some of the world's most glamourous and romantic locations, where power and passion collide.
8 stories per month.

HISTORICAL

Escape with historical heroes from time gone by. Whether your passion is for wicked Regency Rakes, muscled Vikings or rugged Highlanders, awaken the romance of the past.
6 stories per month.

MEDICAL

Set your pulse racing with dedicated, delectable doctors in the high-pressure world of medicine, where emotions run high and passion, comfort and love are the best medicine.
6 stories per month.

True Love

Celebrate true love with tender stories of heartfelt romance, from the rush of falling in love to the joy a new baby can bring, and a focus on the emotional heart of a relationship.
8 stories per month.

Desire

Indulge in secrets and scandal, intense drama and plenty of sizzling hot action with powerful and passionate heroes who have it all: wealth, status, good looks…everything but the right woman.
6 stories per month.

HEROES

Experience all the excitement of a gripping thriller, with an intense romance at its heart. Resourceful, true-to-life women and strong, fearless men face danger and desire - a killer combination!
8 stories per month.

DARE

Sensual love stories featuring smart, sassy heroines you'd want as a best friend, and compelling intense heroes who are worthy of them.
4 stories per month.

To see which titles are coming soon, please visit

millsandboon.co.uk/nextmonth

JOIN US ON SOCIAL MEDIA!

Stay up to date with our latest releases, author news and gossip, special offers and discounts, and all the behind-the-scenes action from Mills & Boon...

 millsandboon

 millsandboonuk

 millsandboon

It might just be true love...

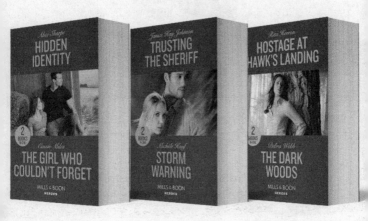

MILLS & BOON

MODERN

Power and Passion

Prepare to be swept off your feet by sophisticated, sexy and seductive heroes, in some of the world's most glamourous and romantic locations, where power and passion collide.